A DEADLY GAME

GAYLE BROWN

Black Rose Writing | Texas

First printing

ISBN: 978-1-68513-332-0
PUBLISHED BY BLACK ROSE WRITING
www.blackrosewriting.com

Printed in the United States of America
Suggested Retail Price (SRP) $21.95

A Deadly Game is printed in Garamond Premier Pro

*As a planet-friendly publisher, Black Rose Writing does its best to eliminate unnecessary waste to reduce paper usage and energy costs, while never compromising the reading experience. As a result, the final word count vs. page count may not meet common expectations.

For all the mothers willing to do whatever it takes
to protect their children—my mom included,
who shows me every day what unconditional love is.

PRAISE FOR A DEADLY GAME

Gayle Brown's accessible writing style and the book's rapid pacing make it an enjoyable read for a wide audience, particularly those who appreciate thrillers with nuanced character perspectives. The final twist is cleverly executed, adding to the overall appeal of the narrative.

A Deadly Game is a compelling read, particularly recommended for fans of the thriller genre seeking a story that combines emotional depth with suspenseful storytelling. Brown's skillfully delivered narrative makes it a worthwhile addition to any thriller enthusiast's collection.

–Literary Titan, 5 stars

Gayle Brown had me hooked from the first page of *A Deadly Game* until the end. This thriller is fast-paced, jam-packed with action, and the suspense kept me on the edge of my seat..The story was excellently written, and the ending was fantastic; there was a major twist that I didn't expect. I was barely over the shock when another truth was revealed that I didn't see coming or expect at all.

–Readers' Favorite

"With unexpected twists, multi-faceted characters, and lightning-quick pacing, Brown's propulsive writing keeps the reader on their toes. Her vivid descriptions, both in atmosphere and emotional turmoil, ensure no one can be trusted. Brown skillfully blurs the boundaries of right and wrong, with the moral quandary of how far is too far to protect one's family simmering beneath the words."

–Marisa Dondlinger, author of *Come and Get Me*

"Gayle Brown's *A Deadly Game* has all the elements of a classic domestic thriller: a missing person, a stalled police investigation, and a seemingly perfect family that's hiding secrets from each other. The characters are so compelling, yet flawed, that you'll wish you could jump in and save them from themselves. The author's skillful plotting will keep you grasping for the truth right up to the final page."

–Regina Buttner, author of *Down a Bad Road*

"*A Deadly Game* is a gripping and surprising novel from a promising new writer."

–J.M. Donellan, author of *Rumors of Her Death*

If you want access to exclusive content, free giveaways, and sneak peeks, sign up for Gayle's Gazette at www.gaylebrownauthor.com

You can learn more about her and her happenings by following her socials: @gaylebrownauthor on Facebook, Instagram, Threads, TikTok

A DEADLY GAME

PROLOGUE

"Jaden! Jaden!" Kyle hollered, his back bumping against his fraternity brother, Ethan. "Dude, you scared me!"

The boys stood face to face. "Sorry, bruh."

It was the perfect night for playing Manhunt; the dark, partly cloudy sky laid the backdrop to the colossal pine trees towering overhead. Branches connected like a primitive roof, filtering out most light, only allowing mere slivers of moonlight to seep through the rustling leaves. Dead ones, previously bright green, now faded and dried out, crunched under the weight of Kyle's worn-out sneakers as he stepped over the bleak undergrowth. "Did you find Jaden?"

"No. You?" Ethan's voice reverberated off the cluster of severed stumps in the woods.

"Not yet." Kyle rocked on his heels, chugging a Pabst Blue Ribbon. Brittle sticks snapped beneath his feet. When finished, he chucked the empty red, white, and blue aluminum can into a thicket of dense trees and stared at the placid water a few hundred yards to his left. "Maybe we should team up together?"

Ethan shrugged. "Sure."

The boys wandered from the murky lake, following the well-trodden dirt trail, shouting Jaden's name, their voices echoing in response.

"How long have we been out here playing?" Kyle asked, bending down and picking up a chalky stone.

Ethan checked his cell phone. "I think an hour. Don't know. Didn't notice what time we'd started."

Kyle lobbed the stone from hand to hand. "Where the hell is Jaden?"

"I have no idea. I looked along the north side of the trail and couldn't find him," Ethan said, gesturing over his left shoulder.

"I went in the opposite direction, and nothing." Kyle tossed the smooth stone higher like a tennis ball. "Guess he's running scared."

Just then, Kyle heard a swoosh from behind. His muscles bunched as he clenched the stone and froze. In a shaky voice, he said, "Jaden?"

Nobody answered.

"What was that?" Kyle whispered swiftly, shifting his dark brown eyes back and forth, scanning the immediate area.

"I didn't hear anything." Ethan's sandy brown curls swayed under the brim of his backward baseball cap. He shook his head. "Dude, you're being paranoid."

With a hefty swallow, his Adam's apple jouncing in response, Kyle said, "Am not. I heard something." He gestured to the right. "It came from that direction."

Ethan shoved his hands into his pockets. "You need to chill. Nobody's gonna find out."

With the woods falling silent once again, Kyle's shoulders relaxed. "Hope not." Bored with the stone, he dropped it, causing a minor dust storm to cloud their sneakers.

Ethan bent down to wipe off his. "I'm sure Jaden's fine. He's probably already back at the frat house."

"Maybe. I'm ready for another beer. You?"

Ethan nodded, readjusting his hat. "Let's head back."

The boys continued north along the rocky trail. Every so often, Kyle thought he heard fraught and distressed voices in the distance, and a few minutes later, when the boys ran into two of their fraternity brothers, Chase and Aiden, Kyle dismissed his paranoia, convinced those were the voices he'd heard.

Gathered together, Chase told the boys, "We can't find Jaden."

Kyle bit his thumbnail. "Us either." Biting deeper into the nail bed, he asked, "Where'd you guys look?"

"Down by the lake," Aiden said. "He better not have cheated by going out of the boundary area."

"If he did, I'll kill him," Chase said, planting his hands on his hips.

Kyle knitted his thick eyebrows together and glared at Chase, who lowered his eyes.

Oblivious to the exchange between the two, Aiden said, "You know how competitive he is. He has to win, no matter what."

Kyle ignored Aiden's comment. "We're headed back to the frat house. You guys gonna keep looking?"

"Nah, we'll head back," Chase said.

The four boys continued on the path, flattening the dirt, Chase and Kyle falling a few steps behind. With enough distance between the pairs of boys, Kyle leaned closer to Chase and, in a barely audible whisper, asked, "Do you think Jaden knows?"

"No way."

Kyle rubbed the back of his sweaty neck. "Then where is he?"

Chase shrugged. "I don't know. Maybe he got the message." He glanced sideways. "Does anyone else know about the fight?"

Kyle shook his head imperceptibly.

Aiden turned around. "What's going on?"

Kyle and Chase exchanged a forewarning expression. "Nothing," Kyle said. He wiped his muddy palms on his fraternity's button-down jersey, smudging dirt across the white fabric.

After walking in silence for ten minutes, the four boys arrived at a clearing in the woods, dumping them back onto the main road of the college campus. Cars rolled by at a steady pace. Waiting to cross, underneath the bright lights of the streetlamps, Ethan, now able to fully see Kyle's face, asked, "Bruh, what happened?"

Kyle dragged a mud-caked finger along his left cheek, tracing a long scrape. He shrugged. "Must've scratched it on a branch while looking for Jaden."

CHAPTER 1

He rolled off her as she rubbed her hand down his muscular back, his body relaxed from pleasure. After twenty years of marriage, Nicole's sex life was still alive. She considered herself lucky—an anomaly in that department; she pitied those who weren't as fortunate.

"That was amazing," Craig murmured, nuzzling Nicole closer into his broad chest.

She twirled a strand of gray chest hair around her finger. "As always, my love." She breathed deeply through her nose, inhaling his familiar musky cologne. "Do you have to go to your lecture today?" She smiled and batted her inky eyelashes like a foolish schoolgirl. "Can't you stay with me all day in our bed?"

"Big day in my class. And as much as I'd love to stay and study you, duty calls." He slipped from under the weighted duvet and plodded off to the bathroom, Nicole drinking in his nakedness. She smiled.

The water turned on, and Nicole curled under the blanket, appreciating the warmth of the down comforter as the rain pelted against the bedroom window. Since she never returned to work after their son Kyle was born, she had nowhere to be. And now that he was grown, she was fortunate enough to laze around most days.

Nicole had dreaded being an empty nester. Not because she feared it being only she and Craig, but because she didn't know what she'd do with all her time since she'd dedicated her life to raising their son, including volunteering as room mom throughout his elementary years. When he entered middle school, she'd volunteered in the office, helping with attendance, admitting late students, and heading fundraisers. Even when Kyle had started high school, Nicole continued her volunteer work.

Considering other women turned their noses up to the idea of not working outside the home—not being a contributing member of the workforce or the family's financial stability—Nicole enjoyed being a housewife. She thought raising a respectable, responsible, successful young man *was* her contribution to society. Grateful for Craig's support, Nicole considered herself blessed with her fortunate circumstance and did whatever she needed to do to keep her husband happy—and satisfied.

Craig, wrapped in a towel, water pooling around his feet on the ceramic tile, stood in front of the mirror, combing his salt and pepper, thinning hair. "Ugh! I think I have more gray hair than brown," he groaned.

"Gray hair makes men look distinguished," Nicole yelled as she stretched in their king-sized bed. "Consider yourself lucky."

"Sure, let's go with that."

"I find it sexy," she said, sneaking behind him and wrapping her arms around his waist. He still looked sexy: well-defined biceps, broad chest, and barely any facial lines. Craig didn't look forty-six except for a small patch of thinning hair, and Nicole was as attracted to him today as the day they'd met.

With her naked body pressed against his taut back, her bare breasts brushing against his damp skin, she kissed his shoulder. He shuddered.

Craig turned and faced her, savoring her body. "God, you're hot," he said, kissing her deeply, arousing her.

"You'd better not start what you can't finish," she said, pulling him closer and running her fingers down his toned arms. Goosebumps cohabited with the hair on them.

"Then I'd better stop now," he grinned, biting her lower lip.

"Hey, what happened to your arm?"

"My arm?" Craig inspected it. "Oh, this?" he asked, pointing to the thin, red line above his wrist. "I scratched it on my crappy filing cabinet. Damn thing's so old and banged up. I reached into the back of the top drawer, and the corner got me."

"Poor baby. Should I kiss it and make it all better?" she teased with a sparkle in her hazel eyes, her lips spreading into a cunning grin.

"Uh, no, but I appreciate the offer." Craig slipped past her, grazing her bare chest. After sliding his arms into the sharp angles of his overly starched white Oxford sleeves, he buttoned it from bottom to top.

"Hmph," she huffed, crossing her arms, acting like a wounded woman. She grabbed a pale-pink satin robe from the back of the bathroom door and tied the sash around her svelte waist. Like Craig, Nicole didn't look her age. Her wavy, brunette hair showed no signs of gray, and the faint laugh lines around her eyes remained unseen to the naked eye. "Maybe I can make it all better tonight?" she said, standing behind him, tightening his blue and red striped tie.

"You can definitely make it all better tonight," he winked.

Nicole's heart fluttered. She thought, *he still gets to me*. Most couples she knew couldn't stand one another, yet she still couldn't get enough of Craig.

"I need a ride to work today," he said before kissing her cheek.

Because he worked close to home, Nicole and Craig shared one car. Most days, he either took the bus or rode his bike. Thanks to their late morning, however, Craig had already missed the next bus, and, at this rate, he'd miss his mid-morning meeting. With the rain, riding his bike wasn't an option either.

"I'm going to the gym, so I guess I can drop you off on the way. Let me throw on my workout clothes," she said, nuzzling her lips in the crook of his neck, a move she knew drove him wild.

"Hey, play fair," he called after her as she twisted her wiry, unruly hair into a self-tying bun and disappeared into the bathroom.

• • • • •

An hour later, Nicole pulled into the gym parking lot.

After Kyle had been born and she gained what she considered, not her obstetrician, too much weight, she began an exercise regimen, one she'd stuck to for over eighteen years. She looked more like thirty, not forty, not only because of her flat stomach, toned thighs, and well-sculpted arms, but also because of her smooth skin, thanks to her stringent skincare routine, occasional facials, and good genetics. She hadn't always looked this good, nor consistently implemented such regimented self-care.

Nicole wasn't part of the "in crowd" in high school. Such groups ridiculed her, starting in middle school. When her hormones began to rage, her face broke out with terrible acne. Her parents, who believed in holistic medicine, refused to take her to a dermatologist. Nicole did her best to hide the pockmarks, but unfortunately, even the best foundations and powders couldn't camouflage the rugged landscape of her face.

Her unhappiness had caused her to overeat, and she gained weight. A lot. So, at sixteen, she got a job to save money for when she turned eighteen. As a legal adult, she could receive the desired medical treatment without her parent's permission–precisely what she did her senior year.

By the time she'd graduated, Nicole's skin had cleared up, and she slimmed down by working out—hitting the gym daily. She ate healthier and treated her body better than she had years before. The boys noticed, and so did the mean girls, but for a different reason: their boyfriends paid too much attention to Nicole, and they didn't like that. Not at all. After those hellish years, Nicole swore she'd forever care for her body, never allowing herself to look or feel like that again.

"Hey, girl. What's up?"

Nicole counted out her last three bicep curls. The muscles popped up under her "I love coffee and working out" muscle shirt, showing off her hard-earned guns. "Hey, Leslie," she said, setting the fifteen-pound weights on the cast iron stand. "What's new?"

"Not much. I haven't seen you in any classes lately. I thought maybe you'd stopped coming."

Nicole swiped a hand towel across her forehead, erasing the perspiration dots. "I've been getting to the gym later these days," she said, lifting ten-pound weights and bending over to start her triceps.

"Everything okay?"

"Yeah." Nicole stood back up. "Craig's classes start later in the day, and sometimes I have to drop him off, like today. And with no little ones at home, we get to sleep in." Nicole smiled, thinking back to their morning.

"I'm so jelly. With Millennia, I'm in the 'up at the butt crack of dawn' stage."

Millennia. Every time Nicole heard the name, she rolled her eyes internally and thought, *What happened to good old-fashioned names like Jennifer, Mary, Susan, Lisa? Not names like Apple, Blue, or Millenia.* She glanced over at the playroom. Giant alphabet-lettered foam mats, baby swings, and walkers littered the colorfully decorated room. She saw the bright-eyed, chubby-legged toddler wobbling back and forth like an amateur preteen walking in stilettos. Millennia picked up a toy and stuffed it in her slobbery mouth.

"Yeah, I don't miss those early morning days. People told me I would, but honestly, I don't. It's nice having a responsible young man who can take care of himself. I don't have to hold a bottle or spoon feed him or change diapers. You know?"

Leslie's lips turned down, and a tiny crease appeared between her eyebrows.

"Oh, my God! I'm sorry. I didn't mean to upset or offend you," Nicole said, placing her hand on Leslie's arm.

"Oh, you didn't. It's just exhausting." Leslie looked down at her neon-yellow trainers.

"It is. The bigger the kid, the bigger the problems, though. Thankfully, my son was a pretty easy teenager."

"I guess you got lucky," Leslie said. She peered up at the clock behind Nicole. "Crap, I gotta run. I only have twenty minutes before Millennia expires in the baby prison."

Nicole laughed. "It was good seeing you. I'm sorry if I upset you," she said, leaning forward to start her triceps.

Swinging her forearm back, Nicole's thoughts wandered to Kyle's teenage years. He really was easy compared to other kids. Sure, he got moody, slamming doors when he'd been grounded for not finishing his homework, thus receiving a zero, bringing down his grade point average right before graduation. Other times, he'd locked himself in his room only to reappear for dinner. Normal teenage behaviors: nothing compared to some stories Nicole had heard.

Other moms had told Nicole scary stories of their sons, like the one who'd snuck out of his bedroom window and had taken the car for a joy ride, only to be escorted home by the police because he drove underage. Another boy was caught at a nearby neighborhood park after hours and had to complete forty hours of community service as restitution for trespassing. Of course, the alcohol on his breath hadn't helped his situation either.

Kyle had done nothing to that degree, at least not to Nicole's knowledge.

After three sets, she moved over to a nearby bench. "Excuse me. Are you using this?"

A beefy guy, with arms bigger than Nicole's thighs, stood beside it.

"Excuse me," she said again, pulling up the waistband on her low-rise, red leggings.

Mr. Beefy was admiring himself in the mirror. Nicole noticed the white stems dangling from his ears. She tapped his deeply bronzed bicep bulging out of his "Don't mess with perfection" t-shirt. "Excuse me," she yelled louder.

He removed an earbud, his shirt sleeve nearly splitting from his flexed arm.

Pointing, Nicole asked, "Are you using this bench?"

"No, go ahead, pretty little lady."

Nicole rolled her eyes. She scooted back on the bench and started her chest presses. Her mind wandered back to Kyle, wondering if she had been lucky with him or if he'd been just sneaky enough to hide his indiscretions.

CHAPTER 2

Two hours later, muscles fatigued, Nicole arrived home to her two-story, four-bedroom Victorian-style house. She and Craig had bought this house, hoping to fill up all the bedrooms. Still, fate had different plans for them—three miscarriages after Kyle's birth, Nicole and Craig had decided to stop trying. Neither one could handle the heartbreak anymore, with Nicole blaming herself.

The acne medicine that she'd desperately wanted—the one that her parents never knew she'd taken—had terrible side effects. Infertility wasn't listed as one of them. Nicole often wondered if it was, even though she'd already given birth once before. So instead of filling the empty bedrooms with siblings for Kyle, they used one as a guest room and the other as Craig's office.

After showering, Nicole threw on a pair of ripped jeans and a canary yellow long-sleeved shirt and texted Kyle.

Hey! It's Mom! How's it going?

Even though he was a college student, Nicole still liked to check on him. "Mom, I'm a grown man," he complained every once in a while. "You don't need to check in on me all the time."

"I know. But you'll always be my little boy," she'd say. Besides, it wasn't *all* the time.

Kyle had finished his first semester with a 3.8 GPA. He would've earned a 4.0, but Intro to Lit had derailed that. Now that it was spring semester and only three weeks in, Nicole was unsure of his new schedule, so she didn't panic when he didn't respond immediately, although she assumed he always had his phone on him. Didn't everyone? *God, we've raised a great kid,* she thought.

Busy in the kitchen baking, Nicole missed her phone ding over the loud music playing in the background. Kneading the dough was therapeutic: she loved rolling it between her fingers, controlling the shape and consistency, and how it responded to her commands. She'd found baking medicinal back in middle school when ostracized thanks to her arch-nemesis, acne. Sweets overtook the sourness of the outside world. But all the taste testing had contributed to her weight gain.

Covered in flour, engrossed in the dough and music (she loved to listen while baking), Nicole had lost track of time and missed the car door closing over the excessive volume pumping from the speaker. She listened to various genres: pop, classical, hard rock, classic rock—but not country music—anything but country music. Since she liked to dance as she maneuvered around the kitchen, the woeful tales of that genre were unfavorable for rocking out, the hardships too depressing.

"Hello, my love," Craig said, startling her. She checked the time on the microwave. "Shit!" She brushed her ghostly white cheek with the back of her forearm. "I didn't pick you up. How'd you get home?"

"Bus." He planted a kiss on her dark-stained lips. "Mmm, chocolate?"

"Yes. And flour. Lots of flour. I'm a mess," she said, holding her arms out, looking down at her clothes.

"You're beautiful to me," he said, grabbing her toned ass.

She blushed.

"What's for dinner?"

"Nothing. I lost track of time," Nicole said, washing her dirty hands under their state-of-the-art sensor faucet. She waved her hand in front of the stainless-steel apparatus, and water flowed. She'd insisted on this luxury when they remodeled a few years ago after Craig received his first economics department promotion.

"We can grab a bite or bring something in," he said, grabbing a beer from their Subzero refrigerator—another unnecessary splurge. Still, it was as durable as it was roomy.

"Let's bring in. I'm a mess. You order, and I'll go shower. Again."

"Maybe I'll join you," he said, pulling her close.

"As tempting as that is, I'll take a rain check. I'm dirty."

"That's how I like you." He nibbled down her neck. Her spine tingled, and the little hairs on her arm stood at attention.

"Babe, I love you, but seriously, not now." She kissed him and headed upstairs, leaving Craig holding only a hard glass bottle.

• • • • •

"I ordered dinner," Craig said as Nicole sat beside him on the plush leather couch, donning her favorite soft sweatpants and a matching baby doll t-shirt, her hair still damp, her skin no longer covered in white granular powder. Even though the roomy sectional seated eight people, she preferred to sit near him.

"Perfect. Wait, what *did* you order?" She hoped it wasn't anything too greasy or fattening.

"Sushi."

"Raw or cooked?"

"Seriously, babe, I know what you like and don't like. Give me a little credit here," he said, clutching his chest.

"Sorry." She squeezed his knee.

"That's why I ordered raw." Craig looked at her, anticipating her reaction.

She frowned. "You know that I hate raw."

He kissed her palm. "Just kidding. I ordered your favorite."

She elbowed him in the ribs. "Whatcha watching?"

"Nothing. Everything." In true Craig fashion, he changed channels faster than she could focus on the screen's image, a habit that drove her crazy.

An image flashed by. "Stop. Go back."

"Why?"

"That last channel. Hurry." Her breath hitched.

Aiming the remote control at the TV on the wall opposite the sofa, Craig hit the down button, displaying the previous channel.

Nicole's eyes flew open as she gasped and covered her mouth. "Oh, my God!"

CHAPTER 3

"A local college student, and a member of the Sigma Omicron fraternity, has gone missing," a perky blonde newscaster wearing a black pencil skirt and a blue blouse plunging to her cleavage chirped into a shiny microphone. She didn't look a day over twenty-one; Nicole wondered if the young reporter was an intern.

Nicole jumped up, her shirt hiking up, exposing her stomach from the fast movement.

Craig furrowed his eyebrows. "What's wrong?"

Nicole looked at Craig, tears pooling in her eyes. "What if it's Ky? That's his fraternity," she said, pointing at the chyron parroting the story at the bottom of the screen.

Craig stood up. He took Nicole's hands. "Babe, calm down. Seriously, I'm sure it's not Ky. Don't you think the police would've notified us?" He wrapped his arms around her, but she retreated.

"Don't tell me to calm down. It could be our son. Our. Son," Nicole said slowly, enunciating each syllable. She clutched her stomach. "He never answered my text from earlier. Where's my phone?" she questioned, her eyes frantically scanning the room.

"Babe, please," Craig called out as she bounded into the kitchen. "There's nothing to be this upset about. I'm sure Ky's fine. He's a college kid. Probably out and about."

As much as Nicole loved Craig and his exceptional qualities—like being reasonable when she couldn't be—sometimes it grated on her nerves. She hated how calm and sensible he could be in times like this.

"Then why didn't he answer me earlier?" she hollered, searching for her phone. Hunting under the upside-down pots drying by the farmhouse-style sink, Nicole saw the bottom half of the phone peeking out from a crumpled dish towel on the marbled countertop. As she noticed a missed text from Kyle, she heard his voice echo from the TV. She whipped her head toward the sound, damp tendrils smacking her flushed cheek. Relieved he wasn't the one missing, she returned to the sofa and plopped down, watching.

"Yeah, it's like totally crazy, ya know?" Kyle said, standing in his baggy cargo shorts and a blue and red Sigma Omicron shirt. "Like, you hear stories like this, but you never think it'll happen to someone you know." His overgrown, wavy hair flopped on his forehead when he leaned forward to speak into the reporter's microphone, his brown eyes glinting in the sun. The one feature that grabbed Nicole's attention, though, was the bright pink line trailing down his left cheek.

"Hopefully, the police will find him safe and sound," the bright-eyed reporter said. "Again, he was last seen playing Manhunt in the woods by Lake Cypress. If anyone has any information, please contact the police. And now, back to you, Jonathon." Blondie flashed a movie star smile at the camera, like she was reporting on a glamorous story, not this unsettling one.

Craig hit the mute button.

"See? Told you it wasn't Kyle. Feel better now?"

"Yes. No. I don't know. I'm relieved it's not Kyle, but did you see that scratch on his face?" Nicole didn't give Craig a chance to answer. "I need to talk to him." She tightened her grip on her phone and texted.

CALL ME!!

Her phone rang immediately, displaying Kyle's name and photo.

"Holy hell," she said, skipping the niceties, firing questions. "What is going on? And what happened to your face?"

"Slow down. Geez. Chill."

"Chill? How can I chill when I don't know if you're safe?" Her voice rose three octaves. The doorbell rang, signaling that dinner had arrived. Craig left the room, leaving Nicole to finish with Kyle.

"Mom, seriously. I can't talk to you when you're hysterical."

Oh great, a mini-Craig. "Fine. Sorry," she said, calmer, easing her grip on the phone. "Better?"

"Yes."

"Who's missing?"

Craig returned, holding two brown bags with chopsticks sticking out the top. "How much did you order?" she mouthed.

With one bag in each hand, he shrugged and headed to the kitchen.

"Jaden," Kyle said, bringing her back to their conversation.

"What happened? Did he run away or did something," she paused, swallowing the lump in her throat with the thought of her following words, "bad happen to him?"

"They don't know yet."

Nicole heard the kitchen drawers opening and closing as Craig rustled the brown bags, removing the Styrofoam containers filled with the colorfully decorated rice rolls. "I can't even imagine what Jaden's parents are going through right now. I don't think I'd be able to handle it," she said.

"Luckily, you don't have to. I gotta run. It's a circus around here, and the brothers are calling an emergency meeting."

Kyle had pledged Sigma Omicron his first semester. This hadn't thrilled Nicole since cliques had burned her. She disapproved of people voting on who was "good enough" for a brand. "It's discrimination," she'd said when Kyle said he was rushing. She'd had her fair share of being left out but soon realized that was *her* issue, not Kyle's, and technically, he was an adult; he could make his own decisions, even though she and Craig were the ones paying for them.

Craig, however, the once wild party boy, had fully supported the idea. Despite his approval, Nicole had another concern—hazing and drinking. She'd heard too many horror stories of rituals, like drinking a shot every fifteen minutes until the pledge passed out. And then died.

"Keep me posted, please."

"Yep. And by the way, you don't need to tell me it's you when you're texting. I know who you are," Kyle said with an exasperated sigh.

Ignoring his snarky comment, Nicole said, "Wait." Kyle hung up before she could find out what'd happened to his face, how he'd gotten that fresh-looking scrape.

When Nicole entered the kitchen, Craig was finished with his first sushi roll. He mumbled, exposing the grains of white rice stuffed in his cheeks, "What's the story?"

"Jaden's missing. That's all I got. Ky had to run to an emergency meeting. I told him to keep me posted." She maneuvered her chopsticks, placing them between her thumb and middle finger, a skill she'd only recently learned and picked up a piece of the Volcano Roll, her favorite. She loved spicy food—the spicier, the better.

"I know that look," Craig said, watching Nicole's brow furrow. "Don't worry. I'm sure it's nothing. College kids wander off all the time."

"Maybe."

"No, not maybe. Trust me, babe. They get drunk, pass out, and wake up elsewhere. Hell, maybe Jaden's holed up banging a hot chick."

"Banging? Real nice, Craig." Her eyes watered from the volcano sauce and wasabi, and she sniffled, stifling a sneeze from the burn.

"You know what I mean. They're college kids. Living it up. Sowing their oats."

She shuddered at the next thought. "Eww, I prefer not to think of our son banging girls."

"He's a guy. It's what they do," he said, stabbing his next sushi victim, a piece of shrimp tucked tightly with asparagus and avocado.

"Not our son. He's a gentleman," Nicole said, reaching for the same piece, their chopsticks dueling it out. Craig won. She pinched the adjacent piece. "I prefer not to categorize my son in the former group."

"Oh, now he's your son?"

She giggled. "Yes."

Stabbing his next piece, Craig's phone rang. He checked the screen. "I need to take this. Sorry."

"What happened to the no phones at the dinner table rule?" she asked, raising an eyebrow.

"It was in my back pocket, so technically—" he said, excusing himself from the table.

The left side of her lip curled. "Loopholes. There are always loopholes," she called out after him. Nicole finished the remaining sushi while thinking about her conversation with Kyle. And that scratch. When finished, with only abandoned rice morsels left in the to-go containers, Nicole tossed them in the trash. "Who was that?" she asked as Craig returned.

He wet a sponge and wiped the espresso-colored table, erasing all evidence that a meal had occurred. "My teaching assistant."

"How's Alex doing?"

"Okay, I guess. Just always trying to please me. It's so annoying."

Craig had constantly complained, semester after semester, saying, "A good teaching assistant is impossible to find." He said they were too disorganized, scatterbrained, undependable, unreliable, or lazy. Nobody could fill the preposterous demands he would conjure up in his head. Nicole used to say, "I think you're expecting way too much from these kids. That's what they are, college kids." Craig would grumble, dismissing her comments, convinced there had to be someone, anyone, who was mature and responsible enough to meet his standards.

"I remember a time, actually, lots of times, when you bitched your T.A. didn't try hard enough, and now this one is trying *too* hard?" Nicole said, drying the table behind Craig.

"I'm not complaining that Alex tries too hard. It's the constant need to please me that drives me crazy."

"I don't find it very hard to please you." Nicole swatted him on the butt.

"That's because you know all the right ways to do it," he said, tossing the dirty sponge over his shoulder. It landed in the sink. "Want to try now?"

"There's absolutely nothing else I'd love more right now than to please you, Mr. Cunningham."

"That's Dr. Cunningham," he corrected.

"Oh, excuse me, *Dr.* Cunningham."

Craig grabbed her hand and led her up the L-shaped staircase. Nicole was excited to finish what she'd started earlier that day, but distracted by

Jaden's disappearance, when they reached the top landing, she said, "I hope they find him," thinking more aloud than speaking to Craig.

"I'm sure they will. Stop worrying and concentrate on the pleasurable things I'm about to do to you, Mrs. Cunningham."

Grateful for such a husband, Nicole tucked the worry in the back of her mind. Craig laid her down on the bed, and they finished the day the way it'd started.

CHAPTER 4

The following morning, Jaden's disappearance was all over the news. Local media trucks covered the campus, reporting that, yes, in fact, Jaden was classified as a "missing person." Usually, a nineteen-year-old, a legal adult, wasn't labeled as such, especially after only a day, because realistically, adults are free to come and go as they pleased. However, Jaden's case was different. He has diabetes, and without his insulin, he could go into insulin shock, a coma, or, even worse, die. Time was of the essence—Jaden needed to be found as quickly as possible—his life depended on it.

The news further reported that the police couldn't pinpoint Jaden's location because his cell phone was no longer transmitting a signal. It was assumed that the battery had drained by now. However, the police confirmed his last known whereabouts—near Lake Cypress. Known for its seductive nature for young adults, Lake Cypress was the place to go to skinny dip in the heart of darkness and get a piece of action far away from roommates, dorm life, and city lights. Lake Cypress wasn't a stranger to secrets. If those waters could speak, the stories it could tell—they'd flow for years.

Other than stating Jaden's name, releasing a current photo of him, and saying they needed to find him as soon as possible because of his diabetic condition, the police remained tight-lipped, not leaking any information. Social media, however, was blowing up.

Photos and messages praying for Jaden's safe return filled the Facebook, Instagram, and Snapchat feeds—begging him to contact anyone to let his family know he was okay. Rumors also jammed up the threads: people claiming he'd committed suicide, others saying he'd run away, others saying he'd been murdered. Nicole's heart went out to Jaden's parents, hoping they weren't reading any of it. She kept putting herself in their shoes, contemplating what she'd do and how she'd feel if this were Kyle.

Worse, Nicole couldn't escape hearing about it. Even while driving to the gym, she heard updates on the radio. Most of the information was mere speculation; people talking amongst themselves, like armchair detectives, saying things like Jaden's parents, George and Cecelia Pierce, would offer a reward. They were desperately worried about their son—the longer time passed, the more dangerous it became to his health.

When she arrived home after her workout, Nicole flipped on the TV to a press conference. Jaden's parents stood front and center of the screen, addressing the public. With a typical middle-aged gut, George, shorter than average height, spoke into the camera. His dark, empty eyes stared blankly into the camera lens. "We love you, Jaden," he said, voice cracking.

Cecelia, shorter than her husband, stood beside him, her face cradled in her palms, shoulders hunched, shaking in waves as she sobbed, a white tissue peeking out from under her black dress sleeve.

George continued to speak. "We are offering a five-thousand-dollar reward to anyone who can help us find our son. Jaden is a sweet, gentle, kind boy and would never disappear on his own, especially without his medication." He hung his head and sighed, sniffling, before he looked back up. "He's smart, funny, and liked by so many. None of this makes any sense." George wiped his nose with the back of his finger and drew a long breath, his chest expanding, stretching his navy-blue Tommy Bahama shirt taut, the fabric straining between the buttons. "If you have any information to help us find Jaden, please, we beg you, come forward. We pray that he's okay. And Jaden, if you're watching this and you left on your own accord, please come home. We need our precious boy returned safely. He can't be without his medication, and we can't be without him. Please," he pleaded one last time, "help us find him now."

Nicole blinked back hot tears. She didn't know Jaden well but knew of him since he was one of Kyle's fraternity brothers. Nicole's heart ached for those parents on the screen. Again, she put herself in their shoes. How were they even functioning? *I need to help them, but how?* Empathizing didn't feel enough. She needed to do more.

Nicole noticed the police and a handful of civilians wandering through the wooded area behind where George had spoken. Since volunteers were welcome to help search, Nicole needed to know who to contact to get involved. She decided to call the police station and speak with the lead detective. Punching in the numbers listed at the bottom of the TV screen, she bit her lower lip.

"Do you have a tip?" the voice on the other end asked.

"I'm not sure," Nicole lied, desperate to talk to whoever was in charge.

"Please hold."

Nicole's heart raced, her palms moist with sweat.

A gruff voice came through. "Hello, this is Lou Newton. I can't talk to you right now. Leave a message, and I'll get back to you as soon as possible. If you need immediate assistance, please press one. Have a blessed day."

This last phrase caught Nicole by surprise.

"A blessed day?" she said to the dead air. "Who is having a blessed day when they need to talk to a detective? Someone's gone missing, and you're saying, 'have a blessed day'?" She rolled her eyes. Too distracted by the ironic phrase, Nicole missed the beep. "Dammit," she said, redialing the number.

After being transferred and listening to the message again, she spoke, "Hi, yes, um, my name is Nicole Cunningham, and I'm familiar with the Jaden boy case. Oh, I don't have any information about it, sorry," she giggled nervously. "Anyway, I was wondering if there is any way I can help. I know that sometimes you need volunteers to help. I've read it in books and seen it on TV, so if it's a real thing, let me know how I can help," she rambled. "Please call me back and let me know what I should do next. Thanks." *Have a blessed day,* she thought as she hung up.

"Shit!" Nicole slapped her forehead. "I didn't leave my number." She called back a third time, listening to his voicemail, picturing Detective Newton as John Krasinski: tall, slim, fit, the attractive boy next door.

At the beep, she said, "Sorry. It's me again. Nicole Cunningham. I forgot to leave my number. You can call me back at 717-555-8121. Please. Thanks. Okay, bye."

She was right back to her awkward teenage self, the one who couldn't find her niche, all plump and pimple-faced. She shook her head as though tossing that depressing thought right out.

• • • • •

While driving to Craig's office to meet him for lunch, Nicole whipped the car around and made an illegal U-turn in the middle of a busy intersection. She needed to talk to Detective Newton, so acting impulsively, she drove to the police station without thinking. Something, unable to put her finger on it, nagged at her. Call it mothers' empathy, women's sympathy, or an intuition of some sort, whatever it was, she needed to be close to this case.

The police station was bustling when Nicole walked in. People outfitted in blue uniforms or plain street clothes, wearing shiny polished badges either pinned to their shirts or hooked around their belts, scurried back and forth. Their shoes clacked on the alternating black and white square linoleum floor. It reminded Nicole of a chessboard. Laughing at the thought, she wondered if they ever used themselves as tokens in moments of boredom. Regretful of thinking anything funny during such a somber time, Nicole cleared her throat.

Phones rang simultaneously and asynchronously, creating a cacophony of bells. "Is this an emergency? Okay, please hold," the brunette sitting behind the Plexiglass said into her headset in a nasally, sing-song tone. Her irritating voice wasn't the first thing Nicole noticed. Instead, it was the girl's nineteen-eighties feathered haircut—hair wisped back and plastered to the sides of her head with what Nicole assumed to be an entire can of White Rain hairspray. The receptionist lifted her finger, signaling she would be with Nicole in a minute.

When the nasally brunette hung up, she asked, "Can I help you?"

"Is Detective Newton in?" Nicole noticed a small chip in the receptionist's front tooth. "I called and left a voicemail earlier. Two actually, but I figured since I was driving by," she lied, "I'd stop in and see if he was here."

"And you are?"

"Nicole Cunningham."

"And why do you need to see the detective?" the girl asked, narrowing her eyes.

"I wanted to talk to him about the Jaden Pierce case."

Raising an unkempt eyebrow, the girl asked, "Do you have any information?"

"I don't think so," Nicole said, her neck knotting up. Worried she couldn't talk to the detective at this rate, she lied. "I'm Jaden's aunt, and I'd like to talk to the detective. Is he here?"

Plaster Hair scrutinized Nicole, eyeing her up and down. Nicole was grateful she had at least showered and changed into something presentable—black Capri pants and a striped scoop neck blouse.

"Let me check," Plaster Hair said, picking up her phone while continuing to inspect Nicole. With a half-eaten neon pink fingernail, the receptionist pressed four numbers on the oversized desk phone and waited. After a minute, she said, "I'm sorry. I only got his voicemail. He must be out. Would you like to leave a message?"

"I already did. Twice. Remember? On his voicemail." Nicole glared at the absentminded receptionist.

"Oh, right." Ms. White Rain's face turned one shade brighter than her remnant nail polish.

"Is there anyone else I can talk to?" Nicole noticed a woman in a maroon suit seated a few desks back, staring at her. The woman tapped a pen rhythmically, watching. Uncomfortable, Nicole shifted her weight from foot to foot.

"Do you have any information regarding his disappearance?" Nasally nose asked again.

"No," Nicole said, leaning against the counter. Not wanting Maroon Suit to hear, Nicole whispered, "Full disclosure, my son is in the same fraternity."

"Your son is in the same fraternity as your nephew?"

"Nephew? What? No."

"But you just said Jaden is your nephew," the receptionist said, reminding Nicole of her little white lie moments ago.

Nicole turned two shades brighter than the receptionist's half-eaten nail polish and continued in a hushed tone, "Oh, right. If I'm being totally honest, I'm not really Jaden's aunt. I keep thinking about Jaden's poor parents and what they must be going through, how they must be feeling. Not that I can totally understand," Nicole said, catching Maroon Suit's gaze. Constantly drumming the pen, she didn't take her eyes off Nicole. "Thankfully, I've never been in their position," Nicole said, louder than intended.

Maroon Suit scowled, her pen hovering mid-strike.

Nicole's face now matched Maroon Suit's outfit. "Oh God, I sound extremely harsh. Sorry. That's not what I meant."

"I get what you're saying," the receptionist said, smiling, setting Nicole at ease.

"Anyway, I know that sometimes the police form search parties or need help putting up signs. You know, stuff like that. I thought maybe I could help. I don't know how any of this works." Nicole looked over the receptionist's head and relaxed her hunched shoulders, seeing that Maroon Suit had moved on.

"Let me see what I can find out for you." The receptionist, Valerie—Nicole just now noticed the name engraved on the metal plate—walked down a corridor, her footsteps fading as she disappeared.

Nicole strummed her fingers on the counter and smiled at a uniformed policewoman walking by. The woman half-smiled, preoccupied with something on her phone. After a few minutes and still no sign of Valerie, Nicole checked her phone.

A text from Craig:

I guess you're not coming?

Sorry! I needed to take care of something. Raincheck?

Yeah. Swamped today anyway. Checked your location. Why you at the police station? All ok?

All good. I'll explain later 😍

😘

Valerie reappeared in the hallway; her black Mary Jane heels joined the other clacking shoes, growing louder as she neared. "I spoke with another detective. Told him you'd like to speak to Newton yourself. I left out the white lie about you being his aunt," she said, rolling her mocha eyes.

Heat rose to Nicole's face once again, spreading to her ears.

"He'll relay the message to Detective Newton, and hopefully, you'll hear back. I'm sure he's a little consumed with more important things." Valerie smirked.

Nicole's heart sank. "I'm sure."

"Thank you for calling the Cypressville Police. Is this an emergency?" Valerie said, putting her headphones back on, answering the next call as she watched Nicole walk out the double doors.

. . . . .

The alarm bell chimed, alerting Nicole Craig was home. "I'm in here," she hollered from the kitchen. Busy wiping a glass cake stand inherited from her grandmother, Nicole gently placed it on the stone countertop.

Craig walked over and kissed her firmly. Nicole wrapped her arms around his neck. "Hello, love of my life," she whispered into his ear, inhaling his familiar cologne.

His arms circled her waist. "Hello, my love. How was your day?" His deep, husky voice tickled her ear.

"Fine. Sorry I skipped out on lunch. How was your day?"

"Busy." He let go and opened the refrigerator door, intently studying the contents. The cool air escaped into the now warm kitchen—the oven had raised the temperature a few degrees.

After a few moments, Nicole asked, "You okay?" The food and Craig were at an impasse.

"Yeah. Why?" he said, holding his gaze.

"I don't know. Maybe the fact that the fridge is winning the staring contest."

"Oh. Sorry." He grabbed a beer and shut the door.

"No need to apologize. Just making sure you're okay. You seem...off."

"Long day. That's all." He rustled through the utensil drawer next to the oven, looking for a bottle opener, scattering about ladles, wooden spoons, and spatulas. Nicole always had to reorganize it because Craig insisted on randomly throwing things in there, never putting them back in their proper place. "Where the hell is the bottle opener?" he growled, chucking the useless items aside, disturbing the contents further.

"This one?" Nicole asked, picking up the shiny metal object from the adjacent junk drawer and handing it to him.

"Why's it in that drawer?" he asked, reaching for it.

"Because that's where you put it. You use it. Not me." Nicole was a wine drinker, never a beer lover. "Are you sure you're okay?"

"Yeah, sorry," he muttered, sitting on the island barstool, untucking his polo shirt from his tan chinos. He gulped a mouthful of beer.

"The bus again?" Sometimes Craig was cranky from waiting for it, or because of the crowded seating arrangements and the inability to sit comfortably, or not at all, for that matter.

"No, the bus was fine."

"Then what is it?" Nicole asked, putting away the cake stand, rising on her tippy toes to reach a high cabinet. Carefully, she balanced it between her hands. It wobbled slightly as she slid it on the shelf.

He hung his head and sighed. "I'm worried I won't get that promotion."

As she closed the cabinet, Nicole faced Craig. "Of course you will. You've earned it."

"Maybe. I don't know. Doesn't feel like it lately." Craig shook his head, like ridding himself of such negativity. Unexpectedly, he flashed his infamous smile, where a dimple appeared on the right side of his lip. Nicole loved that dimple, especially its lopsidedness; the other side was missing its twin.

On their first date, she'd noticed this charming characteristic when he'd taken her hiking—not her ideal first date. Or any date at all. Even though she loved working out and staying in shape, she did not love the outdoors: too many bugs and reptiles. Nicole enjoyed his company, witty humor, and gentlemanliness, so she was a good sport; her interest in him far outweighed the grossness of nature.

He'd catered to her every need that day. He traveled slowly over the dirt, sticks, and stones, never making her feel like an inexperienced hiker. His amusing anecdotes from his college years and his hilariously entertaining stories of hikes gone wrong helped pass the time on the arduous ascent through the narrow paths, the trees encircling them, walling them off from the rest of the world. And before she'd realized it, they'd reached the peak. They were high above the canopy, a vast sea of green below. Nicole felt like if she outstretched her fingers, she could touch the sun. It was like he'd put her on a pedestal, and she knew, right then and there, that she'd marry him one day.

That was one of the most challenging hills they'd ever climbed, except for the fertility issue. Even then, though, they'd leaned on one another. Their relationship had been primarily easy, rarely getting tripped up.

"I have something to tell you," Nicole said as Craig swigged back another gulp of his beer.

"You're pregnant," he joked, knowing that was impossible.

"No," Nicole said, quieter, sitting beside him. Still a tender subject for her, Craig often joked about it, as if humor could remedy her barrenness after Kyle had been born. She knew Craig's intent was harmless—to help lighten a serious situation. Unfortunately, all the humor in the world couldn't remedy it. "I'm going to help find Jaden," she said, holding back the tears desperately wanting to escape from the belly of disappointment.

"You know where he is?" Craig asked, wrinkling his forehead.

"No, of course not."

Craig finished the beer and peered through the transparent, dark-colored glass, checking for any remaining liquid. Reassured it was depleted, he said, "I'm not following."

"I feel like I need to do something. I keep thinking, what if this was Kyle? What if our son went missing? I'd want as many people out there as possible to help find him." She stared at Craig, waiting for a response. He remained silent, picking at the soggy label, the corners now tattered and frayed, only the alcohol content level still intact and legible.

Nicole waved her hand in front of his glassy eyes. "Hello? Anyone in there?"

"Yeah. I'm just processing what you said." He swiveled his barstool and locked his gaze with hers. "Why would you want to help?"

"When I was driving to meet you for lunch, I kept hearing about it on the radio. People are making up rumors. I don't know," she shrugged, "it bothers me. I want to help find the truth. And Jaden."

Nicole studied Craig's expression, watching for his reaction. Nothing. He looked like he was far away, not engaged in this conversation. "So I turned around and went to the police station and offered my help."

"That's why you were at the police station."

Nicole nodded. "I'd called the station first and left a message with the lead detective, Lou something or other. Crap, I hate it when I can't remember a name. Lou...Lou..." she snapped her fingers and rolled her eyes upwards, searching for the forgotten name on her forehead. It worked. "Newton," she said.

Craig mishandled the bottle. It tipped over on the counter and clinked, chipping off a sliver of glass.

"Anyway, I left him a voicemail. I wanted to talk to someone and offer my help, so I drove straight to the station to find out what I could do." To avoid cutting herself, Nicole carefully picked up the dark brown sliver with her thumb and forefinger and tossed it in the trash.

"Was Detective...what was his name?"

"Newton."

"Was Detective Newton there?"

"No, but I spoke to the receptionist. God, her voice was ridiculously annoying." Nicole scoffed, thinking about her. "And she looked like a total Valley Girl. It's like she teleported here straight from the eighties." Nicole laughed louder. "How ironic. Her name was Valerie. Get it? Valley and Valerie?"

"Focus," Craig said, reaching for her hands. He weaved his fingers in with hers, resting them on the countertop.

Nicole shook her head. "Anyway, she found someone else who said they would relay my message. That detective said...huh, I didn't catch that detective's name. I'm not sure Valley Girl, Valerie, even said it, come to think of it."

"Nic," Craig squeezed her hand like it was the magic button to refocus her.

"Right. Anyway, that detective said he'd make sure Detective Newton gets my message. And now I wait. If I don't hear back in a day or two, I'll follow up."

"I love your passion for wanting to help. It's one of the many reasons I love you," he said, standing up, kissing the tip of her thin turned-up nose.

"But?"

He tossed his empty beer bottle in the recycling bin. "But—"

"I knew it. There's always a but."

With an irritated sigh, Craig said, "But I don't know why you *always* feel the need to help everybody."

"I guess it's who I am. I like to help people."

"Yes, you do, but if it's dangerous, then you shouldn't. I love you and don't want anything bad to happen. Ever. I don't know what I'd do if I lost you." His eyes watered, and he cleared his throat.

Nicole's defenses softened. She couldn't be angry at him for wanting her to be careful. And safe; he was only trying to protect her. "I appreciate your concern, but I know what I'm doing. I promise."

"I hope so," he said. "I don't need any trouble finding you."

CHAPTER 5

A day later, and still no sign of Jaden, Nicole followed up twice with the police station, leaving messages for Detective Newton each time. Frustrated with the lack of response, she baked to keep her idle hands occupied.

Despite the police remaining tight-lipped, the story was everywhere now, with the news and social media keeping it alive, swirling with rumors and prayers for Jaden's safe return. As far as everyone knew, the police had no new leads; the only information known was Jaden's medical condition and his last location, Lake Cypress, less than a mile from campus, and the Sigma Omicron fraternity house. Rough terrain covered the area, and the sticky, muddy, uneven grounds made it difficult to pass through. To say it was challenging to comb through the area was an understatement.

Today, the TV was on in the background instead of music. Nicole heard a man say, "We've verified with T-Mobile that Jaden's phone was last located near Lake Cypress when he disappeared two nights ago. We still don't know where he is. The search party is actively looking."

She perked up, stopping mid-roll as she pressed the wooden rolling pin over the freshly made dough for the dessert pizza crust, setting it aside and wiping her hands on the "Kiss the Baker" apron tied around her waist. She turned up the volume and watched while continuing to roll.

"At this time, we're still not suspecting foul play. There is no evidence to suggest this. Presently, we are classifying it as a missing person's case. It wouldn't be our first time dealing with a situation like this: an overstressed, overwhelmed college student taking off, looking for respite. Running away from his problems."

Nicole checked the name at the bottom of the screen. She read the words, "Detective Newton."

That's Detective Newton? she thought, surprised by his haggard appearance. His voice didn't match his face, and he definitely didn't look like John Krasinski. She figured Detective Newton was in his early sixties, much older than he sounded on the phone. He was of average height, with a thick neck and a shiny bald head, like Mr. Clean. Thick, dark, bushy eyebrows rested right above his equally dark brown eyes. As he stared into the camera, Nicole felt he was looking straight through her. His intense stare showed he was a "Don't fuck with me" kind of guy.

"But we know this is different considering Jaden's health, so we are doing everything we can to find him," the detective said, his intense eyes boring a hole through the camera.

"You're not doing enough. You haven't even called me back yet," Nicole said to the TV. "A willing volunteer."

"As Jaden's parents said, we are asking anyone with any information to please come forward. His life depends on it."

Nicole's stomach tensed.

"Rumors are circulating on social media, and we are asking you to please stop posting false information. It's not helping us, the family, or Jaden."

Nicole listened to his update and suddenly wondered if Kyle had been with Jaden that night. She hadn't thought to ask him when they'd spoken on the phone, and since Kyle and Jaden were in the same fraternity, maybe Kyle knew something. If he did, Nicole wanted to know. She left the lump of dough sitting in the middle of the kitchen island and picked up her phone, ignoring Detective Newton's final words of his press conference.

She texted Kyle:

Call me. Immediately!

Watching her blank screen, waiting for the three dots to appear, Nicole bit the inside of her cheek, kicking herself for not thinking about this until now.

The blank screen stared back at her. She wiped the tiny beads of sweat percolating on her forehead with the back of her forearm.

With no response, she typed again.

Where are you? I need you to call me. NOW!!!

Over the years, Kyle had learned that three exclamation points meant his mother wasn't messing around. She was serious, and he'd better answer. Now. No, more like yesterday. Moments later, three dots appeared on her screen. Seconds later, his message popped up:

In class. Can't talk

CALL ME ASAP!!!

Filled with worry, Nicole returned to the dough, transferring her restlessness to the innocent blob. Her knuckles turned white with her rigid grip. She leaned into the pin, placing all her upper body weight into the movement, rolling it back and forth, fear increasing with each pass. For the first time, baking wasn't calming her. Instead, she became more agitated as she manipulated the uncooperative sticky dough waiting for Kyle's call.

While dusting another smattering of flour over the top layer, Nicole jumped when her phone rang. She grabbed it, but it wasn't Kyle. The home screen flashed the words "Unknown Caller." Her doughy finger hit the green button. "Hello?"

"I'm looking for Ms. Cunningham," a raspy voice said through the earpiece.

"This is." Nicole wiped her caked-on, floured finger down her black leggings, leaving white spots, creating her own leopard-looking print.

"This is Detective Newton with the Cypressville Police."

"Oh, hi! Thank you for calling me back."

"Sorry I haven't returned your call sooner," he said, like reading her thought of *it took you long enough*.

"No problem," she lied. "I'm glad you did." She walked back to the TV and turned down the volume. A home improvement show was on now, shutting out what was happening in their sleepy college town.

"I hear you're interested in helping with the search party. Is that correct?" Detective Newton asked.

"Yes. Very much so." Nicole heard his heavy breaths through the phone.

In a gruff tone, he asked, "Why?"

"Because I'm a mom."

Snappier, he asked, "Are you *Jaden's* mom?" dragging out Jaden's name.

Nicole rubbed the back of her neck. "No."

"Then why do you have such an interest in helping?"

Nicole's breath caught in her throat. She hadn't expected such a question. She thought he'd say something like, "Great. We could use all the help we can get." Or "The more sets of eyes we have, the larger the square area we can cover." Instead, he responded with an inquisition, crossly no less. Thinking fast, she spoke the truth. "It's devastating. My heart breaks for his parents. I also have a college boy, so I can totally empathize with them."

Nicole heard muffled voices and papers shuffling in the background. "Sign it now," Detective Newton said.

"Sign what?" Nicole asked, confused.

For the first time since he'd spoken to her, Detective Newton softened his tone. "Sorry, I was talking to another detective here. Anyway, if you're interested in volunteering, you can join the others."

"I don't have to fill out any paperwork?" she asked, surprised at how easy joining was.

"No."

"I don't need to complete a background check or anything like that?"

"No, ma'am." And with his next question, his tone once again turned icy. "Why? Should we do one on you?"

"No. I'm clean as a whistle," she said in a high-pitched voice. "You're saying anyone can walk out there and join? Even someone who may have something to do with Jaden's disappearance?"

"As I said, we don't screen the volunteers." He paused and said, "Do you have something to do with his disappearance?"

"What? No!" Nicole said. "I told you before. I'm a mom, and I want to help."

"That's not my department. I have nothing to do with who joins or not."

"Okay." The tension in her neck released.

Snippily, he asked, "Is that all?"

"Um, yeah, I guess."

The phone went dead. Nicole stood, mouth gaping, rubbing her forehead, utterly disturbed by how the conversation had gone. She looked around the messy kitchen, deciding what to do next: finish here or head to the woods.

She leered at the disheveled lump of dough, waiting for it to speak to her, tell her what to do: salvage or scrap it. "Fuck it," she said, opting for the latter. She scooped up the mountainous ball and tossed it into the trash can like a basketball.

CHAPTER 6

Kyle called Nicole back on her way to the search area. She sighed with relief seeing his name on the screen and answered at the half-ringtone, eager to speak to him.

"Hey," he said.

Nicole opened her mouth to talk, but before she could speak, he asked, "What's up?"

"Jaden Pierce. That's what's up," she said, cutting to the chase, needing to know her son's involvement from that night, *if* he had any involvement, she reminded herself. Eager to find out, she didn't want to dance around and discuss classes, girls, or any other trivial information; she wanted answers.

"Mom, that's not new news." He sounded annoyed, like she was too stupid to tie her own shoe.

She gripped the steering wheel tighter. "Yeah. I know. But I need to know if you were with him the night he disappeared." Less than a mile to her destination—the wooded area—she put on her turn signal and looked in her side mirror. With no car blocking the lane, she inched over.

Dead air lingered between them. Nicole thought she'd lost the call. "Ky? You there?"

"Yeah, I'm here."

"Did you hear me?" she asked, unsure if he hadn't heard her or was avoiding the question.

"No."

Not sure if he was answering *no* about being with Jaden that night or asking if he'd heard her, she clarified, "No, you didn't hear me, or no, you weren't with Jaden?" Gravel flicked up as she drove over the pebbly ground, sending grit and sand swirling around the tires. She parked across the street toward the back of an abandoned area, not wanting to drive over too much rubble and risk scratching or nicking the car.

"No, I didn't hear you, and yes, I was with Jaden." Nicole's heart skipped a beat. Before she could ask her next question, he said, "A bunch of us were."

"Like who?"

"Some of the other brothers."

Once parked, she dropped her head; her fear confirmed. She drew a deep breath. "Do you know what happened to him?"

"No." No explanation. No elaboration. No details. A simple, one-word answer.

Growing impatient, she asked, "Have the police questioned you?"

"Yes."

Upon hearing that word, Nicole's heart dropped into her stomach. "What? And you didn't tell me?"

"It was no big deal. They've questioned all of us."

Terrified for him, she asked, "What kinds of questions did they ask?"

"Things about Jaden, like if we thought he'd threatened to harm himself, or if he'd shown any signs of distress, or if he was in any trouble that we knew of, stuff like that."

As a mom, Nicole felt guilty about asking her next question. She worried Kyle would misinterpret it and think she was unfairly accusing him of knowing something or having been involved since he'd just admitted to being there that night. Still, like a protective mother, she had to ask because she needed to figure out what to do if his answer was yes. Nicole's shoulders tensed. "Did you have anything to do with Jaden's disappearance?"

She could hear Kyle's rapid breathing and held hers, waiting.

In an aggrieved tone, he asked, "How could you ask me that?"

She knew she'd hurt him. Her intent was good—to help him. She needed him to understand this. "I'm sorry. I need to know, so I can help you if you're in trouble. That's it. I promise. I'll love and support you no matter what."

"You think I had something to do with it, don't you?" He sounded deflated.

Nicole was walking a fine line—fishing for the truth and offending her son. Still, she needed to continue to help him if he was in trouble. "I love you. You're my son. My only child. My job is to protect you, and the fact that you're not answering the question concerns me. If you have nothing to hide—" She closed her eyes, anticipating his response.

"Why aren't you answering my question?" he shot back.

"I need to know. No judgments. I need the truth. Please, honey. Tell me. I don't think you had anything to do with it, but I need to hear it from you." She was unsure who she was trying to convince: Kyle or herself? "If we need to hire an attorney or anything like that, I need to know. Talk to me."

Kyle inhaled loudly. "I don't know what happened to him."

A sick feeling washed over Nicole, unsure if she believed him. She wanted to. She really did. More than anything. Such an awful situation, not knowing whether your child is telling the truth. Her mouth went dry as her thoughts returned to that incident years ago.

"Were you involved in any way that night, Ky? I need to know because I can promise you this, the truth will come out, and I don't want you to be in further trouble for withholding information or, even worse, lying." Nicole's heart pounded against her ribs.

Nicole had a motto, "I will trust you until you give me a reason not to." And once given a good reason, the trust was gone. And if she ever trusted again, it would take years to rebuild what'd been demolished instantaneously.

She bit her lower lip. "You know the authorities can charge you with a crime if you withhold information." Not wanting any bystanders overhearing their conversation, Nicole kept the car windows rolled up. Since it was an unusually chilly day for Cypressville, exhaust fumes billowed like fluffy clouds from her tailpipe. She watched them drift in the rearview mirror.

Kyle remained silent.

Waiting for his response, Nicole heard his long, deep sighs.

"I know you're still there. What are you thinking?" She often asked this question when she saw him staring off in the distance, no longer present in his surroundings, or when he would shut down and go completely silent, like now.

"I'm, I'm...scared," he whispered hoarsely.

She wanted to reach through the phone and cradle him on her lap, all six feet two inches of him. She wanted to rock him. Soothe him. Tell him everything would be okay, that he would be okay like she had done when he was a little boy and had fallen off his bike and scraped his knees. This, however, was no superficial cut. This was a serious and dangerous injury, one that could leave a permanent scar.

"You need to tell me everything. I can help you, but only if you tell me what you know." She gave a half-hearted wave to a uniformed officer who parked beside her and opened his car door.

With his following words, Kyle's voice quivered. "Please don't be mad at me. I'm afraid you're going to hate me."

And with those words, her heart cracked open. "Ky, I could never hate you. You're my son, and no matter what, I'll always love you." And that was the truth. Nicole had never fully understood unconditional love, not until she'd become a mother. She'd always love her son, no matter what. She may not like his behavior or choices, but she'd love and choose him above all others. "Just tell me."

Silence filled the line momentarily.

"Okay," he sighed. "We were playing Manhunt in the woods near the lake."

Nicole frowned, interrupting him. "Was this a hazing incident?" She had to ask, her irrational fear screaming.

"What? No. See, this is why I can't tell you. You always jump to the worst-case scenario."

Her chest relaxed. "Sorry. Go on."

"We all split up to hide. Nobody saw Jaden after that."

Suddenly, Nicole was cold. She turned up the heat in the car. "And nobody realized he was missing?"

"No. We figured he'd show up again, but he never did. We tried to call and text him the next morning, but there was no response."

"His phone must've died by then," Nicole said, thinking aloud.

"Exactly."

"What'd you guys do then?"

"We called around to people who'd hung out with him, but nobody had seen or heard from him since earlier that day. I guess our fraternity president called his parents, who said they hadn't heard from him either. From what I understand, when they couldn't reach him, they called the police."

Believing her son's story, Nicole slackened her jaw, and all tension left her body. "Okay," she said. "You should be totally fine then."

"Are you going to tell Dad?"

Swiftly making a mental pros and cons list on the spot, Nicole said, "No, no need to. He knows it's your fraternity, and honestly, he didn't seem too concerned." She picked at a piece of lint on her pants.

Kyle sniffled. Nicole pictured him wiping his nose with the back of his sleeve like he's done since he was a toddler. No matter how often she gave him a tissue, he used the back of his forearm. His third-grade teacher had written a note home, which Nicole thought absurd. *Is it really a classroom disruption?* she'd written back. Mrs. Fluist replied, *Not really, but it's a disgusting habit that should be nipped in the bud before it's too late.* Nicole had rolled her eyes. And yet, his teacher had been right because here he was, nineteen years old, still wiping his snot with his forearm.

"Why would you think I'd hate you? It doesn't sound like you did anything wrong."

"I need to tell you something else," Kyle said.

Nicole held her breath, waiting for the bomb—the one she'd anticipated, the one she feared the most—that he'd lied before, and now he was going to confess. "What?"

"I was drinking that night."

Nicole threw her head back and laughed.

"Why is that so funny?"

"I wasn't born yesterday. I know you drink." She didn't want to tell him what she thought he was going to say.

"Do you think I'll get in trouble for that?"

"I don't know, but I would leave that detail out like you did with me."

"Sorry."

"Don't be sorry. It's not an important detail. I wouldn't worry about it. That reminds me. What happened to your face?" Nicole pictured that long pink scrape marring his usually smooth cheek.

"My face?"

"Yeah. The other night on the news, I noticed a scratch down your left cheek."

"Oh, that. Yeah, I must've scratched it on a tree branch while I was in my hiding spot." Kyle paused and said, "I hope Jaden is okay."

Once again, Nicole's intuition stood at attention, skeptical if her son was disclosing the whole truth. Not wanting to push the issue further, she said, "Me too. Listen, I don't mean to cut you off, but I need to go. I'm helping with the search party."

Kyle's breath bucked. "Are you sure you should? Is it your place to get involved?"

His apprehensive attitude caught her off guard. Why would he care unless, somehow, he was involved? Maybe he hadn't told her the whole truth. She pushed the nagging thought away. "It's everyone's place to get involved. We all need to pull together to help find Jaden and bring him home safely, and the sooner I get off the phone, the sooner I can do that."

"I don't know why you need to get involved in all this, but go do what you feel you need to," he said tersely.

Stunned by Kyle's disgruntlement, Nicole sat in her car, attempting to smooth the tight knot in her stomach. Preoccupied and disturbed by what she'd learned, apprehensive about telling Craig, but eager to help, she checked her appearance in the vanity mirror. She pressed her fingers under her eyes, hoping to flatten the newly formed bags. She dabbed on a thin coat of flamingo pink lip gloss and headed across the street, heavy with uncertainty and doubt.

CHAPTER 7

"Any footprints in that direction?" Roger, a fellow volunteer, shouted to Nicole, scouring over the muddy terrain in the opposite direction, about six trees due west.

"I don't know," she hollered back, her voice echoing off the thick piney stumps. "The rain's made it impossible to tell." It had poured again last night, washing away the fresh dirt, thus erasing any older footprints.

Nicole looked over her shoulder and watched the cadaver dogs sniff the wooded area and down by the lake. Police combed the area, too. The volunteers were the extra sets of eyes to help find anything, like an abandoned shoe, cell phone, or human remains. Nicole had shuddered when she'd heard that part.

Her fire-engine red galoshes squished into the tar-like sludge, sticking her feet in place like glue. It took great effort to lift her foot and move on to the next spot. Inching closer to Roger's location, Nicole scrutinized the ground with every step, surveying at least five yards around her.

Honing in on every detail—the pine needles stacked upon one another, the sticks embedded in the muddy soil like hundred-year-old fossils, and the wet, decomposing leaves carpeting the forest floor, Nicole looked for anything unusual hidden in the debris. Drops of rain splashed down from the two-hundred-foot branches overhead, creating tiny puddles every few inches.

"Do you see anything?" Nicole yelled to Roger as they inched closer.

"Nothing!"

"Holy shit!"

Roger's voice escalated. "Did you find something?"

"No. Sorry. My foot slipped out of my boot. Damn mud is so freaking sticky." She folded over in half and pulled her rubber boot back on.

Pointing to what used to be light gray tennis shoes, now black from the caked-on mud, Roger said, "I hear ya! My sneakers aren't cutting it."

"Eww," Nicole commented. A water droplet landed on her scalp and trickled down her forehead. Using her forefinger like a windshield wiper, she flicked it away. "This weather sucks. I don't think we've seen the sun in two days."

"I know. My wife gets depressed in this kind of weather. She desperately wants to move to Florida, where she says it's sunny every day. I keep telling her it's not sunny every day, anywhere."

"That's the truth," Nicole said, walking toward Roger. While picking up her left foot, she spotted something white, barely visible, layered under the damp soil. She squatted down to inspect it closer. "Hey, I think I found something," she called out.

"What?"

"Hang on." With her thumb and forefinger, Nicole lifted a rectangular piece of plastic. It looked like a license. Her mouth dropped open. Immediately, she recognized the photo staring back at her—Kyle. The scent of rotting leaves burned her nose to the back of her throat, and nausea swept through her stomach. Even the fresh scent of pine trees smelled acrid.

Looking around, and with Roger preoccupied examining his area and no one else in the vicinity, Nicole slipped the evidence into the side pocket of her leggings. "Never mind. It was a stone. Have you found anything?"

"Nothing."

"Should we meet up with the others?"

"I guess. Maybe someone else had some luck."

Nicole's heart hammered against her ribcage, but she tried to remain calm. "I hope. I can't even imagine what Jaden's parents are thinking or feeling at this point." She swallowed hard, keeping the nausea at bay as the license burned against her thigh.

Roger went to speak, but Nicole put her forefinger against her lips, signaling him to stop. She heard whispers nearby. Peering between two trees, she saw Detective Newton talking to another officer.

"It's not looking too hopeful," she heard Detective Newton say with his hands planted on his wide hips. His feet stood shoulder-width apart. "The longer we go with no evidence, clues, or a body, the more challenging this will be to solve. And the goddamn media is crawling up my ass. At this point, I don't know how to keep them off my back."

Nicole waved Roger along as they walked toward a clearing. In a low voice, she said, "He sounds stressed."

As they approached the group of volunteers gathered around, she stepped on a branch, snapping it in half. Detective Newton looked her way. Nicole's breath caught in her throat, hoping he hadn't seen them listening, but above all, that he hadn't seen her confiscate what could be evidence to implicate her son.

"Wouldn't you be?" Roger asked.

Nicole nodded. Beyond stressed is how she felt right now.

"The pressure that guy must be under is unreal. I heard that if the police don't find a body within forty-eight hours, the less likely they'll be found alive."

"That's a cheery tidbit of trivia," she said, rolling her eyes.

Roger tilted his head, his shaggy hair lilting over his ear. "Sorry, I didn't mean to sound like the Grim Reaper, but it's true. And we've crossed that threshold."

"I know." And that's the part that scared Nicole: the longer they went with no sign of Jaden, the less hopeful she became.

• • • • •

"How's Ky doing?" Craig asked, scrubbing a casserole dish.

Nicole leaned against the counter by the sink, watching him clean up after dinner. She knew she couldn't tell Craig what she'd found earlier that day—he still didn't even know Kyle had been one of the last people with

Jaden. Anticipating his less-than-approving tone, Nicole vacillated on whether to tell him just that part.

When she'd come home after helping with the search party, Nicole tucked Kyle's license in her top dresser drawer underneath her bras, hiding it as discreetly as her secret, vowing not to say anything to Craig until she knew why it was in the woods. "Why don't you call your son yourself and find out? I'm sure he'd love to hear from his father."

"I don't know. I feel bad enough that I work on the same campus. I don't want to make it more awkward."

"The only one who thinks it's awkward is you. Kyle's never once complained about it. He *chose* to go here."

The decision to attend the same college where Craig worked had been an easy decision for Kyle. During his senior year, he'd applied to three in-state and two out-of-state schools. Since he'd graduated in the top five percent of his class and scored a fourteen hundred on his SAT, he was accepted to all of them, some even throwing money his way. Ultimately, he decided to attend the College of Cypressville, where Craig was an economics professor, working his way up to the department's dean.

After analyzing each school, Kyle had settled on staying here in Cypressville, which pleased Nicole; her baby would only be a few miles away. Given the proximity, Nicole and Craig vowed to keep their distance and act as if Kyle had gone far away, which they'd successfully done since he started last semester.

It was the perfect scenario for Nicole. Her son was close, and he could come home anytime, which was infrequent, only for the occasional home-cooked meal or the unrestricted use of the washing machine, instead of over-stuffing coins into them at the laundromat.

"I know he chose to go here, but I worry he did it to please me," Craig said, stacking plates into the dishwasher.

"I don't think so. I think he wanted to stay close to home, and the fact that his tuition is free, well, that's an added bonus," she said, slinking behind him, giving him a love tap with her hip.

"I try to keep our lives separate, and because I'm on the faculty here, I don't want him treated differently. Sometimes, I wonder how I'd feel if I attended the same college where my dad worked."

Craig was unaware of the conversation she'd had with Kyle before he'd decided to attend school there. Nicole was worried it wouldn't be the right fit given the same reasons Craig had mentioned, and because she'd dropped out of college and hadn't experienced it to its fullest, she was extra sensitive about the subject. She wanted her son to experience it at all: the parties, the dorm life, the campus life, everything. She'd sat Kyle down and expressed her concerns about him being on the same campus as his father. That it may hinder such experiences, he would hold back, worried about being seen or caught doing the wild stuff that comes with the college experience—caution would limit him.

"I'm not worried about it, and you shouldn't be either," he'd insisted.

Uneasy, Nicole had said, "I want you to have the full experience."

"I know. You've said it like a billion times. Honestly, I'm fine being at the same school." Nicole's motherly instinct, however, whispered differently. Perhaps it had stemmed from her internal issues. Surrendering, she'd decided to trust Kyle to make his own decisions.

"Did I mention I have to be back at work tomorrow night?" Craig said, interrupting her thoughts.

"No. Why?"

Craig squirted another dollop of soap on the sponge. "I'm learning how to create a new grade book for my computer."

"Why?"

While finishing with the last dish, he said, "It'll help with my upcoming promotion. It's unique, and hardly anyone uses it. Totally cutting-edge technology."

"That's cool," Nicole said, skirting past him to get to the dishwasher. Although it was his job, she hated how Craig loaded it. She cooked, he cleaned, but he never stacked the dishes optimally, always leaving too much space in between.

"Hey! I just loaded it," he complained, watching her rearrange it. This was the daily conversation after dinner.

Craig rolled his eyes. "Is nothing I ever do good enough?"

Nicole faced him and noticed the deep scarlet color creeping into his cheeks. "Are you okay?" she asked, confused by the sudden change in his tone.

"I'm fine," he scoffed. "But I'm tired of always having you come behind me and fix what I've done!"

Concerned she'd hurt his feelings, she said, "I'm sorry. I didn't mean to upset you." She reached for his arm.

He retracted it, jerking away from her touch. "Why don't you do it yourself if it bothers you so much?"

Not used to Craig acting defensively since it rarely happened, Nicole struggled with how to diffuse the situation. She reached out, this time sweeping a chunk of hair off his forehead, hoping to calm him. Trying to make light of the situation, she said, "Because it's one of the many flaws I love about you," and kissed the tip of his sharp nose. She turned back around and continued fiddling with the dishwasher, lining the bowls in a straight line.

"Many flaws? Do I have that many?" he said sharply, folding his arms.

"Babe, you have many, many flaws, but they make you, you, and I love every single one of them." She faced him once again and flashed her best smile.

"I guess we all can't be as perfect as you," he said, glaring.

Nicole looked down at the floor, avoiding his glance, and thought, *Perfect? If he only knew what I'm hiding.*

CHAPTER 8

When she rolled over, Nicole noticed the other side of the bed was undisturbed, and Craig had already left for work.

Although she'd tried to remedy the dishwasher situation last night, he'd barely spoken to her, hurt and angry by how he felt she'd treated him. Wanting to give Craig space and time to cool off, Nicole had gone to bed before him, and since his side was still intact, she assumed he'd slept on the couch.

Lying in bed, the sun high in the sky, beaming into their bedroom, warming her body under the heavy blanket, Nicole was grateful she hadn't had to get up early to take him to work. Still, guilt settled in her stomach, remorseful for upsetting him. And for keeping her secret from him. Craig was the love of her life—the last thing she wanted to do was hurt or betray him—keenly gentle with his heart. And feelings. Unfortunately, she'd failed to do this last night.

Nicole was only nineteen when they'd met—much too young to settle down, according to her parents, especially with a man six years her senior. They lectured her about how she and Craig were in different places in their lives. "He's out in the workforce, graduated college. You're only in your second year. Don't throw away your whole life for a guy," they'd warned her. What did they know? They didn't love Craig. She did. And no matter how sternly she'd tried to talk herself out of it, love won. She hadn't intended to settle down at such an early age, but Craig drew her in, throwing away all reason.

"Are you here for the bride or groom?" he'd asked the night they met.

She admired the man standing in front of her, dressed in a sharp gray suit, filling out all the parts nicely. "Neither."

"Then what are you doing here?" Craig said, his eyes flying open. "Are you a wedding crasher?"

Her cheeks flooded with warmth, turning red like the rose in her hand. "Hell no." She laughed. "I'm here helping a friend. She owns the floral shop that provided all the flowers." Nicole pointed to the arrangements cascading the church pews. "Jane, my friend, called me in a panic. Apparently, her assistant developed an allergy to pollen. Ironic, right? Jane called me and asked if I would help." Nicole smiled. "So, here I am."

"And here you are," Craig grinned, his lopsided dimple showing off.

By the night's end, he had her phone number and promised to call. Three days later and with no call from Craig, Nicole doubted his true intentions, especially since she'd seen him dancing with girl after girl at the wedding. Wondering if he was nothing more than a player and liar, Nicole did some digging. Given that she was studying investigative journalism, why not put it into practice?

"What?" Nicole had said to Jane, who'd snubbed the idea of probing. "He seems too good to be true. What's the harm?"

"It's called trust," Jane had said, rolling her eyes. "If you don't have trust now, you've got nothing to build a solid relationship on."

"In this day and age, one can never be too safe."

Upon poking around, Craig had come up clean, settling Nicole's suspicions of his "too good to be true" label. When he called her three days later, Nicole jumped at the chance to see him again. That started their love affair. They still joke about how happy they were that Jane's assistant had suffered from allergies.

But like all couples, Nicole and Craig have had their share of marital strife—no marriage is entirely immune to hiccups. However, no matter the obstacle, they'd always found a way to overcome it; compromise their go-to. Ever pragmatic, Craig often created a pros and cons list specific to the issue at hand, and they'd find a way to meet in the middle. Of course, sometimes, one had to move a little further than they wanted, but they muddled their way through, and the fact they hadn't met in the middle last night saddened Nicole.

• • • • •

There were still no new leads in the case. This jarred Nicole just as much as the fact that she was hiding Kyle's license. She still hadn't confronted him about it, debating how to approach the situation: confront him or quietly slip it back into his wallet. For now, she kept her secret in the back of her mind, like the license in the drawer.

She was restless with the slow progress, and the entire town was as well. Over a dozen volunteers were on the search party team. They stood elbow to elbow, walking in a horizontal line combing over every nook and cranny of a three-square-mile radius, like a till sowing the fields, hoping to find anything to help break the case open. Yet, despite their efforts, not one shred of evidence had popped up. Not a piece of clothing. Not a footprint. Not even Jaden's cell phone. Nothing.

Aside from the search party on land, a team of divers searched the lake. The cadaver dogs continued to sniff the area, and with their training and a strong sense of smell, they turned nothing else up, only Jaden's scent, reaffirming what the police already knew; he was there that night. The police remained close-mouthed, stating it was an ongoing investigation.

Nicole was either helping the search party or baking. If her hands were inactive, she became antsy; the busier they were, the quieter her mind.

Consumed with helping, Nicole hadn't seen the inside of the gym the past few days. Not only did her muscles crave a workout, but her brain also needed the endorphins. She grabbed her protein shake, keys, and gym bag and headed out the door.

Preoccupied with handling Kyle's license situation while driving, Nicole didn't see the oversized black SUV as she moved into the right lane. A horn wailed, and she jerked the steering wheel too far left, nearly swiping the green Mini Cooper now in the spot where she'd just been.

Nicole waved apologetically to the black SUV first. The surly, long-bearded driver ignored her and veered abruptly to the right.

"Sorry!" she mouthed, but he didn't care. He laid on the horn again and sped up. By the time she attempted to apologize to the green Mini Cooper, it was gone. Rattled by the chaos, Nicole pulled into a nearby gas station parking lot. She dropped her face into her cupped hands and muttered how stupid and careless she'd been. When her tirade was over, she merged into traffic, arriving at the gym much later than she would've liked.

• • • • •

Nicole tossed her keys on the kitchen table and strode up the stairs, two at a time to wash the sweat off her body and the unpleasantness of the entire morning—from the road incident to her crappy workout, the day had started less than stellar.

After cleaning up, she hopped back in her car, hoping for a less traumatic ride, and headed to the search area. She walked alongside a newer volunteer, Sylvia. They traipsed over the same trodden path which, no matter how many times they trampled over it—the ground now hollowed out from their repetitive footsteps—nothing new surfaced.

"His poor parents," Nicole said. She couldn't get them out of her mind, and the fact that she held what may be the only piece of evidence in the case so far. She justified keeping it a secret because Kyle *had* admitted he was in the area that night—it was plausible it'd simply slipped out of his pocket: nothing more than a mere coincidence, which is how she justified keeping it all from Craig. However, an unsettling feeling stirred in her core, speculating the worst—her son had something to do with this case. Something far worse than a mere coincidence. She couldn't stop feeling like he hadn't told her the whole truth on the phone.

"I know. I can't even imagine. I couldn't eat, sleep, or do anything." Sylvia said, shuffling her blue sneakers over the dirt. Dust kicked up around them.

"Me either."

"That's why I'm helping. To be close to the case."

Sylvia's foot pushed aside a few decaying leaves near the spot where Nicole had found Kyle's license. Recognizing the area, she swallowed the lump rising in her throat. "I keep putting myself in their position." Moving her gray sneaker to the left, Nicole kicked over a granite-colored stone. "I heard that Detective Newton said the more time that passes, the bigger the search area will become. I wonder when that'll happen."

"Hopefully soon." Sylvia continued scuffing the crumbled dirt. "It's so weird. It's like Jaden disappeared into thin air."

Nicole wondered if this would become another cold case since it'd been a week, and nothing had emerged except for what she'd found—Kyle's license. "Yeah, and not only is the kid without his medication, which is dangerous enough, but I heard that at some point, the police will stop using their time and resources on this when they can't find anything." And as those last words left her mouth, a sinking feeling washed over Nicole.

Maybe *she* was the one holding back the investigation.

CHAPTER 9

After her shift, Nicole threw her cell phone on the passenger seat. She noticed two missed calls and three texts from Craig, one of which read:

I can't make it tonight

She and Craig planned a date night once a week to keep the spark alive. They planned to go to her favorite seafood restaurant tonight, *Catfish Joe's*, an outdoor dive on the coastline known for its local seafood caught fresh off the boat and its spectacular views overlooking the inlet. Nicole was looking forward to it, especially after the fallout from the dishwasher incident. She wanted to make it up to Craig, apologizing for upsetting him.

Disappointed, she opted to answer him later. Paying closer attention to her driving this time, she jumped when her phone rang, Craig's name appearing on the in-dash display.

This time, she answered, not wanting to blow him off further in case it upset him again. "Hi, babe."

"Hey, babe. Did you get my text? I've been trying to call."

"Sorry, I was helping with the search party." Nicole rechecked the rearview mirror.

"How's that going? Any luck?"

Nicole bit her bottom lip and tightened her grip on the steering wheel. She considered telling Craig about Kyle and the license but decided against it. "No."

"Hopefully, something will turn up soon. It's awful here, vigils everywhere. It's so bizarre. No one even knows if he's dead or alive, yet memorials are all around."

Located in the heart of historical downtown Cypressville, Nicole could picture the sprawling campus now—flowers, teddy bears, and balloons adorning the grounds, the plantation-styled brick buildings built back in the early eighteen fifties encompassing the make-shift shrines. With hundred-year-old oak trees branching over the walkways like awnings, protecting students from the hot, humid summer days and the cold, rainy winter ones, it was beautiful. Students strolled about, never rushing from class to class. Instead, they lazed their way through the curved paths, stopping to chat with their peers along the way.

Nicole heard Craig's heavy panting. "Where are you? You sound out of breath."

"I'm going to be late for my next lecture. Alex messed up my grade book, so I was busy fixing it. Thanks to that and the crowds gathered around the campus, I'm hustling."

"Why can't you make it tonight? I was looking forward to sharing oysters with you, if you catch my drift?"

He chuckled. "Yeah, me too, but I'm behind on my lessons and struggling to learn that new grading program from that new professor."

"New professor?" She didn't remember Craig mentioning any new professor.

"Dr. Graham. He transferred here a few weeks ago. Remember? I told you all this the other night."

"I don't think you did."

"I'm sure I told you. You must've had one too many glasses of Chardonnay," he said, blowing it off.

She also didn't remember having one too many glasses of anything.

"We're going to meet tonight. It's the only time we both had that worked for us. Are you upset?"

"No," she lied. "I know how hard you're working for that promotion."

"My success becomes your success. Don't ever forget that."

Nicole noticed his breathing had slowed. "Are you at your class?"

"Yes. Love you."

"Love you, too." She hit the red end button. "I guess I've got plenty of time now to help out again," she said to no one, making a U-turn.

• • • • •

A media frenzy flooded the empty lot across from the wooded area. Every time Nicole tried to park, they circled her car like a shark about to attack its next victim.

"Have they found anything yet?" one reporter shouted.

"What can you tell us about Jaden?" another one asked.

"Did you know him personally? What was he like?" Questions flung at her like darts. Reporters pushed against one another, trying to stick their microphones toward Nicole's car. She kept her windows rolled up and drove slowly through the crowd. She had nothing to report and no desire to talk to the media.

When she crossed the dirt path, she noticed Detective Newton, dressed in a light blue polo shirt that hugged his middle-aged belly, standing mid-circle, surrounded by police and volunteers. Nicole's heart jumped. Maybe they'd finally found something. Perhaps Jaden had resurfaced.

The detective addressed the group, his bushy eyebrows knitted together above the bridge of his pointy nose. "Rumors are milling around that we have a suspect in custody. Let me be clear," he said in a stern tone, "we do not, and if I find out any of you had anything to do with these rumors, it's immediate cause for dismissal. Do I make myself clear?" He waggled his finger to the outer rim, his stormy eyes locking on each person, one at a time.

"Yes," they murmured in unison.

"I mean it. For fuck's sake, we don't have enough evidence of any kind, which, if I'm being totally honest, is really pissing me off." He shoved his hands in the pocket of his khakis and jiggled around some coins as he rocked back and forth on his heels.

Nicole watched the ridges in his forehead deepen each time he furrowed his eyebrows, which happened about every other word. "We've decided to extend the search area by another four-square miles. We still don't know where Jaden is, and at this point, he's been without his insulin for far too long. You do the math."

Several volunteers covered their mouths when they read between the lines, as did Nicole. Nausea overtook her empty stomach, the realness of the situation sinking in.

"I've got the media crawling up my ass, and I don't need any of you adding fuel to the fire," he said, folding his arms across his chest, resting them on top of his belly, pushing his gut further over his waistband, concealing his badge clipped to his belt. "Anyone have something they'd like to say? If so, now's the time."

A slight cough escaped Nicole.

Nobody spoke.

"I didn't think so. I—" Detective Newton started, then stopped. He rushed forward, busting through the circle, as two people careened toward the group, one of them yelling, "I want answers. Now!"

Everyone turned to see the commotion. It was George and Cecelia Pierce. Adrenaline coursed through Nicole's veins; her heart quickened, watching them barrel toward Detective Newton. This was the closest she'd ever been to Jaden's parents. She'd seen them on TV, but never up close, in person, like this.

"Is it true?" George shouted, his steps quickening as Cecelia fell behind, her ankle-length, A-line, salmon-colored linen skirt flowing behind her as she tried to keep up, her short stature making the task impossible.

"Come with me, George," Detective Newton said, putting his arm around George's shoulder, ushering the disheveled couple away from the onlookers.

"No!" George bellowed, shirking off the detective's arm. "I don't want any more of your bullshit runaround answers. I want the damn truth!"

Detective Newton looked around, noticing the bystanders. He reached for George's elbow to escort him further from the rubberneckers. George yanked his arm back as Detective Newton said, "I understand your concern. And I'd be upset if this was my—"

George pointed at the detective. "Bullshit! You don't know what it's like! Has your son ever gone missing, and the inept police can't figure out what happened? Do you even have a son? A child?"

Cecelia spoke for the first time. "George, please." She tugged on her husband's bicep, pulling him back, his finger poking at the detective's chest. "You're not helping," she said. "This isn't going to solve the problem."

A voice of reason, Nicole thought. *Good woman, quite possibly stronger than me.*

George ignored his wife's request like Detective Newton ignored George's questions.

"Mr. Pierce, I need you to calm down." The detective leered straight into George's blazing eyes, neither man blinking.

"I will calm down when you give me some answers." George's lip curled to one side, and he scrunched his nose.

"I assume you're referring to the rumor that we have a suspect in custody?"

"Yes." George relaxed his arms, and Cecelia released her grip. She readjusted the black purse strap on her shoulder that'd slipped off while trying to restrain her husband.

"I assure you, Mr. Pierce, you'd be the first to know if we had any updates. It's only a rumor. That's all." Detective Newton glowered at the crowd nearby, proving the previous point he'd lectured them about.

George slouched his shoulders. "Dammit, I was hoping you had the son of a bitch in custody."

Detective Newton placed his hand on George's back, the canary yellow fabric of his cotton shirt now stained with a sweat mark mid-spine. "I'm sorry. I know you're disappointed, but as we've discussed, we don't even know if any foul play was involved. For all we know, Jaden left on his own accord."

"No way," George insisted, fanning his shirt, glaring at Detective Newton. Cecelia chimed in, "George is right. No way he would've left his insulin behind." Her voice cracked.

Detective Newton waved his arm sideways. "We can't rule out any possibilities. Maybe Jaden left it behind on purpose. Maybe he had reason to want to—"

"Don't say it. Don't you dare say it," George interrupted. "How dare you imply our son would intentionally hurt himself! Impossible."

Nicole saw Cecelia shake her head and dab her eyes. She drew her purse tighter, clutching it against her rib cage, pressing her white peasant top against her pale skin, and looked down.

"I'm not implying anything. I'm merely stating we don't know where Jaden is."

"We need something, anything, from your department showing you're working earnestly on this case. No way you're telling me you don't have any leads after almost a week!"

"Let me make this very clear to you. If we had anything, I certainly wouldn't discuss it here." Detective Newton turned and faced the onlookers. "Do you see how quickly rumors spread? I don't need false information hindering my case. I don't need the media running their mouths and interfering with my case. I don't give a rat's ass about sharing information with the public. What I care about is solving this case. That's it." He turned toward George and Cecelia again. "And like I said before, if I have something to share with you, you would've heard from me. Got it?"

George stood, feet wide apart, brown loafers stuck in place, mouth gaping open. He blinked a few times, clenched his jaw, and snarled. "Oh yeah, I don't give a rat's ass about your policy. I want answers. And I want them now. What about his fraternity brothers? Huh? The ones who were with him that night. They were the last ones to see my son, yet those sons of bitches are still running free. Why's that, Detective?" George spat.

Nicole's stomach dropped to her knees. Kyle was one of those brothers with Jaden that night.

"You need to trust me and let me do my job. I'm handling it."

George dug in. "Have you questioned any of the brothers?"

"I'm handling it."

Nicole rubbed her sweaty palms down the sides of her Capri leggings. Perspiration dotted her forehead. She inched back and headed to her car. Dizzy and queasy, she thought, *the police are going to find out.*

CHAPTER 10

As soon as Nicole was safe in her car, she texted Kyle.

Where are you?

As the three dancing dots appeared, she sighed and relaxed her hunched shoulders.

Fraternity house

On my way

Why?

I'll explain when I get there

The sun blinded Nicole as she drove west. She was a woman on a mission: she needed to get to Kyle and warn him he would most likely be questioned again. And confront him about what she'd found in the woods.

She called Craig next. Voicemail. *Shit.* "Craig, call me the second you get this." She glanced in her rearview mirror, double-checking it was safe to change lanes, not wanting a repeat incident like earlier. She spotted a black SUV, two cars behind her. Squinting, she tried to focus on the driver, but the vehicle darted over to the next lane and slipped behind a semi-truck. Nicole wondered if it was the same car as before. "You're seeing things," she said to her reflection. "All the stress is getting to you." She shook her head, ridding herself of the paranoia. "Besides, all black SUVs look the same," she said, convincing herself she was overreacting, even though it followed her to the campus entrance.

While strangling the steering wheel as she turned onto Fraternity Drive, Nicole's knuckles turned white as her brain worked overtime, thoughts fluctuating between Kyle's role in this and the black SUV. She hated herself for doubting her son, even if it was only for a second. Thanks to that ominous phone call from his middle school, she would trust him one hundred percent if that hadn't happened. But it had. And she didn't. When she pulled into the fraternity house driveway, her head throbbed, and her fingers ached.

Kyle was standing, waiting.

"Get in the car," she demanded through the rolled-down passenger window.

"What's going on?" He folded his lanky body onto the passenger seat.

"We're going for a drive where no one can hear us." She shifted into reverse, looking for the SUV, double-checking to ensure it hadn't followed her. It hadn't—one less thing she had to worry about right now. She backed out of the driveway, accelerating with such force that Kyle's head snapped back, thumping against the headrest.

"You're acting like a madwoman," he said, grasping the door handle, glancing sideways.

Her eyes flitted from the road to Kyle. "I'm about to be mad, all right."

He clenched his teeth. "What. Is. Going. On?"

Now back on the main road, Nicole checked her rearview mirror. No SUV around. Feeling lighter about that, she filled Kyle in on what Detective Newton had said to Jaden's parents. Her neck muscles strained, trying to get the next part out. "You know how I said I was joining the search party?"

"Yeah."

"I found your license. In the mud. In the woods." She turned her head to watch Kyle's reaction.

He turned two shades of green, his hollowed cheeks sinking in further. "What?"

"You heard me. Your license. Did you even notice it missing?"

He licked his partially opened lips. "I thought maybe I'd left it in a pocket or something."

"And did you ever think to, oh, I don't know, find it?"

"I figured it would show up the next time I did laundry." He shrugged. "Did you tell the police?"

"No. Of course not. It's in my drawer."

Kyle exhaled, his birdlike chest collapsing. "Thanks."

"Yeah, well, you're welcome. You're lucky I found it and not the police." A familiar pain settled in her cramped fingers. "I'm hiding what could be evidence."

Kyle stiffened at the word "evidence." A tear spilled down his pallid cheek. "You think I had something to do with it, don't you? I knew you didn't trust me."

"Ky, I do trust you," she half lied, her chest tightening. "But I need to know you're not hiding anything. That you've told me the whole story."

His face changed from pallid to bright red, like a poppy flower. "Like I already said, I was there that night. The police already know that. My license must've slipped out of my pocket."

Conflicted and confused, Nicole didn't know what to believe. "I think the police are going to question you again."

Kyle's eyes flew open. "Why?"

His reaction unsettled Nicole. Needing to read his expressions, she pulled off the side of the road. With the car still idling, she twisted toward Kyle, the seatbelt digging into her neck, and locked her eyes on his. "Does it matter why?"

Kyle looked down at his shaky hands as he picked at a dangling cuticle.

His silence and averted eye contact were answer enough for Nicole; she knew there was more. "Ky, I feel like there's something you're not telling me. Spill it," she said through gritted teeth.

Inhaling, Kyle stuck out his chest and lifted his tear-filled eyes. "I don't know where to start."

Her pulse thumped in her head. "How about at the beginning?"

"Okay," Kyle said, lowering his head again, his chin resting on his chest. "Last semester, I got into sports betting...I'm the fraternity's bookie."

Nicole's eyes widened, her heart racing faster. "You could be arrested for that."

His lips tightened into a straight line.

Afraid she scared him into not being forthright, Nicole softened her tone. "Sorry. I'm just shocked." *And disappointed.*

Kyle continued. "Jaden owed me some money, and no matter how many times I asked him to pay, he didn't. Or couldn't. Or wouldn't. So Chase set up the game of Manhunt. He thought it would be funny if we scared Jaden, mess with him a little, thinking maybe he'd pay up, but instead, he went missing." When finished, Kyle lifted his head and looked at Nicole with tear-streaked cheeks. "I swear, I had nothing to do with his disappearance."

Overwhelmed by this new revelation, thoughts swirled in Nicole's brain as she tried to process it before speaking. She didn't know what to say. Where to begin. She'd suspected there was more, and she was right. Regaining control of her erratic heart, Nicole calmed down.

"Mom?"

"Give me a second." Nicole looked upward, searching her brain for what to do next. She had to make a choice: believe or doubt him. This was her son. Her flesh and blood. A human being she had created. She knew him better than he knew himself. "Okay," she said, deciding she was on board. All in. One hundred percent. Well, almost a hundred. There was still that fragment of a percent.

She stretched her fingers, relieving the tension in her joints. "I believe you. Do you know where Jaden is?"

"No."

"Do you have any idea what may have happened to him?"

"No, I swear."

"Do you think someone else may have something to do with his disappearance?"

Kyle hesitated, crossing his arms against his chest, covering up his fraternity shirt's white and red Greek letters. Then he said, "Maybe Chase? Or Ethan? They swear they had nothing to do it, but besides Jaden, they're the only two who knew he owed me the money."

Nicole tapped her chin with her unmanicured finger, thinking. "As long as you had nothing to do with Jaden's disappearance, I don't see the need to share any of this sports betting mess with anyone. We don't need to rouse the police's suspicions, especially since Jaden hasn't even turned up yet. We don't even know if he's dead or alive."

Kyle remained silent. He stared straight ahead and rubbed his thighs with his balled-up fists.

Watching him, Nicole wondered if she'd jumped on the trust train prematurely. She repeated her last statement.

"True," he said, looking at his knees.

"Good. I called your dad. We might want to lawyer up. He needs to be in the know about you possibly being questioned again. But we don't need to tell him about your license and side business. Not until we absolutely have to."

As Nicole drove again, her phone rang on cue. Craig's name popped up. Upon her answering, he asked, "Where's the fire?"

"Meet us at home."

"Us?"

"Yes, I picked up Kyle." She looked at him. "I think the police are going to question him. Please meet us at home. We'll be there in five minutes."

"I can't just drop everything. I need to prep for that meeting tonight."

"What time?"

"Seven."

"That gives you two and a half hours. We need to make a plan for when they question Kyle."

"*If* they question him. We don't even know if they will," Craig said.

Nicole glanced sideways again. Kyle's leg bounced up and down, his long knobby knee brushing against the glovebox.

"I'm sure they're about to. I'll fill you in at home."

A pregnant pause filled the car. "Craig, please, for our son."

"Please, Dad," Kyle said, his voice cracking at "please."

"Fine. I'll be there in twenty."

"Thank you," they chimed in unison.

Looking in her rearview mirror, for the last time this go around, Nicole swore she saw that same oversized black SUV, once again, trailing two cars behind. Too rapt with the task at hand, she waved it off. For a fleeting moment, however, she wondered if she was being tailed. She would find out soon enough.

CHAPTER 11

Craig walked into the eerily quiet house. Usually, when he came home, loud music was blaring through the Bluetooth speaker, or pots and pans were clanging in the kitchen. Not now, however. Now, the only sound heard was the metronomic ticking of the antique clock resting on the mantle in the family room.

Kyle and Nicole sat facing one another at the high-top table in the kitchen.

When they'd gotten home ten minutes ago, Nicole gave Kyle his license. After the hand-off, they'd come down to the kitchen to wait for Craig and hadn't spoken another word. Kyle fiddled with the saltshaker, sliding it left to right from hand to hand like a hockey puck.

Craig stepped into the kitchen. "What the hell is going on?" he asked, darting his eyes back and forth between the two.

"Sit down," Nicole said, pointing to an empty chair.

Craig plopped down on the stool and folded his arms across his chest.

Nicole inhaled slowly, and after releasing the captive air, said, "I went back to the search area again after you canceled our plans." She paused, noticing Kyle's face—his lips and chin quivered.

She continued, looking at Craig. "And Jaden's parents showed up."

Kyle closed his eyes and winced.

Nicole tucked a rogue piece of hair that'd fallen in front of her eyes behind her ear. "They were causing quite the scene. At least, George, that's Jaden's dad, was. He yelled at Lou, the detective leading the case, Detective Newton—"

"I don't care who is who. Get to the point," Craig said, glancing at his watch, which poked out from under his crossed arm.

"Long story short, George asked the detective about the fraternity brothers with Jaden that night."

"So? What does that have to do with Kyle?" Craig shifted his eyes to Kyle. He looked down at his folded hands resting on the tabletop.

Craig repeated his question. Uncomfortable silence increased the tension in the room. He looked at Nicole. "Nic?"

She dropped her head down.

Craig looked back at Kyle. "Ky?"

Kyle gulped.

"I will ask this for the last time," Craig said tersely. "What does this have to do with Kyle?"

"I was there that night," Kyle whispered, looking down.

"What?" Craig widened his eyes. "Did you know, Nic?"

Nicole's lack of an answer was answer enough.

Craig's lip turned down. "You did, didn't you?"

To cover her mistake, she lied. "Yes, but I thought I'd told you."

"You definitely didn't tell me, and that's a detail I should've been privy to," he snapped, slapping his palm on the table.

Kyle and Nicole both jumped.

"I'm sorry. I thought I had."

Craig met Kyle's eyes dead on. "Did you have anything to do with Jaden's disappearance?"

Nicole studied Craig's face. She couldn't decipher if his sternness expressed anger, disappointment, fear, or a combination of all three.

"No. I swear. I played Manhunt that night, but I had nothing to do with his disappearance. The last time I saw him was when he'd gone to hide." Kyle flipped his head sideways, moving the hair in front of his eyes.

Craig leered at him. "Do you realize how this can ruin my reputation on this campus? I'm done for if you had anything to do with it."

Kyle's face crumpled. The hair he'd just moved fell over his forehead, covering his creased brow. He whimpered.

To redirect Craig's concern for himself to his son, Nicole asked, "Is that what you're worried about? Your reputation?"

"I'd hate to see all my effort wasted."

Nicole eyed Craig, sending an unspoken message—a warning of sorts—that he'd better refocus his attention.

Message received, Craig sighed. "I'm sorry," he said, turning his body toward Kyle. "You're my utmost priority. It's just that I've worked tirelessly to get here, and you know I'm being groomed to be dean."

Kyle kept his head down, his knee jounced, the table vibrating in response. "I know. Believe me, I don't want to do anything to jeopardize your job." His voice cracked, holding back tears.

Nicole reached across the table, placed one hand on Kyle's, and picked up Craig's with her other.

"We are a family. And no matter what, we're always here for one another, right?" She half-smiled, squeezing their hands.

Both men nodded.

"We both believe you and will do whatever it takes to protect you." Nicole looked at Craig, who nodded again, then winked at Kyle. "I'm going to have Dad take you back to the fraternity house on his way back to the office. You will act like nothing's wrong until there is *actually* something wrong." She squeezed Kyle's hand again, reassuring him while giving him a cryptic look, reminding him not to mention anything to anyone about Jaden owing him money.

He nodded.

"If anything changes, though, we need to touch base immediately. Got it?"

Kyle nodded again.

"I know you need to go," she said, looking at Craig, "And I'm sorry for the miscommunication, but we all need to be completely honest with one another from here on out."

Both men nodded. They got up from the table, each kissing Nicole goodbye.

Nicole squeezed her eyes shut as the door clicked behind them and cringed. She'd lied to, or at the very least, withheld information from the man she trusted the most. Troubled, she grabbed her laptop and Googled attorneys, suspecting they were going to need one soon.

• • • • •

Combing over part of the newly expanded search area, Nicole and Sylvia used long sticks to push aside the ground debris, hoping to find anything.

"I feel like I'm living *Groundhog Day*. Another day. More searching, still nothing," Sylvia said, moving a clump of moldy leaves aside.

"I know," Nicole agreed.

Through set jaw, Sylvia said in a high-pitched voice, "I think one of those fraternity boys playing that night knows more than they're saying."

Nicole froze; Kyle was one of those fraternity boys. After learning about his shady pastime, Nicole felt liable for knowing and withholding this vital detail, which may be linked to Jaden's disappearance. To protect her son, she'd compartmentalized it, cramming it into the back of her brain. However, Sylvia's sentence aroused Nicole's conscience; no matter how much she wanted to forget, her moral compass wouldn't allow it.

"Probably got into a fight over a girl. Maybe a case of jealousy gone wrong. You know, the heat of the moment. Passion took hold. At least, that's my theory," Sylvia offered, not that Nicole had asked. "What about you? What do you think happened?"

Nicole studied Sylvia. A disingenuous smile spread across Sylvia's face.

A shiver ran down Nicole's spine. She'd heard of cases where the culprit had joined the search party to keep close tabs. See what the police know and don't know. Was Sylvia one of those people? Did she know something? Was she involved?

Caught staring, setting her eyes on Nicole, Sylvia said, "What?"

"Nothing. I was lost in thought. Sorry." Nicole resumed moving her stick, ignoring the unsettling feeling gnawing at her conscience. "I don't know. They haven't even found his body yet. Maybe he ran away."

"It's been over a week. Don't you think he would've come forward by now? Let someone know he's alive. His parents, at least." Leaves drifted, adding another layer to the carpeted forest floor. Sylvia swatted one as it floated by.

Dragging her grainy shoe horizontally, Nicole moved an empty beer can out of the way. The college kids used these woods to drink and never cleaned up after themselves, leaving behind the abandoned evidence. "Probably. What if he's been kidnapped? Maybe he can't reach out? Maybe he's tied up or something?" She'd watched too many episodes of *Dateline* and *20/20*, fueling her active imagination. Or maybe it was the uneasy feeling in the pit of her stomach.

"I guess, but why wouldn't the kidnappers demand a ransom by now? You'd think they'd call, write, or send a text or email. Do they send ransom notes electronically these days?" Sylvia asked, laughing. "*Everything* is electronic these days."

Uncomfortable with Sylvia's behavior but not wanting to draw attention to this, Nicole played along. "Probably not. Totally traceable."

"Good point. I hope they find him soon."

But Nicole wondered if that was true. "Me too. I've heard the only reason the police are continuing their search is because of Jaden's medical condition. Otherwise, they would've called it off by now." She glanced sideways, watching Sylvia's reaction. She remained steadfast. Stoic.

The women continued combing over every square inch of the area, and after another three hours, Nicole said, "There's nothing here. Let's head back."

With their feet hurting, eyes tired, and feeling morally defeated, Sylvia agreed.

When Nicole returned to her car, a white piece of paper sat on her windshield. Thinking it was a ticket, surprised, knowing she'd parked legally—she removed it and read the ink on the paper.

Mind your own business. You've been warned

Her knees buckled. "What the hell?" she said, looking over both shoulders.

CHAPTER 12

After reading the note the first time, Nicole stood frozen, scanning the parking lot. She tried to steady her breaths, but they came in short, hiccup-y spurts. Still panting, with no one in sight, she scrambled into her car and reread the message, the paper wavering in her hands.

The saliva in her mouth disappeared as she stared at the bold letters. The stale air in the car pressed down on her. She needed to get out of here, but too shaken up, she couldn't. When her hands steadied enough to drive, Nicole crossed town, constantly checking her rearview mirror, making sure she wasn't being followed. Fortunately, she didn't see any suspicious-looking cars.

Her mind raced, befuddled about who would've left the note. Then she wondered if it was meant for somebody else. Maybe her all too familiar silver Sonata, four-door sedan, had been mistaken for somebody else's, and the note had been placed on the wrong car. This thought settled her enough to regulate her breathing, but not enough to calm her nerves.

As soon as she entered the house, she closed the door with trembling fingers, the note tucked deep inside her purse. Covered in layers of grime from walking the dusty trail, she headed upstairs to shower. She sat on the edge of her bed and closed her eyes, rubbing her temples.

A car door closed nearby. Not expecting anyone, Nicole opened the wooden slats on the bedroom window shutter and peered out. She looked in the driveway. No car. She looked down the street, and there, one house away, parked on the opposite side of the road, was an oversized black SUV. Nicole jumped back, the slats snapping shut. Slowly, she backed down onto the edge of the bed. Sweat coated her palms, and her muscles tensed as a disturbing feeling washed over her.

She tried to convince herself she was being neurotic and overreacting—she wasn't being followed—it was all in her mind, the car across the street a mere coincidence. There was no reason she'd be followed. No one had seen her take the license or knew she was privy to Kyle's hobby.

Fifteen minutes later and calmer, Nicole headed to the shower. Hot water danced on her prickly skin as she contemplated who could've left that note, making a mental list of potential culprits, but in the end, she realized none of them were capable of such behavior.

A new thought flashed through her mind: maybe the note was meant for Craig, considering they shared a car. Who, though, would warn him, and why? Perhaps it was related to his promotion—someone vying for the same position—scaring him off, trying to send a message.

Then a different thought crossed her mind. What if she *was* being followed? Maybe the two things were related—whoever was following her had also left the note. Maybe somebody knew what she'd done.

Nicole squeezed a dollop of shampoo into her unsteady hand. She vigorously massaged her scalp, debating whether to tell Craig about her suspicions of possibly being followed and now the note. She didn't want to hear the proverbial "I told you so," but he needed to know if she was in danger. Pondering what to do, Nicole picked up the lilac-scented soap and stood under the steady stream of water. Lost in thought, she slid the purple-tinted bar back and forth over her quivering stomach and washed away the day's events and the remnants of the dusty dirt down the drain.

• • • • •

Since Craig had been working long hours lately, Nicole jumped seeing him standing in the living room when she returned downstairs.

"Grabbed an early bus home," he said, reading her surprised reaction. He walked over and kissed her. She placed her hands on his stubbly cheeks and drew him in for a long kiss, his tongue finding hers in response. He pulled her in and reached under her damp, heather gray hooded sweatshirt from her wet hair draping down and grazed her braless nipple with his thumb.

On edge, she recoiled. "Sorry. I'm a bit preoccupied." She was still wavering whether to tell Craig about the note, and she was perturbed about Kyle's culpability. "We need to talk about what we're going to do if Ky becomes a person of interest."

"Buzzkill," he teased, grabbing her breast fully now.

"I'm serious. I'm really worried. The longer time passes, and Jaden hasn't been found or shown back up, the more anxious I am about Ky."

"You've always been such a worrywart," he said, releasing her flesh. He sat down on the sofa and patted the cushion next to him. "Sit. We can talk first and then finish what I started."

Nicole's lips spread into a smile, choosing to sit on his lap rather than on the cushion where his hand rested. "How about this instead?"

He nuzzled his nose into her neck. "Even better."

"Do you think we need to hire an attorney?" She stroked the back of his head, mussing with his scalp. She loved to run her fingers through his hair, even though it had thinned over the years. Back in the day, however, he had a full head of thick, wavy locks that she could spend hours combing through. Plus, it turned him on.

"Mmm."

"Does that mean we should hire an attorney?"

"It means that feels good," he said, closing his eyes.

Nicole massaged his scalp. "I'm serious. Do you think we need to call one, just in case?"

Craig leaned back against the plump cushions, creating space between them. He rubbed his thumb and forefinger over his chin.

"Honestly, not yet. Ky has done nothing to warrant any suspicion. He admitted to being there. Nothing questionable about that. I don't think we need to do anything until there's a reason to do something. Take your advice from the other night. Don't worry about anything until there's something to worry about."

"I guess." With knowing more than she'd like, an unsettling feeling wrenched in Nicole's gut. Ignoring this disturbing prickle, she opened her mouth to tell Craig about the black SUV and the note but stopped. Not being a car expert, she couldn't swear it had been the same one each time. She hadn't gotten a good enough look to compare them or a good look at the driver. And with this thought, Nicole decided not to say anything. At least, not yet.

"Now, where were we?" Craig asked, kissing her neck. He lifted her hoodie over her head and tossed it on the shaggy throw rug, exposing her naked chest. He kissed along her sternum, his hair skimming her breasts.

She arched her head back. "Mmm...now *that* feels good."

"That's the general idea. Let's finish this upstairs, shall we?" Craig hoisted her up, wrapping her thighs around his waist. He brushed his lips against her smooth skin as he caressed her back.

Nicole's phone rang, interrupting them. She untangled herself. "Hang on, let me see who this is."

Craig huffed, Nicole's back to him.

Her heart quickened seeing the name on the screen. "It's Ky," she said, turning to Craig. Her pulse accelerated as she hit the green button. "Hey, what's up?"

"I'm in trouble."

CHAPTER 13

That phone call instantly took Nicole back to that incident—the one that had planted the seed of doubt in her mind. Since then, Nicole sometimes wondered what Kyle was truly capable of.

At first, Nicole hadn't answered her phone when the school had called because she'd been at a fertility doctor's appointment. Since she and Craig wanted another child and hadn't been successful, they'd decided to explore IVF or any other fertility procedure that would yield a full-term pregnancy.

While paying at the front desk, Nicole looked at her phone. Her heart lurched, seeing five missed calls and two voicemails from the middle school. She bit her lip as she hit redial, worried Kyle was sick or, even worse, severely hurt. She pictured him in the back of an ambulance, alone, on his way to the hospital, her heart pumping faster with each unanswered ring.

After what felt like an hour but was only thirty seconds later, someone answered. Because Nicole volunteered at the school, she recognized the woman's voice on the other end. "Hi, Janet. It's Nicole, Kyle's mom," she said breathlessly. "I see someone there tried to call me."

"Hi, Nicole. Yes, we've been trying to reach you or Craig. Did you listen to your voicemails?"

Nicole silently cursed herself. She'd been so rattled about why the school had called that she hadn't listened to the messages. "No. As soon as I saw the missed calls, I called back."

The receptionist behind the desk asked Nicole for her credit card. She handed it over and asked Janet, "Is Ky okay?" still in the dark about why the school had called.

"He's safe, but we need you to get here immediately."

Nicole's heart pounded in her ears.

"There's been an incident."

"Incident? What kind of incident? Is he hurt? Hang on," Nicole said to Janet.

The receptionist handed Nicole her credit card. She signed the receipt and walked outside. "What's going on?" she asked, her voice too shrill.

"We need you to come to the school, please. I'm unsure of all the details, just that Kyle's sitting in Principal Franklin's office."

"Is Ky in trouble?" Nicole asked, fumbling with the lock on her car door. She couldn't connect the key with the keyhole.

"I'm sorry. I honestly don't know. Please get here as soon as you can. I'll let Mr. Franklin know you're on your way."

"Thanks." Nicole immediately called Craig. No answer. *Must be in class*, she thought. She left him a message explaining what'd happened and texted him the same information at the first red light she had come to.

When she arrived at the school, Nicole's stomach was in her throat. She couldn't even imagine what'd happened. Driving, she tried not to think the worst since Janet had reassured her that Kyle was okay.

Nicole beelined to the office, where Janet greeted and escorted Nicole to the principal's office. A sharp pain stabbed at Nicole's heart when she saw Kyle sitting in a wooden chair, his head hanging down, tears staining his reddened cheeks.

"Ky," she said, squatting down before him, taking his crumpled face in her hands. "What happened? What is going on?" She smoothed his disheveled hair.

Mr. Franklin opened his office door. His thick, black-framed glasses magnified his eyes, looking two sizes too big. He smoothed his partially bald head with his paper-thin skinned hand. "Thank you for getting here."

"What's going on?" Nicole asked, blinking, holding back angry tears. "No one will tell me."

Kyle kept his head down and sniffled.

"Please, come in. Both of you," Mr. Franklin said, fiddling with the lime-green tie hanging loosely across his concave midsection.

Nicole entered; Kyle shuffled behind.

"Please, have a seat." Mr. Franklin gestured to the chair facing his desk. Nicole noticed the purple lines meandering across the landscape of his hands.

Suddenly warm, she fanned away the heat rising from her neck to her face. She looked over at Kyle, who still hadn't made eye contact.

"There was an incident in the boy's bathroom," the principal began, narrowing his large eyes, staring at the top of Kyle's head.

Mr. Franklin filled Nicole in about the alleged incident. Another boy, Max, claimed Kyle had choked him. Max said he'd disparaged Kyle about being a "mama's boy" because Nicole volunteered there. Max admitted to digging in until Kyle couldn't take anymore, thus lunging, wrapping his fingers around Max's neck. When Kyle finally released his grip, Max had fallen to the ground, coughing and gasping, and Kyle had run out of the bathroom. When Max returned to class, he told his teacher what'd happened.

Nicole looked at Kyle. Tears continued to stream down his salt-stained cheeks. He shook his lowered head from side to side. Were those tears of guilt, regret, or fear? She didn't think him capable of such violence, but his silence spoke volumes. "Is this true?"

Kyle continued to shake his head back and forth, never lifting his head.

"Ky, say something," Nicole demanded, her jaw knotting up.

Kyle remained silent, looking down at his clasped hands as he twiddled his thumbs.

Pleading for mercy, Nicole looked back at Principal Franklin with earnest eyes.

Mr. Franklin jutted his pointy chin in Kyle's direction. "Since your son isn't talking, and this is the story we've gotten from Max, this is the information we'll proceed with."

Nicole spoke, shaking her head. "This doesn't sound like Ky to me. There must be more to the story. No way my son would hurt anyone. Ever." She stared squarely into Principal Franklin's unforgiving eyes, his lips tense.

After a brief moment, Nicole put her hand on Kyle's shoulder. "You need to tell us what happened. Now," she said as gently as possible. She didn't want him to feel ganged up on. She knew her son and what he was capable of, and he was incapable of this—a violent act like choking.

Kyle remained silent in the office, on the way home, and as he served his two-day in-school suspension. When he finally spoke about the incident, he told Nicole and Craig, "I didn't do it. I never touched him. Not once. You have to believe me." And with the waterfall of tears and his unsteady voice, Nicole and Craig took his word for it, and to this very day, Kyle has maintained his innocence. Every so often however, Nicole wondered if that was not true.

CHAPTER 14

Craig sped through town, treating stop signs more like commas, merely pausing, rolling through them on a mission to get to the police station.

"I know you're upset, but please, we don't need to die," Nicole said, grabbing the handle overhead as he slammed on the brakes, narrowly running a red light. This reminded her of Cecelia that day in the field. Someone had to be the voice of reason. She and Craig rarely exhibited a blistering reaction simultaneously—one of the two maintained their composure while the other lost control.

"Dammit!" The brakes squealed in response to his heavy foot pushing on the pedal. "Why the hell is Kyle at the police station?"

Nicole assumed he was being questioned about Jaden and the money; the police must've found out.

"He swore he had nothing to do with Jaden's disappearance," Craig said before Nicole could answer.

She didn't want to tell Craig about Kyle's sports betting gig, especially not now. Truth be told, not ever.

A purple vein protruded from Craig's neck. "Hell, we don't even know if foul play was involved or if Jaden left on his own accord."

How quickly everything had changed—was it not thirty minutes ago that they were playful, about to engage in their favorite activity? And now, they were anxious, tensions high, sex a distant memory.

A bright light flashed in the passenger-side mirror, blinding Nicole. She squinted, shielding her eyes from the laser beam-like illumination. When the white spot in her vision subsided, she recognized the culprit—a black

SUV. Again. Not wanting to upset Craig further, she kept a close eye on the car, constantly watching. Craig was already stressed enough, and she didn't need to add any more fuel to his boiling pot of emotions. The car remained two car lengths behind at all times. When Craig turned into the police station, the SUV continued, going straight rather than following them. Once again, she couldn't get a good look at the driver. The car had sped by too fast, Nicole unable to swivel her neck like an owl.

Craig barely shut off the engine as he jumped out of the car. Nicole walked fast, trying to keep pace with him, two feet ahead. His steps were long and fast.

"Where's my son?" Craig demanded from the receptionist, who was not Valerie. Nicole didn't recognize this different young girl.

"Who's your son?" the doe-eyed girl asked, batting her long eyelashes. A thick, black layer of eyeliner extended past the corners of her eyes like a cat.

Nicole scanned the station floor, looking for Kyle. She assumed he was in an interrogation room. A wave of nausea washed over her, thinking how scared and intimidated he must be.

"Kyle Cunningham," Craig said, slamming his fist on the counter, answering the cat-eyed receptionist.

"Let me handle this, Craig, please. I'm sorry," Nicole said, shooing him aside. "My husband is distraught." Nicole attempted to smile. Stressed, it came out more like a smirk.

Craig harrumphed. A matching vein throbbed on his forehead.

"Our son is here. Somewhere." She leered over the girl, trying to find him, but he was nowhere in sight. "Is Detective Newton here?" Nicole asked, looking over the receptionist again, scanning the hodgepodge of employees.

"I'm sorry. You just missed him."

"Oh." Nicole hoped she could talk to him. Get some answers. Find out what was going on. "Who's here regarding the Jaden Pierce case?"

"I believe that would be Detective Cohen. Let me check." Cat Eyes picked up the phone and nodded, alternating between the phrases *I see*, *okay*, and *thank you*. "If you follow me, I'll take you to see your son," she said, smiling, setting down the receiver.

With a genuine smile this time, Nicole said, "Thank you."

They walked through the station, and upon seeing him, Nicole yelled, "Ky!"

Thankfully, he was not in a cramped, windowless, cold room. Instead, he sat on a slatted wooden chair in front of a metal desk at the back of the station. A thin woman with dark, slicked-back hair, wrapped tightly in a bun at the nape of her neck, peered over purple, circular-shaped glasses chained around her neck like a dog collar.

Kyle looked terrified. Nicole reached out to hug him. The woman, whom Nicole presumed to be Detective Cohen, stood up. "Ma'am, please don't touch him."

"Don't tell my wife what she can't do!" Craig boomed, rattling Nicole's chest. "That's our son!"

A dull pain nestled in Nicole's heart seeing Kyle's red, droopy eyes and tear-streaked puffy cheeks.

"Sir," the detective began, "I'm going to need you to calm down," she snapped back.

Kyle slouched down in the hard chair. Nicole wanted to scoop him up and stroke his moppy hair. He dropped his face into his propped-up hands as his elbows rested on his bouncing knees. Except for his age and size, he looked like a scared little boy who'd awakened from a nightmare where scary monsters lurk.

"I have a right to know why my son is here," Craig said. "Did he do something wrong, or are you just harassing him?"

Officers walked by, glancing at the scuttle.

"Your son is a legal adult. We don't need his mommy and daddy here."

Kyle wrapped his long fingers around the crown of his lowered head.

"Craig," Nicole said, grabbing his flailing arm, trying to control its movement. She yanked him aside. So close, their noses nearly touching, she said, "You're upsetting Kyle. Either settle down or let me handle this."

"Fine," he said, not picking either option.

"Fine, what?" she asked.

"I'll settle down." He drew in a deep breath, his chest puffed out, slightly tugging his polo shirt. He turned back to face Kyle and the detective. "I'm sorry," he said. "I'm upset. Please, fill us in."

Detective Cohen grimaced. "I don't have to fill you in on anything. Your son is over eighteen. He gets to decide what you know."

Craig's nostrils flared; his lips pulled back, baring his teeth. A muscle protruded on the right side of his jaw. He stepped closer to the detective, shortening the gap between them. "Go ahead. Ask him. See if you can tell us."

Nicole noticed a small tape recorder on the desk next to where the detective stood. Two buttons were pressed in, and the capstans were spinning.

Detective Cohen stared into Craig's stormy eyes. "Fine. Kyle, can I tell your parents what's going on?"

He nodded.

"We found an empty beer can lying in the wooded area where Jaden was last known to be, and your son's fingerprints were on it. And," she said, crossing her arms in front of her chest, pressing the chain against her white silk blouse, "your son is wearing the same sneakers that match the tread marks left behind in the soil." She leaned against the desk, crossing her ankles.

Nicole's face flushed. "We all know he was there. He already told you," she said, crossing her arms, posturing back.

A low growl came from Craig.

Detective Cohen sneered, her lip curling on one side. "If you'll let me continue."

Nicole did not like this woman. Not at all.

"Kyle's fraternity brothers said your son threatened Jaden, and the two got into a scuffle."

The scrape along Kyle's cheek had faded, but Nicole could still see a faint outline. Was that how the scratch had gotten there? A fight? About the money? Kyle had told her he'd gotten it while hiding that night. Nicole's muscles tensed.

Pressing his lips in a tight line, looking over his shoulder, leering at any onlookers, Craig lowered his voice. "Bullshit. Someone is lying."

"And I think it's your son," the detective retorted. "And let's not forget the fact your son was drinking. Underage," she said, uncrossing her ankles and recrossing them the opposite way.

Nicole stared at Kyle. He kept his head lowered, not making eye contact. With anyone. Nicole's insides twisted, scared he'd be named the prime suspect. She was terrified he was lying, withholding information, or even worse, he *had* done something to Jaden.

Craig asked, "With this alleged information, is he a suspect?"

"Not at this time." Detective Cohen said, unfolding her arms. "But we can cite him for underage drinking. Unless..."

"Unless what?" Craig spat.

The phone on Detective Cohen's desk rang. Craig looked at it while the detective stared at him, ignoring the nagging ring. She tapped her high-heeled black patent leather shoe against the tile. "Unless he wants to admit to anything else."

Nicole didn't want Kyle to utter another word without an attorney present. "Do we need to hire a lawyer?" she asked.

"That's up to you," the detective said, raising an arched eyebrow.

"Is he being charged with anything?" Craig asked.

"Not at this time."

"Then we're finished here."

Detective Cohen glowered at Kyle, who remained still. "I'm not done questioning him."

It was like watching a chess match; Craig and Detective Cohen were the pieces—each trying to outmaneuver the other, strategizing their win, plotting their defenses.

"He's finished now," Craig snapped, reaching for Kyle's shoulder. "I know how this game works. You pry and question and coax people into saying things, twisting the facts. Guess what? My son isn't playing. Not tonight. Not tomorrow. Not ever. Is that clear?"

Checkmate.

Heads turned toward Craig's loud voice again.

Detective Cohen lowered her chin and voice. "Yes, Mr. Cunningham. Very clear," she said, pushing herself away from her desk, standing tall, patting her neat bun.

"Good. Then we're taking Kyle home, and do me a favor, leave my son alone until you have substantial reason to harass him." Craig grabbed Kyle by the elbow, yanked him up, and whispered something in his ear as they turned to leave. "Oh, and one more thing," Craig said, facing Detective Cohen again. "If you have any further questions, you will need to contact our attorney." He turned around, and with Kyle in his grip and Nicole in tow, Detective Cohen watched the trio storm out the double doors.

CHAPTER 15

"Why is there never any goddamned coffee in the house when you need it?" Craig grumbled, slamming the cabinet doors.

Nicole shuddered. "It's in the next cabinet over," she said, pointing to the correct one.

After leaving the police station last night, Craig and Nicole had insisted, more like demanded, that Kyle come home. Exhausted from the emotional day, heads drowning in information overload, they'd decided it was best to get a good night's sleep and devise a plan in the morning.

But for Nicole, sleep never came. Instead, she'd tossed and turned as thoughts swirled like a cyclone in her brain. Not wanting to disturb Craig, much to her annoyance, he'd put his head on the pillow and fell asleep instantly, she'd ambled downstairs and sat at the kitchen table all night, sorting through the week's events, nursing cup after cup of coffee. So much had happened in such a short amount of time. From picking up Kyle's license to hearing about his illegal doings to her suspicions of being followed, and now, after learning last night about an alleged altercation, Nicole hadn't had the proper time to absorb it all.

Craig had come downstairs a few minutes ago with Kyle shuffling in next, his wavy, shaggy hair mussed up, rubbing his eyes, wearing the same t-shirt from last night, lines now imprinted into the red cottony fabric. "What's all the commotion about?" he said, flopping beside Nicole.

Nicole glared at Craig. She hoped he'd read her look, which she gave Kyle as a young boy when he'd defied her reprimand of "knock it off." Thankfully, Craig did. He turned around, scooped the coffee grounds from the metal can, and dumped them into the paper filter. He hit the start button. The machine gurgled and sputtered dark liquid drops into the transparent glass carafe below.

"Nothing," Nicole said to Kyle.

His eyes were red and swollen and filled with tears. "I'm sorry I'm causing so much trouble," he said through quivering lips. A tear plunged down his cheek.

Nicole reached over and wiped it away with her finger. She cupped his face in her hands, studying the remnants of the scrape. "Oh baby, don't be silly. You're not causing any trouble." She tilted her head and smiled.

"I am," he whimpered, exchanging a knowing look with her.

Compassion needled at Nicole's heart. She wanted to fix this. Make it all go away. She looked at Craig. "Would you please tell our son he's not causing us any trouble?"

Before he could answer, Kyle jumped in. "You had to run to the police station last night, I heard you up during the night, and Dad's worried about his promotion. I'm not stupid. I'm not a baby. I can see what this is doing to you both."

"Craig," Nicole said pleadingly.

He crossed his arms across his College of Cypressville jersey and leaned his backside against the counter. "Look, this is a shitty situation. I'm not gonna lie, but I don't know if I'm angrier at the police or you boys for playing the game."

The coffee pot stopped, signaling it had completed its job—to make the dark brown nectar that would carry them through the rest of the day. Craig poured himself a mugful. "That being said, I need time to figure out what to do next. I assume we need to hire an attorney." He looked at Nicole.

"Yes." She'd mentally created a to-do list while up during the night. Hiring an attorney was top priority. Still, she was worried about the part of Kyle's illegal dealings, afraid he'd have to come clean with an attorney, further jeopardizing his innocence. "Are you okay with that?" she asked hesitantly.

Since he was the one knee-deep in this mess, she thought he should have a say in the matter, but as a parent, she felt she and Craig should make the final decision. Ultimately, it was their job to protect their son. And given Kyle's age and the fact that his prefrontal cortex wasn't fully developed and wouldn't be until the ripe old age of twenty-five, Nicole firmly believed the final word should come from her and Craig—it should be their decision, even though, technically, Kyle was a legal adult.

Kyle wrung his hands, kneading his fingers, intertwining them as he sat, unspeaking. Nicole watched him, waiting for an answer. Not wanting to add more pressure on him, she turned to Craig, who blew on the hot coffee. A droplet spewed down the side of his "I like economics and maybe three people" mug, which Kyle had bought for him last Father's Day. "What?"

She wished Kyle was still a young boy and she and Craig could spell out the words in front of him without him understanding what they were saying, but he wasn't. He was a young adult who could hear *everything* they were saying. Nicole lifted her eyelids, widened her eyes, and jutted her head toward Kyle.

"Oh," Craig said, getting the message. "Kyle, an attorney *is* the best move here. I don't think the police are finished with you." He took a few sips of his coffee.

Kyle lowered his head and stared at his hands.

Craig set the half-empty mug on the patterned countertop and sat next to Kyle. "Look, bud, we need to have a plan before you leave here. You can't go back to campus until we do. We'll listen if you have any thoughts or anything you'd like to say."

Nicole waited with bated breath, anticipating Kyle's impending confession.

It didn't come. Instead, he rested his face on his propped-up palms. "This is such a fucking mess."

Nicole flinched. She'd never heard him use that word. Of course, she knew he used it. She wasn't naïve to think he didn't. Still, it surprised her.

Kyle looked at Craig. "I don't want an attorney getting involved, and I don't want to draw any attention to our family and jeopardize your job."

But Nicole wondered if there was another reason he didn't want an attorney involved, something Kyle didn't want anyone to know.

Everything was still, and the only noise in the room was the refrigerator humming in the background. The sun beat in through the kitchen window over the sink, spotlighting the dust particles floating. They sat, staring at one another, as if the answer, the resolution to this quandary, would magically appear and land squarely on the kitchen table.

"What if we create an alibi for Kyle?" Craig suggested.

Nicole raised an eyebrow. "What, lie?"

"Not exactly lie, more like...extend the truth."

"That's called lying, Craig." Nicole's stomach barrel rolled, knowing she was walking a fine line, lying to Craig. And the police. She leaned back and folded her arms across her chest, covering up the words "Strong AF" on her workout tank top she'd grabbed last night when frustrated, sleep eluding her.

"It's not a lie unless we get caught." Craig smiled.

Unable to read his expression, unsure if he was joking or serious, Nicole, unamused, asked, "Are you for real?"

He leaned back in his chair. "Of course, I'm not being for real. I was trying to prove a point. We don't have any other option at this point. We have to hire an attorney." He placed his hand on Kyle's.

Kyle's neck muscles strained. "I guess it's our only option."

Nicole frowned, highlighting the newly formed worry lines on her forehead. Knowing she was withholding information and suspicious of her son, her stomach quivered. She wanted to peel off her skin. Step out of her own body. Escape her guilt. She sat silent, worried an attorney would learn their secrets, and then her son would be in trouble, and so would she.

CHAPTER 16

Kyle, yearning to get back to some normalcy after they'd finished their talk, asked Craig to bring him back to campus, swearing not to speak to anyone about what'd transpired last night. Craig and Nicole had agreed that Kyle needed to keep busy, to be distracted by school, friends, and whatever else a nineteen-year-old college student did.

Before he'd left, Nicole hugged him tightly, whispering in his ear, promising they would find a solution—the best one to protect him. He hugged her back, clinging on like she was his life jacket, keeping him afloat. "It will be okay. I promise," she reassured him.

Neither one of them had divulged Kyle's secret to Craig. And as much as Nicole wanted to ask Kyle what the detective had said last night, she didn't. She didn't need that discussion occurring in front of Craig; no need to enlighten him about Kyle's pastime until it was essential, especially if it could jeopardize Craig's job or upcoming promotion.

And now, she sat in front of her computer, surfing attorneys' sites again. All of them vying for her business, each boasting why she should hire this one and not that one, promising a personalized experience with one-on-one attention and a "we will fight for you and your rights" motto; all of it overwhelming. Eyes tired, head pounding, Nicole sifted through candidates.

After finding three potential contenders based on their expertise, experience, and substantial outstanding accolades, Nicole called and left messages. To her surprise and disappointment, no one could talk to her. A receptionist at each office promised to pass along the message. Nicole reiterated the importance of a quick turnaround time without sounding too desperate. Being in a holding pattern, awaiting a return call, Nicole decided to bake. She thought she should probably go to the gym instead—blow off her frustration, take it out on the weights—but she didn't want to be tied up anywhere in case Kyle needed her again.

Heading to the kitchen, she peeked out the living room bay window, still questioning if she was being followed since she thought she'd seen the car again last night. She inspected the vehicles parked along the magnolia-lined street. No black SUV. She double-checked. It definitely wasn't there. Only the usual suspects—the neighbors' overflow of cars.

She wondered if the SUV was connected to Kyle, and now that he'd been questioned, maybe the mystery person would no longer trail her.

She gathered all the ingredients needed to make a batch of butterscotch-infused brownies, one of Craig's favorite sweet treats. He, unlike her, had no problem indulging himself with sugary treats, which explained his expanding waistline. He wasn't fat by any means, but his belt buckle had moved one notch over and not in a good direction.

As the butterscotch morsels melted in the pan on the stove, her phone rang. She left the simmering pot to answer it and knocked over the measuring cup filled with flour next to her phone. "Shit!" A white, dusty cloud floated, mushrooming out.

Not recognizing the number, Nicole brushed off her hands and hit the speaker button. "Hello?"

"Mrs. Cunningham," a deep voice emitted from the speaker.

"Yes." For a flash second, Nicole panicked Kyle had been arrested.

"My name is Phil Hatcher. I believe you left a message with my receptionist regarding your son."

Nicole exhaled. "Yes. Thank you for getting back to me quickly. I appreciate it." Nicole sat on the counter stool.

"Sure. No problem. What can I help you with?"

Nicole explained their predicament without divulging any names or specifics—especially not what she'd done and knew and asked if someone in that situation should hire an attorney.

"Yes. Absolutely," he said. "Don't ever talk to the police without one present. Ever."

"How much do you charge?"

"I require a five-thousand-dollar retainer fee." Nicole's stomach twisted. Where would they get that kind of money? They didn't have it lying around. Although Craig made decent money, it's not like they were crazy wealthy with a cash surplus on hand. She was skeptical if they could scrape together that amount.

Phil continued, "And when that's depleted, I charge two hundred fifty per hour." Pretty sure they couldn't spare such expense, Nicole would have to talk to Craig. She drummed her fingers, thinking.

"Thanks, I appreciate the information. I need to talk it over with my husband, and I'll get back to you when we decide." Before finalizing their choice, she wanted to hear back from the other prospective attorneys.

"Want some free advice?" Phil asked.

She wanted to say, "Lawyers give something for free?" Instead, she said, "Sure."

"Don't wait too long. Your son may be in deeper than you know, and the longer you wait, the worse it may get for him."

Nicole's already jumpy stomach twitched tighter. "Thank you. I'll take that into account."

"Good luck, and I'll wait to hear back." The line went dead.

A heavy molasses scent lingered in the air. *Shit! The butterscotch!* Nicole slapped her hand on her forehead and jumped from the stool. Forgetting it was on the stove, the butterscotch had burned, stuck to the pan, like chewing gum melted to the sidewalk on a hot summer's day.

She turned off the heat and tossed the singed pot in the sink, unsure the pan could be saved. Between the charred butterscotch and the mound of white powder coating the countertop, Nicole called it quits. Never one to leave a mess, she walked out of the kitchen this one time, leaving behind the crime scene, and called Craig.

• • • • •

Less than twenty-four hours later, Craig, Nicole, and Kyle sat before Phil.

When Nicole had picked up Craig last night from work, she'd explained about calling three different attorneys and only hearing back from two: Phil and another one who was no longer accepting new clients. A sad state of affairs, Nicole had thought—so many people needing legal representation that he wasn't even for hire. Craig said he could scrape together the money for the retainer fee. With no pros and cons list needed, the duo had decided to hire Phil.

Now, looking at the man sitting across from her, Nicole figured the wet-behind-the-ears lawyer to be in his early thirties. His dark blond hair was buzzed short, military-style. He wore a light blue Oxford shirt, one shade lighter than his eyes, and an orange bowtie. Bowtie! Quirky was the word that came to mind when she first saw it.

Seated around a large conference table, big enough to host The Last Supper, and surrounded by four walls decorated with large mahogany diploma-filled frames, Phil talked about his background. He'd graduated from Columbia Law school and had been in practice for seven years.

Nicole mentally computed his age, confirming what she'd suspected—he was in his early thirties but not as inexperienced as previously assumed. She glanced at his ring finger, looking for a wedding band or a tan mark where one would typically rest, but it was bare—no traces of marriage.

After his spiel, Phil asked Kyle why he was there.

Craig spoke. "My son—"

"Mr. Cunningham, with all due respect, if I am going to represent your son, I need to hear from him, not you."

Craig's face burned bright red, a stark contrast to his white Henley shirt.

Nicole jumped in. "Sorry, Mr. Hatcher," she started.

"Please, call me Phil."

"Phil," she corrected, "We are parents first and foremost. Do you have any children?"

He shook his head, his bowtie wiggling.

"If and when you become a parent, you'll understand," she said, squeezing Craig's forearm. "We just want to help our son."

"Kyle is not the first 'child,'" he said, using air quotes, "I've represented. But legally, he is an adult. He's over eighteen, correct?"

Nicole let out an exasperated sigh. "Yes." She forgot that, by law, Kyle was an adult. He was *her* child and still viewed him as such. Nicole and Craig could stay in the room only because Kyle had requested it; he wanted them involved in every step, otherwise, they'd be out of luck.

"If he's my client, then he needs to answer. Not you. Not your husband. Understand?"

Nicole glanced sideways at Craig. His face turned a deeper shade of red, nearing purple. She squeezed his forearm again, reassuring him he needed to let Phil do his job, no matter how much they wanted to take control.

Nicole bobbed her head up and down. "We understand." She side-winked at Craig.

"But we are paying the bill," Craig said, not dropping the issue. Nicole gripped his arm tighter, like a parent warning a child not to enter the busy road; he was about to cross a dangerous line.

Phil squinted and rubbed his clean-shaven chin. "Mr. Cunningham, do we have a problem here?"

"I don't know what you're implying," Craig retorted.

"It seems you have some reason for not wanting my client to speak to me. Any particular reason?"

Craig's lip tightened, and his dark eyes locked with Phil's.

Phil glowered back, not retreating, like in a pissing match, each man exerting his dominance. "Mr. Cunningham, you are wasting my time here today. If you cannot, and will not, abide by my rules, then I think our business here is finished." He rolled his high-backed leather chair from the table and stood up. The chair bumped into the wall under the diplomas.

Nicole panicked. They needed him, and she hadn't had any luck with other attorneys. "Phil, please, can I have a word alone with my husband?" She tilted her head sideways.

"Do as you wish." Phil shut the door behind him, leaving them alone.

Nicole whipped her head toward Craig. "What is wrong with you?" she asked as the door clicked.

"I don't like him," he said, heat radiating from his cheeks.

"Why not?"

"He's arrogant."

"We need arrogance. We need someone to help protect our son."

Kyle sat unmoving, watching his parents bicker.

"I'm begging you, behave yourself. Let Kyle talk. Give Phil a chance." Nicole's brown and green speckled eyes filled with tears. She hated turning on the waterworks, but she was desperate.

Through clenched teeth, Craig said, "Fine."

"Thank you," she said and kissed his cheek. "Ky, go tell Phil we're ready now."

Kyle, who hadn't uttered a word, left to get Phil.

Nicole laced her fingers with Craig's and set their entwined hands on his lap.

Kyle returned with Phil, and before taking his seat, Phil asked, wagging his finger, "We all good here?"

Nicole was afraid Craig would have a change of heart and start again. When he said "yes," Phil retook his seat, and she slid down her chair, resting her head on the back.

For the next forty-five minutes, Phil questioned Kyle. When he got to the part about the fingerprints on the beer can, Phil asked, "Do you have a previous record? One I'm not aware of?"

Kyle wiggled in the chair and widened his eyes. Nicole knew what he was anxious about—the sports betting. "No. Why?"

"Because unless you have a prior, the police don't have a fingerprint on record to match yours with."

"What do you mean?" Nicole asked, confused yet relieved Kyle hadn't revealed his hobby.

"The police have a database. It's called the IAFIS—"

Craig interrupted. "The what?" he asked sternly. "Speak English."

Phil narrowed his eyes and folded his hands, leaning his forearms on the table. "The IAFIS—the Integrated Automated Fingerprint Identification System. It's the national database the FBI keeps of fingerprints and criminal history, which is what I was about to say if you would've let me finish."

Craig squeezed Nicole's hand tightly. She grimaced in pain.

"Anyway, as I was saying, if Kyle here doesn't have a previous record, his fingerprints aren't in that system. The police were bluffing, probably trying to get you to confess. Scare tactics. Common practice."

Craig tugged at his shirt collar.

"Anything else I should know?" Phil asked, checking his watch, their time almost up.

Worried about Kyle's following answer, Nicole bit the inside of her cheek.

Instead of saying anything, he lowered his head.

Phil raised an eyebrow. "Something you're not telling me?"

Silently, Kyle shook his head, and Nicole's jaw slackened. Although it probably wasn't in his best interest, Nicole sighed, relieved he said nothing more.

Phil stood up and escorted them out of the room, reassuring them Kyle would be fine, even suggesting he go back to the police station, but this time, with his attorney present, promising the police wouldn't be happy to hear what he had to say. Craig refuted, but Phil insisted, stating he knew what was best for his client.

Nicole only hoped so.

CHAPTER 17

Preoccupied with Kyle, Nicole hadn't helped volunteer over the past few days. There was still no evidence, clues, or body after ten days. The town was restless, wanting updates, information, and, most of all, Jaden's return. Rumors circulated, bogus theories were tossed into the nebulous mix, and people were pointing fingers in all directions, the police neither confirming nor denying any of it.

An apple-sized knot cohabitated with this morning's omelet in Nicole's stomach, waiting for three o'clock. That's when Detective Cohen would interview Kyle again, this time with Phil present.

Nicole would be there, but not Craig since he'd be teaching then. They decided that was for the best, so Craig wouldn't be seen with Kyle at the police station. Worried about his upcoming promotion, Craig wanted to lay low—he didn't want to draw attention where unneeded. It was easy to blend in on a campus of fifteen thousand students and over a thousand professors.

Nicole watched the clock, each minute feeling more like an hour. She closed her eyes as if willing the hands to move faster. Only three minutes had elapsed when she opened them. "This is useless," she said, staring at the clock on the mantle. Aggravated, she decided to go to the gym rather than agonize over watching the clock. She haphazardly threw her towel, water bottle, and a change of clothes in her gym bag and left.

She approached the car in the driveway and noticed a white piece of paper tucked under the windshield wiper. A pain pricked through her stomach like a pin pushing into a pincushion. Nicole looked left, then right, for anyone nearby. The street was empty. Just cars, mailboxes, and houses.

"What the fuck?" she said, grabbing the folded note from its resting place.

Her heart accelerated as she unfolded the paper. Her eyes darted back and forth over the words:

Stay out of it. You're playing with fire, and you'll get burned

She opened her mouth. A small moan escaped. "Who is doing this?" she said to the paper. It didn't respond, but it certainly knew the answer. She crumpled it up into a small ball, and on wavy legs, she threw it in the large blue recycling bin on the side of the house.

Whoever had left this note knew where she lived. She was now, more than ever, convinced that she was indeed being followed. Finally acknowledging what she'd suspected all along, she opted to keep it to herself. She didn't want to burden anyone with this, convincing herself it could wait.

She weaved in and out of traffic, looking forward to her upcoming workout. Apprehensive and to be extra cautious, she constantly checked her rearview mirror, looking for any car that might be tailing her, every black SUV arousing her suspicion.

When returning to her car after her workout, Nicole breathed a sigh of relief, seeing an empty windshield. Cautiously optimistic that she wasn't being followed, she repeated the same attentive behavior on the way home. Driving down her street, she inventoried all the cars in the vicinity. The dubious SUV was nowhere to be seen. She practiced the same prudent behavior on her way to pick up Kyle, constantly watching for suspicious cars. Nothing.

When arriving at the police station, Nicole and Kyle walked toward Phil. Today, he wore a purple polka-dotted bow tie and a pink and white pinstripe Oxford shirt. Nicole rolled her eyes at the mismatched combination, but somehow, he pulled it off.

"You ready?" Phil asked Kyle.

Nicole looked sideways at Kyle; his pasty white face told her no, he wasn't. He rubbed his palms on his dark jeans and nodded. She placed her hand on his shoulder. "You've got this. Just a few moments of uncomfortableness to make it all better," she said, like when he'd get a shot as a young boy. Cowering behind her leg, shielding himself from the needle-yielding nurse, Nicole used to say, "It'll only hurt for a second, but it'll keep you safe and healthy forever."

He nodded again.

As the doors opened, familiar noises hit her ears. Valerie sat behind the counter, headphones on, chattering away. She held up her half-polished finger, signaling, "give me a minute," and smiled at Nicole.

Nicole gave a halfhearted wave. Phil leaned against the counter, his black leather briefcase dangling from his hand. Kyle shifted his weight from foot to foot, like fighting for balance on a rocky boat.

"Hi!" Valerie said. "What can I help you with today?" Nicole noticed a small gap between Valerie's bottom front teeth. It looked like a piece of spinach.

"We have a three o'clock appointment."

"Do you know who you're meeting with?"

Nicole turned to face Phil. He was looking upward, rocking on his heels, and whistling. Puzzled by his lack of participation, she said, "Detective Cohen, I belie—,"

Phil cut in. "No. We're here to see Detective Newton." He slid his business card under the rectangular gap in the Plexiglass.

"I'll let him know you're here." Valerie smiled, revealing her chipped tooth, ignoring the card. While she called the detective, Phil continued to whistle.

He's an eighty-year-old man trapped in a thirty-something body.

When she hung up, Valerie interrupted his trilling. "You can head back to his desk. It's over there." She pointed to the back left corner. "I'm sure he'll recognize you," she said to Nicole.

The corral door buzzed open, and Nicole pushed her way through. Phil grabbed her elbow, pulling her close, startling her. Applying pressure, he hissed in her ear, "Why would the detective recognize you?"

Nicole jerked her arm away and wrinkled her brow. "We've seen one another while I've helped with the search party."

"What?" he stammered. "You're part of the search party?" He pushed in front of her, blocking her path, facing her, his blue eyes blazing. "That would've been a significant detail to disclose."

"Why?"

Before Phil could answer, Detective Newton walked toward them, swapping glances between Phil and Nicole, scratching his forehead. "What are you doing here? With him? And him?" Detective Newton asked, pointing to both Kyle and Phil.

Kyle averted the detective's stare and looked down at his scuffed-up sneakers.

"We have an appointment. Apparently, with you," she chuckled.

Neither man saw the humor; Phil pursed his lips, and Detective Newton drew his eyebrows together.

Rubbing the back of his neck, Detective Newton asked, "You're Kyle's mother?"

"Yes."

"That can't be," he said, shaking his head.

Confused, Nicole asked, "Why not?"

"Kyle is a person of interest."

"So," she said, shrugging, her shoulders nearly touching the earrings dangling down.

"So you can't be a volunteer if you're related to anyone possibly involved."

Disappointment jabbed her heart. "Wait, I can't be a part of the search party because Kyle is my son? When I spoke to you on the phone that day, you said anyone could help and that the search party wasn't your department."

"It isn't, but if it's a conflict of interest, it becomes my department."

"Kyle's not even a suspect."

"Sorry. Conflict of interest. That's my policy, and you're officially done."

"Bingo," Phil said, putting his forefinger on his sharp nose. "And that's *exactly* what I was trying to say." He set his briefcase down next to his saddle-brown wingback shoes.

"Shit." She pressed her fingers to her temple and lowered her head.

"I'm sorry, Mom," Kyle said, lifting his gaze to hers.

Not wanting to add undue stress on him, she smiled. "It's okay. No worries." Truth be told, it wasn't okay. She wanted to help.

"Now that we have that all squared away, please, have a seat," Detective Newton said, gesturing to the chairs in front of him.

"Would you prefer to do this in a conference room?" Phil asked, hitching his thumb over his shoulder.

"No, here is fine."

Phil set his briefcase on his lap. "My client would like to tell you what he knows about the night Jaden went missing. He is volunteering information and willing to help fill in any gaps if he has further knowledge regarding this case."

"How refreshing," Detective Newton said, sitting down, his chair rolling back from the pressure of his weight.

Nicole couldn't tell if he was speaking genuinely or sarcastically. He pressed two buttons on a tape recorder and placed it down on his desk.

Fumbling through his opened briefcase, Phil pulled out a yellow legal pad. "As I understand it, my client isn't a suspect, correct?"

"Yes."

"And you brought him in for questioning the other night without an attorney present. Is that correct?"

"Yes." Detective Newton leaned back in his chair, tipping it to almost falling, and folded his hands together, resting them on his extended belly.

"And Detective Cohen continued to question him, anyway. Is that correct?" Phil looked down at the pad resting on his thigh, crossing off words with a red pen as he went.

"Yes."

"Do you have anything linking my client to this case?"

Detective Newton put the chair's front legs back down and leaned his elbows on his desk, his rotund stomach pinned against the desk's ledge. "Who is questioning who here?"

Nicole watched the men as they bantered.

"Detective Newton," Phil said, ignoring the question, "my client is innocent until proven guilty."

"But Kyle was there that night. We have a beer can with his fingerprints on it," Detective Newton sneered.

"Let me assure you; they're not my client's. Since he has no priors, his fingerprints aren't in the database. You didn't match *any* fingerprints to Kyle."

Stunned, Detective Newton blinked slowly, his mouth hanging open.

"I thought so," Phil said, smirking. "Your associate was merely bluffing. Now, back to my question. Do you have anything substantial to indict my client?"

"His sneakers match the tread marks found the next day."

"That's not enough. We all know Kyle was playing in the woods that night. He's admitted to that."

"But we have witnesses saying they heard your client threaten Jaden."

Nicole's heart stopped.

Phil's eyebrows shot up, and he looked at Kyle, who'd been looking down the whole time. His eyes flew open as he lifted his head, turning white.

Phil regained his composure and acted like he knew this information. "Still not enough proof. It's merely hearsay, third-party information."

Displeased with Phil's statement, Detective Newton looked at Kyle. "We also heard that you and Jaden had some sort of physical altercation."

Again, utterly oblivious but pretending to know, Phil frowned and glared at Kyle, who looked down at the checkerboard linoleum.

Detective Newton asked, "Any of this ringing a bell?"

Phil jumped in and said to Kyle, "You don't need to answer that." He then addressed the detective. "He's not on trial."

"If I were you, and he has nothing to hide and wants to clear his name, I'd let him talk. Unless, of course," Detective Newton paused and then said, "he has something to hide. Do you?" he asked, looking at the top of Kyle's lowered head.

The police station exploded with the sounds Nicole had become accustomed to hearing: ringing phones blaring, voices conversing, footsteps echoing against the concrete walls. Yet, as those last words left Detective Newton's mouth, it was like the entire station had stopped.

Phil placed his slender-fingered hand on Kyle's arm. "You don't have to answer."

Kyle, pulling his shoulders back and sitting up straight, looked directly into Detective Newton's dark eyes. "I want to. I need to get this off my chest."

CHAPTER 18

"Is Ky off the hook?" Craig asked.

Nicole heard whispering in the background. "Who's that?"

"Dr. Graham."

After Nicole dropped Kyle off at the fraternity house, she updated Craig. She told him about the entertaining interaction between Phil and Detective Newton and how Phil had questioned the detective more than the detective had interrogated Kyle. Craig didn't seem as amused as she was. He wanted the crux of the meeting.

When parked in the driveway, Nicole switched the call from Bluetooth to her cell, stepped out of the car, and checked her surroundings, ensuring she hadn't been followed. With no wayward vehicle in sight, she went into the house feeling safe.

"Not yet," Nicole said, setting down her purse, "But after he answered the detective's question, I don't think he'll be looked at as closely."

More whispers crossed through the phone line. "Hang on, Nic."

Static crackled, the crunching sound annoying Nicole. She squinted as if that would help her decode the words being spoken. She held her breath, hoping that would help, too. It didn't, but the angry voices stopped.

"Sorry, I'm back."

"Everything okay? It sounded pretty heated."

"All good here. Dr. Graham was trying to explain something to me. Guess I'm not the best at this new technology," Craig chuckled. "Anyway, you were about to tell me why the police may back off, Ky," Craig said, bringing their conversation back to the forefront.

"Yes. Newton said he'd heard that Ky had threatened Jaden, and that there'd been some sort of fight between the two, but Phil interjected, saying it was nothing more than hearsay. And when Newton asked Ky if it was true, Phil reassured Ky he didn't have to answer, but Ky said he needed to get it off his chest."

"And?"

"Kyle told Newton that it was the other way around. That *he'd* been the one who'd overheard some conversations between Chase, Ethan, and Jaden a few days before Jaden disappeared. Something about money. Kyle said he'd tried to keep the peace between the boys, and when he interceded, he'd accidentally been scratched in the crossfire. Kyle also said it was Chase's idea to play Manhunt that night. Something about messing with Jaden."

"Huh. I wonder if those boys will be looked at a little closer now?"

"Don't know and don't care. Not our problem, thankfully."

The clock on the mantle struck the top of the hour, a soft chime filling the quiet house. When it finished, a rush of air echoed in Nicole's ear. She pictured Craig's chest sinking with relief.

"Do you think it went well?" he asked.

"Yes, definitely."

Another rush of air reverberated in her ear. "Thank you for taking care of all this. I love you, babe."

Nicole smiled. Her heart swelled hearing his words, but her stomach shrunk, second-guessing Kyle because each time he talked about that scratch, the story changed.

• • • • •

Nicole checked out the front window one last time, promising herself that it was one of two things if the suspicious car was nowhere in sight. Either 1. She'd been paranoid, or 2. It'd been purely coincidental that she'd seen the black SUV more than once, quite possibly different ones, for that matter. She pulled the wooden slat down. The street was free and clear. She told herself now that she was off the search party, she would no longer receive any more alarming notes.

Disappointed she'd been booted, Nicole wanted and needed to stay involved just in case Kyle was responsible in some way. Although he'd sworn he wasn't, Nicole now wondered if Chase or Ethan had been, and maybe Kyle knew about it and was protecting his fraternity brothers. She needed updates. She paced the floor, thinking, when an idea came to her. Sylvia. But Nicole hesitated. After watching her in the woods, Nicole was uncertain how trustworthy and blameless Sylvia was.

With no other alternative, desperate for insider information, Nicole picked up her phone and typed:

Hey! Guess what?

Purposely cryptic in her message, Nicole left the question open-ended, hoping to incite curiosity. Three dots danced on the screen. It worked. Sylvia typed:

What?

I've been booted from the search party

Is that even a thing? Who kicked you off? Jaden's parents?

No, Newton

What? Why?

My son was playing Manhunt the night Jaden went missing

OMG! Your son knows Jaden?

Yes. Fraternity brothers. Been a whole thing

How awful!

Newton said I'm off the search party. Conflict of interest

That sucks. Did you know Jaden 2?

Not really

Does your son know anything? Was he involved?

Nicole tensed up at that question. If Sylvia were guilty of something, would Kyle become her scapegoat?

No. To both

Nicole didn't repeat what Kyle had said at the police station. No need to give Sylvia a match if she was the gasoline.

That must be a huge relief. Would've been helpful if he did know anything, but good he wasn't involved

Yeah, I'm pissed I can't help

I get it

Maybe you can send me updates?

Nicole waited, hoping Sylvia would take the bait, but the dots stopped dancing. She stared at the screen, transfixed, waiting. Annoyed at herself for possibly pushing the issue too far, she tossed her phone on the table. It dinged as it landed.

Sorry! Had to let the dog out. Sure, no problem!

Nicole typed as fast as her pulse raced.

Thank you!!

NP! Good luck with your son!

Thx!

At least she would still be in the loop for now. Unsure who to trust, Nicole decided maybe she would keep searching herself, only not while anyone else was watching.

• • • • •

Craig and Nicole enjoyed some respite after the past few crazy days. Kyle had also settled down and continued his everyday college life while the search for Jaden grew colder. Since the police had backed off from Kyle thanks to Phil, worth every penny Nicole had said to Craig, Nicole hoped their life would get back to normal.

Postcoital pleasure consumed Nicole as she watched Craig dress for work. She preferred morning sex—it released endorphins to kick-start the day. "What's on your agenda today?" she asked, folding the down comforter over her naked body.

"You know, the usual." *God, he looks handsome.* He was wearing a seafoam green polo shirt, which brought out the specks of green interspersed in his mostly brown eyes, and black chino pants. He liked to dress casually every so often, so he wouldn't intimidate his students, especially the freshmen. Craig took pity on their frightened faces as they packed into the great lecture hall, finding anyone to sit by that they knew. Only on special meeting days did he wear a full suit.

"How are things going with Dr. Graham? It sounded like you two were arguing the other day."

"When?" Craig faced the mirror and tilted his head, rubbing his hand over his chin, inspecting his shave job.

"When I called you. After Kyle's trip to the police station. Remember?" Nicole flipped on her side and propped her chin on her hand.

"Oh, that. Yeah, it was nothing. Trying to learn something new, that's all. Sometimes I get frustrated." He smiled, his lip dimpling. He reached for his cologne bottle on the shelf beside the vanity and squirted some on.

Nicole inhaled the scent. "You're a highly intelligent man. You'll get it."

Craig checked his watch—not a digital one like everyone used these days—his was a Cartier with fancy Roman numerals decorating the face. Nicole had splurged and bought it for him when he'd gotten the job here at the college. It was used; she didn't want to break the bank entirely by purchasing a brand-new one. "Shit, no time to eat today," he complained, tucking in the back of his shirt.

Nicole thought a polo shirt should be untucked, but Craig insisted on tucking it in no matter how many times she'd advised him to leave it out.

She flashed him her sexiest smile. "Sorry."

He softened his tone. "Totally worth it," he said, leaning on the bed to kiss her forehead.

Grabbing a handful of his shirt, Nicole pulled him down lower. Nose to nose, she said, "Love you. Have a great day."

As he scrambled down the stairs, he shouted, "You too! Oh, and don't worry about picking me up. I'll grab a ride since I'll be home late again."

Nicole heard the lock click behind him.

CHAPTER 19

Nicole poured a fresh cup of coffee into a travel carafe sitting on the counter. She decided to hit the gym today. Finally. Feeling more like herself, she vowed to settle back into a more consistent workout routine. She flipped on the TV to see if there were any new breaks in the case since she'd heard nothing else from Sylvia, not that Nicole minded—something about that woman didn't feel right.

With her face nose deep in the refrigerator, digging for the oat milk, she'd given up regular cream years ago—no sense in erasing all her dedication to the gym, Nicole heard familiar voices coming from the television. It was George and Cecelia Pierce. Nicole wondered if there'd been a break in the case. More curious to find the answer, rather than the need to lighten her coffee, she abandoned her quest and scurried over to the TV. The Pierces were not on the news. Instead, they were on *The Claudia Welch Show*, a nationally syndicated televised talk show.

Claudia, who'd been on the air for over ten years, sat in an oversized chair. She looked like a small child engulfed by the ginormous, teal-colored cushions. George and Cecelia sat right across from her in twinning chairs. The audience was applauding whatever Claudia had just said. Glued to the screen now, Nicole backed up and sat on the sofa, forgetting all about the fresh cup of coffee on the counter.

George was slumped down in the fabric cushions, and Cecelia's cheeks were black from the mascara cascading down her splotchy cheeks. They both stared at Claudia, watching her rant.

Nicole always disliked that talk show host. She found Claudia condescending with her "higher and mightier than thou" attitude. *What is her area of expertise, anyway? Is she a licensed therapist or anything of the sort?* No. All Claudia was, at least as far as Nicole knew and heard, was a nosy, overbearing, pompous TV personality, not the least qualified to offer anyone advice.

Nicole had to watch, despite her contempt for Claudia. She needed to hear why on God's green earth Jaden's parents were on the show. No matter the circumstances in her own life, Nicole solemnly swore she'd *never* sit across from Claudia, much less air her dirty laundry—which, fortunately, had few stains—on such a public forum.

When the applause subsided, Claudia continued, "I totally get what you're saying. It's preposterous and blasphemy." She pressed her perfectly manicured hands together and clapped, her cherry-red fingernails looking like beacons of light. The audience followed suit. The Pierces sat stiffly. They didn't even blink. Nicole squinted, checking to see if their chests were moving up and down, confirming that they were authentic humans and not wax statues.

Claudia raised her scrawny arms and flapped them like a hummingbird, signaling the audience to settle down. Once it was quiet again, George spoke directly into the camera. "We are thoroughly disappointed with how the Cypressville police have handled our son's disappearance."

Nicole covered her mouth with her cupped hands.

The audience erupted again.

George raised his voice and shouted over them, "They have not been searching aggressively enough. They have not expanded their area far enough. They have not done their due diligence following up on any tips!" He pounded his fist in his open palm with each *not*. "We know it has to be one of his fraternity brothers who had something to do with all this."

George stopped his rant and sucked in his hollow cheeks, closing his eyes. After a brief moment, he exhaled, opening his eyes. "We heard the police found a beer can in that area with the fingerprints of one of the brothers, along with sneaker prints, and we've also heard that a fraternity brother had threatened our son. When we discover who that was, there'll be hell to pay."

Cecelia bobbed her head up and down like a spineless rag doll.

"This is not a threat!" George shouted over the lingering noise. "This is a promise. If the police don't give us the name of that fraternity brother, we'll sue the pants off them! We have a right to know! It's been eleven goddamn days, and we've still got nothing!" He slammed his clenched fist on his knee. The audience waited for him to go on, but he didn't. Instead, he leaned back in his chair, panting, sweat shining on his forehead.

The camera panned over the audience. Not one person remained seated; every guest was standing and cheering. They clapped, hooted, hollered, and whistled loudly. Claudia's lips curled into a dubious smile. She pointed her nose down and peered over her saucer-sized, red glasses, admiring the crowd.

"Holy shit. This is not good." Wetness pooled under Nicole's arms more than during her extraneous workouts. Unable to watch anymore, she turned off the TV and searched for her phone, finding it resting next to her keys, next to the abandoned coffee. Her nervous hands misdialed Craig. "Fuck," she muttered, starting over. She bit her lip, waiting for him to answer. It went to voicemail. "I need you to call me as soon as you get this message," she panted.

"Shit, shit, shit." She paced in front of the TV, texting Kyle.

Call me ASAP!

While waiting to hear back, Nicole scrolled through her social media accounts. Well-wishes, prayers, and rumors still filled the news feeds, and now, thanks to the Pierce's appearance on *The Claudia Welch Show*, more accusations flew—various names, including Kyle's, were being listed, and the hashtag "Justice for Jaden" flooded her feed.

A faint beep came from the kitchen, alerting Nicole that she'd left the refrigerator door open. She hadn't even noticed when she'd picked up her phone, aggravated by what she'd just witnessed. She saw the travel mug sitting on the counter and dumped the cold, brown liquid down the drain. Her stomach felt like an ocean churning in a powerful storm; mixing anything else with the waves of nausea would end in disaster. Halfway through emptying the cup, her phone chimed.

Kyle texted:

What's up?

Where are you?

Chapter meeting. Our president in a snit. Nationals involved. May suspend us. It's a cluster!

Sorry. More bad news. Jaden's parents on Claudia Welch today. Did u see?

No. I heard. It's all over my Insta feed

Kyle's name was on that feed. She didn't ask him if he'd seen it, and since he hadn't mentioned it, she didn't want to bring it up. No need to incite further panic. She would handle it for him. Nicole texted:

This is bad. I'm calling Phil

Why?

It's gone national now!

Oh, I didn't think about that. I wouldn't worry. It's NBD

NBD?

No big deal. Gtg

Nicole's heart pounded against her rib cage as she rolled her eyes at his last acronym. Disinterested in its meaning, she cleared her throat, trying to regulate her breathing, settling it back into a rhythmic pattern with her heart. Tiny hairs prickled the nape of her neck. Why wasn't Kyle panicking? Something was off. Very off.

CHAPTER 20

"You need to call me the second you get this," Nicole spoke loud and fast into her phone. She shifted her weight back and forth, foot to foot, and twisted the bottom of her oversized fuchsia tank top with her free hand. "I mean it, Phil. It's urgent," she reiterated. When she ended the call, she checked her messages. Again. Nothing from Craig yet.

She texted him for the fifth time.

Uptight, Nicole left where she'd been standing for the past five minutes and paced the floor, racking up thousands of steps. She remembered reading an article in one of her health magazines about how pacing helped ease anxiety. Supposedly, it got the creative juices flowing and pleased the brain by creating a path over the same pattern, and right now, Nicole needed an overload of creative juices—she needed a plan—a way to minimize the damage the Pierce's had just created.

At the half-ringtone, Nicole dove for her phone. "What's wrong now?" Craig asked in a sharp tone.

Nicole filled him in on the morning's events.

He sighed. "I don't think you need to worry. They're rumors. Not facts. Stop reading the comments. Stay off social media. And I'm sure nothing will change just because Jaden's parents are randomly spewing shit on a tabloid TV show. It's all about the ratings."

"But what if the police name Kyle as the person the Pierces are referring to, just to appease them?" She lifted her hair and flapped it up and down, trying to fan her sweaty neck.

"They won't. They can't. They have nothing substantial. It's all speculation and hearsay like you'd said before. Sit tight and wait for Phil to call you back. Besides, you said Ky said it was Chase or Ethan who'd threatened Jaden."

Nicole stopped pacing. That was true, but with Kyle's conflicting narratives, something still didn't feel or sound right. Silencing her intuition, she asked, "Do you think I should've called Phil?"

"It can't hurt. Besides, we need to get our money's worth," he chuckled.

Nicole could feel the heat rising in her neck. "How can you find any humor in this?"

"Sorry. I'm only trying to help. I wish I were there to help calm you down. It'll be okay. I promise. I know Ky had nothing to do with Jaden's disappearance."

"Okay," she said, loosening her grip on the phone. Craig had calmed her nerves and quieted her brain. Anxiety draining from her body, Nicole realized maybe she was overthinking and panicking unnecessarily.

Somewhat relieved, Nicole decided to go to the gym. If there was nothing to worry about, she didn't want to lose another day of working out. She slung her Nike "Just Do It" workout bag over her shoulder and headed toward the door. Juggling her keys in one hand and her phone in the other, Phil's call came through.

"Have you heard?" he asked.

The bag slid down her arm and landed on the floor. Phil must've seen the show and knew what was going on. Nicole frowned. "Yes," she said, thinking his question was about the shit show she'd witnessed. "If you saw it, then why didn't you answer my call after the show?"

"Show? What show? I'm talking about the news. Turn it on. Now."

"Hang on." Nicole set her keys on the table by the front door and turned the TV back on. Detective Newton stood at the podium, the sun reflecting off his freshly shaven head. He wore a navy polo shirt with the words *Cypressville Police* embroidered in a fancy white font above the police department's logo. A few gray chest hairs peeked out from the unbuttoned collar.

Her body stiffened. Once again, every muscle from head to toe went rigid. Worried, Nicole hoarsely said, "They're going to name Kyle."

"What? Why?"

Nicole repeated what'd happened on *The Claudia Welch Show*. "That's why I called you," she said, blinking back hot tears.

"Oh boy. I had no—"

"Shh!" Nicole said, cutting him off. "I want to hear this."

Detective Newton rested his hands on the sides of the wooden lectern and leaned forward to speak into the microphone. A shrill pitch pierced the silence. The people standing behind him on the raised platform plugged their ears. "Sorry," he said, backing up a few inches, covering the microphone with his hand. When the sound subsided, he tapped it. *Thump, thump, thump*. "Is this better?" he asked.

People nodded as they settled their arms back to their original resting positions—either by their sides, folded across their chests, shielding their eyes from the sun's glare, or as with the media personnel, pens poised over tiny notebooks.

Detective Newton began, "Contrary to the Pierce's unfounded accusations, we are doing *everything* to find Jaden."

Nicole stood firm, teeth clenched, unblinking, waiting for what he said next. Her loud, spastic heartbeat droned in her ears.

They were near the wooded area that Nicole had helped scour. A sprinkling of pine needles drifted down, landing on the stage. If it weren't for the unfavorable circumstances, anyone watching would marvel at the beautiful scenery.

A few muffled coughs came from the crowd. "Look," Detective Newton began, "I want to make something very clear. This is a police investigation. At this time, we have—"

An onlooker sneezed. Detective Newton paused and said, "Bless you." Motors murmuring could be heard off in the distance.

"Come on!" she yelled at the TV. Nicole could hear Phil breathing heavily through the phone.

Detective Newton cleared his throat and continued, "We have nothing to share with all of you except—" He plugged his nose with his thumb and forefinger. Either something smelled in the marshy wooded area, or he was wiping his nose, Nicole couldn't tell. "Except that Jaden's last known location was somewhere near this area," he said, pointing behind him. "Unfortunately, we don't know his last *exact* location, but we do know it was in this vicinity."

As if reading everybody's mind, he said, "And yes, we've expanded our search area." The detective looked skyward, squinting at the sunlight penetrating his eyes. "We have air help now. Helicopters are flying over the area in addition to drones." He pointed his index finger upward. He inhaled, extending his pregnant-like belly; more tufts of hair peeked out from the top of his shirt. He sighed. "Despite all we're doing, unfortunately, we still have a missing person."

The captive audience, including Nicole, waited for his next piece of information. The detective put his hands in his pockets and rocked on his heels. She wondered if he was finished. A tall, broad-shouldered man wearing a matching navy-blue polo shirt leaned forward and whispered in the detective's ear. He nodded in response.

On pins and needles, Nicole waited for the detective to mention Kyle's name.

"This is an active investigation, and you need to let us do our job and not waste our precious time. Time we can spend on finding Jaden rather than addressing unfounded accusations flying around on media outlets, including social media, where rumors are running amuck." He wrapped his white knuckles tightly around the podium edge.

Nicole saw the fire in his rounded cheeks. "I think they're going to name Kyle."

"No way. It's all circumstantial. They have nothing solid."

But Nicole knew the truth about the gambling money, and she didn't know if the police knew as well.

The broad-shouldered man leaned forward and whispered something into Detective Newton's ear again, only this time the detective shook his head, disagreeing with what the man had said. Detective Newton uncurled his fingers from the lectern and folded his arms under the badge logo on his shirt. He finished with, "I have no further comments."

Nicole's shoulders slumped. "He didn't say anything about Kyle," she whispered.

"I told you."

A thunderous roar of questions shot out simultaneously, breaking the thick silence following the detective's last statement. Nicole turned off the TV.

"Thanks for staying on the phone with me," she said.

"That's why you pay me the big bucks."

"I need to go. Can we talk in a little bit?"

"Sure."

Nicole wrapped her arms around herself. She was unsure if Detective Newton had set her mind at ease by not mentioning Kyle's name or if he'd created another level of anxiety—the anticipation of if or when it would happen.

CHAPTER 21

That afternoon, Nicole tore through the white-washed oak cabinets, assessing what ingredients she was low on. Deciding to go shopping, to get out of the house and escape her reality, she feverishly wrote a grocery list, trying not to think about what was happening in her life.

Cautiously, she approached her car in the driveway, perturbed about whether another note would be there. Relieved by the naked windshield, Nicole reversed out of her driveway. Her phone dinged as the car rolled back. Annoyingly, the in-dash display didn't show messages when in reverse—a safety issue the manufacturers had incorporated—and instead, it showed distorted images of what was behind her. Her car beeped, alerting her to the rear cross-traffic.

She checked the mirror and saw a black SUV pass by. It didn't slow down, stop, or park on her street. She wondered if she should follow it. *Why not?* She only had time to lose. Concentrating on the task at hand, Nicole had forgotten all about the message on her phone. She weaved behind a bigger car, hoping to hide hers while in pursuit, staying close enough not to lose it but not too close to be seen.

Traveling in the opposite direction from the grocery store, she decided her ingredients would have to wait. She continued along the main street of town, tucked behind two cars at all times. She desperately wanted to get a closer look at the driver and see if it was indeed the same person.

As luck would have it, she got her chance. The driver took a quick left turn from the middle lane, and Nicole followed suit, nearly running a car off the road. Focused on getting a clear view of the driver, she didn't acknowledge her reckless move, and as the SUV veered off, Nicole's heart sank. It wasn't the same man. It wasn't a man at all. It was a woman; a "Baby on Board" sign waved from the rear passenger window confirming it was the wrong car. Nicole sighed, guilt washing over her. She should've gone to the grocery store. What if she'd caused an accident because she was tailing a black SUV when she didn't even know if one was following her? As often as she'd tried to get a good look at the license plate, she'd been unsuccessful; either the black SUV was too far away, or it hadn't even been the right car, like now.

The gas tank lit up on Nicole's dashboard. Not only had she wasted her time following the wrong car, but she'd also wasted gas. She pulled into the nearest gas station and laid her forehead on the steering wheel, cursing her irresponsible behavior.

Once again, her phone dinged. A red circle with the number two popped up on her in-dash display. She hit the little icon on the screen, and Siri said, "Message from Sylvia. Call me when you can. Would you like to reply?"

Nicole's stomach tightened. "No."

Siri continued, "Message from Sylvia. They found something. Call me. Would you like to reply?" Siri asked again.

"No." Adrenaline increasing, Nicole commanded, "Call Sylvia."

When Sylvia answered, she told Nicole that another volunteer had found an empty syringe. Nicole wondered if it'd indeed been another volunteer or Sylvia.

Unsure of what to say, Nicole thought quickly. "Do they think Jaden was drugged?"

"I don't know," Sylvia said. "It could be from his insulin, too."

That thought hadn't crossed Nicole's mind. Feeling uneasy, she scanned the cars pulling in and out of the parking lot, double-checking for the SUV. "Of course, I totally forgot about that."

"I'm sure they'll send it to a lab and process it."

Sylvia seemed knowledgeable about how all this worked. Nicole ignored her intuition and said, "Maybe this is the break we've all been waiting for. Especially his parents."

"And the police."

Certainly, Sylvia wouldn't add that part if she were guilty, would she? "And the police," Nicole said, thinking about what Detective Newton had said about the police not giving out any information. She wondered if this new finding would somehow be leaked to the public. Leaked information and rumors were impossible to contain.

"Thanks for the update," Nicole said. She turned off the car, and as she pumped the gas, a frightening thought crossed her mind; what if Kyle's fingerprints were on that syringe? With a tight grip on the nozzle, lost in thought, unsettled with this notion, Nicole hadn't paid attention again to what she'd been doing and missed the click, signaling that her tank was full. Oblivious, she overfilled the tank, the liquid fuel spilling down the side of her car.

• • • • •

Nicole tried to call Craig on her way home to update him on the newest finding. Her heart sat in her throat, worried that Kyle's fingerprints may be on that syringe. Craig didn't answer. "Fuck!" she shouted at the windshield. "Doesn't anyone answer their phone?"

By the time she arrived home, Nicole had settled herself down by practicing her old Lamaze breathing that she'd used while delivering Kyle, who she decided not to call. "Nothing to worry about until there's something to worry about," she'd said to him. She only wished she could follow her advice.

Once inside the house, she tossed her purse on the kitchen counter and called Phil. She wanted to hear his thoughts on the syringe being found. At least he answered. "What's up?"

Nicole relayed the newest discovery to him. Then she asked, "What if Kyle's fingerprints are on that syringe? What if the police call him in for questioning again? What if he becomes a suspect? What if—"

"What if the world ends in ten minutes?" he responded, ending her rant. "We can play the *what if* game all day long, but until any of that happens, you need to relax."

Annoyed with his attitude, Nicole realized he had a valid point.

"Kyle told his version of the story. That's what we need to go off of, and besides, unless the police have probable cause to make an arrest, they can't force Kyle to give his fingerprints. And they have no probable cause. And they don't have a copy of his fingerprints, remember?"

"But I'm completely terrified," she said, picking at a leftover smattering of crusty dough stuck on the quartz counter.

"I can hear that," he said snippily.

Now more annoyed with his tone and wanting to snap back, Nicole bit her tongue, resisting the urge. She allowed him to continue.

"You have absolutely nothing to worry about."

"But what if the police—"

"What if? What if? We'll deal with what comes our way, not the what if's," he said in the sharpest tone yet.

Nicole's blood raced through her veins, warming her entire body. She was utterly annoyed by Phil's tone and attitude. She wanted to say, "We're paying you to help us, not have a freaking attitude toward me." In better judgment, she sighed. "Okay." Rationally, she knew he had Kyle's best interest at heart. At least, she hoped he did.

Phil warned her to stay off social media. However, Nicole couldn't. An unsavory yearning tugged at her—she needed to see what was being posted.

Scrolling through, rumors filled the feeds: Jaden ran away with a girl, Jaden had run away because he hated his parents, a serial killer murdered him, he'd committed suicide, and so on. Nicole rolled her eyes at the laughable posts, like the one saying Jaden was a serial killer and he was on the lam. Skipping further down, she looked for Kyle's name. It appeared in some posts, but so did Chase and Ethan. And then a new name appeared. One she hadn't seen before, but one she immediately recognized.

CHAPTER 22

Nicole hadn't been sleeping well. Too exhausted to do anything productive, she put on her favorite black leggings and a lilac, off-the-shoulder t-shirt, gathered her hair in a loose ponytail, and headed out to a local coffee shop, *Brews Brothers*. On the drive over, her brain worked overtime, stuck in a loop, consumed with all that weighed on her guilty conscience.

Two silver bells tinkled overhead as Nicole opened the door to the shop. The smell of coffee hit her so strongly that she could practically smell the caffeine. The shop was bustling for a Monday—the line six people deep. When she reached the counter, a perky brunette barista asked, "What can I brew for you?"

"I'll have a small skinny vanilla latte, please," Nicole said, smiling at the freckled face girl.

She didn't look a day over fifteen. "Awesome choice."

Nicole half-smiled and slid her chipped credit card into the tiny machine.

"That'll be up in a moment. Thank you." The overly peppy employee shooed Nicole aside. "Hi, what can I brew for you?" she asked the next customer.

Standing at the end of the counter, waiting for her drink, Nicole mindlessly checked her phone, reading through emails. Occasionally, she peered out at the crowded tables. She saw two young moms, hair piled high on their heads, chatting away as two toddlers sat in highchairs, blueberry muffin crumbs blanketing the table and tile floor. Other people had their heads in their phones as they sipped their overpriced, oversized coffees.

As she continued to scan the room, one man, in particular, caught her attention. A jolt shot through her body when she recognized the face, but she couldn't place where she'd seen him. He looked up, locking eyes. Nicole's stomach bunched.

Feeling uneasy, she pretended to type on her phone. She peered up again—he was still staring. *Hurry up!* she thought. *What is taking so long to make a damn cup of coffee?* Realizing other people surrounded her, Nicole relaxed a bit because, rationally, she knew he couldn't, nor wouldn't, do anything here, in a public place.

Placing her unsteady finger on Craig's name, just in case, ready to dial him if need be, Nicole could feel the man's steady gaze upon her. And when she looked up to confirm that he hadn't taken his eyes off her, she still couldn't recall, no matter how frantically her brain worked, where she'd seen him before: the gym, the police station, the search party? Nothing struck a chord.

"One skinny vanilla latte for Nicole!"

Grateful for the distraction and the fact that her drink was finally ready, Nicole grabbed the coffee and bolted for the door. She kept her head down, face in the phone, hoping the creepy guy wasn't watching her, but she felt his eyes on her back as she left the shop. Rushing out, she spilled a few drops of the hot liquid on her hands, not stopping to contend with the minor mishap. She wanted to get out of there as quickly as possible.

While Nicole nervously fumbled with the keys to unlock the car door, a white piece of paper tucked under her windshield wiper startled her. She dropped her coffee—five dollars of hot liquid pooled around her feet, staining her sneakers. "Shit." She left the empty cup on the ground. She stretched over the side mirror to grab the paper and scanned the parking lot. Carefully, she unfolded the note and read:

I know. Let this be your one and only warning

Nicole covered her mouth with her empty hand. "Oh, my God." Had someone seen her pick up Kyle's license? Did someone else know about Kyle being a bookie? As far as she knew, only two people were in the know: she and him. A disturbing thought quickly flashed through her mind: was her own son the note bandit? Technically, he *was* the only other person who knew she knew. Sickened by this thought, Nicole pushed it away. It's not like he knew she was here. At this coffee shop. Right now. She looked over her shoulders. If he'd been here, he was long gone by now.

Nicole bent down, her shuddering knees knocking together, and scooped up the abandoned cup. She examined the parking lot for a trash can, and that's when a familiar-looking black SUV caught her eye. The pavement spun. She steadied herself against the car. That's where she'd seen that man before; he was the driver of that black SUV—the one following her—the same one parked across the street by her house.

She'd thought she was being paranoid. She'd thought she was being neurotic. She'd thought it was unreal, that she'd imagined it. All of it, but the car was here. The man was here. In the flesh. It was as real as it got. She now knew that she wasn't paranoid; she was being followed.

She sped out of the parking lot, watching her rearview mirror, lucky she didn't cause an accident, too busy concentrating on what was behind her rather than what was in front of her. Certain the man was real, and following her, Nicole didn't know what to do, unsure if she should call Craig and finally come clean, but her concern for his well-being far outweighed her concern for herself; she didn't want to add more stress on him.

She considered calling Detective Newton, but that would only make it more real. A part of her hoped and thought that it was nothing more than a mere coincidence that she and that guy had both been at the same coffee shop at the same time. She didn't know what she would even say to the detective. *Hey, I noticed I may or may not be being followed ever since Jaden went missing, and oh, also, my son may or may not have been involved because I found his license in the same woods, and I'd kept it to myself. Plus, my son admitted Jaden owed him money because, get this, my son is the fraternity's bookie.* That didn't sound like the best option.

She didn't want to call Kyle. She didn't need him to know what was happening and that she suspected it had something to do with him. Besides, what could he do for her? It certainly wasn't his place to comfort his mother: it should be the other way around.

Sylvia crossed her mind. Something about Sylvia heightened Nicole's suspicions. She was unlikely to reach out to Sylvia, disclosing something like this. Besides, it's not like they were friends. Come to think of it, Nicole didn't have friends anymore. She had many acquaintances, but no real true friends, not like her best friend, Jane, back in the day. Married life and parenthood had taken away her friendships. She'd been consumed being a wife and mother first—all her time dedicated to her family—not lunching with her besties or cocktailing it up with work gals. It was either wife, mom, or on the rare occasion, Nicole time.

With no viable options, Nicole drove home without calling anyone.

• • • • •

Nicole, not a big drinker except for the occasional glass of wine, wondered if it was too early to imbibe. She hadn't even finished her overpriced coffee, and already she needed a drink—a good stiff one—none of that lightweight Chardonnay she usually drank. That wouldn't do; a light, white wine couldn't ease these nerves. She needed a heavyweight. Whiskey. Dignified, austere, strong.

Nicole flipped on the TV, hoping a mindless program would drown out the voice in her head, the one telling her to be on guard, that something about that guy was bad. When she heard that wretched Claudia Welch's voice, she switched to the local news.

Nicole rummaged through the mahogany wood bar next to the sofa, searching for the bottle that would lift the world off her shoulders. While pouring the brown, oaky liquid into a highball glass, she heard George's voice on the TV. She stopped mid-pour, abandoning the bottle and glass.

The camera focused on George and Cecilia, but George was the one addressing the public. Cecelia clutched him tightly, her arm looped through his bent elbow. Her floral maxi skirt flowed in the breeze, and tiny beads of sweat glistened around George's receding hairline.

"We are begging anyone with any information that you may have about our son's whereabouts to please come forward." Cecelia leaned forward and dabbed her wet eye with a tissue, not letting go of George. He paused, swallowed hard, and continued. "We know with each passing day it is less likely that we will—" He broke again and cleared his throat.

A familiar lump settled in Nicole's throat. She forced it back down and folded onto the sofa.

George didn't finish his last sentence. Instead, he said, "Jaden needs his medicine. We need to find him. We've been to his apartment, and his diabetic supplies are still there. That means that...that means that—" George stopped again and coughed into his fist. "We need to find him now. We're offering fifty-thousand dollars to anyone who can help us."

"Damn," Nicole said to the TV. "That's a lot of money."

George continued, "We're hoping the syringe the police found will be the break we've been praying for. While we wait to find out, please call the tip line with anything, no matter how small you think it may be. You can do it anonymously. No questions asked. Anything may—"

After hearing enough, Nicole turned off the TV. She picked up the whiskey bottle and poured herself a drink, needing it now more than ever.

Thoughts of Kyle's bookie confession flooded her brain. The guilt of knowing she may hold crucial evidence strangled her conscience. She debated whether to call and finally report it, ridding herself of the inner turmoil wreaking havoc on her conscience. She could do it with no one knowing, anonymously, as George had said. No one would ever have to know. Not Craig. Not Kyle. Only her, but she didn't know if it was worth risking her son's reputation. And her culpability.

CHAPTER 23

"Hey, babe. I'm home," Craig called out.

Nicole pried an eye open and peered at the cable box. Startled by the time—six-thirty, she shot up, the room spinning. She clutched her throbbing head and moaned in pain, trying to remember what'd happened. The last thing she remembered was finishing her third drink and lying down to rest her weary eyes.

"Babe? Where are you?" Craig yelled from the kitchen.

"Shh," she said, still holding her head in her hands, the pounding growing louder.

"Are you okay?" he asked, rushing over and kneeling beside her.

"I don't know," she whispered. It wasn't solely the epic hangover making her feel sick. It was everything. Kyle. The license. The gambling. Jaden. The threats. The SUV. The notes. All of it. She thought a few drinks would erase it but sitting here cotton-mouthed and bleary-eyed, she realized the truth was the only thing that would cure what ailed her. She lifted her head to look at Craig when she noticed a tall, slender man standing a few feet behind him. The unfamiliar man looked about the same age and height as Craig. The man's dark brown eyes roved, looking at anything but Nicole. His gangly arms hung by his side, and she noticed how his dark, shaggy hair curled over his ears.

Her neck burned red with embarrassment. "I'm sorry," she croaked like she had a wad of cotton balls stuffed in her mouth.

"Don't be sorry," Craig said. "If you're sick, you can't help it. I should've called first and checked if it was okay for Dave to join us for dinner."

Nicole assumed the strange man, avoiding her eyes, was Dave. "No, no. Don't be silly. Of course, it's okay." She stood slowly, steadying herself as the room slowed its spinning. "I'm Nicole. Craig's wife," she said, extending her hand to Dave. "It's nice to meet you."

His large hand grasped hers. "It's nice to meet you, too. If it's an imposition, I can leave. Come back another time," he said, hitching his other thumb over his shoulder.

"No. It's all good. I had a migraine earlier," she lied. "I must've fallen asleep. I'm better now." She smiled, hoping her greenish face didn't suggest otherwise. "I didn't make anything for dinner, but I can whip something up, or we can do takeout."

Dave said, "If you aren't feeling well, I don't want you to go out of your way. Takeout is fine."

"Great," Nicole said, looking at Craig. "Any suggestions?"

"Whatever is fine with me," Dave said. "And my treat."

"Oh no. I couldn't let you do that. It's our house. Our treat." Nicole smiled.

Craig suggested their favorite Italian restaurant, *Casa De Roma*.

Nicole excused herself upstairs to clean up before the food arrived. She splashed cold water on her ashen face and popped two ibuprofen, hoping to obliterate the pain radiating from the back of her eyes. While fixing her mussed-up hair, a strong garlic scent wafted through the slatted vent on the bathroom floor, along with irritating voices. She finished up and headed downstairs.

Both men sat at the table, cluttered with round aluminum containers. When Nicole entered the kitchen instantaneously, they stopped talking.

"Did I disrupt something?" she asked, confused by this strange behavior.

"No. Dave was going over more of that program with me."

Nicole's eyes widened. "You're Dr. Graham?" she asked. It hadn't dawned on her to ask what his connection was to Craig. The residual whiskey sloshing through her brain prevented her from asking any questions.

"The one and only," he said, smiling. Nicole noticed his tight, straight, white teeth that looked like a fence for his tongue.

Nicole sat. "Craig's told me how gracious you've been in helping him learn that new program."

"It's nothing," Dave said, blushing. "Your husband is a dedicated man. As difficult as it is to learn this program, your husband is relentless."

"That's my husband," she said, looking at Craig, taking his hand in hers. "Dedicated and stubborn."

"Hey, I resemble that remark," Craig said, chuckling.

The ibuprofen started working, and suddenly Nicole was ravenous. They all dug into the food, and the men sipped on red wine, but she passed, having had enough alcohol for one day.

"So, how long have you been at Cypressville?" she asked, stabbing her fork into her gnocchi. It squished.

"This is my first semester."

"And what a semester it's been so far," Craig said.

"How so?" Nicole asked, covering her food-filled mouth.

"With the whole Jaden thing."

Fork midair, Nicole froze, no longer hungry. She set the fork back down, resting it on the side of the container.

"I'd say it's been...different," Dave said. "What a pain in the ass it is walking around the campus. Damn vigils and memorials are set up all over the place. Students not paying attention in class *if* they even show up. They're all consumed with Jaden, even if they didn't know him." Dave picked up his wineglass and took a big gulp. He rubbed his tongue across his perfect teeth. "And that damn detective keeps hounding me."

Nicole choked. "Detective? Why?"

"Jaden was in my class."

That explained why Dr. Graham's name was on some social media posts. "Why would the detective hound you if Jaden was your student? It wouldn't matter, would it?"

Craig shot her a dirty look.

She bugged her eyes and mouthed, "What?"

"You don't have to talk about it if you don't want to," Craig said.

"I don't mind. It's not like I'm a suspect, at least not yet." Dave laughed.

Nicole was confused if he was serious or joking. And if he was joking, she didn't find his comment humorous.

"At first, they questioned me to get general information about Jaden: how was he as a student? Was he struggling? Did he exhibit any odd behaviors? Stuff like that. That was the first time."

"You've been questioned more than once?" Nicole asked.

"Yes. The second time was because another student went to the police and said they saw Jaden and me arguing. The student claimed he'd heard us in a heated argument, but I explained the story to the police. That kid didn't know what the hell he was talking about. He'd only overheard part of the conversation. Miscommunication on his part."

"On whose part, Jaden's or the student who reported you?"

Craig shot her the death stare this time.

"The student. Jaden was perfectly clear on what the issue was."

"Nicole," Craig said in a warning tone, "This isn't any of our business, and you're making our guest uncomfortable."

"Which was what exactly?" she asked, propping her head in her hand, resting on the table, ignoring Craig's warning.

"It's not like there's even a body yet, you know?" Dave said, shoveling a forkful of chicken parmesan into his mouth, bypassing Nicole's question. "For Christ's sake, the kid could've run away. I don't know why the police have their panties in such a wad."

Disgusted by his comment, Nicole said, "Because somebody's child has gone missing. Missing," she said, drawing out the word.

"I guess," Dave said, shrugging. "This wine is incredible. Where's it from?" he asked, picking up his glass and polishing it off.

Nicole didn't say another word or ask another question. When Dave left, she said, "I don't like him."

"Why would you say that? You don't even know the guy."

"I heard enough here tonight. He was too flippant about the whole thing."

"He didn't mean it the way you took it."

"I think he knows more than he's saying. And if our son is under fire for something that guy did, all the more reason for me to dislike him. All I'm saying is between what he said here tonight and what I've read on Instagram and Facebook, I don't trust him."

"You can't believe everything you read on social media. You know that. He's a good guy. Trust me. I know. He's spending his free time helping me to get promoted. It's not like there's something in it for him. He's doing it because he wants to. That's a stand-up kind of guy."

Nicole threw the last empty container in the trash and headed for the sofa since her head hadn't fully recovered from her excessive whiskey intake. "There's something off about the guy. I don't know what it is. Besides, don't you find it odd that Jaden went missing around the same time Dave started here?"

Craig didn't answer.

CHAPTER 24

The following afternoon, Nicole finished at the gym, pulling her belongings out of her locker, when her phone rang. It was Phil. "Are you watching TV?"

Any time Phil asked this question, it usually meant something was up. She fidgeted with the lock in her free hand. "No, why?"

"Then you don't know, do you?"

She tightened her grip on her phone, annoyed with how he often dragged out his forthcoming information, wishing he'd get to the point. "No. I don't know. Why don't you tell me," she snapped.

"No need to get all snippy," he huffed. "I can hang up and call you later if you prefer?"

"Please. Just tell me. I'm sorry I snapped. I'm kind of busy." Not the whole truth. Although she needed to get dressed, she was more eager to hear what he had to say. Plus, every minute on the phone literally counted—five dollars per minute, to be exact.

"A witness came forward."

Nicole dropped the phone. It bounced off her foot and landed face-down on the locker room floor. "Is it that kid from Dr. Graham's class?" she asked, returning the phone to her ear.

"What kid from whose class?"

Nicole told Phil about what Dr. Graham had said the night before. "I don't know anything about that, but from what I've seen on the news, it didn't sound like the witness was a kid."

Nicole calculated the timeline. She realized it couldn't have been that kid from Dr. Graham's class. If the professor had already been hounded by

Detective Newton, and the witness had come forward after the Pierce's reward offer, then no way it could be the same person.

"I need to go," Nicole said. Abruptly, she hung up, quickly dressed, and gathered her belongings. She rushed to the hanging TVs on the gym floor, thankful for closed captioning. As the words appeared underneath the news reporter, the same blonde girl from the first day with that Hollywood smile smeared across her face, Nicole read them.

Besides the occasional typo, Nicole got the gist of the story. The reporter said sources heard that Detective Newton was about to close the case because, as he'd said, it'd gone cold; they didn't want to waste any more of their time, money, or resources on something that wasn't turning anything up as Nicole had heard before. After the Pierce's press conference, a witness had come forward stating he was near the woods that night and saw a guy exiting the area around the same time the boys said they'd given up on finding Jaden.

"Excuse me, miss," a voice said from behind.

"Huh?" Nicole asked, not turning around.

"Are you using this bench?"

"What? No. Sorry," Nicole said, moving away from the area she was blocking.

She continued reading what the anchorman was saying to the reporter. The witness wished to remain anonymous, and the police weren't saying a word about who it was or if his story was valid. The news promised to keep everyone informed as more information rolled in.

Nicole walked to her car, face in the phone, texting Kyle to see if he'd heard, assuming he had. She sat in the driver's seat, leaned her head against the headrest, and sighed. When she reached over to plug in her phone, a white piece of paper flapping under the windshield wiper on the passenger side caught her eye. Because her head had been buried in her phone when she'd first approached her car, Nicole hadn't noticed it.

She couldn't stomach the thought of reading another one, but she couldn't drive with it blocking the view. She walked around the front bumper and removed it, praying it was an advertisement. It wasn't. Immediately, she recognized the font as she read,

Watch your back or you may be next

A real threat. A scary threat. Possibly a death threat. Nicole didn't know how long she could hold out without telling anyone what was happening.

• • • • •

Nicole watched her surroundings as she drove home, a behavior that had become second nature. She was relieved when she didn't see anything to be worried about.

Safely inside her house, she locked the front door, something she rarely did. After all, they lived in a safe neighborhood, and locking the door was unnecessary in the middle of the day. Once setting her bag down, Nicole checked her social media. The only information flowing was what she'd already heard, nothing new or different from what the news had already reported.

And that's when Kyle called her back. "All I know is a guy came forward."

"But nobody knows anything about him. Is he young? Old? What did he see?"

"I have no idea. I'm not the police."

"What's wrong with you?" she asked, more annoyed at this attitude than concerned.

"There's so much shit going on here. Our fraternity is upside down. People are freaking out. The longer no sign of Jaden, the more scared everyone is."

"I get that," she said. And she did. She felt the same way. "But somebody must know something about the witness or what he saw."

"Rumors are milling around campus. Some people claim they heard the witness saw a tall, thin-looking dude coming out of the woods."

Nicole pictured Kyle. He fits that description. She hated herself for visualizing that.

But Dr. Graham did as well.

"Others are saying it was an older man, hunched over and wearing a baseball cap. I also heard it was too dark for the witness to identify what or who he saw. Nobody knows. But I know whoever it was is getting fifty thousand dollars now."

Nicole shuddered at her next thought. "Do you think this witness is saying something now because of the money?" She hoped that wasn't the case, the cruelty and greediness of that unfathomable.

"It's possible, I suppose," Kyle said, sighing. "That'd be a sick joke. Getting Jaden's parents' hopes up like that."

"Exactly. You read my mind," she said, looking out the front window. Nothing. She went back to the sofa. "Somebody knows something, but that somebody isn't talking to the public," she said aloud, intended more as a statement to herself than Kyle.

He ignored it. "I need to run. We're having another chapter meeting in ten minutes."

Nicole sunk deeper into the cushions and closed her eyes. Her heart hurt: a deep throbbing pain pulsed in her body. She felt helpless. She needed answers. Now. And if the police wouldn't give them to her, she'd get them herself. It was time to take matters into her own hands, like she'd done with the license. All she had to do now was come up with a plan.

CHAPTER 25

The Grand Hotel lobby looked like something out of a fairytale, like Cinderella's castle with two tall towers bookending a smaller building in the middle. Nicole had decided her plan started here—where Jaden's parents were staying while in town. Since that first day, they hadn't returned to their hometown, a two-hour plane ride away. Instead, they'd been living here at the Grand Hotel for weeks. The only time they'd left was when they'd appeared on that awful *Claudia Welch Show*. Otherwise, George and Cecelia remained here, close to Jaden's last known location, waiting.

Nicole walked over to a large, red velvet chaise-style sofa in the center of the atrium, wedged between a stone fireplace and a coffee shop, and folded herself into the posh cushions. She wore a dark blue baseball cap, donning the word "Hawks," the college's mascot, low on her forehead, her dark-tinted Ray-Ban sunglasses barely visible. Hoping not to look too obvious or suspicious, Nicole dressed the part; if she was going to snoop, she didn't want to be recognized.

Footsteps and voices echoed in the atrium. Not even all the lush flora towering overhead, palm trees with leaves as green as a freshly cut Christmas tree and stumps as wide as a cement pole, helped absorb the sound. "Welcome to The Grand Hotel," a deep voice carried to where Nicole sat. She looked up and saw a young man, probably around twenty-five years old, with sandy brown hair grazing his neck, greeting what she assumed to be a media person with a bright green lanyard dangling around his neck. His accomplice carried an oversized black valise that housed a news camera.

While sitting, Nicole pretended to be occupied with her phone as she peered over her Ray-Bans. She watched people pop in and out of the revolving door like a Pez dispenser. Some people were here for pleasure, like those in shorts and tank tops, carrying beach bags stuffed to the brim with brightly striped towels, wearing flip-flops that squished against the marble floors. Others, dressed in three-piece suits, were here for business. And the ones with credentials swinging around their necks—they were here to cover the Jaden case.

"What am I doing here?" She stood up to leave when suddenly she heard loud voices coming from the elevator vestibule.

"No comment," a man shouted.

Nicole gawked to see what the ruckus was all about. To get a better look, she walked toward a gaggle of reporters shoving their microphones and cameras at a man. It was George. He was wearing jeans and a black sweater. He held up his hand, repeating, "No comment," as he walked forward, cutting the mob in half. Cecelia wasn't with him, an unusual sight.

Nicole walked swiftly toward the commotion, her white and gray striped sneakers squealing intermittently as the rubber squished against the floor.

"What's going on?" Nicole asked a fellow onlooker dressed in a dark blue business suit.

"I heard a witness came forward in that missing kid case."

This was not new news to her. "Really?" she said, acting surprised, keeping in character. "Do they know who it is?"

The man shrugged, his shoulder pads almost touching his ears. "Don't know."

Nicole watched the throngs of people move like a fluid blob, gliding through the hotel lobby while smothering George with questions. He continued saying, "No comment," all the way out of the building.

With Cecelia nowhere in sight, Nicole knew exactly what to do next.

• • • • •

"Hi," Nicole said to the bright-eyed, twenty-something man behind the reception desk. "I'm Cecelia Pierce's sister. I came all this way to help her deal with this," Nicole said, nodding over her shoulder at the media frenzy. "That's why I'm dressed like this. Like my poor brother-in-law, George, I don't want to be hounded by the media."

"Yeah, poor guy. They never leave him alone, always following him wherever he goes," the young man replied.

"I'd get a restraining order, but that's just me." Nicole removed her sunglasses and flashed her best smile as she hung them on the neckline of her plain white t-shirt. "Anyway, I'm surprising my sister, you know, to help comfort her during this tough time. I don't want to call or text her asking for her room number. Would you mind giving it to me?"

He shifted his eyes from side to side. "I'm sorry, ma'am. I can't do that. It's against hotel policy."

Nicole lowered her eyes and looked at her unpolished fingernails.

"I can ring her room, though, and tell her you're here. I'm sure she'd still be super surprised," he said, dipping his head lower.

"No, no, I want to see the look on her face when she sees me." Regardless of the frigid temperature in the lobby, Nicole's palms were warm. A trail of sweat dripped down her neck, and the loose hairs that had slipped from her ponytail clung to her clammy skin. "Can you imagine the state she's in? Have you seen the bags under her eyes? Poor thing hasn't slept in weeks." Nicole shook her head in pity.

The play-by-the-rules employee stared at Nicole as she hammed it up. She noticed the name etched on his gold-plated name tag pinned above the right chest pocket of his black Grand Hotel blazer. "Dylan, could you imagine if your child went missing? Oh my, how presumptuous of me! Do you have any children?" she asked in a syrupy voice, placing her hand on her chest.

"Yes, ma'am. A six-month-old baby boy."

"Wow. Congrats. They're the best, aren't they?" she added with more sweetness.

"Oh, yes," he gushed, his mouth spreading into a broad smile, revealing his crooked front tooth. "My wife and I are so smitten with him."

"I'm sure you are. Now imagine if he went missing, no matter how old he was. You'd be a basket case, right?" Nicole leaned her elbows on the counter and batted her eyelashes, her cleavage peeking out from the V-neck of her shirt.

Dylan swallowed hard. "Ma'am, I can't even imagine. I'd lose my mind."

"I'm sure you would just like my sister's losing hers. She has no one else. Our parents died a few years ago. Terrible accident." Nicole shook her head again, tsking. "Poor Cecelia still blames herself."

Nicole was knee-deep, shoveling further and further, Dylan hanging on to her every word.

His eyes flew open. "How awful," he gasped.

"I know, right? I keep telling her it wasn't her fault, but she can't let it go. And now... this." A forced tear appeared.

"Oh, ma'am, I am so sorry," Dylan said, putting his hand on his chest.

"Please, can't you bypass hotel policy?" she asked, elevating her eyebrows. "Just this once. I know Cecelia would be forever grateful."

Dylan stood stone-faced. Nicole wondered if she'd convinced him yet. "Please?" She let the tear spill down her cheek.

Dylan leaned closer and lowered his voice. "Okay, but please don't let anyone know it was me. I could lose my job, and I can't afford to be out of work with the baby."

"No. No. I'm sure you can't."

"We decided my wife should stay home for at least a year. We didn't want to put D.J., that's short for Dylan Junior, in daycare."

"Sure. Sure. I get that. Mum's the word," she said, zipping her lips like a schoolgirl keeping a best friend's secret. Honestly, Nicole didn't give two craps about Dylan's family life or his job. She only cared about seeing Cecelia, so she acted caring, nodding and sympathizing with him. "Do you have that room number? I'm anxious to get to my sister."

"Oh, yes. Sorry. Didn't mean to spill my life's story to you." He tapped on the keyboard, staring at the monitor before him.

"No worries. It's all good. You're helping me out in a big way, so it's the least I could do." She smiled and winked.

Dylan blushed. "It's room 16545." He leaned further over the desk and pointed. "Take the second set of elevators on the left."

"Thank you so much." Nicole laid her hand on his. "You've done a good thing here," she said, patting it.

His cheeks reddened further.

Nicole beelined to the elevator door as it closed. "Wait!" she shouted. A hand wrapped around the rubber casing, holding it open for her. She stepped inside, and as she did, Dylan was chasing behind, yelling, and panting, "Hold up! Hold up! I need to see your ID!" Lucky for her, the door closed before he reached her.

As the elevator soared up, Nicole breathed a sigh of relief, and as the door opened on the sixteenth floor, she was hopeful for the first time in weeks.

CHAPTER 26

The long, narrow hallway reminded Nicole of a horror movie where the main character has to run down the never-ending corridor, trying to escape an ax murderer. Like that person, Nicole's pulse quickened as she followed the numbered plaques plastered to the light-blue and beige pin-striped walls nearing the room. Her t-shirt was heavy with sweat, making it feel more like a jacket than a shirt.

With each step closer, Nicole rehearsed what she'd say, repeating the conversation in her head, assuring to keep all the facts straight. She couldn't slip up and let Cecelia know who she *really* was and why she was there. She had to stay focused. In character. Never wavering. Solid in her lie.

At Cecelia's room, Nicole took a deep breath, raised her fist, and as she exhaled, she knocked lightly on the door. She held her next breath, waiting. Silence. She slid her sweaty palm against the denim fabric on her thigh, then knocked a little louder a second time. Not wanting to look suspicious, like a hoodlum and possibly scaring Cecelia, Nicole removed her baseball cap and fastened it on a belt loop.

A rustling sound came from the other side of the door, but Cecilia didn't open it or respond. A third knock. This time louder. The door across the hall opened. Nicole turned and smiled, giving a halfhearted wave. The older gentleman grinned and closed the door.

"Come on, Cecelia," Nicole muttered, wiggling her legs back and forth.

Footsteps neared. "Hello?" Cecelia questioned through the thick door separating the two women.

"Hi," Nicole nervously replied. A sweat drop rolled into her waistband and down her pant leg.

Cecelia raised her voice. "If you're the media, go away. I have nothing to say."

Nicole cleared her throat. "I'm not with the media. My name is Amber Bentley. I came here to talk to you."

"I don't know any Amber Bentley. Now go away."

Nicole could hear the pain in Cecelia's voice. The sound of footsteps moved away from the door. Nicole was losing her chance. And Cecelia. "Cecelia!" she shouted.

The footsteps stopped. Through the closed door, Cecelia asked, "How do you know my name?"

"I've seen you on television. You're pretty well-known." Nicole silently praised her quick thinking.

No response.

"Please, can I come in and talk to you? We have a lot in common."

"I'm not up for talking. Go away and leave me alone."

Nicole detected the melancholy in Cecelia's voice.

"Cecelia, please," Nicole said, cracking her voice, pretending to be broken up. In a quieter, somber tone, she said, "My daughter went missing, too."

Silence blasted Nicole's ear. Not thinking it possible, the dead air hurt more than any loud noise. Her heart struck against her chest as if it could leap right out. Once more, Nicole lightly rapped on the door with her knuckles. "Hello? Hello?"

The door clicked, and Cecelia's pale, deathlike, sunken face appeared through the narrow gap.

"Hi," Nicole grinned as a peace offering.

"What do you want?"

"I want to talk to you. I need to talk to you." Nicole forced her eyes to water again.

"Why?"

Nicole noticed the lines carved around Cecelia's empty gray eyes and the deep grooves on her forehead. She looked like hell. Then again, she was going through hell.

"I told you. We have a lot in common, and if you let me in, I can explain. I don't want to do it out here," Nicole said, looking up and down the hallway. Murmured voices drifted down the hallway from the elevator vestibule. "I don't need anyone overhearing my story or seeing me break down for the thousandth time."

Cecilia's face softened, and she opened the door wider.

"Thank you." Nicole entered the spacious suite furnished with a robin-blue and salmon-colored floral couch, mahogany coffee table, a matching dinette set in one room, and a playhouse-like kitchen right down to the mini-sized refrigerator to the right. A king-sized bed sat in the center of a separate bedroom off to the left, a crumpled, basic beige and brown plaid comforter spread over the mattress.

"Wow, this is quite the room," Nicole said, admiring its size and layout.

"I guess if we're going to live here for God knows how long, we need to be as comfortable as possible."

Cecelia wore a white and black, polka-dotted floor-length house dress with a silver zipper spanning from top to bottom, and her uncombed, short, wavy hair was sticking out on top.

Nicole reached out and put her hand on Cecelia's forearm, peeking from the three-quarter sleeve. "I'm so sorry. For everything. I know exactly how you feel," Nicole said, sitting on the stiff, flowery sofa.

"Thank you. I appreciate that. You said your daughter went missing too?" Cecelia asked in a softer tone.

Nicole nodded.

"I'm sorry for you, too."

"Thank you. It never gets easier." Nicole sniffled, staying in character.

"Can I get you some tea? Or coffee?"

"Tea would be great."

Cecilia filled the single-cup coffee pot reservoir with tap water from the small sink and placed a white ceramic mug under the spout. She hit the brew button.

Nicole started slowly and cautiously, wanting to build trust with Cecelia before getting to the real motivation for her visit. "How are you holding up?"

"You know what it's like. I don't sleep at all. And if I doze off, it's in fits of nightmares and restlessness. I'm exhausted. Frustrated. Scared. Angry. All of it." Lost in thought, Cecelia's brow folded in, and her mouth turned down.

Nicole nodded again.

Shaking her head, Cecelia dunked a tea bag in the steaming water. "Sugar?"

"No thanks."

Cecilia handed Nicole the mug. She steeped the tea bag, plunging it up and down as the water turned dark brown, like a murky lake. "I hear you. Unless you've been through it, no one can understand your feelings. And the nights are the *worst*."

Cecelia nodded. "Exactly. And you feel helpless."

"Yes." Nicole took a sip of her tea. Scalding, it burned her tongue. She blew on it before trying again. "How is your detective handling all of it? Are you happy with his progress?" she asked, knowing good and well the answer.

Cecelia looked down at her hands resting in her lap. "No. Not at all. My husband and I feel like the police aren't doing enough." Her cheeks turned a deep sienna. "Do you watch *The Claudia Welch Show*?"

"Never heard of her," Nicole lied.

"George, that's my husband, but you probably already know that from the news," Cecelia rambled, "and I went on her show. We were hoping to light a fire under their asses." She put her hand up to her mouth. "Excuse my foul language." Her cheeks reddened. Not as deeply this time.

Nicole rolled her eyes inside her head. "I've heard much worse." She giggled for good measure. "Did it work?"

"What?"

"Going on the show?" Nicole wondered if Cecelia was usually this spacey or if she was taking a sedative to help keep her calm. Her brain seemed hazy.

"Oh, right. Yes, I think so, but I don't truly know. George does most of the communication. It's too difficult for me. Being a mom—" She stopped, her eyes glazed over, empty, as though her soul had left her body, and all that was left was an outer shell. She blinked, snapped to, and continued. "You understand what I'm saying." A tear spilled down her pale cheek, all redness drained from moments ago.

"Yes, totally. I feel like I've lost a piece of my heart. No, more like my whole heart. After my daughter was born, I told people that being a parent is like watching your heart walking outside your body." Nicole set her mug down and scooted forward on the sofa, nearly touching knees with Cecelia seated in an adjacent wingback chair.

The women sat in silence for a few moments. Treading carefully, not wanting to seem too eager but impatient to move on, Nicole asked, "Have they found anything yet? Any clues that will help solve the case?"

"I don't know." Cecelia's brows indented further. She stared blankly off into the distance again.

Nicole kept losing her; she needed to reconnect, so she said, "When my daughter disappeared, the police went balls to the walls for a few weeks, but then—" She stopped, purposely leaving the sentence unfinished, imitating Cecelia's behavior.

Watching Nicole, Cecelia sat erect, hands on her lap, waiting.

With Cecelia's full attention again, Nicole shook her head, mimicking snapping back to the present. Going in for the kill now, she asked, "Do they have a suspect yet? They must have one by now."

Cecelia averted her eyes and stared out the large bay window overlooking the town. Clouds floated past the sun, casting shadows across her hardened face.

Nicole wondered if she knew something and wasn't talking, or perhaps a sedative was kicking in. Nicole waved her hand in front of Cecelia's eyes. "Hello? You there?"

Cecelia blinked. "Oh, sorry. I was lost in thought for a minute."

"Do you want to talk about it?"

"No. Yes. I don't know." She hesitated momentarily, then said, "Just when I think there's a break in the case, it turns out to be nothing."

What was Cecelia talking about? Was it about the witness that had come forward? She didn't want to push or come across as prying, although that was precisely what she'd come to do—get information. Still, she tried to appear like a fellow mother who'd lived through the same ordeal. "That's extremely frustrating, isn't it? The false hope." She waited, giving Cecelia a chance to elaborate, but when she didn't, Nicole asked, "What'd they find?"

"A syringe."

Despite the fluttering in her tight chest, Nicole tried to appear calm. "Syringe?" she asked, pretending to be daft. Since the police hadn't divulged what they'd found, Nicole assumed they hadn't received the report yet.

"Yeah. The police found one in the woods where my precious boy went—" Cecelia looked off into the distance again. This time, she continued without Nicole coaxing her. "The police told us they matched Jaden's prints on the syringe, which we'd expected because it turns out it was his insulin shot."

Cecelia rubbed her hands back and forth on her lap. "He'd always wanted to get the pump. Unfortunately, our insurance wouldn't cover it, and with paying for his tuition and whatnot, it wasn't feasible for us to get him one. He hated having to use needles all the time."

Not wanting to seem too knowledgeable about the fingerprint database and certainly not wanting to offend Cecilia by asking if Jaden had a prior record, Nicole acted innocent. "How do they know it's Jaden's?"

"Because he had diabetes."

"No, not the syringe. The fingerprints."

"Oh, sorry." Cecelia put her hand to her mouth again and blushed. "We let the police fingerprint his apartment to match them."

This ended the concern that Jaden had been drugged or poisoned. "Makes sense." She followed up with her ulterior motive. "Did they find any other fingerprints on the syringe?" Nicole sipped her tea and peered over the mug, waiting for the answer.

"That's the weird part. The police said they did."

Familiar sweat percolated down Nicole's stiff neck, wetting her collar. Realistically, she knew Kyle couldn't be identified through those fingerprints. Still, she was nervous, waiting to hear if someone else had been named. Setting her tea down, Nicole folded her hands around her knee, steadying her fingers.

"But the police don't know whose they are. Something about a directory with fingerprints."

Nicole wasn't about to correct Cecelia's mistake of calling it a directory. Clearly, she knew about the database.

"And I guess whoever's fingerprints were on that syringe wasn't in that directory."

Nicole deflated, letting the breath she'd been holding escape, hoping Cecelia hadn't seen this. Nicole was confused if this news was comforting or disturbing; nobody was named, and that was the problem; nobody was named—it was all still so nebulous.

Cecelia started to speak again but stopped.

"I wonder why the public hasn't heard the results?" Nicole said, pretending to think out loud.

"Because the police said they want to keep quiet. They keep telling us it's an ongoing investigation."

Nicole rolled her eyes and huffed, pretending she'd been treated the same way in her fake daughter's disappearance. "I know. The same thing happened to me. It's so annoying. And frustrating, isn't it?"

"It is." Cecelia paused again and sucked in her lower lip. "The other thing bugging me is Jaden's fraternity brothers who were with him that night. The night he went—" She stopped, unable to say the words. She looked out the window again, avoiding Nicole's eyes.

"What about them?" Nicole asked slowly, drawing out the question. Did Cecelia know something more? Something about Kyle? Something the police may have told only her and George, as they'd done with the syringe.

Reengaged, Cecelia said, "I'm sorry, I'm being rude and selfish. We keep circling back, constantly talking about my son. Tell me more about your daughter's disappearance. When did she disappear, and did they ever find her?"

CHAPTER 27

"How's your sister?" Dylan yelled to Nicole as she rushed by the reception desk, ignoring his question, hightailing it out of The Grand Hotel. The sun was lower on the horizon, and with her cap still looped around her waist and her glasses still dangling from her collar, Nicole shielded her eyes from the blinding light. Although she didn't come out with as much as she'd hoped for, she was content with what she did learn: another set of prints was on that syringe, and the police couldn't identify whose. Regrettably, however, Kyle still wasn't out of the woods yet.

Nicole had to think fast when Cecelia hounded her about her daughter's disappearance. Luckily, Nicole's phone had rung, a welcomed reprieve, saving her hide from Cecelia's suspicions of her true intentions. Nicole had pretended the call was from her husband, but it was a solicitor. Nicole explained to Cecelia that there was an unexpected family crisis, and she had to leave immediately. Apologizing for her sudden exit, Nicole left abruptly and in what she thought was the nick of time.

Driving home, constantly watching her rearview mirror and without seeing any black SUV, Nicole breathed a sigh of relief. She didn't think she could handle any more today. After her lies, her nerves were shot.

"Hey! I'm home," a voice called from across the house. Nicole jumped. She wasn't expecting anyone. It was Kyle from his bedroom.

Nicole stood in his doorway. "Welcome home," she half-smiled. Part of her was happy to see him, but another part was uneasy, skeptical of his innocence. "What are you doing here?"

Sprawled out on his bed, he wore a pair of board shorts and an AC/DC t-shirt, his tall, lanky body hanging over the edges of his "big boy" bed. "Am I not allowed to come home?"

"Of course you are. Anytime." She looked at his drawn face. "You okay?" she asked, pushing his legs aside, sitting next to him, squeezing onto the little bed. She hated seeing his saddened expression.

"I guess."

"I know this is distressing and that you keep feeling guilty—from being a bookie to playing that stupid game that night to possibly affecting your dad's promotion." Kyle flinched at her latter statement. "But it's going to be okay. You're going to be okay. We're going to be okay. I promise." She stroked his rumpled hair. "Have you heard anything new about the case?"

His bottom lip quivered. "Chase, Ethan, and Aiden were all brought in for further questioning. Thankfully, the police said they don't have substantial evidence to incriminate."

"Like you."

A tear escaped, wetting his blue and white striped pillowcase. "Like me."

Her intuition and heart contradicted one another; her gut said something was off—that her son may have been involved, yet her heart said otherwise—he was innocent, and she should trust him. "I'll do whatever I have to do to protect you. I've always kept you safe, and I don't intend to stop now." He looked up at Nicole with an unfamiliar expression, one she hadn't seen before. "Is there something else you want to tell me?"

He opened his mouth, closed it in a straight line, and turned his head away, his hair matted against the pillow. Facing the wall, he asked, "Is it okay if I spend the night tonight?"

"Of course." She waited a minute to see if he'd say anything else. When he didn't, she kissed him on his forehead. Closing the door behind her, she wondered what that strange expression had been: guilt or angst?

• • • • •

Nicole followed suit when Kyle and Craig left the house the following day. After a night of pondering what to do next, with only sleeping two hours, she had an important errand to run.

As much as she disliked the national chain stores, Nicole decided that was the best place for her needs. Not wanting to be recognized by locals, she drove to the next town. Standing in the middle of the electronics department, ensuring no one she knew was there, she tapped a sales associate on the shoulder. "Excuse me, I'm interested in buying a mobile phone."

The blue-aproned employee with a thick black mustache, Ralph, as his name badge stated, asked, "What kind? Smartphone? Flip phone?"

Nicole shrugged. "Something simple to use. Probably a flip phone," she said. "It's for my elderly mother. I don't think she could figure out how to use all that fancy technology on a smartphone. Nor does she need it." Nicole realized she was getting good at lying. It was almost as easy as speaking the truth.

"An emergency use phone?" Ralph asked, his mustache dancing up and down as he spoke.

"Yes," Nicole said, snapping her fingers.

"We have these flip phones over here," Ralph said, leading her to a case next to the register, displaying three different brands, all similar in design.

She leaned on the glass top, inspecting the devices. "I want to surprise her and pay for the usage." Nicole didn't want a monthly bill linked to her name; she didn't need it traced back to her. "How would I go about doing that?"

"You can do a pre-paid plan." Ralph combed his furry lip cover with his thumb and forefinger.

"So I pay in advance?"

"Yes."

"Does it have to be with a credit card, or can I use cash?"

Ralph's expression changed, and he smiled sheepishly. "Are you sure this phone isn't for you, little lady?"

Nicole didn't like his tone. Or his insinuation. "I'm sure. And I'm not a little lady." An elderly man who'd been looking at phone chargers turned his head in her direction and frowned. Nicole smirked.

Oblivious to the encounter, Ralph said, "Suit yourself."

"So, can I pay with cash?"

He nodded.

"Great." She smiled. "You know what? Maybe I'll get one for my father. Oh, and maybe my mother-in-law, too. We're always worried about their safety and well-being. It's like having small children all over again." She laughed. "Worried all the time if they'll fall or wander off. These will give us peace of mind." She flashed her glamorous, toothy grin, catching the elderly man's eye.

Ralph unlocked the door. "So that's how many?"

"Three."

He handed her the phones. "Do you set it up here?" she asked.

"No, you do it when you turn the phones on. You'll need to buy the pre-paid card over there," he said, pointing to a carousel of cards, "depending on how much data you think you'll need. You can reload them as often as you'd like."

"The phones or the cards?"

"The phones. Using the cards. You can buy more cards to add more money to the phones."

"Perfect." She selected the cheapest amount since she wouldn't use each one for more than fifteen minutes. She paid in cash with the money she'd withdrawn from the ATM on the way over, knowing Craig would never notice the missing money. Being an economics professor, one would think he'd pay closer attention to their bank balance, but he never did. He'd said that he wasn't worried unless it dipped below a certain amount. And with two-step authentication, he wasn't concerned about being hacked. Nicole was surprised, however, that the amount listed on the receipt was lower than expected; she'd have to ask him about that.

Feeling giddy, armed with her purchase, Nicole left, ready for her next move.

CHAPTER 28

Still parked in the lot, Nicole's fingers trembled nervously, holding the missing person's brochure. She stared at the phone number on the bottom—the tip hotline. When she'd walked into The Grand Hotel, she'd picked up the flyer from a large rack near the revolving door and tucked it safely in a zippered inside pocket of her purse, never thinking she'd need or use it. Yet, here she was, sitting in her car, hoping her story would be plausible enough to raise suspicion.

Nicole's heart pounded, waiting for someone to answer. "Missing person hotline. How may I help you?" a friendly voice said.

Nicole cleared her throat.

"Hello? Hello? You there? Do you have a tip?"

"Yes. Sorry." She cleared her throat again. "I'm a bit down in the dumps with a cold," Nicole said, recovering quickly.

"What's your tip?"

"Is this call anonymous?"

"Yes, ma'am."

"Good."

A pregnant pause filled the line.

The friendly voice broke the silence. "Do you have a tip, ma'am?"

"Yes."

"Go ahead, please."

Nicole closed her eyes. "So, I was passing by one of my classes, and my professor was inside with Jaden." She stopped and swallowed.

"And?"

"And, like, my professor and Jaden were going at it. I couldn't hear everything they were saying, but I did hear Dr. Graham threaten Jaden, something about how he'd better keep quiet and if he didn't, he'd make sure Jaden could never talk to anyone. Ever." Nicole was so nervous that the phone almost slipped from her slick palm, so she cranked up the air conditioner to combat the sweat.

She heard the tapping of computer keys. "And you heard this for yourself?"

"Yes."

"And when was this?"

Watching a mother fasten her toddler into his car seat, Nicole longed for those days right now. "A day or two before Jaden disappeared," she said.

"Okay. Is there anything else you can remember that might be helpful?"

Nicole did, and would save that for another time, not wanting to reveal her entire hand on the first phone call. "No, that's all I know."

"Okay then. Thank you for your time and civic duty."

"You're welcome." Nicole was satisfied with her work.

"Oh, and ma'am?"

Nicole tensed, worried she'd messed up. She held her breath, waiting.

"Yes."

"Feel better."

I already do. Nicole tossed the first phone in the dumpster next to where she'd parked.

• • • • •

Curious about any updates, especially after her phone call, Nicole flipped on the TV. That Barbie-looking reporter stood near the woods, her blonde tendrils spilling over her shoulders as she looked directly into the camera, squinting from the midday sun, microphone in hand. It was like she was speaking only to Nicole—an old girlfriend, spilling the tea.

"It turns out the witness who'd come forward wasn't credible. Therefore, the Pierces have upped their reward by another ten thousand dollars. Anyone with any information is encouraged to contact local authorities or call the hotline on the screen below. Jaden's parents need your help. Their son's life depends on it."

Nicole sat engrossed. Darlene, the name written underneath Barbie, put her hand up to her earpiece. "Now back to you, Jess," she said, and the camera switched to the news desk in the studio.

"Hey, you," Craig said, startling Nicole.

"You scared me!"

He stood in front of her, blocking the TV. "I can leave if you prefer," he joked, hitching his thumb over his shoulder.

She stood up and hugged him. "Sorry."

He dropped his dark brown leather briefcase with his initials engraved on the metal latch on the coffee table, answering her embrace.

"I was totally into the news. I didn't hear you come in," she said, tightening her arms around his waist. She leaned against his chest, listening to his strong, steady heartbeat. They stood, bound together, arms entangled, holding on, the quiet a welcomed relief. She inhaled his familiar musky scent. Craig was the kind of guy who let the girl pick out his cologne. He didn't care what it smelled like as long as she liked how he smelled. "How'd you get home?"

"Alex dropped me off."

"Why didn't you tell me he was here? I would've come out and said hi."

"Next time." He kissed the top of Nicole's head and sighed. "I know I haven't been the best husband lately."

"What are you talking about? You're always a great husband," Nicole said, but her mind wandered back to the night he'd jumped down her throat, flipping out about the dishwasher, and to the few times he was curt with her on the phone. She looked up at him, excusing his behavior, saying, "To say we've been under some stress is an understatement."

"Yeah, true." His eyes clouded over. "I feel like the walls are closing in on me, and I don't have the strength to push them back open."

She squeezed him again and rested her head back on his chest. "Oh, babe," she said, leading him to the couch. "I'm sorry. How can I help?"

"I guess you can't. They're my struggles to contend with. You can't learn that damn program for me. You can't get that promotion for me, and you can't solve the looming Jaden case." He leaned back and rested his folded hands on top of his head.

He was right. She couldn't learn that program for him. She couldn't get him that promotion. And she couldn't solve the missing person case. What she could do and *was* doing was protecting her family the best way she knew how.

Watching him broke her heart. He looked lost. "I love you with every fiber of my being. You and Ky are my world. And whatever you need from me, I'm here." She placed her hand on his knee.

"There is *one* thing I need from you," he said, wiggling his eyebrows up and down. He led Nicole to the bedroom, shrugging her clothes off one stair at a time. By the time he was down to her hot pink lace panties, he'd passed by her jewelry box, where the two other burner phones would remain until the next time.

CHAPTER 29

As Nicole drove down her street, she noticed a strange car parked in the driveway, but not the black SUV. She thought maybe it was Alex's car, and Craig had come home early, an unusual occurrence for the middle of the day. Since she'd only been gone for thirty minutes to grab some groceries, and if Craig had returned home during that time, she worried he might be sick.

"Babe? You home?" she yelled as she balanced the heavy brown bags.

"In here," he called out from his office.

She dropped the groceries on the speckled quartz kitchen counter.

"Oh, sorry," she said, an uncomfortable feeling washing over her as she stood in the doorway. She thought she'd made her feelings clear. She didn't understand why Dr. Graham was here again. In their house. Still, he sat in a chair, his gray and blue College of Cypressville sweatshirt bunched up, making him look heavier than he was. "It's all good," he said, smiling.

Nicole noticed a scar slashing through his right eyebrow, slicing it in half.

"It's much quieter here. Fewer distractions," Craig said, rolling up the sleeves of his green baseball-style shirt, staring at his computer screen. "We keep getting interrupted in our offices between phone calls, students, and teaching assistants." He glanced sideways at Dr. Graham.

"Yeah. It's way better here, especially without Alex hovering about," Dr. Graham said, clasping his large hands behind his head, leaning back.

Craig shot him a look, one Nicole couldn't interpret.

"Anyway, we'll stay out of your hair," Craig said, typing.

"Okay." Nicole smiled. "I'll be in the kitchen if you need anything. I've got some stuff I need to catch up on." For some unknown reason, Nicole didn't trust Dr. Graham. Her skin tingled whenever he was around. She needed to find out if there was any truth to her intuition. She decided to Google the man sitting beside her husband.

After she put the groceries away, Nicole opened her computer and started her search. Every so often, she heard voices coming from Craig's office. Sometimes they were soft and even-toned, other times, they were harsh and emotional. Nicole kept telling herself that Craig had said how intricate the program was, and since Dr. Graham had confirmed this, that must be the reason for such heated moments. The knot in Nicole's stomach disagreed.

She couldn't distinguish their exact words, only their tones and inflections. Too busy trying to concentrate on the men's conversation, Nicole couldn't focus on what she was reading in front of her. After twenty minutes of scanning articles about Dr. David Graham and nothing out of the ordinary, curiosity got the better of her. She tiptoed near Craig's office, her breath as still as the dead of night. She leaned in and listened.

"If you put this number here on this spreadsheet, the average will pop up here," Dr. Graham said.

"But what if I want to weigh the grades? Then how do I account for that?" she heard Craig reply.

Dr. Graham continued to explain how it all worked, and she heard the clickety-clack of the keyboard. She realized that her paranoia was getting the better of her again. She turned to walk away when the following statement stopped her.

Dr. Graham asked, "Do you think your wife knows?"

"No, but if you keep bringing it up, she will. You need to keep your voice down. She doesn't trust you as it is," Craig snapped in a hushed tone.

Nicole pressed her ear against the door. The men had lowered their voices to an inaudible whisper. She could only make out a few sporadic words, not cohesive sentences, and it was Dr. Graham's voice, saying things like *threatening...money*, *last warning*, and *paid...price*.

Her heart bucked. What was he referring to? Had Dr. Graham done something to Jaden? Did he know about the gambling money? She tiptoed back to the kitchen, releasing all her breath.

She knew she couldn't ask Craig what that conversation had been about—then he'd know she'd been snooping—it hadn't been for her ears. More determined than ever to find out what it was about Dr. Graham that heightened her senses, she continued reading the articles, one by one, combing through them, trying to unravel her suspicions. She couldn't concentrate again, her mind preoccupied, untangling what she'd overheard, her brain incapable of multitasking.

Just as she was about to give up, a headline caught her eye. It was an editorial written by a student at Brighton University, Dr. Graham's former campus. Bathed in dread, her wavering finger pointed to the screen as she raced over the words. Pointedly, her intuition wasn't off.

• • • • •

Nicole lifted the jewelry box lid and pulled out the second burner phone. The third one would remain there until the next time.

After reading the editorial, she'd been on edge, waiting for Craig and Dr. Graham to leave. She'd switched gears and paid her credit card bill (she had a separate one from Craig to buy him gifts—she felt like if she used his card, then it was like he was buying his own present) when she remembered about their bank account balance. While she was scrolling through their transactions, Craig had walked in and kissed her goodbye. She'd closed her laptop, left it abandoned on the kitchen table, and watched the car pull off the driveway. The moment they'd gone, Nicole went upstairs to retrieve the phone.

Back downstairs now, she dug through her purse, unfolded the crinkled brochure secretly tucked inside, and redialed the tip line number.

"Missing person's hotline. How may I help you?" Relieved, Nicole noticed it wasn't the same voice as before, even though she'd disguised her voice the last time. To be safe, she spoke in a higher pitch. "Hi, yeah, like, I think I may have some information that may, uh, like, help with the Jaden case."

"What's your tip?"

"Like, I don't have to give out my name or anything like that, do I?"

"Not if you don't want to." The voice on the other end explained about the reward money.

"Oh, like, I don't want any money. Like, that's a lot of money, you know," Nicole side commented, "but that doesn't matter to me. I just want justice for Jaden." Nicole remembered seeing that hashtag on social media and used it for exaggeration.

"What's your tip?"

"So, like, my best friend had something happen to her, and I've read some of the posts on my Insta feed, and now I'm wondering if it's not connected to Jaden somehow. Um, like, I'm not sure it is, but I thought the police might want to know." Nicole paused.

"Any information is good information."

"Great. So, okay, like, my best friend would kill me if she knew I was calling. I promised her I wouldn't tell a soul, but you know, like, I don't think the professor should get away with it."

"Like I said, any information is good information, and she doesn't have to know you're calling."

"Great. That's such a huge relief, you know? Anyway, so, uh, she told me that her professor—" Nicole paused for a dramatic effect. In her high octave tone, voice cracking, she said, "He, uh, he...took advantage of her." She stopped again.

"In what way? How?"

"He...he... groped her, and when she told him to stop, he'd said if she didn't let him touch her, he'd give her an F in his class." Nicole sniffled, pretending to be the concerned and upset best friend.

"I'm sorry that happened to your friend. I'll need the name of this professor."

"I'm, like, so upset, you know? I thought I'd said it already. His name is Dr. Graham."

"Can you spell that for me?"

Nicole did. Then she said, "And I know Jaden was a student in Dr. Graham's class, too. My best friend told me she overheard Jaden and the professor fighting one day. Says she walked past his office and heard the argument." Nicole knew connecting the stories would solidify what she'd called in earlier. That would be two strikes against good old Dr. Graham—multiple tips now tied to him. "My friend was going to confront the professor about what he'd done, but when she heard the arguing voices, she left."

Nicole heard the tapping of the keyboard. "Thank you for this information," the voice said.

"Like, uh, sure. No problem. Feels good to get it off my chest, you know? I've lost so much sleep over this, sick about the whole thing. I was torn about what to do, but since Jaden is still missing, I thought maybe it's all connected somehow."

"Any information is good information," the voice on the other end said for the third time. "If you remember anything else that may be important, please call back."

"I will."

Nicole flipped the phone closed and buried it in the bottom of her purse. Next time she went out, she would dispose of it in a dumpster as far away as possible.

CHAPTER 30

Nicole knew the perfect dumpster. Not that any dumpster wouldn't do, but there was one in particular. One that was tucked between two large boulders behind her favorite health food store, and since she needed to replenish her favorite organic, low-fat protein powder, she decided that would be the perfect one.

Before entering the store, Nicole, dressed in black cut-offs and a black tank top with her hair piled high on her head, snuck around back, lifted the heavy lid of the vast green receptacle, and chucked the phone in. She heard the clunking sound as it landed. Trash pickup had been earlier that morning, so the phone was one of the first items tossed in, a fact that relieved Nicole. It would be buried deep down at the bottom, underneath heaps of leftover food, mounds of stuffed trash bags, and mixed in with a sizeable amount of unidentifiable waste.

Satisfied it was properly disposed of, Nicole rounded the building next to the end store anchored in the plaza and blended in with the mass of people milling around. This shopping center was always a zoo. Nicole hated shopping here, the crowds too much, but this is where her favorite nutrition store was, and to get her preferred supplemental powder, she had to endure the chaos.

Cold air blasted her face as she walked in. It was a welcomed relief since the weather had substantially changed from a few days ago. The air was now saturated with humidity, making it feel warmer than the thermometer read; not unusual for Cypressville this time of year. It often became hot, muggy, and sticky long before the calendar said spring.

Fit For You was the biggest nutrition store Nicole had ever seen, more like a big-box store, although not a chain. A local couple owned it. They had everything here to enhance a healthy lifestyle—from fruits to supplements—they had it all.

Picking up random bunches of bananas and inspecting their yellow piqued color, Nicole noticed the guy from the coffee shop, the SUV driver, standing by the oranges, staring at her. He pretended to examine the fruit piled high before him, but his eyes focused on her.

Nicole froze. The only parts that moved were the blood speeding through her veins and her eyes as she looked down at the bananas again. She didn't know what to do. She could yell, "help!" but why? The man hadn't technically done anything. Not yet. He was in a store. Shopping. Or so it appeared.

Not wanting to draw attention, she continued perusing through the bananas. When she picked the perfect bunch, she dropped it in her cart and moved on. Her fingers turned white, gripping the handle tightly, and her breaths came in short bursts. She debated whether to continue shopping or leave her cart abandoned in the middle of the store, making a mad dash for the exit.

Conflicted between the two, Nicole thought to pull out her cell phone, pretending to answer it. With no one on the other end, she continued to push her cart with one hand, muttering to herself, "Keep walking, don't panic. Keep walking, don't panic."

Nicole thought about rushing by him, picking up an orange from the bottom of the pile, causing an avalanche, and sending the entire stack rolling everywhere, creating a diversion. Or she thought she could ram the man with her cart, incapacitating him, while she got away. Neither idea seemed reasonable nor plausible. Instead, she continued shopping, and much to her surprise, she moved closer to him while pretending to talk on the phone.

She didn't make eye contact, dropping her head like she was examining her cart's contents, and wheeled past him at a pretty quick clip but slow enough to notice a protruding mole on his forehead, precisely under his dark brown, receding hairline. She noticed his bulging muscles under his snug-fitting t-shirt that said, "I love Cypressville." If he was trying to blend in, it wasn't working. That shirt screamed tourist.

She moved up and down the aisles with a purpose, hastily tossing in what she'd come for, watching over her shoulder, looking out for the man. Her muscles smoothed when she hadn't bumped into him after a few aisles, so she put her cell phone away. It wasn't until she got to the car that she totally calmed down.

"What the hell is this?" she said, pulling another note from her windshield. She looked around the parking lot for Creeper Dude, which she now named him. Thankfully, he was nowhere in sight. She squinted toward the plaza sidewalk. Scads of people roamed about, but she didn't see him, and nobody was near the car. She ripped the paper off the window and unfolded it.

Not everyone is who they say they are. Consider this your last warning

Nicole wondered if Creeper Dude had left it. He knew she was here. And because this was the second time he'd been in the same place as she was, like at the coffee shop, when a note appeared on her windshield, she wondered if he was the responsible party. And if he wasn't, then who was?

She was too shaken to drive. Still, Nicole had no other choice; she had to get out of there. She threw the car into reverse with unstable limbs and hightailed it, knowing time was up: she had to tell Craig. After this second "chance" encounter, fourth note, and confident she wasn't being paranoid—convinced that she *was* being followed—it was time to bring him into the know. Her quaky finger dialed his number.

• • • • •

"This is just what we needed," Craig said.

"I totally agree. Let's make a toast. To us and what lies ahead." Nicole raised her glass of champagne, the expensive kind from the south of France, and waited for Craig to lift his. "Why aren't you clinking?"

"I'm just wondering what you mean by what lies ahead?"

When Nicole had called Craig, she opted not to say anything over the phone. It was too long of a story, and thought it necessary to tell him in person. So instead of being forthright, she asked him to meet her for a romantic dinner at their favorite upscale restaurant, *Donatellos,* saying she had something important to tell him. She figured that with a few drinks and a hearty meal, it'd also be an opportune time to ask about their bank account.

Nicole's low-cut sundress tied at the top of her shoulders brought out the green in her hazel eyes. Mood eyes, that's what she referred to them as; depending on her mood, they changed color. Sometimes they were greener, sometimes browner, often a slight combination of both, like tonight.

"I'm talking about your promotion. Your future. All great things coming your way."

"I'll definitely drink to that," he said, grabbing the fluted stem, the golden bubbles fizzing to the top. He met Nicole's glass, still suspended midair.

The server took their order, Chicken Cacciatore for him, Shrimp Francese for her, and the moment the server walked away, Craig cut to the chase. "Is there something you want to share with me? Something you haven't told me?" His right eyebrow arched.

Whenever Craig doubted something or someone, his right eyebrow lifted like that. Nicole wondered how often he made that expression in class—his skeptical face.

Unsettled by how he'd worded his question, Nicole feared Craig was privy to her deceptiveness. Why else would he express it that way? "Now it's my turn to wonder what you mean," she said, rubbing her finger around the rim of her champagne glass.

"You said you had something you wanted to tell me. That's why we're here, isn't it?"

Not sure he was ready for the truth, unsure if he'd had enough to drink yet, or herself for that matter, thinking it may be too soon with only a few sips into their first glass of champagne, Nicole read his body language. With his body sagging against the booth, his hand draped loosely around his glass, and his lips parted slightly open, she knew he was relaxed—no better time than now.

"I didn't want to say anything until I was absolutely sure, but—"

Craig's eyes widened. "Oh, my God. Are you pregnant?"

Nicole let out a hearty belly laugh. An older couple next to them glared. She covered her mouth. "Sorry," she said through her palm. "No." Something struck her, though. Pain. It rippled through her heart. Or perhaps her gut. She couldn't tell where or what it meant. Would it be so catastrophic if they had another baby? Kyle *was* nineteen years old, and sure, she'd be a high-risk pregnancy. It wouldn't be disastrous, however. Ideally, it would fill the void, the vast emptiness that she'd buried deep down when they'd resigned themselves that Kyle would be an only child, albeit not by choice.

Warmth rose to her cheeks, stirring from that dormant place where she'd stuffed it. She gulped the champagne to numb the dull ache. "No, I'm not pregnant," she said, taking another big swig. If being pregnant was the thing to flip him out, if that were what he considered scary, then maybe her being followed wouldn't be as big of a deal as she'd thought.

Eyebrows creased, he asked, "Then what is it? What did you want to tell me?"

"Never mind. It's nothing." She finished her drink, holding the stem so tightly that it could snap in half.

"Please. Tell me," Craig said, leaning his elbows on the table. He'd rolled up his chartreuse Oxford shirt sleeves partway, exposing his muscular forearms, the Cartier watch now gleaming in the candle's flame.

Nicole averted his stare.

"Wait," Craig said, scooting in further. "Are you upset that you're *not* pregnant?"

"No," she lied, not only to him but to herself as well. "That ship has sailed. We are way too old for that."

His shoulders dropped. "Thank God. I thought you were pregnant, and then I thought you were upset about *not* being pregnant. I may need a shot to calm my nerves." He laughed.

Nicole hiccupped. "Why? Would it be so terrible if I was pregnant? If we had another child?" Her face flooded with anger.

"Yeah, Nic. I'm in my late forties, for Christ's sake, and I'm knee-deep in my job, hopefully about to get a huge promotion. I'm settled. We're settled. The last thing we need is another baby to upset all that." He leaned back.

A piece of Nicole's heart fell to her feet. She hung her head and let out a long exasperated sigh.

"You're acting like you *want* another baby. You say you don't, but you're getting all, I don't know...something. Look at you. What gives?"

She restrained the tears, yearning to escape. "Nothing, I'm fine."

"You're not acting fine."

Nicole sat back, shoulders connected to the back of the booth, and lifted her eyes to Craig's. Her cheeks glowed a hot pink. She glared at him. Annoyance, anger, disappointment—a dangerous, volatile cocktail of emotions churning in her inner core. She grumbled a deep growl, loud enough for other patrons to hear.

"You're causing a scene," Craig snarled. He didn't like public displays of emotion. Nicole sat stone-faced, a low rumble reverberating from her chest.

His lips tensed. "Nic, say something."

She continued to stare.

"What. Is. Wrong?" he asked through gritted teeth.

Nicole folded her arms. "Nothing. Absolutely nothing."

"Then why are you acting like this?" he asked, gesturing to her.

Nicole threw her napkin on the table. "I'm not hungry anymore." She slid out of the booth.

She left Craig to sit alone, the single flamed candle in the center of the table casting shadows on his bewildered face.

CHAPTER 31

She didn't know why she'd come undone at dinner last night. With everything else going on in her life right now, she didn't have the time or emotional space to deal with the essence of the issue. She'd apologized to Craig when she'd come downstairs to find him sleeping on the couch again, blaming it on the champagne, saying she hadn't had time to eat, and it'd gone straight to her head. She promised to make it up to him.

Worried about what was happening to their marriage following another contentious incident, which seemed to occur more frequently, Nicole hadn't mentioned being followed or the notes. She vowed to tell him tonight. Becoming more frightened the closer this creep encroached on her world, it was time to bring her husband into the loop.

Nicole took a hot shower, the water sluicing over her stressed muscles, hoping to wash away the sick feeling. Thinking that if she scrubbed forcefully, she could eliminate the uneasiness lurking below the surface. It didn't help. All she was left with was bright pink skin. She sat on the bed with a towel wrapped around her wet hair, mindlessly scrolling through her emails. A text message from Kyle popped up on her screen.

Did you see the latest?

No, what?

It's all over the news. Turn it on

Nicole scrambled to get dressed, throwing on a ratty pair of gym shorts and a College of Cypressville t-shirt, and hightailed it downstairs, skipping steps, slipping on the last one, grabbing the handrail to steady herself.

She turned on the TV, her heart practically leaping out of her chest, and there, on the screen, was Darlene, the familiar blonde bombshell dressed in a white, flowy dress. Her hair was pulled back in a neat ponytail high on her head, and sweat droplets glistened on her upper lip. She spoke into the microphone, "Police aren't releasing any details, nor are they confirming if he is a suspect. Sources say that the college's own Dr. David Graham has been brought in for extensive questioning."

Nicole gasped.

"We have reached out to Detective Newton for comment, but he hasn't returned our calls. Dr. Graham came here this semester from Brighton University, where he allegedly coerced a student into a sexual relationship. The professor was never officially charged, but he'd been relieved of his position. In the end, the female student recanted her story. Since the higher-ups didn't want that kind of publicity on their campus, he was let go."

Nicole pulled up her Instagram and Facebook accounts, checking them as fast as her finger could move.

Her phone dinged again.

Mom, did you see?

She switched apps to answer.

Watching now

Darlene continued. "Apparently, Jaden was a student in Dr. Graham's class, and there've been reports that the two were seen arguing the day before Jaden's disappearance."

Nicole covered her mouth, her eyes widening. Her tips had worked. The police were breathing down Dr. Graham's neck.

Kyle texted:

Do you think he did it?

I don't know

Could you imagine a professor killing a student?

Nicole couldn't. Students are supposed to trust their professors, not fear them. She texted back:

No, I can't. Where r u?

Class

Nicole wondered how students learned anything these days, unable to pay attention if always on their electronic devices during lectures. Craig had a zero-tolerance policy in his classroom. Students were asked to leave if he heard one ding, chime, or ring. "It's disrespectful," Craig had said. Nicole agreed. "Besides," he'd said, "these kids are paying out the ass to be in class. You'd think they'd want to get their money's worth."

Nicole had pointed out that it was mostly the parents' money, not the students'. She was sure they'd be more attentive if they were the ones paying.

The news showed footage of Dr. Graham being escorted into the police station as Nicole looked back up. The banner underneath read, "Local professor brought in for questioning. Is he guilty?" Oh, how she would like to know the answer to *that* question.

Her phone dinged again. This time it was from Craig.

Have you seen the news?

Yes

WTF? Did you have something to do with this?

Nicole, reading the anger in his text, didn't know how to answer—she'd had everything to do with it, but she couldn't tell him that.

What? No! How can you even ask that?

Another free-flowing, blatant lie.

Because you said you don't trust the man and now he's at the police station

We'll talk when you get home

Yes, we will. This conversation is far from over

That familiar, sickening feeling washed over her. If all eyes were on Dr. Graham, then why did Nicole feel like she was the one being scrutinized?

• • • • •

Nicole had just finished drying her hair when her cell phone rang. Her stomach dropped hearing the sound, afraid of what she'd hear next and from whom. It was Phil. "Hi," she said in relief.

"Hey. Did you hear? They have a person in custody." He sounded unusually chipper.

"Uh, yeah, I did. I watched it on TV." *And my husband is pissed at me about it.*

"Then why do you sound like you lost your beloved pet? If this is the guy, then Kyle's good to go. You should be happy."

"I am," she lied.

"You certainly don't sound it."

"I'm preoccupied with some personal stuff." Not a *complete* lie.

"Perk up. This could be great news for all of you."

Nicole knew that if the police didn't find substantial evidence to keep Dr. Graham in custody, he'd be released, and Kyle would still be in the mix. "Is Ky out of the woods?" she asked.

Phil laughed. "Funny."

Nicole looked at her reflection in the dresser mirror and asked, "What?" She didn't know what he found so amusing.

"Woods. You said woods. Get it?" *He* is *an old man trapped in a young man's body*. She pictured him wearing a striped button-down shirt, ironed so stiffly that the sleeves could stand outstretched on their own, and a clashing bow tie to boot.

"It's like a dad joke," he continued explaining.

"I get it." She rolled her eyes, hanging the towel on the door hook. "Pardon the pun."

"Anyway, I called the station to talk to the detective, but I was told in a not-so-nice tone might I add, that he was busy and didn't have time to talk to any lawyers or media."

Wondering if she'd made things worse for herself, Nicole thanked Phil for the phone call and for keeping her abreast with the newest update.

Before hanging up, she said, "Hey Phil, how do they even know if Jaden is dead or alive? They haven't found a body yet, and there's no physical evidence against anyone. No proof. Nothing."

"What'd you mean?"

Nicole was second-guessing her actions. "I don't know. Maybe Dr. Graham had nothing to do with it. Maybe Jaden disappeared on purpose." If her actions had taken the heat off of Kyle but simultaneously created a further rift between her and Craig, she didn't know if it'd been worth it. It was a no-win situation.

"That's up to the detectives to determine. That's their job. To figure out what happened. And I suppose that starts with Dr. Graham."

• • • • •

Ever since Craig's text, Nicole felt awful. She tried to bake, occupy her mind, and pass the time waiting for him to come home. She tried to drown out her inner voice with the loud music, but it only caused more angst, so she opted to bake in silence. Distracted, lost in thought, replaying what she'd done and how Craig had reacted, she accidentally used baking powder rather than baking soda, causing the cake to taste saltier and more acidic. It ended up in the trash.

While she measured out the salt, sugar, and baking soda a second time, paying careful attention to which canister was which, she rationalized her behavior, hoping it would make her feel better. Like her first cake had been unsuccessful, so was her attempt to soothe herself—nothing would make her feel better until she talked to Craig.

The front door slammed while her arms were stretched out to put the cake in the oven. Nicole jumped at the sound, spilling batter over the cake pan's rim. "Shit," she mumbled, unsure if she was cursing at the near mishap or that she had to face the music with her husband.

"Nic?" he yelled from the living room.

"I'm in here," she replied, untying the apron around her waist.

She could see the anger in his eyes. Usually, he'd kiss her the second he walked through the door. Not today. Today, he brushed past her, opened the refrigerator, grabbed an IPA beer, and sat on a barstool at the kitchen island.

Nicole leaned on her elbows, her chest grazing the quartz countertop. "Hey," she said, starting the conversation.

He tipped the bottle back and emptied a quarter of the honey-colored liquid in one big gulp.

"What happened?" she asked, acting daft.

"Like you don't know," he said in a biting tone. "That asshole detective brought Dave in for questioning. That's what happened."

She looked down at her wedding band, which she hadn't taken off since the day they wed. Even during her pregnancy weight gain, she'd left it on. "Yes, I know."

After another long swig, he said, "Because apparently, somebody called the tip line and made up some bullshit story about him, claiming he groped a former student or was blackmailing one or some ridiculous accusation like that." He brought the bottle up to his lips but didn't drink. Instead, he said, "It's bogus. Bullshit. A load of crap."

Nicole wondered how Craig knew it'd come from the tip line. "But what if it is true? What if he did have something to do with Jaden's disappearance? If he didn't, then the police will let him go, right?" She paused, waiting for an answer.

Craig looked down at the long-neck bottle, not responding.

She continued. "Jaden was in his class, and shortly after he started here, one of his students goes missing. Like I said before, it's odd."

"Pure coincidence. That's it. And if I don't learn this whole new program, I can kiss that promotion goodbye. I need him to be innocent. I need him to be free. I need him to help me get that job. I've dedicated myself for years to be in this position!" Craig tossed his empty beer bottle into the trash.

Nicole fished it out and moved it to the recycling bin. "You're brilliant and diligent. You deserve that promotion, and I know you'll get it. The department can't hold it against you if Dr. Graham isn't here to help you. Seriously. It's out of your control if he gets arrested. Isn't there someone else who can help you?"

"No," he said, sitting upright, crossing his arms across his chest. "There isn't anyone else. It's new and innovative, and only a select few people use it. Dave is one of them. If he's not here to teach me, I'm screwed."

Nicole walked behind him and wrapped her arms around his chest, placing her arms over his. She rested her chin on his shoulder. "I'm sure the police are crossing their *t*'s and dotting their *i*'s. They'll release him if he's truly innocent."

"He is innocent." Craig sighed. "All I know is that if I ever find out who made those calls, they'll be sorry they ever did. Mark my words."

The kitchen suddenly became small. Nicole felt trapped inside the four walls, unable to move. There was no way she could ask how he knew it'd come from an anonymous call, and there was no way she could ever let Craig realize it'd been her. She would take this and the fact that she'd been more involved than he knew to her grave. Too disturbed by his last statement, Nicole forgot all about the cake and burned it, ruining another yet again.

CHAPTER 32

To say Nicole needed a workout was an understatement. She would've spent the next twenty-four hours in the gym if she could. Since that was unrealistic, she settled on two hours. Grateful for no notes on the windshield, no run-ins with Creeper Dude, and no sightings of the SUV, Nicole was relieved as she parked on the driveway.

Given his sour mood last night, Nicole never had the chance to tell Craig about her ordeal. Again.

When she opened the front door, she heard voices in the kitchen and froze. There were no other cars out front. Maybe Craig was home again, working on the program. She panicked momentarily, wondering if Dr. Graham was here, too. If so, she couldn't look him in the eye. Then she had another thought. Maybe Craig was agitated about Dr. Graham being questioned, too agitated to even work.

"Hey, Mom," Kyle called out, interrupting her feverish thought process, setting her mind at ease that Dr. Graham and Craig weren't here.

Nicole's shoulders relaxed, and her Nike gym bag slid off her arm, landing near her feet.

"Hey, what are you doing here?" she asked, entering the kitchen. She stopped, surprised to see two other guys sitting at the kitchen table.

"You remember Ethan and Chase?" Kyle said, pointing to the respective owners.

The boys smirked and waved.

She recognized their faces from pictures Kyle had shared with Nicole—they were fellow fraternity brothers, and all dressed similarly: baggy cargo khaki shorts, various rock band t-shirts, and high-top sneakers. Comparable-looking backpacks were propped up against each barstool by their feet.

"We came by to study. The campus is a hot mess with Dr. Graham being questioned and all the Jaden vigils. Can't get any peace and quiet," he said, fanning through the pages of a textbook.

Exactly what Craig and Dr. Graham had said. "No problem. Should I go upstairs so you boys can study?" Nicole asked, gesturing to the ceiling with her thumb.

Kyle looked at the other two boys. They shook their heads. "No," Kyle said. "We'll go to my room."

"Are you sure? I don't mind," Nicole said, grabbing a protein shake from the fridge. "I can take this upstairs and shower." Sweat stained her black and green camo tank top and matching leggings.

"It's all good," Kyle said, closing the book.

The three boys scooted their chairs back and stood up.

"Any goodies we can hijack?" Kyle asked, grabbing his backpack.

Nicole thought back to last night's disastrous baking event. "No. I haven't had a chance to bake lately," she lied. No sense in confessing what'd happened and why it'd gone awry. "But you're welcome to whatever's in the pantry."

Kyle pilfered through the closet and fridge, tossing various snacks to the others. "We'll be in my room," he said, walking out, Ethan and Chase on his heels. From the back, they looked like clones, with similar height, similar hair, and similar gait.

"How long will you be here?" she called out after them.

Kyle stopped, the other two boys colliding into him. "'Til we're done."

• • • • •

Every so often, Nicole walked past Kyles's bedroom door. Sometimes she stopped and leaned her ear against the door, listening to their conversation. Because Dr. Graham hadn't been formally charged yet, the police had released him late last night, and nobody had publicly commented about his questioning, Nicole needed to continue her quest for answers. What if the boys knew something? Maybe one of them knew what'd happened. More than they were letting on.

Muffled voices crossed through the barrier, dividing her from them. "Chase," she heard. She pressed her ear harder against the wood door, standing still, trying to hear better, eavesdropping with little success, the boys unaware of her presence.

She could only hear parts of sentences, like *made a pact, not taking the blame, the money, scared him off, was your idea, your fight, didn't tell the police.*

All sorts of fragmented sentences, making it sound like they did know more than they were letting on. No matter how hard she strained to decipher what was said by whom, she struggled. With their deep, nineteen-year-old voices, they all sounded the same. Nicole felt sick. Were they protecting one another? She didn't know what would be worse—Kyle having had something to do with it or the fact that he was covering something up?

She heard zippers, papers, and bodies moving and darted from the door and sat back down at the kitchen table, breathless. That's when she noticed a backpack still propped against a chair leg. She waited for the boys to emerge from Kyle's room. When still alone after a few minutes, she kneeled next to the abandoned bag.

She unzipped it gingerly, not wanting to make any noise, and jammed her hand into the open bag, shuffling items around. A notebook, a textbook, a binder, and some loose pens were all she found. Nothing unusual or out of the ordinary. She rezipped the main compartment and opened the front pouch, holding her breath, listening for any movement from the boys.

Once confirming the coast was clear, she peeked inside. Stuffed at the bottom was a wad of white paper. She pulled it out and unfolded it, reading. When finished, she placed her palm on her forehead. "This can't be."

She reread the paper to confirm what she'd seen the first time. It was definitely what she thought it was—a threatening note, like the ones left on her windshield—in the same font. Why was it in the backpack? Was it meant for her? Even worse, was this Kyle's backpack?

She heard the bedroom door creak and footsteps approaching. With moments to spare, she stuffed the paper back as she'd found it and jumped into her chair. She pretended to be surfing the Internet when Chase walked in.

"I forgot my backpack," he said, bending down to pick it up.

Nicole smiled.

He slung it over his shoulder and headed back to Kyle's room.

Nicole sat stunned. Baffled and upset, she couldn't imagine why Chase would have that note. Then she remembered what Kyle had said about Chase setting up the game that night and how he'd coerced Jaden into playing. Nicole's head ached. Was Chase somehow involved? Guilty of something? She held her throbbing head in her hand, shaking it from side to side.

"What have I done?" she moaned to the computer screen, contemplating if, maybe, she'd pushed the police in the wrong direction once again.

CHAPTER 33

Kyle stayed for dinner while the other two boys returned to the fraternity house. Nicole didn't breathe a word to him about what she'd found in that backpack. With no proof of who'd left her those notes, there was no way she could confront Kyle, especially having to admit that she'd snooped.

On edge enough already, she was about to tell Craig about Creeper Dude. It was time, especially after finding that note. She'd blown it off too many times before, but now she knew she had to do it after her latest discovery. She couldn't keep this packed inside with all her other secrets. She had to unload something, release the pressure building within, and this information seemed like the least damaging item to purge. If their son was the responsible party, Nicole didn't know how she'd deal with it. While Kyle was holed up in his room, Nicole filled a pot with water, and Craig walked in from work.

When he saw her, he asked, "What's wrong?"

She set the pot on the burner and turned the heat to a medium flame. Facing him again, she verbally vomited all the information about being followed in one fell swoop. It all tumbled out—from the first time she'd suspected it—until the last note she'd pulled off her windshield; she rid her conscience without stopping to even take a breath.

When finished, Craig stared at her, his arms stiff at his sides. "Why am I just hearing about this now?"

Nicole shrugged.

Agitated, pumping his fists, Craig wandered back and forth in front of the kitchen island, processing all the information she'd just dumped.

"Stop pacing. You're making me nervous," she said, leaning back against the island counter, watching Craig wear a path.

He ran his hands through his somewhat graying hair. "So you've seen him, in person, twice, and this is the first time I'm hearing about it?"

"Yes, but—"

He stopped to face Nicole. "But what? Don't you think you could've mentioned it before or maybe the first time you saw the car parked there," he said, pointing toward the front window in the living room, a giant purple vein protruding on his forehead, matching the color of today's polo shirt. "Or maybe, call me crazy, the first time you realized he was following you?" Craig paced faster now.

"You're upset with me. I get it, but please, be rational. Hear me—"

Craig cut her off. "Rational? You want me to be rational? You think I'm being irrational?" His fiery eyes doubled in size.

Another rift in their once sturdy marriage. "No. That's not what I'm saying."

"But you're implying it."

This was going off the rails.

"Dad, please stop yelling at Mom. It's not helping anything," Kyle said from behind Craig.

Neither Nicole nor Craig had heard Kyle enter the kitchen.

Turning to face his son, Craig said, pointing, "Don't even get me started about you."

Nicole jumped in like a mama bear protecting her cub. "Craig, please. This isn't Kyle's fault."

Planted firmly in place, Kyle stood, feet spread wide, arms crossed over his shirt, covering the DMB letters. He was not backing down, standing his ground.

"Not his fault? Not his fault?" Craig spat in Kyle's direction. He turned to face Nicole. "How can you even say that? If he hadn't been playing that stupid ass game that night, and been one of the last people with Jaden, then maybe, just maybe, we wouldn't be here, in this kitchen, having this discussion."

Craig stopped to catch his breath, planting his hands on his hips. After a momentary pause, he said, "And oh yeah, maybe you wouldn't be scared for your safety while being followed by God knows who." His red cheeks puffed in and out.

Kyle looked at Nicole for an explanation. "Followed?"

Not wanting to burden him with any more guilt, she downplayed it by saying, "It's nothing."

Craig started again. "Nothing? Nothing? It's not nothing. Your mom's being followed by some raving lunatic in a big black SUV, it would appear since Jaden went missing?" he questioned, looking at Nicole to confirm the timeline.

She nodded. "He's hardly a raving lun—" Nicole started to correct Craig, but he cut her off.

"And for some reason, one I'll never understand, this is the first time I'm hearing of it. And he's stalked her in the store and coffee shop and God knows where else. Maybe he's been elsewhere, and you didn't even know." He stopped again.

Nicole and Kyle remained silent, watching Craig's every move.

Drawing air through his nose, Craig closed his eyes. After regaining his composure, he said, "This is all a mess. I'm frustrated that I can't fix it, and I'm worried about your safety. And Kyle's."

Nicole blinked. "I understand your concern, but we don't know if Kyle's even in danger. We don't even know if he has anything to do with me possibly being followed or with Jaden's disappearance."

Kyle, stunned by Nicole's indirect accusation, gulped. "You don't believe me?"

Nicole's mouth hung open. She didn't know what to do or say. She desperately wanted to, but after hearing the whisperings from his bedroom earlier and finding that note in Chase's backpack, she was unconvinced of his innocence. Again. Still. She didn't think Kyle could hurt a fly. At this point, however, she couldn't swear he wasn't involved.

She'd mulled over all the possibilities while sitting at the kitchen table earlier that day. Maybe it was a tussle gone wrong? Perhaps it was an accident, and Kyle was too afraid to say anything. Maybe he was an accomplice?

Several plausible possibilities existed, none of which Kyle mentioned, owned up to, or confessed. Instead, the three of them stood in the kitchen in silence—the water she'd set to boil not the only thing steaming—doubt, suspicion, and hurt also bubbled in that room.

• • • • •

Kyle had left before they ate, too angry with Nicole to eat. She dumped the pasta water into the sink. Neither she nor Craig was hungry after their cantankerous conversation.

Nicole found Craig reclining on the sofa. He'd changed into blue nylon shorts and a white undershirt. His tall stature stretched end to end. She folded onto a cushion and scooped up his lean legs, placing them across her lap. "Are you okay?" she asked softly.

"I think so." He rubbed his temples. "I hate when we fight."

"I wouldn't say we're fighting." Hadn't she thought the same thing an hour ago? "You're upset. I understand." She stroked his leg.

"Our kid may have murdered someone."

Nicole laughed.

"What's so funny?"

"Our son murdering someone?" And there it was again—the swinging pendulum of emotion—one minute accusing Kyle, the next, defending him. "Come on, you know, Ky. He's a gentle, kind, caring kid. Excuse me, young man," she corrected herself. "He couldn't even kill an ant. Remember? We had to set it free outside."

When Kyle was six, he found an ant crawling in his bed. He'd melted down when Craig went to squash it, crying, "Don't hurt it! You'll crush him, and he'll die." Tears had spilled down his baby-like cheeks. "He's a tiny ant. You have to save him." Craig had rolled his eyes, but did as his son requested, redirecting the ant onto his finger, setting it free on the sidewalk.

Craig laughed at the memory. "Yeah, I do, but that's when he was little. We think we know him, but what if we don't?" He flopped his arm over his forehead.

Nicole was relieved to know that Craig had the same doubts. "We still don't even know if Jaden is—" she said, incapable of finishing the thought.

"I know. You're right."

"And we do know our son. We know he could never hurt anyone. And even if it were an accident, or if he'd witnessed anything, he would've told us by now. We've raised him well. He's good, through and through." She just needed to heed her advice.

Craig smiled. "Yeah, he is."

Nicole leaned her head back on the sofa cushion and outstretched her legs, crossing them at the ankle. "Feel better?"

"A little."

"Craig," she said, stroking his legs. He loved when she did that; the fastest way to relax him and turn him on, but sex was the last thing on her mind, guilt coursing through her body. Nicole contemplated telling him about everything she'd withheld to date and how she'd found the note in Chase's backpack.

"Mm," he said, closing his eyes, enjoying her fingernails moving up and down his leg.

"I need to tell you something else," she said, mustering up the courage to continue.

He popped up, jostling her. "Oh, that's right. We never finished our conversation about you being followed. Now, what are we going to do about that?"

CHAPTER 34

The following day, Nicole sat in her car, windows rolled up, watching from across the street. She parked far enough away, undetectable. Detective Newton, dressed in Cypressville's police detective uniform—a navy-blue polo shirt with the department's logo embroidered on the breast and khaki slacks—was talking to another detective dressed the same. Nicole hadn't seen this unfamiliar man before. He was taller than his counterpart and looked about the same age, but with an excellent head of hair.

Newton gesticulated while speaking, deep in conversation, and the unidentifiable one was nodding, listening intently. Nicole wanted to roll down her window and listen to what they were saying, but the cold rain came down fast and sideways, making it impossible. Plus, she was too far away to hear.

With most people returning to their everyday lives, the search party had basically dissolved. Most volunteers had dropped off, with only a few stragglers remaining. Nicole longed to be one of them. Disappointingly, she had to settle for the daily news reports to keep her abreast of any updates or the occasional text from Sylvia. Over time, Nicole distanced herself from Sylvia, apprehensive about her involvement, rarely hearing from her anymore. Because of this, Nicole was across the street, hoping to be here at an opportune time, trying to get a glimpse of anything going on.

The Cypressville Police Department, in addition to Detective Newton, had called off the search since no leads had yielded any concrete evidence, clues, or anything worthwhile in almost three weeks; the witness turned out to be bogus. As expected, he'd only come forward for the money, which he hadn't received since no accurate information had been given. Dr. Graham had no legitimate proof against him, and the second set of fingerprints on the syringe couldn't be identified. With Detective Newton classifying this as a cold case, Nicole didn't know why he was out here today. Maybe he knew more than he was disclosing.

With Detective Newton turning in her direction and pointing, Nicole ducked down. He didn't know her car, but he certainly knew her. Craig had strongly urged her to contact the detective about Creeper Dude, saying it may be connected to the Jaden case since she'd noticed it happening after he went missing. Nicole had profusely contested the idea, stating, "I don't want to bring any attention to our family."

Genuinely concerned for her safety, Craig had said she needed to do something, get the authorities involved. It'd happened far too many times at this point not to act.

"Maybe it'll stop now," Nicole had pleaded to Craig, who wouldn't hear any more of her excuses. He gave her an ultimatum, "You tell them, or I will." It wasn't up for further discussion.

Defying Craig's demands, Nicole watched the man she should be talking to. "If he walks this way in the next three minutes, I'll tell him," she said to herself. After three minutes and no movement from the detective, she said, "Okay, five minutes. If he heads this way in five, I'll do it." She continued to negotiate with herself. Her phone rang, hitching her out of her seat. "Shit!" she laughed. It was Phil. She sent it to voicemail.

She'd hoped it was Kyle. He wouldn't answer her calls or respond to her texts after her accusatory statement. Worried about him, she'd used *Find My Friends* earlier that morning to ensure he was okay. When she'd checked, he'd moved from the fraternity house to the library; she knew he was alive. And safe. And not at the police station, as she often feared.

She continued to watch the activity around the wooded area. The tall pine trees swayed in the wind, shirking needles in reply. Patches of green grass peppered the dead vegetation as spring neared. The two detectives wandered in between the brush, blocking her view. It all seemed surreal, like she was watching a movie, not her life.

Her phone dinged. Phil had left a voicemail. She read the transcription rather than listening to it: *Call me.*

"Wow. Very detailed message, Phil," she said, tossing the phone back on the seat. Since the case had zero breaks, she knew it must not be urgent. "Maybe good old Phil needs more money."

Detective Newton, and today's sidekick, disappeared into a thick patch of woods, vanishing. Nicole lost sight of them. "Looks like I'm not telling Lou today," she said when a tap on the window startled her, her second jump scare of the day.

She put her hand on her heart. "You scared the shit out of me," she said, opening the passenger window slightly, not wanting to let the rain in.

"What are you doing here?"

"I could ask you the same question," she replied.

Nicole unlocked the door to let Phil in. He shook off his umbrella, folding into the passenger seat. "Well, why are you here?"

"I wanted to see what was happening," Nicole half-lied. She was here to tell Detective Newton about Creeper Dude and the notes, but she also wanted to see what was happening.

Phil wiped the raindrops dripping from his nose. "This is *not* a good idea."

The rain continued to fall rapidly, blurring her vision through the windshield. Between that and the layer of fog blanketing the glass, she couldn't see further than the hood of the car.

"Dodging my calls, I see?" he said, his forehead wrinkling, dropping his hairline closer to his brow. He picked up her phone and handed it back to her, water droplets dappling the screen.

Nicole wiped them off with the bottom of her shirt. "How did you know I was here?"

"I didn't."

"Then why are you here?" she asked, arching her eyebrows.

"Because I had a few free minutes between meetings, and believe it or not, I actually care what happens to my clients. So, whenever I can, I drive by here and observe what's going on. Keeping an eye out for any funny business."

"Lawyers can do that?"

"Can we? Yes. Should we? Probably not, but I'm trying to protect my client by making sure they," he said, pointing toward the woods that had swallowed up Detective Newton and his accomplice, "are following the rules. Proper procedures."

Nicole wrinkled her nose. "Why?"

"I'm not saying they're all bad. I've seen or, more aptly, have heard a few law enforcement members who have, in desperation, to quiet the public or family members, bent the rules, if you will," he said, tilting his head at an angle.

"Ah, got it," Nicole said, putting two and two together.

"And since my clients pay good money, I like to do a good job for them." He straightened his bowtie; little Shih Tzus decorated the fabric today. Nicole grinned.

"And since you *are* the mother of a person the police have their eye on, and since you have been clearly 'kicked off,'" he said with air quotes, "the search party, I highly suggest you stay away from here. You could make things way worse by snooping around. A big no-no."

Nicole laughed in her head at his choice of words, like she was a two-year-old putting a Tide Pod in her mouth.

"You could draw more suspicion to Kyle. I can see the headline now, 'Meddling Mom Messing with Investigation.'" He swiped his hand from left to right as he uttered the words. "Really, you should know better." He shook his head.

He should only know the extent to which I've meddled. Nicole stared out the front window, saddened by all she'd done. Even though Phil had been stern with her, she did like him. Good guy. Ethical. Put his clients first. She lucked out, finding him on her first try at searching for an attorney.

"What's wrong?" he asked, watching her expression.

"Nothing." She placed her hands on the steering wheel and studied the simple gold band around her ring finger, shame needling her heart. She felt like she was betraying her family—keeping secrets from Craig and doubting her son.

Getting back to his interrogation, frowning, Phil asked, "Tell me, why are you here?"

She side-eyed him. "Are you a detective, too?"

"No. Just a good attorney. One who asks the important questions, and you're avoiding mine."

"Is it against the law to park here?"

"Stop evading the question. Why are you here?"

Relentless is how Nicole would later describe Phil.

She sighed and repeated the story about Creeper Dude and the notes.

"And you're just telling me this now?" he asked.

"Now you sound like my husband," she said, shaking her head.

"What do you mean?"

Because she hated being unable to see out the front window, even though she was parked and not going anywhere, Nicole turned on the windshield wipers. "I mean, my husband asked me the same question when I'd finally told him."

"Finally? Do you mean to tell me you didn't tell Craig straight away?"

"No." Nicole looked out the driver's window. It was fogging up, too. She cranked up the air.

"Why not?"

"I don't know. At first, I didn't think it was anything. I thought maybe I was paranoid. That it was only my imagination, but when it happened a few more times, and I saw the SUV parked across the street from our house, I realized maybe it was real and not all in my head."

"This guy knows where you live?"

Nicole nodded.

"This is super important information. You absolutely should've told me. And Craig. And the police." Phil let out a long, slow sigh.

"Why?"

"Why? I can give about ten reasons. The first one is your safety. The second one," he said, his voice rising while he demonstrated counting on his fingers, "is this guy might know something about Jaden's disappearance."

Nicole never realized it could be related to Jaden's *actual* disappearance. She'd considered the possibility that it had something to do with Kyle's involvement, never that it could be related to Jaden going missing. "Shit," she groused.

"Shit is right. This guy might've witnessed what happened that night. He might have some information about Kyle. He might know that Kyle is innocent. He might know what happened to Jaden. He might be the one who did something."

Upset, Nicole hung her head. She wanted to kick herself for being so stupid and not connecting the dots further. Raking over the scenarios in her mind about why she was being followed, she never once thought about all the things Phil had suggested. This mysterious man may hold the key to clearing her son's name, and instead of luring Creeper Dude closer, she'd done everything to avoid him, and now he was nowhere to be seen.

While Nicole's mind swirled, Phil pulled his cell phone from his pocket and punched in a phone number.

"Who are you calling?" she asked.

CHAPTER 35

Nicole and Phil sat in the cramped interrogation room, waiting. It'd been a while since Nicole had been here—since she'd heard those familiar sounds outside this room. "I don't see why I have to do this," she said to Phil, who sat beside her, rifling through a stack of papers.

"We've been over this. You need to let Detective Newton know about being followed. We don't know if it's related to Jaden disappearing or Kyle's possible connection."

Nicole wondered if Phil suspected her son on any level with that statement. "*If* Kyle has any connection, which I don't think he does," she said, once again defending him. Or maybe she was trying to convince herself of his innocence every time she said it aloud.

"Yes, *if* Kyle is involved in any way. And I agree, I don't think he is." He went back to reading through his papers.

Nicole was relieved to hear Kyle's attorney believed in his client. She drummed her fingers on the table; the colorless cement walls leaving nothing to look at.

"Stop. You're driving me crazy," Phil said, placing his hand over her fingers, stifling the movement.

"How much longer do we have to wait here?"

"Until Detective Newton comes in, and we've finished talking to him."

"Hmph," Nicole said. She leaned back in her chair and crossed her arms like a pouting child.

The door flew open, and Detective Newton, with his belly hanging over his black leather belt looped around his khakis, dropped a pile of file folders on the table, looking flustered. "Sorry. Crazy day," he said, sitting in a metal chair across from them.

"No problem," Phil said. Nicole shot him an annoying look. She disagreed with his *no problem* attitude. Everything about this was a problem, starting with her not wanting to be here.

"So, what can I do for you?" The detective scooted in. The chair scraped along the cold linoleum floor, creating a loud screech that echoed off the cement, subway-style wall.

Nicole plugged her ears.

"Where's your client?" Detective Newton asked, looking confused.

"We're not here for him. We're here about her." Phil jutted his chin toward Nicole.

"Her? Why? Oh...we were perfectly within our rights to ask her to leave the search party. It was a conflict of interest. That's our department's policy. Other agencies may not have the same rule, but that's our rule here." He leaned back, his excessive weight causing the chair to scuttle along the floor, emitting another high-pitched squeak. "I don't need a lawsuit on top of everything else. I've already got one angry family regarding this case, and I certainly don't need two."

Phil laughed. "That's not why we're here. And actually, I'm not technically acting as her attorney. However, I will if you put me in that position. That may not be other lawyers' policy, to represent two family members simultaneously, but that's mine," he said, mimicking the detective.

Detective Newton didn't look amused. "You could be disbarred for that."

"Au contraire mon frère. If it's not a conflict of interest between the same family members, then I'm perfectly within my rights," Phil said, waving his hand across his face like swatting at an annoying gnat.

Detective Newton went to say something else, but Phil cut him off. "We are here because Nicole has something she needs to tell you. She may need your help. Let's say I'm here as her...moral support."

Nicole rolled her eyes.

The detective looked at Nicole. "What is it you want to tell me?"

Nervous, Nicole gripped the side of the chair. "I'm sure it's nothing. I'm sure I'm just being paranoid."

"Let's assume you're not."

"I think I'm being followed."

"You think, or you know?"

"I'm pretty sure."

Detective Newton fiddled with one of the file folders in front of him. "By who?"

"If I knew that, I wouldn't be here, would I?"

The detective narrowed his eyes and refrained from responding to her snarky question. Instead, he went on. "How long has this been happening?" He pushed aside the file folder and grabbed a steno pad. He wrote as she spoke.

She shrugged. "I don't know. A while, I guess."

"Days? Weeks? Months? Years? Ballpark it."

"A few weeks or so."

"What kind of car?"

Nicole rolled her eyes upward. "An oversized black SUV."

With his head down, scribbling on the notepad, Detective Newton asked, "Make and model? I'm going to need some details here."

"I don't know," she shrugged again, her neck knotting. "They all look the same."

"Hyundai? GMC? Toyota? Cadillac? Think."

"I'm not sure," Nicole said in a shaky voice, rubbing the side of her face.

Detective Newton tossed the pen. "Listen, I can't go off that it's an oversized black SUV. I need details. I need a make. Model." His voice grew louder as he tapped his forefinger on the paper.

Phil jumped in. "If she doesn't know the difference, then she doesn't know the difference."

Detective Newton stared at them both. He huffed. "If I show you some emblems, would that help?"

Nicole sighed. "Maybe." It was worth a shot.

The detective jotted down another note, writing swiftly. "Okay, I'll see if I can get images of different car emblems." He set the pen back down. "Did you get the license plate, by any chance?"

"No. I was too busy trying to avoid him. I never had time to see it up close."

"You said him. I assume it was a male driver?"

"Yes."

Detective Newton picked up the pen again and asked, "Can you describe him?"

Nicole squirmed in her chair. "I've gotten a few good looks when I've bumped into him at the grocery store and coffee shop."

"Wait," the detective said, pen poised over the paper. He looked up at Nicole. "He's followed you into places? You've come face-to-face with him?" He put his pen down again.

Nicole cleared her throat. "Yes. Well, not technically."

Detective Newton stared at her, waiting for more.

"Oh, you want me to explain?" she said, his expression changing from inquisitive to annoyed.

"Yes. That'd be helpful."

Nicole heard the irritation in his voice. "He was already in those places when I got there. At least, I think he was. Now I'm not sure. Maybe he followed me in?" she shrugged again, sitting on her hands.

"And you haven't reported this. At all?"

"No."

"Why not?" *What is it with these men*? *First Craig. Then Phil. Now Detective Newton*. She gave him the same explanation.

"So why are you here, telling me this now?"

"Because he's making me do it," she said, thumbing toward Phil, who was rifling through his briefcase. "I told him about it today, and then he called you."

"I see." Detective Newton twirled the ballpoint pen between his fingers like a miniature baton. "Mrs. Cunningham—"

While crossing her legs and placing her hands in the crease, she said, "Please, call me Nicole."

"Nicole, let me be frank with you. I do not think you're being paranoid. This is not in your head. It most certainly is real." Nicole was relieved, yet scared; with the detective validating her suspicion, it truly was happening, thus making it even more frightening.

"I'm going to see if I can find a list of cars and emblems. When I return, we'll see if you can figure out the make and model of the car. Then I'll get a full description of the perp." He stood up, gathering his papers and pen. He opened the door, "And Nicole—"

"Yes?"

"Your son is still a person of interest, and because of that, you absolutely should've come in sooner. This guy might be following you because of your son's involvement in Jaden's disappearance."

Snapping the lock of his briefcase, Phil interjected, "Speculation only. You have no evidence to back up such accusations."

Newton continued. "Okay, let's say, for argument's sake, that your son didn't have anything to do with it. We may have lost our only chance to catch the son of a bitch because you waited too long to report this."

The door clicked behind him.

Nicole looked at Phil with a pained expression. She'd made a grave mistake. And she knew it. *Great. One more way I've screwed with this case,* she thought.

CHAPTER 36

Nicole was mentally spent by the time she finished with Detective Newton. After reviewing what felt like over a hundred cars—all different makes and models—she was confident it'd been a GMC Suburban. After confirming the vehicle, a sketch artist drew a rough image from Nicole's description of what she'd remembered about the man.

Double-checking, ensuring she told him everything and left nothing out, Nicole told the detective about the notes. He asked her if she still had them. She didn't. Unfortunately, she'd thrown them all out.

When finished, Detective Newton thanked her and dismissed them.

As Phil and Nicole left the conference room, she said, "I just want to go home and lie down."

Phil put his hand on her lower back, ushering her toward the exit. Nicole was happy he was here with her. Craig never made it due to unforeseen circumstances.

She hadn't expected it to be such a big deal or mentally taxing. What she'd thought to be of minor importance had become quite significant. "I hope I helped them out here today. I hope I wasn't too late," she said to Phil as they walked toward the front of the station.

"Amber, is that you?"

Nicole heard a familiar-sounding voice. "Amber? It's me, Cecelia Pierce."

Cecelia was here. At the police station.

"Amber!" Cecelia called out again, only louder this time. "It's me, Jaden's mom," she shouted, waving her hand, drawing attention, and causing onlookers to gawk.

Phil leaned closer to Nicole and asked, "Why is Jaden's mother calling you Amber?"

"Don't ask," she whispered harshly. "Just get me out of here."

"I will, on one condition."

"I don't have time for conditions." Nicole lowered her head and covered her face, pretending to cry uncontrollably.

"There, there, it'll be okay," Phil said, patting Nicole's back. "Ma'am, is there a side door we can slip out of?" he asked a young woman in a blue uniform sitting at the nearest desk.

She looked quizzically at the pair. "Yes, it's to your left," she said, pointing toward a door.

Thankfully, Cecelia was still on the other side of the corral door waiting to be buzzed in, but still shouting, "Amber! Amber!" and waving her arm higher overhead, her cream-colored silk blouse swaying in a rhythmic motion.

Cecelia must have felt a deep connection to Nicole after their little chat about their missing kids. Apparently, Nicole had done an excellent job role-playing. Too good.

"Walk faster," Nicole said.

"You owe me." Phil steered her to the left, toward the door. Nicole pretended to sob loudly into her hands. Briefly, she peeked through her fingers and saw Cecelia shaking her head at the policewoman, now on this side of the Plexiglass, saying, "Poor thing. They must've found her daughter. I hope she's okay."

When they reached outside, Phil said, "What the hell was that all about? And why did she call you Amber?"

"Trust me, you don't want to know." She was too tired to explain. And embarrassed. And ashamed.

"If you've gone snooping around, let me be the first to warn you yet again, stop. Don't do it. I work for *your* family. I am on *your* side. Those people in there," he said, gesturing toward the red brick building they'd left, "not so much. They have a job to do and trust me, they don't care who they hurt along the way. They want answers no matter the cost." Spittle flew from his mouth, littering the air.

Sometimes the man terrified her.

"I mean it, Nicole. Don't go sticking your nose in where it doesn't belong. Understand?" He pointed his index finger toward her chest.

Lowering her eyes, she said, "Yes, I understand."

• • • • •

Nicole climbed the stairs, eager to peel off her jeans and crawl into bed. It'd been a hell of a day, and she was grateful for a quiet, empty house. All she wanted to do was to shut the blinds and hide under the covers. She shrugged off her pink shirt and threw on one of Craig's oversized t-shirts. Having his scent near her body comforted her. Feeling heavy from the day's events, she slid under the covers and dozed off.

Jolted out of a deep sleep with a nightmare, Nicole sat up drenched in sweat. Craig's shirt stuck to her body like duct tape. She dreamed Creeper Dude was following her, and he was married to Cecelia and was Jaden's birth father. They hunted down Nicole because Kyle had killed Jaden and sought revenge. She ran to reach Craig, who said he would protect her, but she couldn't get to him. He kept moving further and further away. Creeper Dude had captured her, and that's when she'd awoken.

Heavily panting from the nightmare, sweat droplets trickled down Nicole's back. She checked her surroundings. She was home. Safe in her bed. It hadn't really happened. Still, it had felt incredibly real.

She headed downstairs to the kitchen, thinking a cup of tea might settle her. Steeping the chamomile bag in the boiling water, Nicole's mind wandered back to Cecelia at the police station. Nicole felt guilty about leading Cecelia on, pretending to be the mother of a missing child, and playing on Cecelia's vulnerability for her gain. That's not who Nicole was.

Then her mind flashed to Phil's warning. "Stay out of it," is what he'd said. She hadn't. Now the damage was done. She was withholding what could be possible information and or evidence and lying to her husband. She was becoming someone she didn't like.

All she had wanted to do was make it better. Fix it. Protect her son. Keep him safe. Out of the public eye. Far away from the police's investigation. She convinced herself that any mother would do the same—whatever it took to help their child, no matter the cost, even if that meant snooping, tampering, and lying, or as Nicole defined it, withholding the truth, therefore, technically, not lying.

But she realized her plan had failed. Backfired. Instead of feeling relief, she felt guilt. Mounds of it. Pressing down. Suffocating her. Remorse squeezed her conscience like a vice grip. An innocent man could go to jail. She'd made sure of that when she'd made those anonymous phone calls. And if Chase had anything to do with Jaden's disappearance, and she didn't speak up, he walked free. If she accused Chase, however, she also risked implicating Kyle, who may have done something directly or indirectly to Jaden. It was a complicated labyrinth with only one way out.

Burdened with regret, remorse, and apprehension, Nicole knew what she had to do next. No matter how difficult, she had to come clean. Tell the truth. And she would start with Craig. *The second he gets home,* she thought, *I'll confess everything.* He'd always been her rock. She knew he would comfort her, help her, and make it all better.

Resolved in what came next, albeit uptight to tell him, yet hoping it would rid her guilt of her wrongdoings, Nicole rinsed her empty tea mug and tidied up, too restless to sit while waiting for Craig, expecting him home any minute now.

She heard an engine shut off and a car door close as she picked up an empty glass off the coffee table. She froze. Hadn't Craig told her he was going to take the bus? Maybe he'd caught a ride instead. Either way, he was home. It was time to be held accountable. Thunderous waves roared in her ears as she waited for the front door to open. It didn't. Instead, a knock came.

Not expecting anyone, Nicole walked toward the door. Maybe it was Phil checking in on her, ensuring she was okay after her harrowing day. Or perhaps he was coming to apologize for lecturing her, reprimanding her like that, especially after what she'd been through at the police station. She opened the door, expecting to see a familiar face. It was familiar all right, only not the one she expected.

Nicole screamed and tried to close the door, but the burly man put his tree trunk of an arm out, stopping it. Nicole shouldered his opposing force, but he was much stronger. The door wouldn't budge. She thought about running, but where? He'd follow her, and she assumed him to be much faster; no way she could escape.

"My husband will be home any minute now!" she yelled, pushing all her weight against the door. This was the only defense she could think of. It was all happening too fast, and she didn't have time to think. This was the best she could do given the sudden circumstances.

"You mean Craig," he said in a deep, throaty voice.

Nicole's arm hairs elevated. "How do you know my husband's name?" She lessened her force on the door and peered around the opening. Creeper Dude, dressed in tight-fitting jeans and a black muscle t-shirt, rested his arm back by his side. Nicole noticed the large black GMC Suburban behind him, parked on the street beside her mailbox. She saw a woman sitting in the passenger seat, looking straight ahead. Confused, Nicole pointed and asked, "Who's that?"

"If you let us in, we can explain."

CHAPTER 37

Gabriel said he'd been hired by Trista, the woman wearing her hair in a sleek bob with a long oval-shaped face, sitting across from Nicole.

"Why did she hire you?"

Gabriel looked at Trista, who said, "What I'm about to say will sound absolutely crazy, but I need you to hear me out."

"It sounds like I'm going to need a drink first." Nicole walked over to the liquor cabinet and selected Fireball. She poured a shot's worth into a crystal glass and tipped it back. The heat burned her esophagus, hitting her stomach, warming her insides.

"Miss," Gabriel said.

"Nicole. My name is Nicole, although I'm sure you already know that," she said, pointing at him, clutching the emptied highball glass, "since you've been following me for God knows how long."

"Nicole," he said, using her first name this time. "Trista hired me to follow your husband. Not you."

"Then why the hell were you following *me*?" The liquor radiated throughout her body, all the way to her fingertips, settling her nerves and giving her the courage to lash out.

"Because your car is registered in your husband's name."

"So?"

"So, when I did my due diligence and investigated him—"

"Stalked, more like it," Nicole interrupted. She burped, a slow burn working its way back up. She put her fingers to her lips.

Gabriel continued, his thick necking expanding as he spoke. "Your car's license plate came up under his name. That's why I followed you."

"That's because we share one car, Sherlock." Nicole plopped on the sofa, slumping back. "Why then, when you realized I wasn't Craig, did you keep following me?"

"Trista asked me to."

Nausea took hold. Nicole knew what she'd done and prayed he wasn't acquainted with her indiscretions. Worried, she asked, "Wait, did you investigate me?"

"I ran a background check on you. Squeaky clean, I must say." He laughed, combing his long reddish-brown frizzy beard with his thumb and forefinger.

Nicole didn't find his statement complementary or amusing. She felt vulnerable, like she was standing naked in the middle of a crowd.

Antsy, Nicole stood back up and started pacing. "What do you want from me? Why continue to follow me when it's Craig you're looking for?" Nicole asked, addressing Trista.

Without hesitation, Trista said, "Because I hoped you'd lead me to him. According to Gabriel, however, there was only one time when he'd seen Craig with you, and that was the night you'd gone to the police station."

The room felt overly warm all of a sudden. They knew way more than Nicole would've liked. She stretched her collar, allowing cooler air to seep in.

"Gabriel wasn't about to confront Craig there. That certainly wasn't a good place to do it." Trista blew a wispy, rogue, dirty blonde chunk of hair away from her liquid blue eyes.

Nicole started to relax, thanks to the alcohol. "Why not knock on our door like you did today?"

"I sat out in front of your house numerous times," Gabriel said.

"I'd noticed," Nicole muttered.

Trista twirled the gold stud in her ear. "Never once did Gabriel see Craig come home. Is he ever home?"

"Yes," Nicole defended, "all the time." She poured another shot, enjoying the fiery burn of the brown liquid sliding down the back of her throat, warming her down to her toes. "If you did your due diligence, you'd know Craig is an economics professor here. Why not go to his office?"

Gabriel looked at Trista. "Want to answer that, or should I?"

"You can," she said, nodding her rounded chin in his direction.

Ambivalent to which one was causing the heat—the anger from this woman's presence or the Fireball seeping into her bloodstream—Nicole's face flushed.

"I tried to approach him, but that man is never alone," Gabriel said, shifting his weight from one foot to the other. He hadn't sat down yet. Instead, he stood by the TV, constantly fiddling with the beard that covered half his neck. "He's either in-class lecturing, meeting with students, or working with his assistant. You, on the other hand, seem to be alone. A lot."

Nicole's cheeks burned hotter, spreading to her ears. "Thanks for pointing that out. Why didn't you approach him when he was with someone?"

Trista jumped in. "I asked Gabriel not to."

"Why not?"

"Because what I'm about to tell you isn't what you would want to reveal in a public setting."

The glass in Nicole's hand swung around as she spoke. "And what is it that you want to tell me? You still haven't gotten to that part."

Trista smoothed her pants. "Because you keep asking questions. If you'd let me get this out."

Nicole pinched her thumb and forefinger and ran them along her lips, mimicking a zipper.

Trista took a deep breath. "Your husband is my daughter's father."

Without blinking, without responding, Nicole froze.

"Nicole?" Trista asked, snapping Nicole from her trance.

"I'm sorry, what? It sounded like you said Craig is your daughter's father."

Her lips turning down, Trista said, "I did."

As she processed the information, Nicole's heart squeezed, and pain ricocheted against her ribs. Unsteady on her wobbly knees, she ambled back over to the couch and flopped down, her arm falling to her side, the glass hitting the floor. "I don't understand. I just don't understand. This doesn't make any sense." Nicole shook her head. She sat on the sofa, arms now empty, and crossed them over her chest like a shield, deflecting the words she'd heard. "You're lying!" She narrowed her eyes, glaring at the younger woman sitting at the other end.

"Why would I lie? What do I have to gain?" The woman's sharp blue eyes cut through Nicole.

Nicole had read stories like this in books and magazines, never believing they were true. Sure, she'd seen it on TV, on talk shows like *The Claudia Welch Show*, but she didn't think it happened in real life, especially not hers.

Gabriel chimed in. "I understand you're upset, and it's a lot to take in, but I promise you, it's true."

"I would know if what you're saying is true. I'm Craig's wife." That old, familiar, unsettling feeling in Nicole's gut said otherwise. It roiled, making itself heard. "He would've told me. I know my husband," she insisted. "We don't have secrets." While the words escaped her mouth, she realized how untrue this statement was: she's been sneaking around behind his back, trying to help her family, withholding relevant information.

"You may not understand why I'm doing this. Or even believe me. Hannah, that's my daughter, our daughter," Trista corrected, "has been asking me about her father lately. She's twelve and curious about him. I didn't want to continue lying, so I told her the truth, and now she wants to meet him. Being a mom, you can understand. Don't you think my daughter has a right to know her father?"

Nicole remained silent. She tried to put herself in Trista's shoes, as challenging as it was. If the roles were reversed, what would she do?

Trista continued. "It may not seem like it, but I have scruples and wanted to spare Craig from learning about this in a public place. Not that I owe him shit." Trista wrinkled her forehead, devoid of worry lines. "But I do have a conscience, and I can't imagine how I'd react if I were in your position. I'm sure the shock of this is overwhelming."

"That's an understatement," Nicole said, her blood racing through her veins.

"I felt you should know, and I was worried Craig wouldn't tell you. So when Gabriel figured out it was you he was following and not Craig, I told him to continue. I wanted the chance to talk to you. To tell you myself. I'm doing this woman to woman, mom to mom."

Nicole huffed. "I don't believe it. I think you're making this all up, lying. Are you trying to extort money? Is that it? You need money?" Nicole stopped, another thought occurring. "Are you the one who's been leaving those notes on my car?"

Trista crinkled her button nose. "Notes? What notes?"

"Warning me to keep my nose out of other people's business. Basically threatening me."

"No. I had nothing to do with those. And no, I don't need money." Trista glanced at Gabriel.

"Don't look at him. Look at me," Nicole demanded, feeling drunk on adrenaline and whiskey. "You must need something. Or want *something*."

Trista pinched the bridge of her nose. "I want my daughter to know her father. I want to foster a relationship between the two of them. They've both missed out on too much time already, and I don't want them to lose out on anymore."

"But why now?" Nicole still couldn't figure out why, after all this time, Trista had come forward. It didn't make sense.

"Because it's what my daughter wants. I want to honor her wishes. Do right by her. And as moms, we'd do anything for our children. Yes?"

She should only know. From the rush of spicy cinnamon infiltrating her brain and reeling from Trista's revelation, Nicole said, "I still think you're making this all up."

No matter how much Trista explained it to Nicole, she didn't believe it, even with Gabriel backing it up. Not one word. Not for one second.

CHAPTER 38

Still in shock, disbelief, and denial, Nicole hadn't kicked Trista and Gabriel out despite the ludicrous accusation. Instead, she'd put on a pot of coffee because she was the kind of person who offered people something to eat or drink when in her home. Nicole and Gabriel sat at the kitchen table while Trista excused herself to use the bathroom. Nicole found it nervy of the woman to ask to use it. Still, she pointed down the hallway, directing Trista toward it.

With her nerves somewhat calmer, thanks to that third shot of whiskey, Nicole stared at Gabriel while they waited for Trista. When she finally returned to the table, Gabriel went to speak, but the front door opening stopped him.

Craig shouted from the entry, "Whose car is that?"

"Come and see for yourself."

Craig entered the kitchen. His face drained of all color. His eyes flew open wide, and while watching his face crumble, Nicole knew Trista wasn't lying; she'd been telling the truth. Nicole knew her life, their life, would be forever changed.

"What are you doing here?" he sneered, baring his teeth that matched the color of his face.

Trista raised an eyebrow and looked at Nicole. The Fireball threatened to reappear. She swallowed it with all her might, doing everything to keep the liquid where it belonged. Pressure crashed against her temples like she was a thousand meters underwater. She wanted to punch Craig. Hit him.

Scream. Her tightly pressed lips, however, locked up her voice. She couldn't move. She couldn't even look at him.

"I came looking for you," Trista said calmly, her voice steady, neither wavering nor expressing emotion.

Nicole, on the other hand, was sweaty, nauseous, and dizzy. Her hands trembled.

Craig stood stoic. Only his eyes darted back and forth between the two women.

"Surprise," Trista said, lifting her arms like a guest at a birthday party.

"No. No. You can't be here," Craig said, his voice rising. "How'd you find me?"

Nicole's lips were no longer glued shut. They parted, her mouth dropping open. The initial shock wore off, her voice strong and clear. She jumped in before Trista could answer. "You know her? It's all true?" Nicole's eyes filled with tears, but she refused to cry. "How could you do this to us?" She ignored the lingering lump in her throat. Between the rage and disappointment, it was hard to contain the hot tears stinging the back of her eyes.

"I don't know what she's told you. And who the hell is this?" Craig asked, pointing to Gabriel.

"This is Gabriel, the man who's been following me. The man Trista hired to find *you*."

"And you let him in?"

Nicole flicked away the trickling tear, not answering his last question.

Craig stared at Nicole. "Whatever she's telling you, she's lying."

"I'm not convinced she is," Nicole whispered through dry lips.

"Nic, I'm your husband. You know me. She's psycho." He glared at Trista.

"I wish I could believe you, but I don't know what to believe right now. Who to believe." Another tear rolled down, trailing its predecessor.

Craig walked over and laid his hand on Nicole's fingers. She yanked them away. "Don't touch me."

Trista shot a look at Gabriel as if to say, "Whoa."

"I want to hear it. I want to hear you say it," Nicole sneered.

"Say what?" Craig acted like he had no idea what Trista had told Nicole.

"You had an affair. With her." Nicole tilted her head toward Trista. Trista looked smug. Now Nicole wanted to punch her, too.

"No. No, I didn't."

"Liar! You slept with me. More than once."

Nicole's stomach roiled, the whiskey churning.

"And knocked me up," Trista added.

Craig, who hadn't regained color in his face, turned green. Nicole thought he might be the one to get sick, even though the syrupy, brown liquid sloshing from below was aching to get out.

"So it's true?" Desperate to get to the truth, Nicole ignored the sickness below. "You are her daughter's father?"

"What? No," Craig protested. "This psycho," he said, hitching his thumb toward Trista, "followed me around all semester. I was half tempted to have her removed from class and file a restraining order." He sat down in the last empty chair at the table. Redness crept in, mixing with his ashen face.

"Why didn't you?" Nicole couldn't wait to hear his answer.

"Because, because," he stammered. Craig hung his head low, like a puppy being punished for soiling the carpet.

Nicole watched his face contort as he squirmed uncomfortably in his chair. She was convinced Trista was telling the truth, and Craig was lying. He tried to deny it emphatically, but Nicole didn't believe him. He had no choice but to accept defeat, admitting to his unscrupulous behavior, but he refused to take all the onus for what'd happened.

"Trista says there is one way for you to prove it. To put an end to any speculation," Nicole said.

"How?" Craig asked, looking down at his lap.

"A paternity test," Gabriel said.

Craig's head popped up, sheer terror on his face. "No, absolutely not."

"If you have nothing to hide, if none of this is true, then why not take the test?" Nicole asked.

Craig didn't respond. He fixed his eyes on Nicole's devastated face. His silence spoke volumes—it was all the answer she needed. "Craig, let me make this simple. If you don't take the test, I'll think it's true, and I'll never trust you again. Ever." Nicole suspected she'd never fully trust him again, regardless. He'd had an affair, that much he admitted. That was enough to withdraw all the reserves from her trust bank, leaving a zero balance.

Craig's eyes watered. Nicole never saw him cry, usually unemotional, rarely outwardly expressing his emotions. Despite her anger, Nicole's heart went out to him. His betrayal devastated and hurt her, but he was still her husband. Her Craig. The man she'd loved for over twenty years. The man she devoted her life to.

Silence filled the room, the air saturated, thick with emotion. All eyes were on Craig.

"Fine, I'll do it. For you, Nic. Not for you," he said, glaring and pointing at Trista.

"Thank you," both women said simultaneously, albeit for different reasons.

"When should I do it?"

"Now," Gabriel said. He reached into the back pocket of his tight jeans and pulled out a clear plastic bag filled with the necessary supplies.

Gabriel collected the sample, and the trust between Nicole and Craig sloughed away like the sample being scraped from the inside of his cheek.

CHAPTER 39

When satisfied with what they'd come for, Trista and Gabriel left. The duo was more than happy to, after Craig, in a not-so-friendly manner, asked them to go, leaving Nicole alone with the man standing in front of her whom she no longer knew. He was like a complete stranger. Definitely not the man she'd married.

"I think you should leave, too," Nicole said, not wanting anything to do with him for the time being. She needed time to process everything that'd happened.

In a quivering voice, he refused. "I'm not leaving. We need to work through this. I love you, and I don't want to lose you. You are my whole life."

"You should've thought about that before you went and put your dick where it didn't belong," she spat back. Anger surged through her entire body. She was too angry to even cry.

Stunned at her comment, Craig stood in disbelief but didn't argue. He sulked off to the bedroom as Nicole sat on the sofa, unmoving, shocked by the preceding events.

After an hour of staring at the walls, Nicole decided to sleep in Kyle's room—there was no way she could be near Craig in any capacity—infuriation overriding her deep love for him. Sleep evaded her, ladened with anguish, hurt, and despair. She lay awake, staring at the ceiling or tossing and turning, restless, filled with mixed emotions.

Now knowing who Gabriel was, Nicole toyed with hiring him to follow Kyle and watch his every move. She considered the possibility that it might finally settle the nagging question: was her son somehow involved? She wanted to know the honest answer. With her brain too tired to think anymore, she finally drifted off to sleep after four a.m.

When she awakened, Craig had already left for work, leaving a note on the kitchen table professing his love for her, expressing his anguish for "being such a dickish asshole," as he'd worded it. Nicole ripped it up and tossed it in the trash, as she'd done with all those threatening notes.

Chilled from the events from the night before, Nicole walked into her closet looking for her favorite sweatshirt, hoping it would comfort and warm her. She rummaged through the hangers, unable to find it. She racked her brain where she'd put it. Come to think of it, she couldn't even remember the last time she'd seen it. With the long stretch of warm weather, she hadn't needed it.

"Think, Nicole, think," she said, tapping her chin with her finger. Sometimes, when lost in thought, she'd mix up clothes while folding laundry. Once, she accidentally put her red lace panties in with Craig's pile. He teased her. "Kinky, but not my style." She'd laughed at her absentmindedness and giggled, picturing Craig in her bright red string bikini underwear. And now, as preoccupied as she's been, maybe she'd made the same careless mistake again.

She nosed through Craig's drawers. A stickler for keeping each one neat and orderly, Nicole made a mental note to leave them exactly as she'd found them—he'd notice if one sock were moved even an eighth of an inch.

The sweatshirt wasn't there.

Since Kyle hadn't taken all his clothes to school with him, leaving behind some stuff in his drawers, Nicole checked his room next. She rummaged through his shirts, checking deep down in case the sweatshirt was at the bottom. While shifting a pile to the right, something thudded against the bottom of the wood drawer. Nicole lifted the stack higher to see what had made the unexpected noise. A shiny object jutted out between two shirts near the bottom. Reaching her hand underneath, cold metal met her fingers.

CHAPTER 40

Nicole leaned her weight against the bathroom vanity, staring at her reflection. She didn't know what to do. She didn't know if there was anything to do. Maybe this wasn't a big deal. Maybe she was overreacting, but the last time she'd thought she'd been overreacting, as in being followed, she was right. Last night proved that.

Not wanting Kyle to know that she'd rifled through his drawers in case he went looking for it, Nicole had placed the watch as she'd found it. At least, she thought she had. Now she wasn't sure. She returned to his bedroom, opened the drawer, and double-checked, ensuring the watch was sandwiched between the bottom two shirts.

While sitting on the edge of his bed, Nicole tried to recall if she'd seen Kyle wearing it, or any watch, since he wasn't big on jewelry. One time, when she and Craig had taken a weekend trip, she'd picked out a thin, gold rope chain she thought Kyle would like. All his friends wore similar necklaces back then, and Nicole assumed he'd want one, too. However, when he opened the box neatly wrapped in shimmery silver paper, he politely thanked her and tossed it in his nightstand drawer. The chain never saw the light of day again. Nicole only knew it was there when she stumbled upon it while cleaning his drawer a few years back.

When her fingers had first clasped the smooth metal mere hours ago, she'd thought that's what it was, his necklace, that it'd gotten misplaced or shuffled through the years, but it wasn't that. It was a watch, an expensive one she didn't recognize nor had seen before. Nicole had inspected the brassy timepiece, turning it this way and that, noticing illegible letters etched on the back.

Nicole had removed her cell phone from the side pocket of her camo leggings, turned on the flashlight, and held it close to the shimmery backside. She couldn't read the engraving, no matter how much she'd examined it. It looked like an inscription with the words "to our" at the top and what she thought might be the letters *P.P.* at the bottom. Maybe it was *B.B.,* but because the lower curves had worn off, she couldn't tell. Perplexed by what she'd found, wondering why Kyle had it and where it'd come from, she'd returned it and left the room.

Now, after checking a third time, making sure the watch was exactly where it should be, Nicole collapsed on Kyle's bed. She folded over and propped her chin in her hands. She couldn't confront him because he was upset enough with her comment the other night; he'd never believe it'd been an innocent discovery. He'd assume she'd been nosing around, searching for proof of his culpability.

Her brain worked overtime processing the discovery. Nicole entertained the idea that Kyle had a girlfriend, and maybe it was a gift for her. Or perhaps, Nicole thought, Kyle was holding it for someone else. Perhaps it was a surprise gift, and someone had asked him to keep it safe and hidden. With the letters rubbed off like that, Nicole realized it must be an older watch, making those theories improbable. Maybe it was collateral for a bet that someone had placed? Or perhaps it was repayment?

Nicole's stomach flurried thinking about Kyle's illegal hobby, and then a new theory formed: what if this watch was linked to Jaden somehow? What if Kyle was hiding a piece of evidence?

Nicole sat erect, rubbing her forearms. She doubled over, and her shoulders shuttered as she silently cried. The tears didn't stop. They flowed freely, escaping their prison, where she'd locked them up since the night Jaden had gone missing. She hadn't allowed herself to break down fully. Feel. Mourn. Mourn the loss of their calm, peaceful life. That watch, however, pushed her to the brink. Sent her over the edge, plunging into a deep, emotional abyss.

When her eyes dried, finally devoid of tears, she left Kyle's room and the watch, went to the bathroom, splashed cold water on her red, splotchy face, and headed downstairs, never finding the sweatshirt. She sat at the kitchen table thinking, contemplating, and deciding what should she do next?

She knew what she needed to do, but it was the last thing she *wanted* to do. He wasn't exactly the person she felt like speaking to. With no option, she picked up her cell phone and dialed his number. After being on hold for five minutes, he answered.

"Good afternoon, Detective Newton," Nicole said, her phone nuzzled between her ear and shoulder as she scooped coffee grounds into the filter. If she ever needed coffee, it was now—the past eighteen hours felt more like three days. "I need to update you on the guy who was following me."

"Did you see him again?"

"You could say that." She didn't want to air her dirty laundry to the police, but she had to let him know it had nothing to do with the Jaden case. "He came to my house and—"

"Your house? Are you okay? Did he hurt you?"

Not in the way you think, she thought. "No, I'm fine. Apparently, he was hired by—" Nicole didn't know how to refer to Trista. Ex-girlfriend? Ex-lover? Craig's Baby Mama? What was the appropriate label here?

"By who?" The detective asked, annoyance creeping in.

Nicole sighed and closed her eyes. "Someone my husband used to know. I guess this person had been trying to find him, and Gabriel, Creeper Dude's real name, followed me instead of my husband. We share a car, and because the license plate is registered to his name, Gabriel thought he'd been following my husband, not me. Turns out it was a former colleague of my husband's that'd hired Gabriel," Nicole lied. She didn't need to divulge all the nitty-gritty details.

"So, this guy isn't connected to Jaden's disappearance?"

"No." Nicole was unsure which option was worse: the real reason Gabriel had been following her or if it was connected to the case and her son's possible involvement. They both sucked.

"Thanks for letting me know. We were in the throes of tracking him down, this Gabriel guy. Do you want me to continue investigating him, make sure he's who he says he is?"

"No, but thanks for the offer. I'm sure he's telling the truth. He has nothing to do with your case." Nicole took a sip of her coffee.

"Is he a threat to you or your husband in any way? Maybe you need to file a restraining order?"

While the warm coffee trickled down her throat, Nicole wondered if she could file one against Craig. It may be the only way to keep him away from her. "No, we're good," Nicole lied again. "But thanks for your concern. I appreciate it."

"You should watch who you trust. Let that be a warning."

Nicole's heart stopped. *Let that be a warning.* One of those threatening notes had said something like that, hadn't it? Nicole's shoulders tensed. Hadn't Phil implied some cops aren't on the straight and narrow? Some were unethical. Nicole wondered if Detective Newton wasn't one of them, especially after seeing him in the woods, even though the investigation had been called off.

"Got it," Nicole said, dumping the coffee down the drain. Suddenly, it tasted sour.

"Remember, my job is to put people's safety first."

Nicole didn't believe him.

• • • • •

Awaiting the paternity test proved to be challenging for Nicole. During the past two days, every time her phone buzzed, dinged, or rang, she jumped and grabbed it at the first sound. She was on pins and needles, waiting.

While pulling the last cookie tray out of the oven, her phone rang. She dropped the hot pan on the stovetop and pounced on the phone before it finished a complete ring. Not paying attention to the name, not giving it enough time to register, she was disappointed when she heard Phil's voice on the other end.

"It's nice to talk to you, too," he said sarcastically.

Nicole imagined what bowtie he was wearing today—stripes, polka dots, animals, stars—something quirky for sure and not matching his outfit. "Sorry, I was hoping it was someone else. What's up?"

"Craig called me."

Nicole nearly dropped the phone. "Why?"

She was still avoiding him, walking out of the room any time he entered, and she continued to sleep in Kyle's room. She was unready to deal with their situation because she didn't know how she wanted to deal with it: forgive and forget or leave.

"He told me someone showed up on your doorstep the other night."

Before Phil could say another word, Nicole asked, "What else did he say?"

"He said it was the guy who'd been following you."

Nicole noticed Craig hadn't mentioned anything about Trista to Phil. He'd repeated that a guy had been there, but Nicole found it convenient that Craig hadn't mentioned anything about his ex-lover. Nicole didn't understand why he'd want Phil to know. "I wonder what he wanted?" she said out loud, tossing a potholder into a drawer.

"Who? The guy or Craig?"

She closed the drawer with her hip. "Craig."

"That's the part I found odd. He asked what a man's responsibility would be to an illegitimate child."

Nicole stood in place. Craig would only ask that question if he knew what that paternity test would reveal. He was not a "put the cart before the horse" kind of guy—he dealt with things as they came. "Why would he ask that?" Phil asked, snapping Nicole from thought.

Her blood boiled, furious that Craig had called their attorney, their criminal-law attorney, asking for personal advice. "I don't know," Nicole lied.

An awkward silence filled the space between them.

"Are you okay?" Phil asked, finally breaking it.

"Yeah," she said sullenly.

"Are you sure?"

"Yeah."

"And Craig's okay?"

"Mm-hmm." Nicole poked her finger into the center of a cookie. It squished down, leaving an indent.

"Alrighty then. Oh, by the way, who *was* that guy that showed up?"

"I don't want to talk about it." And she really didn't. Nicole reassured Phil it had nothing to do with Jaden's case or Kyle and that she was perfectly safe.

"Okay, as long as you're safe and Craig is fine, I'll let you handle it."

Oh, I'll handle it, and trust me, when I'm finished with Craig, he'll be anything but fine.

CHAPTER 41

Nicole texted Craig:

Call me ASAP

No response.

Unable to sit around and wait, Nicole drove straight to his office. She wanted to confront him about why he'd called Phil asking for advice. She didn't think the test results could come back that fast. She vaguely remembered Gabriel mentioning something about twenty-four hours, but she hadn't paid attention to that detail between the ringing in her ears and the night being all a blur. And if he'd said twenty-four hours, it was now almost forty-eight.

Maybe Craig had gotten the call, and he hadn't told her. It's not like they were speaking, and besides, if he'd kept one thing from her, a very critical thing, like an affair and an illegitimate child, maybe he was holding the results from her, too.

Nicole drove around looking for a parking spot. No luck. The campus was crowded in the middle of the day as students roamed between the buildings. When she rounded the red-bricked, cathedral-style building a second time, she noticed a mound of flowers and teddy bears amassed under an oak tree. Signs with *We love you, Jaden* and *Justice for Jaden* encircled the shrines.

She spotted an alleyway alongside the building and parked, knowing it was illegal to park without a permit. She didn't care. A parking ticket paled compared to her desire to talk to Craig. She knew being in a public place, especially his place of employment, would curtail their emotions; they'd have to keep them in check and act like civilized adults.

As Nicole rushed into the building, her steps quickened the further down the hall she walked. Anxiety spread down to her fingertips. After her less-than-kind comment, this would be their first time speaking to one another.

His office was within sight as Nicole rounded the corner. She saw her reflection in the gold-plated plaque with "Craig Cunningham" etched on it. The eyes staring back at her blazed with heat. She knocked on the door. No response. She rapped her fist sharper on the dark, stained paneled door. Silence answered again.

He must be in lecture. And as bitter and angry as she was, she was smart enough not to bust into his class and cause a scene. She didn't know what to do or where to go. She didn't want to leave, but she didn't want to wait in the hallway either, her options limited.

Opting to text him, Nicole pulled her cell phone from her purse when she heard voices nearing. One of them was Craig's. She straightened up and smoothed her hair, hoping she didn't look as crazed as she felt.

She needed to know if Craig had a daughter. A pain pierced through her heart. A daughter. Craig may have a daughter. Another child. After their conversation at dinner that night, when Craig had panicked and freaked out, thinking she was pregnant, Nicole realized maybe she was unready to close the door on having another child. Craig, however, had undoubtedly acted like he was. And now, here she stood, in his office hallway, waiting to find out if he had another child. If it turned out to be true, Nicole didn't know how she'd process it. Would she ever accept that Craig got what she desired, no less with another woman?

The footsteps drew closer. Nicole inhaled, drawing in as much breath as possible. She let it out slowly until her lungs were empty, just like she felt.

"Hey," Nicole said, giving a quick wave to Craig.

He stopped dead in his tracks. "What are you doing here?"

Nicole didn't think it was physically possible, yet somehow, Craig's face drained of all color and reddened at the same time.

"I texted you. We need to talk. Now." Too busy focusing on Craig, Nicole hadn't paid attention to the figure standing next to him. It was a woman. No, more like a girl. Super young. Blonde hair, blue eyes, a figure like an AirPod—all boobs, no butt. The girl looked chic, like fashion was as second nature to her as breathing. Her classy black pumps accentuated her bulging calves, and the hemline of her houndstooth skirt showed enough thigh to leave little to the imagination. The neckline of the hot pink, V-neck cashmere sweater plunged further down than it should have, revealing mounds of cleavage.

Embarrassed by how she looked in her worn-out leggings, oversized sweatshirt, and messy ponytail, Nicole ran her fingers through her hair and smoothed her shirt. She felt small—two feet tall at best, wishing she looked better. More put together, not like a madwoman stalking her husband.

She wanted to run, but that would only make her look more unhinged. Instead, she stepped forward and extended her hand to the young knockout. "Hi, I'm Nicole." She spread her lips wide, attempting her best smile. "Craig's wife. Uh, Doctor Cunningham's," she corrected.

Nicole noticed a strange expression cloud over the girl's light eyes. Without skipping a beat, she extended her perfectly manicured fingers to meet Nicole's unpolished ones. "I'm Alexandria, Craig's teaching assistant."

Everything went black.

• • • • •

Nicole held the wet paper towel on her clammy forehead. "How could you not mention that your assistant is a female?" Nicole tried to shout, but it was futile. She groaned at the pain stabbing the back of her head. "No, I stand corrected. She's a girl. A young girl," Nicole said between clenched teeth. "You never once mentioned that Alex was short for Alexandria."

They were home now after Nicole had nearly passed out upon learning his infamous, pain-in-the-ass teaching assistant was a woman. Nicole's knees had buckled, and Alex had been the one to reach out and help steady her. Craig had stood, aghast, like the kid who'd been caught with his hand in the cookie jar before dinner.

When Nicole had regained her balance, Craig sent Alex away, telling her he'd be leaving for the day. *And he may not be coming back at all when I'm through with him,* Nicole had thought.

"I did tell you, babe."

Nicole cringed at the word "babe." She was anything but his babe.

"You just don't remember." He sat down next to her on the lip of the cushion as Nicole lay on her back with the paper towel plastered to her forehead.

"Craig, as God was my witness, you never once said your teaching assistant was a girl. Sure, you bitched and complained about your 'teaching assistant,'" she said, using one hand to air quote while the other one held the damp cloth, "but never once did you use a gender pronoun." Nicole's face heated, the throbbing in her head worsening. "Even that night when *she* dropped you off, I'd suggested I should've gone out to say hi to him. You never corrected me or mentioned *he* was a *she*."

"I don't see why it matters. I've had plenty of female assistants over the years. What's the big deal?"

Nicole chose her words carefully. Once they left her mouth, she knew there was no taking them back. She didn't want emotion to override reason, but it was taxing not to let it. Angry and disgusted with Craig, she still loved him and hated hurting him. She'd regretted lashing out the other night and didn't want to repeat the same behavior.

To avoid his eyes, Nicole closed hers. "I think you purposely withheld this minor detail. I think you didn't want me to know this time." Tears fell down her hot cheeks through closed eyelids. These days, they were impossible to contain. Nicole wiped them away with the back of her free hand.

Craig gasped.

She shot the arrow, and he was wounded. She opened her eyes to see his head hanging low and his hands clasped together. "I didn't purposely leave it out. I understand why it might seem that way after what's transpired here over the past few days," he said, standing up. "You know me, Nic. You have to trust that."

He stood to walk away. Nicole sat up. "Wait," she said, setting the wadded-up towel on the coffee table.

"What?"

Nicole grabbed the table before her, wanting off this dizzying ride. When the room righted itself once again, she said, "I thought I knew you. I thought I knew us. Not anymore. I used to feel sorry for other couples who weren't like us. Happy. In sync. Unable to get enough of each other." She paused and swallowed the lump wedged in her throat. "I devoted my entire life to you. To us. To our family. But now—" Unwanted tears flowed.

"But now, what?" Craig asked with a pained expression. His hollow cheeks sunk further.

"But now, some woman shows up on our doorstep claiming you're the father of her twelve-year-old daughter. Now I'm wondering if she wasn't another female assistant that you forgot to mention?" Nicole looked up at Craig. Pain mixed with the tears pooling in his eyes.

"She wasn't. I swear."

"Then who was she?"

"I don't think this is the best time to get into it. You've had a lot to deal with these past few days. Let's revisit this when you're feeling better."

He turned and walked away again, and as he did, Nicole said, "I don't know if I'll ever feel better." She heard the door click, and Craig was gone.

All alone now, Nicole crumpled on the sofa, a sobbing heap of emotions. She pounded her fists on the cushions. Ignoring her splitting headache, she cried until no more tears fell, the reservoir running dry, at least for now. She'd thought they'd run dry the last time, but since the dam opened, the spillway hadn't stopped.

She hadn't found out the paternity test results. She hadn't found out if they were even in yet. She hadn't found the answers to what she yearned to know. Not feeling any closer to the truth, she lay still, unable to move. Spent. Broken. Exhausted. And that's how Kyle found her, two hours later, when he walked through the door.

CHAPTER 42

Cypressville was known for its beautiful landscapes, architectural history, and erratic weather. It could be gloriously sunny one minute and then torrentially pouring the next. In town, an old saying was, "If you don't like the weather, stick around for five minutes." And with its proximity to the ocean, it was common for strong storms to roll through: cold fronts in the winter, warm fronts in the spring, and hurricanes in the summer.

The small college town was prepping for a major storm, one that had unexpectedly formed off the coast, the meteorologists dubbing it "The Storm of the Century." A frontal boundary mixed with tropical air was moving up from the south, and meteorologists warned residents to be prepared for heavy wind damage, massive flooding, and power outages.

Consumed with the task at hand, readying their home from the impending storm, Nicole and Craig had to work together to prepare everything in time. Spending time with Craig was the last thing she wanted to do, but it was out of necessity. Several trips back and forth to the local home-improvement store to buy the necessary supplies took up all their time over the day. With no word yet on the paternity test results, Nicole suspected the storm would delay the results even longer. A massive storm like this was like dominoes; one piece affected everything in its subsequent path—power lines, gas, the food supply, all of it. A one-day storm potentially knocking down everything behind it.

Craig was out back tying down some trees. Nicole watched him through the kitchen window. Dressed in a tight-fitting, chestnut brown short-sleeved t-shirt, he leaned over, his biceps flaring, showing their size as he wrapped thick twine around the tree trunks. When he stood back up, he wiped his forehead with the back of his forearm. Although filled with bitterness and anger, Nicole was still attracted to him. *What is wrong with me*? she thought.

A powerful gust of wind picked up, and a cluster of leaves swirled in a cyclone formation around his feet. A branch snapped off the tree, and Craig reached out with his gloved hand to stop it from becoming a harmful projectile. He saw Nicole in the window watching him, and he flashed her that smile that made her melt. She jumped back, out of eyesight, not wanting to send him the wrong message.

To keep busy, she put fresh batteries in the flashlights and lined up the candles on the dining room table along with the lighters. She finished cooking, using the perishable foods in the fridge. If they lost power, they could reheat the food on the grill.

Kyle opened the front door as Nicole bustled around the kitchen. The wind created a tunnel effect from the back screen door opening, causing the front door to slam shut, startling her. She dropped the meatloaf on the floor; the juices splattered, dotting the floor and her exposed legs with grease freckles. "Shit."

"Sorry," Kyle said, kneeling beside her, helping her gather the misshapen meat.

"Don't worry about it. If the power goes out, we would've had to waste it, anyway." She tossed the hunk of junk in the trash.

"I'm sure you heard classes were canceled," Kyle said, wetting paper towels to sop up the greasy dots.

Nicole cleaned off her shins. "Yeah. That's why your father's home. He's out back tying down the trees."

When Kyle had come home to find Nicole in pieces, she'd explained she hadn't been sleeping and was overtired and hormonal. At the mere mention of hormones, Kyle didn't ask another question. He'd taken her word for it. She hadn't wanted to say anything to him yet, on the off chance that the paternity test returned in Craig's favor. No need to bring their son into their mess.

"You feeling better?" he asked, stepping on the trash can lever and tossing in the stained paper towel.

"Yes, much," she lied. She knew he could see the truth on her face. The dark circles cohabitating under her eyes and her hollow cheeks revealed the honest answer. "I figured you'd hunker down with the fraternity brothers," she said, washing the abandoned pan.

"Yeah, I am. I want to grab a few things before I go back."

The watch. Was he here to retrieve the watch? She hadn't completely forgotten about it, but with her focus on the other events as of late, it hadn't been top of mind.

Kyle went to his room. Nicole heard drawers opening and closing. He kissed her on the cheek as he passed back through the kitchen, his sneakers leaving tread marks on the wet floor.

She noticed his empty hands. "Where's your stuff?" she asked.

"Got what I need," he said, patting the right front pocket of his cargo shorts. And like the gust of wind that had whooshed through earlier, he was gone.

• • • • •

The storm rolled through Cypressville, leaving a path of destruction. It lasted less than twelve hours, but the residents would have weeks of cleanup. As soon as it cleared out, the next morning, Nicole and Craig were raking up the trail of limbs, branches, and twigs in their driveway when Craig received the news from Gabriel. With ninety-nine percent accuracy, Craig was Hannah's father.

Nicole dropped her rake, ran into the house, and became ill in the kitchen sink. That morning's breakfast washed down the drain with the hope that it wasn't true.

Kyle, who'd come home to help clean up after the storm at Craig's request for the extra set of hands, heard the commotion and ran out of his room to find Nicole bent over the sink. "Oh, my God. Mom, are you okay?"

She didn't know how to answer. Should she tell Kyle about Hannah? Should Craig? Or should they do it together?

She wiped her mouth with the back of her hand. "I'm okay. I guess the exhaustion got to me." She needed time to absorb this news and find out what came next. After splashing cold water on her face, she went to the bay window and watched Craig pace in the driveway, muttering to himself, running his hands through his hair.

Nicole stood in front of Kyle, blocking his view. She didn't need him asking any more questions, like why his father was pacing like a madman in the driveway.

"Hope you feel better," he said, returning to his room. "If you need anything, let me know," he shouted over his shoulder.

When Kyle had left yesterday to return to the fraternity house, she'd checked his drawer; the watch was still there. She didn't know what he'd taken and didn't care. The watch hadn't been moved.

"Hey, you need to help us clean up," she called after him.

"Yeah, yeah. I know. I'll be out in a few." He shut his bedroom door.

Craig found Nicole, head down, retching over the kitchen sink.

"Are you okay?" he asked, rushing to her side, rubbing his hand on her back.

She shirked him off. "I'm anything but okay!"

"Shh. Kyle will hear," Craig said, jutting his head toward Kyle's bedroom.

"I don't care anymore. He needs to know. He'll find out, anyway. Unless you're going to hide the fact that you have a daughter?" Nicole choked. She felt sick again. Anger burned in the depths of her soul, taking control. She shoved her finger into his chest, tapping the center of the hawk logo on his shirt. "You son of a bitch! How could you do this to us? How? We've got enough shit going on, and now this? What happens next, Craig? What? Huh? Have you thought any of this through? Do you have her part-time? Does she live with us? Do you pay child support? Does Hannah even want a relationship with you?" Questions flew out of Nicole's mouth faster than Craig could answer.

"I don't know," he said quietly.

"And Trista. What about Trista? You know, she's a part of our lives now, too. Forever. Did that thought ever occur to you? Huh?" she continued to peck at his chest, Craig allowing her. He'd screwed up in the most significant way possible; one indiscretion with a lifetime of consequence.

"I'm so sorry, Nic." His eyes watered. Nicole wondered why he was sorry—for what he'd done, or that he'd been caught? She blew a frizzy, rogue hair from her mouth. "It's too late for sorry. I want you out."

"You can't be serious."

Nicole noticed sweat droplets dripping from his hairline down his forehead. "Oh, I am. Dead serious."

"Nic," he pleaded, "Don't do this. We can work through this. We'll figure it out. We can do a pros and cons list."

"I don't want to make one of your precious lists. There are zero pros to this situation," she said, making a circle with her hand.

"Love. Our love is a pro."

"You don't know what love is." She was getting good at throwing daggers.

Craig extended his arm toward Nicole, stepping closer. "I know I love you. And Kyle. I love our family."

Nicole retreated, her backside pressed against the counter by the sink. "If you loved us, you wouldn't have done what you did. And I only found out because your baby mama showed up. If she hadn't, then I'd still be in the dark. Blind to your betrayal."

Kyle came out again, "What's going on?" He looked at Craig and Nicole standing squarely in front of one another.

"Tell him," Nicole ordered Craig, pointing to Kyle.

Craig stared at her, his eyes begging her not to make him do it. "Tell him, or I will," she demanded, folding her arms over her heaving chest.

"Tell me what? What the hell is going on?"

Craig remained tight-lipped.

"You have a half-sister," Nicole said, brushing past Craig, storming out of the room.

CHAPTER 43

"I can't believe I have a sister," Kyle told Nicole.

"Half-sister," Nicole corrected him, reminding her she hadn't been the one who'd provided a sibling for Kyle. That other woman had. It was the tenth time Kyle had said it in the past few hours. Craig hadn't given Kyle the gritty details, but Craig finally confessed about Trista and Hannah. Kyle was as disappointed and disgusted with Craig as Nicole.

Given the current mood, feeling ganged up on and not welcomed in his own home, Craig had packed a bag and left, honoring Nicole's wishes. She didn't know where he was going, nor did she care. She assumed, most likely, he'd hole up in his office or head to a local motel or somewhere close to campus since she'd insisted on keeping the car. Hell, maybe he was going to shack up with that tart, Alex. Wherever he went was fine, as long as he was far away. Nicole needed time. And space. Lots of both.

With Craig gone, Nicole and Kyle sat on the couch. "I know," she said. "It's so...surreal." They were watching mindless mid-morning shows like *Renovate My Home*. Nicole loved seeing how an unsalvageable house transformed into something worth saving.

"It's like nuts," Kyle said, shaking his head for the umpteenth time.

Nicole sipped her coffee, her best friend these days. It was the only thing keeping her awake and functioning after many sleepless nights. "I know. It's surreal."

"Is that all you can say?"

Nicole chuckled. "No, I can say more. Lots more, but I'm trying to control myself. He's still your father, and I don't want to disparage him, although, technically, he deserves it."

"I'm furious, too."

Music played on the TV, and the words *Breaking News* flashed on the screen. Nicole leaned forward and held up her hand, stopping Kyle from saying more. "I want to hear this."

Darlene, that friendly reporter, stood in front of the woods, and the first thing Nicole noticed was the bright yellow *Crime Scene* tape wrapped around the towering pine trees. Previously absent, that was new. "We have breaking news in the Jaden Pierce case," she said somberly, the first time she was anything but chipper.

"Do you think they found him?" Kyle asked, his mouth turning down.

Nicole glanced sideways, watching if he somehow knew the answer. That uncomfortable, tiny thread of doubt weaved into her brain. She shook her head, ridding herself of the thought and refocused on the TV.

"A local man was fishing on Lake Cypress when he hooked what he thought was a big fish. Unfortunately, it wasn't. It was a piece of clothing."

Nicole gasped.

Kyle put his hand over his mouth.

Darlene continued. "Police believe it to be a piece of Jaden's shirt. It matches the description of what he was last seen wearing the night he disappeared."

Once again, Nicole looked at Kyle, trying to read his reaction. He stared at the screen, unblinking, his eyebrows knitted together like concentrating on a laborious task.

Darlene continued, "Despite not finding anything the last time, police are sending in a dive team again. They believe the storm may have turned up whatever was embedded at the bottom of the lake. They're speculating if maybe the murky water may have hidden the body. We will have to wait and see. Darlene Moore, reporting live from Lake Cypress."

Nicole's phone blew up, dinging rapidly like a trolley car. Sylvia, Phil, and Craig were all sending messages about what she and Kyle had just watched. Nicole typed furiously, responding to two of the three, opting to ignore Craig, carefully choosing her words with Sylvia.

Kyle's phone dinged, too.

Slowly, Nicole looked over at him. He was green—an ugly, putrid, horrific shade of green. "Are you okay?" she asked. His hands shook as he typed. Perspiration dotted his upper lip, and he focused on his phone.

"Kyle!" she said, getting his attention.

He jumped. "What?"

"Are you okay?"

"Yes, fine. Why wouldn't I be?" He didn't look fine. He looked uneasy. Worried.

"I don't know. You don't look right. What's wrong?"

"Oh, here we go again. You think I had something to do with it, don't you?"

Nicole gently placed her hand on his arm. His defensive stance fueled her suspicions, but she had to lie. She couldn't afford to offend him again. "I don't. You're acting...off."

"My fraternity brother may be dead at the bottom of Lake Cypress. Obviously, I'm off."

Nicole hadn't thought about how that would affect him. "I'm sorry. This must be painful for you."

"More than you know," he said under his breath.

Not wanting to push the issue further, Nicole jumped on her social media accounts. They were blowing up with the latest update, people sending messages, everyone praying for the best possible outcome, but it didn't look like that would be the case.

• • • • •

The entire town waited on edge for what felt like days. In reality, it'd only been eight hours. Nicole was a mess, anxiously awaiting, wanting, and needing a definitive answer. The whole town needed an answer. She knew she'd feel awful if Jaden turned up dead. However, she needed respite from the constant wondering. Somehow, knowing was comfort—freedom from being in limbo.

She didn't have to wait any longer.

Sullen, Detective Newton stood at dusk, the sun setting behind him. "It is with great sadness that I stand here today to let you all know we have recovered Jaden Pierce's body. Our community mourns the loss of such a young soul. Unfortunately, we don't know how he died. This is an ongoing investigation, and we ask for your full cooperation. Let us do our job. We will find out what happened to him, and if foul play was involved, I promise you, whoever is responsible will pay."

Kyle sniffled. Nicole wrapped her arms around him. Consumed with her motives and sorting through Craig's lies, Nicole had overlooked that Jaden was her son's friend. Not only had Kyle been dealing with being questioned, but he was also dealing with the loss of a friend. A brother.

Nicole comforted Kyle as he sobbed in her arms. "I'm so sorry, baby," she repeated, rocking him as he wept.

"I can't believe they found him. I don't know what I was thinking. I thought he'd taken off on his own, you know. Or he'd come back safe."

Kyle's raw emotion gave Nicole a sliver of hope. There was no way he could react this way if he'd had anything to do with it, could he? He was either genuinely innocent or an outstanding actor. "I know, I know," she said, not letting go.

"But now, he's dead. Gone. I can't believe it." Kyle continued to cry.

"Me either, baby. Me either." Nicole squeezed him tighter.

Recovering the body may have put part of the mystery to rest, but learning the cause of death would trigger a whole new nightmare.

CHAPTER 44

Discovering Jaden's body brought a bigger media frenzy to Cypressville. Stations from all over the state, and others, swarmed to cover the case. They hovered like a flock of vultures circling their prey. It'd been less than twenty-four hours since they'd pulled Jaden's body from the lake, and already everyone was irate, impatient, wanting answers. Unfortunately, the preliminary report would take a few more days to come back. It would be weeks before they had the final autopsy. Not good enough for the public, especially not for Jaden's parents.

Nicole remained glued to the TV, skipping workouts, baking, or even showering. She stayed put on the sofa, eager eyes fixated on the screen. Rumors continued to circulate, speculation filling the airwaves. Misleading information flooded social media, accusations flying, none with any substantial proof to back them up.

Nicole's phone hadn't stopped since the news broke, notifications blowing up, alerting her of social media updates, news stories, and text messages. She checked her phone after each ding, beep, or buzz. More times than not, it was Craig, like now.

Please, please, please, hear me out!

She considered blocking his number but ignored the barrage of messages instead.

"How long until you answer him?" Kyle asked. He'd spent the night again last night. He returned to the fraternity house briefly to grab a few things. Without Craig home, Kyle had told Nicole he didn't want her alone.

She was relieved to have him here. She could help comfort him during this difficult time.

Nicole scowled at the screen and tossed the phone on the table. "I don't know. I haven't decided."

"I hope it's soon. He hasn't stopped texting me either, begging me to get you to talk to him. It's annoying," Kyle said, lifting his phone and showing her his screen.

"Sorry."

Nicole didn't know what to say to Craig. He'd pulled the rug out from underneath her, and she hadn't been able to get her footing since. *My parents must be rolling over in their graves,* she thought. They'd warned her about marrying a man she barely knew. Nicole had vowed to prove them wrong by devoting herself to her marriage every day, no matter the circumstances, and for twenty years she succeeded, holding to her promise. Sadly, unbeknownst to her, Craig hadn't done the same. Her marriage was a lie. What she thought was solid, strong, and indestructible, built on a sturdy foundation of commitment, was built on a platform of deception.

She needed time. She didn't want to act rashly. Polar opposite emotions lived in her heart once again. This time, however, they were anger, disappointment, and disgust, all sharing the same space with the love that had slowly etched its way in, carving itself deeper until permanently inked, like a tattoo. A few days' passing can't undo that kind of love.

"Maybe hear him out," Kyle suggested.

"Why should I? And why aren't you angrier with him? He did this to you, too. You have a half-sister. One you've never even met."

"I am angry. Don't think I'm not. But he's still my father, and he didn't cheat on me."

Nicole winced, her usually smooth forehead wrinkled.

"Sorry."

"It's okay," she said, touching Kyle's forearm. "It's still fresh and new. It's impossible to process it all."

"I'm just saying, maybe hear him out. And then, after you do, if you still feel the same, you can ignore him," Kyle said, twirling his phone against his lap.

"Who made you the love expert? Have you been watching that shitty *Claudia Welch Show*?" Nicole gestured to the TV.

"No," he said, shrugging. "Psychology courses, I guess."

"You're a wise young man." She kissed his forehead and picked up her phone to find three more messages from Craig.

• • • • •

Nicole chose a very public place to meet Craig; he'd jumped on the chance to meet her when she'd suggested they meet the following evening at an outdoor restaurant known for its local seafood, *Captain Tom's*. With a large crowd consistently present, it was the perfect place to drown out their conversation, making it private, yet public enough, to have people around her if it went south—a safety net of sorts.

She was already seated when Craig arrived. He looked amazing. Freshly shaven, hair combed back, and wearing a mint-green polo shirt with two top buttons open. He flashed his infamous smile, showboating his dimple and polished white teeth.

"Hi," she said in a small voice, sitting on the opposite bench at the picnic-styled table. Not very comfortable for sitting, it completed the local backyard-style restaurant's theme, right down to the faded, chipped red paint, now almost pink, from years' worth of sun damage. It looked like one of those accidentally found priceless antiques, one that had been dumped thinking it was trash, only to be worth a fortune.

Nicole read the sadness in Craig's eyes. More hurt piled on her heavy heart. With almost too much weight to bear, she felt like it might crack under pressure. A waft of his familiar musky cologne tickled her nose, carried by the gentle breeze. It took her back to when they were happily married, at least she thought they were, and with that thought, whatever sympathy she'd had moments ago vanished, like the scent disappearing with the wind. She looked down at her lap, not wanting to look him in the eye, not wanting to succumb to his despair or charm. She needed to stay strong.

"You look beautiful," he said, folding onto the bench.

She blushed, lowering her head. "Thanks." Wearing her Gingham jumper that hugged her curves in all the right places, she felt anything but.

He lowered his head. "Thanks for meeting me. I know this isn't easy for you."

He had no idea how unbearable this was not living it from this side. He wasn't the recipient. Instead, he was the instigator, the one who'd caused it. She picked up a menu pretending to read it even though she knew what she'd order, always choosing the same thing here—crab cakes, her favorite, the menu simply acting as a barrier.

"What are you going to get?" he asked, trying to make small talk.

Nicole didn't want any part of it. "My usual."

He also perused the menu, commenting on today's specials, the prices, the font, anything to keep the conversation flowing. Nicole's one-word answers stopped that. Her walls were up, and his idle chit-chat wouldn't tear them down. She wasn't sure if anything would.

After ordering, Nicole cut to the chase. "Why did you want to meet? What could you possibly have to say to me to fix this?"

Craig leaned in closer, not wanting to shout over the loud conversations around them. "I'm incredibly sorry that I've hurt you, Nic. You are my world, and I fucked up."

"Yeah, you did." She looked up at the sky. At the next table. At the wood floor. At anything to avoid his eye contact.

"I know. And I know I've forever changed our lives, but I need you now more than ever. I'm terrified of losing you. I need you by my side through all this: meeting Hannah, navigating time-sharing, my new job, all of it."

"You got the promotion?" This news surprised Nicole. She wondered how he'd suddenly learned to work with Dr. Graham's program, and she thought Craig wouldn't find out about the promotion until the end of the semester.

"No. Not yet, but *when* I do—"

Nicole thought how presumptuous of him to assume he'd get the job.

"I'll need you," he continued, touching her arm across the splintered table.

Dodging his advances, she leaned away, the slivered surface scratching the soft inside of her forearm. "I will give you this last chance, and I mean it. This is the last chance for you to come clean. No more lies. The truth. All of it." She stared at Craig. Her mood eyes displayed their mossy green color, signifying the fire.

"Fine," he sighed.

Trista had been one of his students when he'd taught at the community college in Dorado, the town she and Craig had lived in before he took the job here in Cypressville. The affair hadn't lasted long—a little over two months. Trista had come to his office begging him for help in his class, so he worked with her to help her pull up her grade. While doing so, Trista fell in love with him. Given their ten-year age difference, she saw him as her knight in shining armor, a savior.

Craig said they'd started sleeping together shortly after their one-on-one sessions began, and when he'd called it off, Trista came to him, begging him to take her back. He'd tried to explain that what they were doing was wrong on so many levels, including betraying his wife and jeopardizing his job. And that's when Trista told him she was pregnant.

At first, Craig had thought she was bluffing, but when he found out that she was indeed pregnant, he questioned if it was even his. When Trista assured him, yes it was, Craig suggested terminating the pregnancy. She'd refused, threatening to tell Nicole and the higher-ups if he didn't take responsibility. Still unconvinced it was his because Trista had recently broken up with a boyfriend, and with no way to prove it, Craig worried she'd follow through with the threat. He'd paid her ten-thousand dollars to quiet her, and they both agreed never to speak of what had happened.

Craig had been fired from that job and hadn't resigned like he'd led Nicole to believe. Ultimately, Trista had gone to the dean, and Craig had been let go. Immediately following his dismissal, he'd applied to the College of Cypressville, where he was hired on the spot, leaving Trista, their baby, and his secret behind as he moved his wife, young son, and himself to a new town. A new school with a clean slate, never once looking back.

Nicole sat stunned. Her mouth hung open. She didn't know. About any of it.

"Say something."

Nicole blinked. "What do you want me to say? What could I possibly say after hearing all that?" Emotions churned like a bubbling cauldron: shock, anger, disbelief, outrage, intermixing, ready to boil over. "What are you hoping I'll say?"

He shrugged. "I don't know. Maybe you forgive me?"

"Forgive you? You think you can unload years' worth of lies and expect me to what? Immediately forgive you? It'll take years to process all of this, and even then, I don't know if I can ever forgive you."

A group of girls celebrating a birthday at the table behind them stopped talking and watched as Nicole continued. "You lied, my greatest pet peeve. You broke my trust. You broke us." Her face reddened. She hit the table with her hands, causing Craig to jump. "You did this. You," she said louder, waggling her finger at him. The girl at the end of the celebratory table, wearing a tiara with the words *Birthday Queen*, giggled.

"You're making a scene," Craig said, leaning in.

Nicole side-eyed the gawking girls. "I. Don't. Care. I loved you. Supported you. Not anymore. I'm done."

"It was one mistake. Please, I'm begging you."

Nicole closed her eyes and calmed herself. "Really, Craig? One mistake? I don't believe you. I think you're lying to me now. Here. Today. Again."

"I'm not. I swear. Why would you even think that?"

"Let's start with Alex," she said, "and then we can move on to the money missing in our account."

CHAPTER 45

Thank God for Google—Nicole's new best friend, replacing coffee's previous title. And, in fact, her only friend these days. She typed in an address, the one she'd looked up online. If Craig wouldn't give her the answers, she would find them herself.

Nicole's mind wandered back to the disastrous dinner while driving toward her destination. She thought about all Craig's lies—she hadn't believed a word he'd said. She hadn't bought his excuse, swearing he'd told her that Alex was a female, and she certainly hadn't bought his cock and bull story about the money being used in a "guaranteed to double your money" scheme that one of his former colleagues had insisted he invest in. Nicole knew Craig was more intelligent than that. He was an economics professor. To her, everything he said was a lie.

And then a sickening feeling washed over her. Hadn't she done the same thing? Hadn't she snuck behind his back? Lied to him. She squashed the thought like a pesky bug, justifying it by saying it'd been for a good reason—to help their son. Their family. She didn't feel it was breaking her rule if good intent was behind it. Besides, she didn't think she was lying. She merely omitted some facts. Bent the truth. What Craig had done was entirely different; he'd outright lied to protect himself. Nobody else.

Nicole vowed to find the truth. Without sneaking around this time. She didn't like who she'd become when she interfered before. She learned her lesson. Being deceitful made her feel worse, dishonest, and devious. She couldn't behave that way again because she didn't want to feel that way again. This time she would go straight to the source—Alex.

Alex lived in a quaint apartment village on the outskirts of campus. Most students lived in the dorms their first year and moved further away from campus each subsequent one. Nicole pegged Alex to be at least a first-year grad student by how far away her apartment was from campus.

Nicole climbed the stairs to the second floor, looking for apartment 202. Her heart beat fast from the uphill climb and the adrenaline pumping in her legs. She knocked loudly, sending the dog next door into a barking frenzy.

Footsteps approached. "Can I help you?" a voice said through the closed door.

Nicole's stomach fluttered like tiny butterflies furiously flapping their wings, trying to escape, but these were no butterflies, these were nerves. "Yes, I'm looking for Alexandria. Is she here?"

"Hang on." The footsteps faded, and then no sound at all. Nicole waited. Sweat pooled under her arms, even in the cool breeze. The footsteps started again. The lock clicked, and Alex opened the door. "Mrs. Cunningham," she said, opening her eyes wide, revealing how blue they were. Almost violet. "What are you doing here? Is Dr. Cunningham okay?"

"He's fine. Um, I was wondering if I could talk to you for a few minutes?" Nicole peeked inside the apartment, taking in the décor. Alex had exquisite taste.

"Sure. Come in." She opened the door wider and ushered Nicole inside.

Nicole entered the posh little apartment. It was decorated in complementary grays and blues, more elaborate than Nicole's college days. The modern farmhouse style made Nicole wonder if Chip and Joanna Gaines had decorated it. Black orbital light fixtures hung over the kitchen island, matching the hardware on the rustic barn door that separated the living room from the den. A thick shaggy rug, which looked like a Maltese dog, sat on the floor in front of the stone fireplace. "I love your apartment. It's beautiful," Nicole said, taking it all in.

Alex blushed. "Thanks, but I can't take any credit. My roommate, Olivia, did all the decorating. She's studying interior decorating."

"Ah, makes sense," Nicole said, admiring how coordinated everything was, down to the color-coordinated, fuzzy throw blankets draped over the backside of the plush sofa.

"Please, have a seat." Alex gestured toward it. Nicole sank into the soft, feather-filled cushions.

"What did you want to talk to me about, Mrs. Cunningham?"

"Please, call me Nicole."

"Okay, Nicole," Alex said, arching her perfectly plucked eyebrows. She sat on a low-backed, wood and metal barstool, matching everything else.

"I want to talk to you about my husband." Nicole studied Alex's face, watching for any change in expression. Nothing.

"What about him?"

With no substantial proof, solely acting on a hunch, Nicole said, "I know about you two."

Alex squirmed in her chair, readjusting her frayed denim shorts (too short in Nicole's opinion and inappropriate, given the cool weather) by pulling them lower on her bronzed thighs. Snubbing Nicole's accusation, Alex remained silent, locking eyes with Nicole.

"Did you hear what I said?" Nicole asked nervous Alex might kick her out with that bold allegation. Nicole knew if asked to leave, she'd never get what she'd come for; Alex's version of her and Craig's relationship.

Alex's neck strained when she tried to swallow, her cleavage peeking out of her baby doll t-shirt moving in succession. "Yes, I heard you." She averted her eyes and looked out the window.

"And?"

Sunlight streamed into the apartment, highlighting Alex's blue eyes. "I can't believe he told you. He swore he wouldn't say a word to anyone. Ever."

An unwelcome pain stabbed at Nicole's heart. "How long has it been going on?"

With that question, Alex burst into tears. She dropped her head into her hands and sobbed. Nicole almost felt bad for her. Almost. After all, she was young and vulnerable, and Nicole suspected Craig preyed upon that. It certainly seemed to be his pattern. He'd done it with Nicole when she'd been around the same age, Trista at his previous school, and now, Nicole assumed, Alex.

Nicole watched as Alex shook, sobbing. She hiccupped and sniffled, finally looking up. Dark black mascara trailed her porcelain skin like an old, tired, worn-out prostitute.

"I called it off a while ago, but Craig wouldn't leave it alone."

Nicole didn't think any parts of her heart were left to break. She was wrong. Another sliver cracked off.

Alex sobbed harder.

"Alex, I need you to take a breath. Calm down. I can't understand what you're saying." Nicole couldn't believe she had to comfort her husband's mistress despite her entire life being turned upside down.

"Sorry. I am sorry. I am so, so sorry," Alex sniveled.

"Believe it or not, I'm not upset with you. I just need to hear your side of the story." Nicole readjusted the wide collar of her red and white striped pullover.

Alex nodded. She gulped down air, like fighting for her last breath. Her shoulders shook with each greedy mouthful. When her breathing regulated, she sighed and told Nicole the story. "I was a student in Craig's...is it okay if I call him that instead of Dr. Cunningham?"

Nicole nodded. *No need to be formal when you've seen my husband naked.*

Alex continued. "I was a student in Craig's class. One day, last year after class, he'd approached me and said how impressed he was with a paper I'd turned in, so much so that he wanted me to apply to be his teaching assistant for this year. I was honored. And shocked. With hundreds of students in his lectures, he sought me out."

And your boobs. Nicole couldn't stop the thought, looking at the chesty girl.

"I met with him the next day to start the process."

"Did he do anything inappropriate that day?"

"No, no way. If he had, I assure you, I never would've followed through with the assistantship. It wasn't until I was officially hired for the position that he started flirting, making sexual innuendos, stuff like that."

"Why didn't you quit then?"

"Because, at first, it felt nice. I was flattered that this high-powered professor found me attractive. It sounds sick now that I'm saying it, but at the time, it was like...a game, I guess. Harmless fun, you know?"

Nicole was unsure if that was a rhetorical question. Before she could find out, Alex continued. "He told me he wasn't married. I didn't know until a month after we'd started sleeping together."

Nicole blinked back hot tears. Another sliver of her heart dislodged.

"Sorry, I can stop if you'd like. I wouldn't blame you for not wanting to hear the rest."

"No, no. It's okay. Please, go on." Nicole willed back the tears. She needed to hear it. All of it. No matter how much it hurt.

"When I found out he was married, I told him I was done. I was angry. Humiliated. Disgusted. But he wouldn't let it rest." Alex stopped.

Nicole seized the opportunistic pause with a question. "When you found out he was married, why didn't you quit? Or go to the higher-ups and report him?"

Nicole saw Alex struggling, grappling with something else. Something she appeared to be holding back. Panicked that Alex would stop, Nicole softened her face and tone, afraid of not getting the answers. "You can tell me anything. Everything. The damage is done. I assure you, you can't make it any worse."

Nicole was done with Craig. For good, another indiscretion giving her the final permission to sever all ties, once and for all. How many other women had he lured in? She wasn't sure she could handle the answer. "Why didn't you quit or report him?" Nicole asked again.

Alex rubbed her palms on her long-tanned thighs. "Because—"

Nicole had a repulsive thought. What if Alex was pregnant? Another illegitimate child, the only thing that could make this worse. "Did he knock you up?" Nicole asked abruptly.

Alex's eyes popped. "Oh God, no! We were careful every time," she said, turning pink.

Nicole cringed.

Alex looked down. "Sorry. I can't imagine how horrendous this is for you."

Nicole didn't want or need this girl's sympathy or empathy. She needed answers. "Because why?" she asked, picking up where Alex had left off.

Alex closed her eyes. "Because Craig was blackmailing me."

"I don't understand."

"Craig threatened me if I didn't meet his demands."

Nicole rolled her eyes inside her head. "I get how blackmail works. What I don't understand is what did he have over you?" Nicole thought there was no way this young girl had lived enough of a life to have done anything Craig could use against her.

"Jaden's disappearance."

Nicole's breath caught in her throat. Her brain churned, trying to compute what Alex was saying, but Nicole couldn't, no matter how hard she ruminated. "I'm not sure I'm following."

Alex sighed. She placed her foot on the barstool next to her other lean leg and folded her fingers, hooking them around her propped-up knee. "Craig told me if I didn't meet his demands, he'd go to the authorities and tell them I'd killed Jaden."

That was a lot to unpack. Nicole had a long list of questions to follow up with and needed to figure out where to start. While she quickly prioritized them mentally, Alex continued.

"I'm sorry, Nicole. For everything. I'm sorry I slept with your husband. I'm sorry I left those notes. I'm sorry for all of it."

All the questions swirling in Nicole's brain moments ago stopped. Everything appeared fuzzy. Nicole felt like she was in an alternate dimension. She knew what notes Alex was referring to. Nicole didn't want Alex to see how stunned she was. Nicole bit the inside of her cheek, regaining control. "You were the one who left those messages on my car?"

Alex nodded. "Yes."

Confirmation elicited another long list of questions, but Nicole needed to clarify a previous statement first. "None of this makes sense. Why was Craig blackmailing you?"

Alex wiggled in the chair, readjusting her shorts again. "Because he said he knew he wouldn't get that promotion if anyone found out he'd been sleeping with me. He said he'd lose his job and that he couldn't afford that."

Nicole noticed Craig hadn't been worried about losing his wife or family, only his promotion and job.

"He promised me that if I told anybody, he'd make sure they never believed me. He said he'd deny it and that no one would ever take my word over his, and I believed him. You hear stories like this all the time. Girl reports boy, he denies it, says she's made it up. I was afraid people would say I'd asked for it. That it was my fault." Tears dotted her pink cheeks.

Nicole felt bad. She empathized with what Alex was saying. It was true. Nicole had seen and heard it enough times, men using their power like that. She sat listening, her breath coming in short, quick waves.

Alex shivered and hugged her knee tighter. "One day, I told Craig I didn't care anymore if he went to the authorities. I was going to report him. For all of it. The affair, the blackmailing, everything. That's when he started paying me to keep quiet."

"That's where the money went," Nicole said aloud, unaware of her voice.

Alex ignored Nicole's comment. "Craig said he'd make it worth my while to stay quiet. I needed the money because, let's be real, what college student doesn't?" Alex stopped and stared at Nicole. "I know what you're thinking. How could I do this? That I knew better."

"I wasn't thinking any of those things."

"I did know better, but I was in too deep. I didn't know how to get out. I didn't know if I'd get in trouble, and I didn't want to be expelled."

"Fear drove you."

"Exactly," Alex said, dropping her leg back down.

Still confused about one last thing, Nicole said, "I still don't understand why Craig would tell the authorities that *you* killed Jaden. Why you?" Nicole's stomach knotted tight, waiting for the answer.

Alex locked eyes with Nicole. "I slept with Jaden."

CHAPTER 46

The thrumming in Nicole's ear made her wonder if she'd misheard what Alex had said. "I'm sorry, did you say you'd slept with Jaden?"

"Yes."

More to unpack. Another long list of questions. Nicole didn't know where to begin with this new piece of information. She started with when.

"Last semester."

"Were you still sleeping with him when he went missing?"

"No."

"Do the police know you were involved with him?"

"No, because it ended before he'd disappeared."

Nicole narrowed her eyes, staring at Alex.

Alex raised her hands. "I had nothing to do with Jaden's disappearance."

Nicole's brain was in overdrive. Unsure if she believed that, she needed to probe further. She stood up, too anxious to sit. She paced the floor, wearing a path on the shaggy rug. "How long did you say you were together?"

"We weren't technically together. It was more like a 'friends with benefits' type situation," Alex said, miming air quotes.

"Did anyone else know about you two?"

"Some of Jaden's fraternity brothers."

Nicole wondered if Kyle was one of them. She asked if Alex knew Kyle, but Nicole didn't disclose that he was her and Craig's son.

"Yeah. Met him a few times. It seemed like he and Jaden weren't the best of friends."

Nicole cocked her head. "What do you mean?"

"I don't know. Jaden complained on a couple of different occasions about Kyle. Something about Chase and Kyle ganging up on him. He never elaborated what the problem was."

Chase and Kyle. Kyle and Chase. How involved were these boys?

Pointing her finger, Nicole asked, "Did anyone else know about you and Jaden?"

Alex looked at the ceiling. "Yes. Dr. Graham. Another professor in the economics department."

Nicole stopped pacing upon hearing his name.

Watching Nicole's behavior, Alex asked, "Do you know Dr. Graham?"

"Yes. He's been to my house. He's been helping Craig with a new computer grading program. They've spent a lot of time together." Nicole thought back to the men's heated argument at her house, how they'd stopped talking when she entered the room. Was that what was discussed? "How did Dr. Graham know?" Nicole asked, trying to make the connection.

"Because Jaden was in his class, and he'd overheard Jaden bragging about how he'd slept with me last semester. Dr. Graham knew me because I'm Craig's assistant. Jaden told me that Dr. Graham had confronted him, threatening him, telling him to knock it off, but Jaden told him we'd already ended it."

"That must've been the argument that the student had reported to the police," Nicole said, filling in the gaps. "But why would Dr. Graham care if you slept with one of his students?"

Alex shrugged. "I don't know."

Nicole paced again. "Alex, I need you to think. You might be holding the answer to what happened to Jaden. Think."

Olivia walked out of her bedroom. She looked at Alex's disheveled face and asked, "Everything okay out here?"

Nicole and Alex exchanged glances. Neither woman wanted Olivia to know what they were talking about.

"All good," Alex said, smiling.

"Okay. It sounds like things are strained out here. I'm in my room if you need me," she said, glaring at Nicole.

Nicole smirked.

When Olivia left, Nicole finished with pacing, leaving the rug looking mangier than before, flopped back down on the couch, letting the plump pillows engulf her. She wished the sofa could swallow her up, take her away from this surreal life.

Think, Nicole, think. She knew she was missing something, but what? What was the missing link? "Maybe Craig had another girl on the side?"

"I don't think so. He never would've cheated on me." Alex looked wounded by Nicole's accusation.

Nicole lifted an eyebrow. "You're number two that I know of. It's not entirely impossible."

Alex's face crumbled. "I guess."

Nicole dug deep in her brain, trying to figure out why Dr. Graham would care if Jaden had slept with Alex. A thought transpired, and Nicole felt sicker than she had, if that was even possible. She held back the vomit rising to the surface. She needed to compose herself and remain strong because she needed to follow through with the next step.

"I need you to do something." Nicole stood up, walked over to Alex, and squeezed her hands gently. And with determination, desperation, and fire in her eyes, Nicole said, "I know this is asking a lot, but I need your help."

"I don't like that look," Alex said, retracting her hands.

"You said you're sorry for everything. If you want to make it up to me, this is how you can do that."

CHAPTER 47

Nicole lifted the lid of her jewelry box. The last flip phone, the very device that Alex would use to call in the last tip, the one that would lead police to whom Nicole suspected to be the actual responsible party, remained tucked inside as she'd left it. Not that she had any definitive proof, but Nicole had a hunch, and she wanted to point the police toward who she now presumed to be responsible for Jaden's demise.

She and Alex had argued about what Nicole wanted to do next. Alex had been adamant, saying that it was a dreadful idea. She was terrified. Frightened by the repercussions. She'd begged Nicole not to make her do it, but Nicole had given Alex twenty-four hours to make the call or, Nicole had threatened, she would make Alex's affair public.

"You have to come clean," Nicole had said. "The police need to know."

"I can't," Alex had pleaded, tears welling up again. "They might expel me, and I can't take that risk."

Nicole argued, "It's the right thing to do."

"I'm too scared," Alex had sobbed.

Nicole wondered how many tears lived inside this girl. Wasn't she dry by now?

"I know I wouldn't want all this on my conscience. Do you?" Nicole was taking this as an opportunity to clear her conscience for all her wrongdoings. A second chance to fix what she'd done and Alex held the power. And if she wouldn't do it, Nicole would. She had to. She owed it to those she'd put at risk and to herself. If she wanted a clean slate, and she did, this was her golden ticket.

Alex had shaken her head, aggressively protesting.

Nicole explained why making the call was essential. Why it mattered.

Finally, dry-eyed, Alex stared at Nicole. "I'm sorry. I had no idea. About any of it. Honestly."

"I'm sure you didn't."

Alex had finally agreed to it once Nicole had told her it could be done anonymously on an untraceable device. The women finalized the plan, and Nicole left to retrieve the phone.

Checking the time on the clock on her nightstand with just enough time to grab what she needed, Nicole headed out.

• • • • •

A warm, gentle breeze blew Nicole's hair hanging in a low ponytail, tickling the back of her neck. The night sky, blanketed by a thin layer of clouds, remnants from the storm that had rolled through earlier that day, covered the moon and stars, leaving a dark slate above. Goosebumps appeared on her arm under her pullover. She rubbed her hands over the sleeves, trying to push the bumps back down.

Alex closed the phone. "Done," she said, handing it back with shaky hands.

"Go toss it in that dumpster," Nicole said, pointing to the large receptacle a few yards away.

As she watched Alex dispose of the last burner phone, Nicole thought about how beautiful this young woman was. Her tall, lanky legs moved fluidly, with grace and ease, like a ballerina floating across the stage. Her blonde hair fell halfway down her back, a mix of curl and straightness, creating the envious beach waves most girls die for. Nicole glimpsed at Alex's flat stomach under her light pink cotton baby doll shirt as she reached and dropped the phone into its final resting place.

"Are you okay?" Nicole asked as Alex stood in front of her once again.

"I guess so. What an absolute nightmare this has been. I hope it's over. Finally."

Nicole wiggled her foot, removing a piece of gravel from her open-toed shoe. "I'm sure it's been tough. I'm sorry you got caught up in all of it. Given different circumstances, I think you and I could've been friends. Although you're probably young enough to be my daughter."

Alex laughed. "You don't look your age at all. Craig was a fool for cheating on a knockout like you."

Nicole blushed. "Thanks for the compliment, but I'm realizing it has nothing to do with me and everything to do with him."

The women walked in silence back to their cars. They'd chosen to meet at this particular bar's parking lot because people were constantly coming and going. They would blend in—no one would question why they were standing outside, talking on a phone.

"So, what do we do now?" Alex asked.

"I guess we wait."

Alex nodded.

"This is where we part ways," Nicole said, standing beside her car. "If we should cross paths again, I think it's best to act like we don't know one another. At least for now. Until this is all over."

Alex nodded again and turned to open her car door.

"Alex?"

"Yeah?" She stopped and faced Nicole.

As she lifted the door handle, Nicole said, "Thanks. For everything. You've helped me out, and I am sorry for what's happened to you."

"Thanks. And I feel the same. You've opened my eyes a lot, and I've learned my lesson. I will never get sucked in like that again. I hope Craig pays the price for what he's done."

"He already is," Nicole said, smiling.

CHAPTER 48

When Craig called, Nicole let it go to voicemail. When he sent messages, she ignored them. She had nothing to say to him and didn't want to see him, wanting absolutely nothing to do with him, finally wising up to his ways and remaining steadfast. He continued to plead with her, begging her to take him back. He said he would change. She ignored every bit of it, not buying anything he was selling. Not anymore. He told her he'd hit rock bottom. Little did he know, the bottom was about to fall out from underneath him, making rock bottom look like high ground.

On the living room floor after a much-needed sweat session at the gym, stretching in front of the TV, still wearing her sweaty maroon leggings and a light yellow, snug-fitting tank top, Nicole heard Detective Newton's voice and looked up. It'd been three days since Jaden's body had been pulled from the lake and one day since Alex had made that unfavorable phone call.

George and Cecelia Pierce stood beside the detective in front of the police station. A bouquet of microphones, attached to a podium, pointed in their direction. Cecelia's sunken cheeks quivered as she sucked in her bottom lip. George stood, shoulders back, chest puffed out, his arm around Cecelia's shoulder. Detective Newton spoke first.

"Good Evening. We will keep this very brief. Jaden's parents would like to make a statement to the public." Detective Newton stepped aside, allowing George to stand front and center. New lines were etched into his pale skin, framing his dark, sunken eyes—the only light in them was coming from the camera lights reflecting in the welling tears.

George inhaled while unfolding a piece of paper from his pocket. He rubbed the paper, smoothing it out against the podium surface with his unsteady palms. His voice shook as he spoke. "Cecelia and I thank you all for your support throughout this horrendous experience. We are heartbroken. Our lives will never be the same. We've lost our son." He looked up from the letter, choking back tears. He looked down and continued to read. "May none of you know the pain and anguish we are living. We wouldn't wish this on our worst enemy. We are devastated that our boy was found—" He choked back the tears. "Dead. We'd held out hope, thinking he'd show up alive, and that this had all been a mistake. A bad dream. But it's worse than that. Losing a child is a parent's worst nightmare. Jaden was a son, grandson, nephew, friend, and well-loved by everyone."

Nicole watched Cecelia. She looked anemic, fraught with grief, staring blankly with vacant eyes. George continued. "We are asking again, if you have any information to help the police with this investigation, please come forward. We need answers. Our boy deserves justice." Cecelia handed something to George. He held up a picture. "This is our boy." George shook his head, hanging low. He looked back up. "Whoever did this to our precious boy will pay."

There, in that picture, on Jaden's wrist, was the identical watch hiding in Kyle's drawer. Nicole's heart jumped to her throat.

• • • • •

Seated at the kitchen table, Nicole stared at the watch in her hand. She was surprised to still find it where she'd left it—in Kyle's drawer, figuring with the body being found, he might've taken it by now. She turned it over, studying the faded letters etched on the back. Could it be? Was it a *P* and a *B* for *precious boy*? Was this Jaden's watch? Nicole didn't know what to do. What if she'd pointed the police in the wrong direction again? Worse, what if Kyle had done it? Nicole thought she'd made the final connection. Maybe she hadn't.

If this watch was evidence, she couldn't withhold it. Nicole had vowed to help, not hinder. Still, turning it in could implicate her son. If she didn't turn it in, she could obstruct justice.

Lost in thought, the ringing phone startled her. Familiar with the phone number by now, Nicole wondered if she should tell him what was going on. She let it ring a few times, debating. She'd wait and see how the conversation went before making that decision. On the fifth ring, she answered. "Hey, Phil."

"Hey, Nicole." He didn't sound like his usual self.

"Everything okay?"

"I'm not sure. I just got a call from Kyle saying he needs me to go to the police station with him. Detective Newton wants to speak to him again."

Nicole dropped the watch like it was on fire and had burned her hand. "What? Why?"

"I don't know. Was hoping maybe you did."

Nicole placed her hand on her tight chest. "I have no idea." Nicole thought maybe she did, although she didn't want to say anything to Phil yet.

Nicole hung up, put the watch in an envelope, tucked it into her purse, grabbed a cardigan sweater, and headed for the station.

• • • • •

Phil stood in the police station lobby, briefcase in hand, wearing a yellow bowtie with black stripes reminding Nicole of a bumblebee. He stood next to Kyle, who looked pale and like he'd slept in the wrinkled clothes hanging on his body.

With the watch hidden at the bottom of her purse, Nicole hugged him. "You okay?"

Kyle nodded.

"Something you want to tell me before we go in?" she asked, raising an eyebrow.

Kyle shook his head. He was silent, like when he'd been accused of strangling Max. Nicole's nerves flooded every limb of her body. She grabbed her purse strap tightly so no one would see her hand trembling.

Valerie ushered them into an interrogation room—a slightly bigger one this time. Kyle's knees jounced up and down while they waited for Detective Newton. Nicole put her hand on his knee, telling him to relax. His jitteriness was making her nervous. None of them knew why the detective had called Kyle in.

Phil shuffled through some paperwork in his opened briefcase. *Why doesn't he use a computer?* Nicole thought. The odd way he dressed might be a clue to his old-fashioned ways.

The door opened, and Detective Newton breezed in, harried, flustered as usual, dressed in his typical outfit. He set down a Styrofoam cup filled to the top with coffee, which splattered on the papers he'd set down. His badge was barely visible, as usual, hidden under his belly. "Sorry, I'm late. Thanks for coming in on such short notice," he said, sliding back on the tan metal chair.

Nicole's butt hurt from the hard, non-cushioned surface. She readjusted her position, trying to get comfortable, her leggings sticking.

"No problem," Phil said. "Kyle has requested his mother be present, too."

That was the only way Nicole could be in there, and she wanted to be there, to hear exactly what the detective wanted. On edge, Nicole's heightened senses could hear the watch ticking inside her purse like a bomb waiting to explode.

Phil stopped shuffling the papers from his hands and put them back into the briefcase, closing the lid. "What can we do for you?"

"I have a few more questions for Kyle."

Nicole balled her fingers into tight fists.

"Okay, but why?"

"Because we've had a new lead. Hopefully, a break in the case."

Nicole's heart lurched. *Was it the tip Alex had called in?*

Detective Newton addressed Kyle. "Did you see anyone else in the area that night? Someone you haven't mentioned. Anyone other than a fraternity brother?"

Kyle looked up at the ceiling, searching for the answer from above. "No, not at all. I didn't even see all the guys in the woods. We couldn't find each other, but I accidentally bumped into Ethan, and when we ran into the others, we went back to the house."

"Did you hear any struggle? Any cries for help?"

Kyle paused.

"What is it?" Nicole asked.

"Mrs. Cunningham, if you can't sit here quietly, I will have to ask you to leave," Detective Newton reprimanded.

Nicole frowned.

"Kyle, is there something else you haven't told us?" the detective prompted.

"I'd forgotten about this part. After meeting Ethan, I thought I heard something or someone running through the woods. Ethan said he didn't hear it, so I thought I'd imagined it." Kyle ran his fingers through his messy hair. "And right before we'd bumped into Chase and Aiden, I heard voices but assumed it was theirs."

Nicole watched Kyle's body language for any signs of lying. She paid attention to the shiftiness of his eyes, any fidgety behavior, and any changes in his complexion. She observed it all, acutely cognizant. Knowing her son, and from what she saw here, she believed him; he made direct eye contact, sat perfectly still, except for running his fingers through his hair, a typical behavior for him, like his father, and his skin never once changed color.

Then why was Jaden's watch in his drawer? Nicole's head ticked rhythmically, like the second hand of that watch.

Detective Newton nodded. "Okay. But what about the threats against Jaden? We can't get a straight answer from any of you boys. You say it was Chase or Ethan. Ethan says it was you or Chase, and Chase says it was you or Ethan. Why the cover-up? What are you boys hiding?" he asked, leaning in.

Phil went to interject, but the door opening interrupted him. Detective Cohen popped her head in, dressed in a navy skirt suit, her hair slicked back again in a tight bun at the nape of her neck. "Lou, we have a problem."

Detective Newton scowled. "Can't you see I'm in the middle of something here? Handle it."

Loud voices traveled into the room, garbled, unintelligible, yet loud enough to decipher the angry tone.

"I think we may need your help," Detective Cohen said, looking back toward the chaos. Detective Newton pushed back his chair and huffed, annoyed with the interruption.

Not wanting to waste any more unnecessary time, Phil asked, "Are we finished here? Are we free to go?"

"No, I'm not finished with your client," Detective Newton barked, pointing. "Wait here."

Detective Cohen held the door open for Detective Newton. And that's when Nicole saw the figure causing all the commotion.

CHAPTER 49

"Craig?" Nicole asked, even though he was too far away to hear her.

Kyle's eyes widened, his pupils dilating into the size of pinholes. "Why is Dad here?"

Nicole wrinkled her forehead. "Did you call him to meet us?"

"No. Did you?" Kyle asked Phil.

"Me?" Phil asked, pointing to himself. "Not me. I thought maybe you did," he said, pointing to Nicole.

Nicole crossed her arms over her chest. "No way. I have nothing to say to that man."

Through the open door, they heard Craig screaming, "Let me go! You have no right to bring me in here! You can't do this to me!" The entire station stopped and stared at him.

With what he was yelling, it didn't sound like he was there for Kyle. Nicole peered around the doorjamb, leaning in front of Detective Cohen, who stood near the interrogation room door, her bun severely tight, not a single strand of hair out of place.

Craig was handcuffed. He continued shouting, profanity sprinkled in every few words as he struggled to be restrained.

Nicole whipped her head back to Kyle and Phil. "He's in handcuffs."

"What?" Kyle said, his mouth dropping open as he ambled to the doorway.

Phil lifted his eyebrows.

"Sir. Sir, I need you to settle down," Detective Newton commanded.

"I want my lawyer!"

Back in the room, dodging Craig, Nicole looked at Phil. "Don't look at me," he said, "I'm not his lawyer. I'm Kyle's." He hitched his thumb, demonstrating.

Nicole breathed a sigh of relief.

Phil continued. "If your husband had anything to do with Jaden's case, that would be a conflict of interest, and there is no way I could represent him and your son."

"I don't get it. I don't understand. Why would they arrest Dad?" Kyle said, blinking rapidly, following Nicole.

Nicole wanted to tell him what she'd suspected, why she'd had Alex make that final call. To protect her son, though, she acted surprised. This time, Nicole's motive was altruistic; she wanted justice for Jaden and her son absolved of all suspicions. She did what she had to do to help uncover the truth—the absolute truth—not the one she'd tried to make up on all those occasions, attempting to keep her son out of it. This new truth would free everyone, including herself from her guilt.

"I don't know, but I'm sure we'll find out soon enough," Nicole said. She walked past Detective Cohen, who hadn't moved, and asked Detective Newton, "Why is he here?"

"Do you know this guy?"

"That's my husband," Nicole said, pointing toward Craig.

"What are you doing here?" Craig asked, leering at Nicole and Kyle.

Before Nicole could answer, Detective Newton looked at her. "I'd say you have a family of persons of interest. Do you want to add yourself to the list?"

Nicole's stomach barrel rolled. Technically, she was withholding what may be evidence, making her no less guilty.

Overhearing the conversation, Phil hurried to her side and jumped in. "Excuse me, you still have nothing on my client, so don't you dare accuse Nicole. She's done nothing wrong."

Nicole silently grimaced. That wasn't entirely true.

"If anything, she's been a victim of all this," Phil continued.

Detective Newton raised his salt-and-pepper furry eyebrow. He was still restraining Craig. "Really? How's that?"

"You know she'd been followed, fearing for her life by that crazy guy, only to find out that this scumbag—" Craig snarled, baring his teeth like a rabid animal. "Fathered another child with another woman."

Nicole wanted to shrivel up, make herself tiny or unseen. She loved Phil's loyalty, but she wanted to clock him for outing their family drama in such a public way. She'd told him that information in secrecy when he'd hounded her a few days ago, not letting the issue drop, no matter how many times she'd told him she didn't want to discuss why Gabriel had shown up on her doorstep.

This news flash piqued Newton's interest. "Well then, good sir, I guess you have lots of questions to answer." Detective Newton grabbed Craig by the elbow, who fought back, pulling away. Compromised in the cuffs, the detective won the battle and threw Craig into another room across the hall. "Cohen! Come sit and watch my newest victim."

Detective Cohen went in with Craig, and the other three headed back to theirs, retaking their seats. Kyle sat wide-eyed and utterly confused.

Nicole reached into her purse to pull out the watch tucked safely in the envelope. However, before she lifted it, Detective Newton spoke. "I think we may have enough of a lead to release you," he said, smiling at Kyle, "unless—"

Nicole wrapped her fingers around the evidence, keeping her hand stuffed in her purse, waiting to hear the caveat. Phil asked, "Unless what?"

"Unless you're in on it with your old man. Perhaps you all are," he said, eyeing Nicole.

She bit her lip as her fingers remained wrapped around the envelope. How could she possibly turn the watch over with that last statement? Having Jaden's watch in her purse did indeed make her look involved. She had to think fast.

Kyle jumped in, saving her from having to say anything at all. "I swear I don't know what the hell is going on here. I had absolutely nothing to do with Jaden's death, and I have no idea what my dad has to do with any of this. I've told you everything I know. I'll take a lie detector test to prove it." Kyle's leg rocked up and down again.

"I may hold you to that," the detective said. "Let me see what your dear old dad has to say, and then I'll let you know. No one is going anywhere until I'm through with him."

"How long will that take?" Nicole asked, her hand still wedged inside her purse.

"My advice? I'd get comfortable if I were you."

And while they waited, Nicole figured out precisely what to do about the watch.

• • • • •

Kyle dozed off with his head on his arms folded on the cold metal table. Nicole checked her watch: 3:30 a.m. Dark circles settled under her heavy eyes. She'd been awake for almost twenty-four hours with all that'd happened over the past day, exhaustion an acquaintance, an old hat these days, like the long, sleepless nights with a newborn. But that exhaustion paled in comparison—what she wouldn't give to feel that level of tiredness right now.

She yawned.

"You look like hell," Phil said, leaning back in his chair. Nicole was pretty sure she'd lost all feeling in her butt after the close relationship she'd formed with the bridge chair. "Thanks. You sure know how to compliment a lady."

"Good thing it wasn't a compliment. I mean it. You look like you're about to collapse." They spoke in hushed tones not to disturb Kyle. Nicole watched the rise and fall of his back with each breath. "I'm okay. Honestly. I just don't know what the hell is taking so long."

The door finally opened for the first time in hours. The only other time they'd seen another human was when someone had come in to see if they needed a bathroom break or something to drink. That'd been at least two hours ago.

"Sorry. That took longer than I'd expected. You're free to go," Newton said, leaving the door open to let them leave. He looked like Nicole felt.

"What did Craig say?" she asked.

"Enough to fully clear your son."

Nicole released all the breath she'd been holding over the past few weeks. Tension melted from each taut muscle down to her pinky toe, processing those words. Craig had done one thing right: he'd had the decency to help their son. Of course, he could've done it four weeks ago, preventing all of this.

"Did he have anything to do with Jaden's death?" Nicole asked.

Kyle's head popped up.

"I can't discuss any details with you," Newton said.

"Phil," Nicole pleaded, "doesn't Detective Newton have to let me know? I'm Craig's wife." For this, she played the wife card.

"No, he doesn't. If Craig doesn't want you to know, the detective doesn't have to tell you."

"So, are we free to leave?" Phil asked.

Detective Newton nodded.

"Great, let's get out of here." Phil stood up. "I think we all need a shower and a decent bed, not these metal contraptions you call chairs." He collected his materials.

"Wait," Nicole said, looking at the detective. "I have something I need to give you." She reached into her purse.

"What?"

"This." Nicole handed him the envelope.

Detective Newton took it. The envelope looked tiny in his cumbersome hand. "What is this?" he asked as he lifted the gold, shiny metal object and dangled it before his eyes.

Phil looked quizzically at Nicole. "What is *that*?" he asked, pointing at the watch.

"I believe it's Jaden's watch," she said.

Phil flopped on a chair. "And I believe I'll be sitting back down."

"What are you doing with Jaden's watch?" Kyle asked, his eyes narrowing, his eyebrows connecting right above his nose.

"I could ask you the same thing," Nicole said in a last-ditch effort to see what, if any, connection he'd had with Jaden's death.

"I've never seen that before." Nicole saw the expression on Kyle's face. The innocence in his eyes. He honestly didn't know how that watch had ended up in his drawer. That left only one explanation for how it'd made its way there.

And like the last piece of a puzzle clicking into place, Nicole explained what she thought had happened. Kyle slumped over, putting his face in his hands. Phil scratched his jaw. And Detective Newton wrote as fast as Nicole talked, jotting everything down. When he asked why she hadn't turned the watch over sooner, she lied for the last time, this time to protect herself since she hadn't made the connection until earlier that day. "I just found it. I was going to turn it in, but when I got Phil's call to meet him here, I brought it with me instead."

"Why didn't you turn it over when you first arrived?" Detective Newton asked, staring at her. "You know, you can be charged for withholding evidence."

Phil jumped in. "Look, in theory, yes, she could." He glared at Nicole. She took in his displeasure. "But she turned it in, and if it helps your case, she should be regarded as a hero of sorts for doing her civic duty."

Detective Newton sat in silence, staring at the watch.

"I have one more thing that I think can help," Nicole said.

"Oh yeah, what's that?"

Nicole told him. "And if I do that, we can call it good."

The detective knew he needed what she had. "Fine. Bring it in first thing tomorrow. Well, technically, today. If it's not here by noon, I'm pressing charges for withholding the watch."

"Fair enough. You have my word." She made an "X" over her heart like she used to do as a young girl, promising her parents that she'd behave.

As he left the room, Kyle asked, "Does my dad want to see me?"

Detective Newton shook his head. "I'm sorry. He doesn't want to see anyone."

Kyle frowned and slouched. "That's okay. I get it."

But Nicole saw he didn't.

CHAPTER 50

Nicole stood, staring at the bed that she once shared with Craig. A man who'd turned out to be somebody she didn't know at all—a monster. The entire drive home, she'd struggled with the fact that her husband, Kyle's father, could have potentially allowed their son to take the fall for what he'd done. What kind of man does that?

Nicole had dropped Kyle off at the fraternity house on her way home, although he'd insisted on going home with her, worried about her. She promised she'd be okay and that he needed to live his life. She knew he had a lot to process and deal with, and she assured him he was welcome to come home with her, but *only* if he needed her and it wasn't the other way around. He opted to return to his brothers, his confidants who would help him navigate these rough, unchartered waters.

Crawling under the covers, the ones she'd pulled over her body a thousand times through the years with her husband lying next to her, the man she'd admired, adored, and loved unconditionally, she questioned how she'd never seen the other side of him, the one that not only could harm another human being, but the one that could also blame his son or any other innocent person.

Craig had acted like the doting husband. The man she'd dreamed of. Had she not been looking with clear vision? Had her brain tricked her into seeing what she wanted to see? What she wanted a man to be. What she needed him to be. Her brain couldn't sift through it all. It was too much for any one person in such a short amount of time. She knew sleep would elude her again tonight. Still, she set her alarm for ten o'clock in case she dozed off, not wanting to be late in delivering what Detective Newton needed—the final proof.

• • • • •

"We have made an arrest in the Jaden Pierce case." Detective Newton stood once again at the podium, addressing the public. "We are still waiting for the preliminary report, but thanks to an anonymous tip called into our hotline, we followed a strong lead and made an arrest. The alleged suspect is one of the College of Cypressville's very own, Dr. Craig Cunningham."

A collective gasp escaped from the crowd. "We are very saddened by the loss of an innocent life and the downfall of a well-loved faculty member. Professor Cunningham will be held in custody until his bond hearing. We will continue our investigation while we wait for the autopsy. Jaden's parents have something they'd like to say." The detective moved aside, leaving the podium vacant.

George, looking destroyed, his face pale, wan, and pinched, and Cecelia, looking worse than that, stood in front of the microphone. George cleared his throat. "We want to start by thanking whoever called in the tip that led the police to Professor Cunningham. We are forever grateful for your help in this case. It has been a living nightmare. Every. Single. Day. Waiting, anticipating, wondering." Cecelia clung to her husband's arm, wiping the stream of tears with a white lace handkerchief. She wore dark sunglasses to shield the shadows harbored under her eyes. She sniffled. George patted her arm. "You can't imagine the pain and the loss we are suffering. You can't imagine it unless you've lived it yourself."

George continued. "We've lost our son. His fraternity brothers lost one of their own, a brother and a friend. We are left with a hole in our hearts. We will never have the chance to celebrate another birthday, Christmas, or any other holiday with our son." George stopped and hung his head. He gripped the side of the podium to steady himself.

He lifted his head. "We will never see our precious boy walk through the front door. We have been robbed of seeing his smile. His eyes. The way he laughs. Walks. Talks. We will never hear his voice again. We have lost an entire lifetime of watching our son grow. We'll never get to see him get married." George paused again, his neck straining.

"He'll never have children of his own, who would've been...been...our grandchildren." He stopped again. His bottom lip quivered as he sucked in air. The crowd waited in silence as he regained his composure. He continued. "My family's lineage stops here all because of that monster. A professor. A man who is supposed to teach, guide, and help his students. Not hurt them."

Cecelia dabbed under her eyes behind her oversized sunglasses. A few stray tears dodged the lacy square and splashed onto the breast of her form-fitting black dress, leaving spots of dampness.

The camera panned over the crowd. Not a dry eye could be seen. Sniffles echoed.

Salty tears streaked Nicole's face. Even Detective Newton was choked up. Nobody moved. Nobody spoke. Silence deafened the airwaves. Helping to steady her, George ushered Cecelia aside.

Detective Newton pushed a tear teetering on his lower eyelid back with his knuckle as he took George's place at the podium. He inhaled and said, "I think we can all agree this is a tragedy. We will continue to keep you updated as we get more answers. Justice will be served, and we won't stop until it is."

Nicole turned off the TV. Her husband was a tornado, always leaving a path of destruction in his wake.

• • • • •

Cecilia sat at a small round table in the corner of the bar by the front door of the atrium. Nicole saw her instantly when she walked into The Grand Hotel. Her off-white maxi skirt flowed behind her as she walked toward the bar, and her ballet-style flats clicked on the tiled floor.

Recalling her last escapade here, Nicole shuddered. "Thank you for meeting me," she said as she approached Cecelia sitting at a table.

Cecelia stared blankly at Nicole, who slid into the opposite chair. "I can't tell you how much this means to me," she said, hailing the server over. A good stiff drink would do her wonders.

"I'm not sure what you want from me this time," Cecelia said. She looked worn out, with freshly carved, deep lines encasing her gray, forlorn eyes and the newly loose skin drooping from her sunken cheeks.

"I'm sorry for everything," Nicole started, tucking her hair behind her ear. The lobby was still inundated with media personnel. After Jaden had been found, nobody had left. They all stayed, waiting for more details. Far too many unanswered questions loomed for anyone to go. "And I'm sorry for the loss of your son."

Cecelia looked down at her folded hands in her lap, resting on her white linen pants.

"I can't even imagine what you're going through."

"At least you don't have to, seeing as you don't have a daughter who went missing," Cecelia spat, twirling her thumbs.

Nicole knew she deserved that. Ultimately, she'd lied, and yes, her child was alive, safe, and sound. "I apologize for that as well. I was desperate, not that I'm excusing my behavior. I was out of my mind with worry, trying to protect my son while uncovering the truth. And my husband—" Nicole took a long swig of her Moscow Mule, stopping, the term *husband* repulsing her. The cold liquid trickled down her dry throat.

Cecilia sat still, unblinking, watching Nicole squirm uncomfortably in her chair. "Mostly, I'm sorry for my husband's actions."

"Did you know? Is that why you came here lying about who you were? You knew your husband had something to do with it, and you needed to protect him, too?"

Her words cut like a knife. Still, Nicole didn't blame the woman. She was angry. At everyone. And everything. And rightly so. Cecelia had lost her only child. Unimaginable. "I swear," Nicole held up her hand in a scout-like manner, "I had no idea. Apparently, I'm a fool. My husband hid a lot from me." She paused, looking upward. "More like outright lied to me. For years. I thought I knew him. Clearly, I didn't. I don't." She stirred her drink, twirling the black plastic straw around the copper mug. She gulped down more, self-medicating her pain and anguish.

"I'm sorry to hear that. I am sorry you had to live with such a... such a—"

Nicole finished Cecelia's thought. "Sleazeball? Asshole? Monster? Pick one. Or all three."

The two women sat in silence, each lost in their thoughts, processing their tragedies: Nicole, the loss of her husband and marriage; Cecelia, the loss of her son at the hands of Nicole's monstrous husband. Strangers at the start, the two women now had a unique bond—they'd both lived through the same harrowing ordeal, albeit on opposing sides. Yet, they both had lost someone they'd loved, just in different ways.

CHAPTER 51

"Turn on the news. Detective Newton is about to address the media."

Phil called Nicole as she walked through the door after running by the pharmacy to pick up the sedatives her doctor had called in to help her sleep. Whenever her phone rang, she still jumped, thinking it might be Craig. She didn't want to talk to him, even though he'd attempted to contact her numerous times when allowed to use the phone, but she didn't want to hear anything he had to say. Evidently, Kyle felt the same.

"I'm not sure I can watch. Knowing my husband's responsible for Jaden's demise is more than I can handle. I'm having night terrors. I wake up drenched in sweat. It's awful."

"I can come over if you want." Ironically, Phil had become more than Kyle's attorney through it all. He'd become a good friend.

"Thanks, Phil. I appreciate that. But I need time alone. I need to figure out what I'm going to do next."

"Meaning?"

"Meaning I can't stay married to Craig. Even if he hadn't been involved in Jaden's death, he had an affair. Multiple affairs, if you include Alex, and fathered another child that he knew about and abandoned. I don't want to be involved with someone like that. I can't love that kind of person."

"Need a good divorce lawyer? I can hook you up," Phil chuckled.

Nicole laughed. "Yeah, probably going to need one of those." She turned on the TV and watched as Detective Newton, dressed in his usual polo shirt and khakis, walked to the podium. "It's starting. Chat later?"

"Absolutely. Hang in there."

It was late afternoon, one week since they'd found Jaden's body, and once again, a crowd had accumulated, waiting. "We have received the preliminary report in the Jaden Pierce case," Detective Newton said, reading the note before him, periodically looking back at the camera. "Jaden suffered blunt-force trauma to the head, routinely involved in an accidental death or homicide. Therefore, we cannot rule either one out yet. We are still questioning the suspect in custody, trying to piecemeal what happened that fateful night. The medical examiner found traces of Professor Cunningham's DNA underneath Jaden's fingernails."

The morning after Craig had been detained, Nicole retrieved one of his empty beer bottles from the recycling bin and brought it to Detective Newton. The lab then matched Craig's DNA from the beer bottle to the DNA found under Jaden's fingernails.

"We have obtained a search warrant and are actively combing through the professor's computer and cell phone. We are also questioning his coworkers, who are fully cooperating."

Bile raced it's way up into Nicole's throat. She closed her eyes, willing the tears and sickness away. It was true. Craig had harmed Jaden. No, killed him. Deep down, she knew Craig had had something to do with it. Still, she'd hoped it wasn't true, that it'd all been nothing more than a misunderstanding. That her life wasn't completely turned upside down. That they could go back to how it'd been before all of this. Unfortunately, though, it was real. And they couldn't. Even if Craig hadn't been involved in Jaden's death, Trista had shown up, alerting Nicole that her whole marriage had been a ruse. There was no going back.

Detective Newton continued, snapping Nicole from her thoughts. "We also have the toxicology report. Jaden's alcohol level was .16, twice the legal limit. Like I said, this is an ongoing investigation, and we will continue to update you as we learn more. Thank you." He gathered his notes and walked off without answering any further questions.

Stunned, Nicole sat bleary-eyed, staring at the screen while a news reporter reiterated what the detective had just said.

After hearing all this, Nicole was finally done with Craig, or at least so she thought.

Mining through the hurt and despair embedded in the cavern of her heart, Nicole cried more tears over the past day than she'd cried over the past twenty years combined. Convinced she'd run dry, the tears proved her wrong. And as much as she didn't want to see Craig, she needed closure. Irate, Nicole went to the jail to confront him one last time.

When alone in the tiny little room, neither spoke for a few minutes.

Craig looked like hell, like he'd aged ten years in four days, the bright orange pantsuit not helping the cause. Gray stubble peppered his long, drawn-out face, and his cheekbones protruded beneath his haggard skin. Where once was light in his brown eyes, only darkness remained.

Breaking the awkward silence, Craig spoke first. "Nic, you have to believe me. I didn't kill Jaden."

"I can't believe you're still lying to me," she said disgustingly. "After everything you've been caught doing, and even with your DNA being found under Jaden's fingernails, you have the balls to sit here and deny your culpability."

"I swear on my life, he was alive when I left those woods."

"At least you admit to being there. How big of you." Nicole rolled her eyes and huffed, blowing a wispy hair from her forehead.

"I went there that night...because...because—"

"Let me finish that sentence for you. Because you're a lying, cheating bastard who slept with the same girl as Jaden. Does that sound about right?"

Craig hung his head. He folded his shackled hands together, intertwining his fingers.

"I didn't mean to hurt him. I was so, so," he stammered, "angry. And jealous. And when Jaden fell back, I panicked. I checked his chest before I left, though. He was breathing. You have to believe me."

Nicole stared through him like he was invisible. And in some ways, he was. She couldn't see who he was anymore. "That's the funny thing. I don't have to believe you. You've lied far too many times. Besides, even if you're telling the truth, you left that poor boy for dead. You've lost all credibility with me. And with everyone else, for that matter."

"Please," tears pooled in his dark eyes. "You're all I've got left. Kyle won't even speak to me."

"You should've thought about that before you did what you did. Now, if you'll excuse me, I have nothing left to say, and I'm done listening to your lies." Nicole scooted the chair back and stood up.

More disenchanted with him than when she'd first walked in, Nicole walked out and closed the door on him for good.

CHAPTER 52

THAT NIGHT

Jaden squatted behind a tall oak tree, holding his breath, his heart beating against his chest like an angry prisoner pounding his fists on a wall. Footsteps rustled the leaves, and faint whispers came from a few yards away.

This is as good of a spot as any, he thought as the footsteps and whispers faded. His breath slowed, and his chest relaxed. "They'll never find me here," he whispered. Branches overhead swayed in rhythmic motion as a breeze whirled by.

He waited, hunkered down, at the base of the hundred-year-old tree, his back pressed against the dry, scratchy bark. His high-top sneakers sunk deeper into the thick, muddy soil. Moonlight danced on the tranquil lake. He knew he'd slip off the bank and fall into the murky water if he moved any closer. *That would suck,* he thought, as his overloaded bladder nagged at him.

No longer hearing footsteps or whispers, only the sound of water lapping against the lake's bank and the trees answering the call of the wind, Jaden wondered where the others had gone. They promised they'd come looking for him. Reluctant to play at first, he'd finally agreed when Chase had made it sound fun.

Not wanting to be found yet, he dared not move, but he needed to pee, thanks to the six beers and three shots. If he didn't honor his bladder's request, he would have a different problem altogether. He looked around, scouting a good place to relieve himself.

He spotted a small nook nestled between two thick trees to his left, near the lake's edge. If he hurried, he could be back in plenty of time without being caught. Confident, he dashed over to the hidden area. "Shit." He fumbled with the stuck zipper on his sky-blue chino shorts. Intoxication took hold, making a seamless task impossible. After clawing at the cold metal for a minute or two, he leaned back and stretched the teeth, the zipper moving downward. A steady stream of urine splashed into the lake, creating ripples across the glass-like surface.

"Ahh," he moaned.

When finished, he zipped his shorts. Desperate to return to his hiding spot, Jaden stumbled toward the tall oak tree. "Shit." He tripped over a stick embedded in the dirt. *Shouldn't have had that last shot.* He laughed, trying to regain his balance. Unsteady on his feet, he continued teetering toward the tree. A twig snapped, and Jaden turned around. Convinced he'd been found, he was startled to see an unexpected man and not one of his fraternity brothers.

"What are you doing here?" Jaden asked, recognizing the man, unable to place from where, though, thanks to the alcohol clouding his brain.

The somewhat familiar-looking man said with heat in his eyes, "Trying to find you. Heard you boys were out here tonight." He looked crazed. Intense. Fierce.

Suddenly, Jaden realized who it was—Kyle's father, an economics professor from campus. "Did Kyle invite you? That sonofabitch," Jaden slurred. "You're too old to play with us. Besides, you're not even a member of our fraternity." Jaden put his arms out to balance, like a small child playing airplane.

"I'm not here to play."

"You here to help your son win?" Jaden laughed, slapping Craig on the arm.

"No," Craig snarled, showing off more of his white teeth. "I'm here for you."

"Me?" Jaden snorted, placing a finger on the Sigma in the middle of his shirt. A goofy smile spread across his face. "Why me?"

"Because," Craig growled, "you slept with my girlfriend."

"Girlfriend? What are you talking about?" Jaden stepped back, losing his balance again, and landed on his backside. He struggled to stand, but Craig pushed him back down.

The smile faded from Jaden's face. "I don't know who your girlfriend even is," he said, sobering, his senses alerting him he was in danger. Craig approached; Jaden still sat on the ground. "Look, man, I'm serious. I don't know who or what you're talking about."

"My T.A., Alex. And don't play dumb with me, you little prick." Craig lunged at Jaden, who crawled away in just enough time to avoid Craig's advances. Jaden clambered to his feet while Craig lurched forward and grabbed them, knocking Jaden back down.

Craig shouted, "She's mine. I love her, you sniveling little asshole!" He tugged at Jaden, who clung to a nearby root. Craig, however, overpowered him.

The hair on the back of Jaden's neck stood at attention when he saw the rage in Craig's eyes. He knew if he didn't think fast, he would die. He continued talking—hoping to calm Craig. "Look, man, I was through with her. You can have my sloppy seconds. She's used trash."

Jaden hoped that would settle Craig. It didn't. His eyes looked wild, like a rabid animal.

Between the alcohol and adrenaline, Jaden couldn't think clearly. He was desperate. Desperate to get out. Desperate to save his life. He started rambling again. "We're not together anymore. You can have that whore."

"Whore? You think she's a whore? How dare you!" Craig straddled Jaden's midsection. Jaden extended his arms toward Craig's face, trying to scratch his eyes. Instinctively, Craig wrapped his hands around Jaden's neck, while Jaden dug his nails into Craig's arms.

Craig released his grip, pain radiating up his arm. "Fuck. You scratched me!" he yelled.

As Craig writhed on the ground, Jaden escaped, running as fast as possible. He weaved in between the trees, stumbling on the oversized roots. But Craig was faster and caught up.

"Please, sir, please don't do this. You can have her." Jaden heard voices off in the distance. *If I yell loud enough, they might hear me.*

There was no time. Craig lunged at Jaden once again. And as he stepped back, avoiding Craig's advance, Jaden fell backward on a protruding root. A loud thud permeated the silent forest when his head smacked against the ground. He lay motionless.

Kneeling next to Jaden, Craig panted, repeating, "Hey. Hey. You all right?" Sweat dripped in his eyes as he leaned over and turned his head sideways, watching the rise and fall of Jaden's rhythmic breathing.

Reassured that Jaden was alive, Craig stood up and craned his neck, double-checking, ensuring no one had seen what'd happened. Satisfied the coast was clear, he walked out of the woods, leaving behind Jaden's unresponsive body.

CHAPTER 53

TWO MONTHS AFTER THAT NIGHT

Nicole sat waiting in the coffee shop, the same one that Gabriel had watched her in almost two months ago. She hadn't wanted to meet, but Trista had sounded distressed, something about Hannah. Although it wasn't her problem, Nicole felt obligated to intercede since it wasn't Hannah's fault that her father was a criminal. She was an innocent child, a bystander of her parents' misconduct.

Kyle had mentioned to Nicole that he'd like to meet his half-sister. Maybe Kyle had reached out to Trista, unbeknownst to Nicole. Maybe that's why Trista wanted to chat. Maybe she wanted to work out a schedule so Kyle could get to know his half-sister. Nicole wouldn't stand in the way. She wanted her son to be happy, and if that meant fostering a relationship with Hannah, then Nicole was a hundred percent on board. Besides, her heart went out to the poor girl; she'd finally found out who her father was, and now, because of his uncontrollable jealousy, she'd lost him.

Maybe Trista wanted child support, which would be difficult, given that Craig sat in jail, awaiting a trial one day in the distant future. Between his confession that he'd pushed Jaden down and the DNA underneath Jaden's fingernails, the prosecutor said there was enough evidence to charge Craig with involuntary manslaughter.

The tinkling bells above the door rang, and Nicole saw Trista, dressed in black tights and an oversized lilac tunic sweater with tiny flowers embroidered on the top, her perfectly straight hair with a small fringe bang sweeping across her forehead, smile, and wave. She pointed to the coffee counter, and Nicole nodded. She would have to wait another few minutes to find out the real reason for today.

As she waited, Nicole recalled those first few days after Craig's arrest. Alex had agreed to testify against him in exchange for probation. Since she didn't know that Craig had been the one to kill Jaden, but since she'd accepted bribes from a killer, left threatening notes on Nicole's car, and withheld her relationship with Jaden from the police, they threatened jail time unless Alex testified against Craig. She happily agreed, not only to save her hide, but she said she'd do anything to make Craig pay for what he'd done.

Dr. Graham had accepted the same deal since he'd withheld information, like the fact that Craig paid him to keep quiet when he'd been questioned the previous two times. Nicole figured that's why their bank balance was lower than expected; Craig had been paying Alex and Dr. Graham.

Nicole was most grateful for and relieved that no one had ever learned about Kyle's illegal pastime and that Jaden had owed him money. Craig's arrest had come just in the nick of time, allowing that secret to remain hidden from the police, Phil, and Craig. Additionally, Nicole was pleased that no one knew the extent of her involvement because, in the end, it hadn't hindered the case at all—she was acting like a mom, like she'd justified to herself.

"Sorry. I can't live without my coffee," Trista said, setting her cup down, snapping Nicole from thought.

"No problem." Nicole smiled, rubbing the back of her neck. Sitting face to face with Craig's ex-lover, who'd produced a half-sibling for Kyle, wasn't Nicole's first choice of where to be.

"I appreciate you taking the time to meet me." Trista's lips spread into a friendly, welcoming smile. "This won't take long." She blew through the hole in the coffee cup lid and took a slow sip. "Damn, that's hot."

Nicole didn't want to talk about the temperature of the coffee, the weather, or any other superfluous topics. She wanted Trista to get to the point.

As if reading Nicole's mind, Trista said, "I guess you're wondering what this is all about?"

Nicole tilted her head. "You said it's about Hannah."

Trista looked Nicole squarely in the eyes and lifted the coffee to her lips again, shaking her head slightly from side to side, her sleek hair swinging. When she set the cup down, one side of her lip curled.

"No?" Nicole questioned.

"No."

Nicole lifted her eyelids a little wider.

Trista looked around, checking over both shoulders, and leaned in closer. She folded her arms on the table, her fingers curled around the brown cardboard, circling the white paper cup.

"Then I'm confused," Nicole said, linking her eyebrows. "I figured you wanted to discuss where Hannah fits into our family now that Craig's in jail."

"The thought has crossed my mind," Trista said, leaning in further, practically laying her entire upper torso on the green table. "But truthfully, I thought you should know something else about Craig."

Nicole couldn't imagine what more she could learn about her soon-to-be ex-husband. She didn't know *if* she wanted to know anything else. Curiosity knocked, however, wanting answers. "What?"

Suddenly, Trista's expression changed, her blue eyes clouding over. "I know *exactly* what your husband did to Jaden."

Nicole's heart skipped a beat. "How?"

A smirk erupted, spreading ear to ear. "That night," Trista said, "I followed your husband into the woods." She paused, watching Nicole.

Nicole's forehead wrinkled. "Wait, I thought you said you'd hired Gabriel to follow Craig, so how did you see him? How did you know he was there?"

With an inexplicable expression, Trista said, "Oh, I hired Gabriel, all right. But that lunkhead almost blew the whole thing. You see, I knew there was no way Craig would ever agree to a paternity test if I approached him. He'd deny all of it, so I hired a heavy to confront and coerce him." She stopped and blew into the lid again. Smiling and pointing her pinky finger at Nicole while her other fingers remained wrapped around the cup, Trista said, "Gabriel kept following *you*. You can't find good help these days."

Nicole curled her white knuckles around the edge of her seat to stop the room from spinning.

Trista continued, ignoring Nicole's pale face. "I'd already found Craig on my own. Thanks to Google, I'd done my own reconnaissance work and found out he was a faculty member here."

Nicole found that ironic; her best friend, Google, was also Trista's. "I don't understand," Nicole said, her brow furrowing deeper.

"Once I found Craig here at the college, I started following him, even saw him canoodling with that knockout assistant of his." All the sweetness had drained from Trista's voice. "When he went to the woods that night, I assumed he was meeting her for a little horizontal mambo."

Nicole recoiled.

"But imagine my surprise when I saw him arguing with Jaden."

Nicole couldn't swallow. With a sour taste overtaking her mouth, she rubbed her pasty tongue along her cheek.

"After Craig pushed Jaden down and left, I ran over to check on him. And guess what? The poor kid was still alive. Imagine that! Your husband had been telling the truth, at least about that part." Trista let out a low-boil cackle.

Nicole's chest tightened.

"There I was, faced with a choice: save Jaden or get revenge on Craig."

Nicole clenched the seat tighter, her forearms straining.

"Guess which path I chose?"

Nicole, paralyzed with fright, couldn't answer.

"Pushing him into the lake was no easy task," Trista said, rolling her eyes. "Kid was heavier than he looked."

Acid burned Nicole's throat as she found the strength to speak. "You killed an innocent kid? For what? Revenge?"

"I don't see it like that."

The walls closed in on Nicole and sweat beaded on her neck.

Trista rambled on. "And the watch? How fortunate that you were the one who'd found it, turning it in, crucifying your husband. I'd hoped the police would eventually find it. That was my intent, anyway, when I'd shoved it in that drawer."

With all her might to lift her heavy tongue, Nicole licked her dry lips and stuttered, "How...how'd you put it there?"

Trista raised her right eyebrow. "Remember when I used the bathroom?"

Nicole wanted to scream. Yell for help. Shock, fear, or perhaps even the need to hear more stifled her.

"Thank you for throwing your husband under the bus like that. And the beer bottle? Nice touch, Nicole. The final nail in his coffin." Trista leaned back, abandoning her coffee, and crossed her arms over her chest.

Nicole continued to stare, mouth gaping, unable to blink, incapable of moving, the thumping in her head and ears ballooning with each passing word.

Trista leaned in again. "And here's the best part."

Nicole's eyes widened. She couldn't imagine what else was left.

"I saved womankind, and my daughter, from that monster."

Nicole didn't know where her voice came from. She whispered hoarsely, "You're the monster."

"But am I? We do what's necessary to protect our children. And our own kind. I saved Craig's next victim, so really, I'm the hero of this story. Unfortunately, Jaden was the sacrificial lamb."

Nicole shook her head slowly and blinked, too stunned for tears.

Trista pushed her chair back and stood up with a cryptic smile. "No need to thank me, by the way. Watching Craig rot in jail is thanks enough."

The room continued to spin, and white dots danced in Nicole's vision, her breaths coming in short, rapid waves. She relinquished her grip on the chair and dropped her head in her hands, covering her face. She heard ringing in her ears. Altogether shocked and appalled, Nicole didn't know if it was from the pressure mounting in her head or from the bells chiming overhead as Trista opened the door and vanished.

EPILOGUE

Fifteen minutes after Trista's confession, Nicole still couldn't move. She was stuck, not only physically but mentally as well, transfixed in thought about all she'd done during the investigation. How she kept secrets, tampered with potential evidence, misdirected the police, and acted entirely against her moral code, even pretending to be someone she wasn't, all to protect Kyle.

But she'd had it all wrong; her suspicions invoked unscrupulous behavior. And those actions led to guilt, such guilt that she couldn't and didn't want to live with, yet here she was once again, faced with a harrowing decision: should she go to the authorities and tell them what she'd learned or keep it to herself?

If she reported Trista's story, Craig might go free. If she didn't, he'd pay for a crime he didn't commit—murder. Not that Craig was completely innocent in Jaden's demise. After all, he'd attacked Jaden, leaving him unconscious, allowing Trista to strike. Craig had insisted Trista was crazy. A liar. Unhinged. And he was right, but both of them were liars in their own right. Nicole didn't want to be like either one of them. And that's when she remembered the trending hashtag, "Justice for Jaden." This was her chance to make it right once and for all.

With her heart pounding against her ribs, Nicole punched in the numbers she'd come to know by heart, calling the one person she could trust. After the fourth ring, when she was about to hang up, she heard Phil's voice.

"Hey, what's up?"

Nicole detected surprise in his voice. After all, it'd been six weeks since they'd last spoken.

"Hi, Phil," she said, voice shaking. "I need you to meet me at the police station."

"Why? What happened?"

Wanting privacy, Nicole walked outside on shaky legs and told Phil Trista's story.

He let out a long, low whistle. "Wow. That's a lot to take in. Are you okay?"

"No, but I will be once I talk to Detective Newton."

"It takes a courageous person to do what you're doing, especially after everything you've been through."

With the sun beating down on her, Nicole felt cold. "Thanks. Courageous isn't a word I'd use to describe myself, but I appreciate your compliment. Can you meet in ten minutes?"

"I've already made a U-turn and am headed in that direction." Phil paused momentarily and said, "I imagine this will cause another media frenzy. Are you ready for what comes next?"

Nicole pulled out of the parking lot. "Jaden's parents deserve to know the truth. And no matter what happens next, at least I know I've done the right thing."

And as she drove to the police station, for the first time, in a long time, she was at peace.

ACKNOWLEDGMENTS

This novel would not be in your hands today if it were not for the incredible team behind me.

To my fabulous agent, Cindy Bullard of Birch Literary, I am forever indebted to you, a true champion of my work, and as brilliant as you are patient. Thank you for taking a chance on me and knowing when to tell me, with the utmost kindness, after my umpteenth round of revisions, to step away; it's ready. I'd still be revising if you hadn't put your foot down (in the nicest way!).

Thank you to Reagan Rothe and the entire team at Black Rose Writing. You are all an integral part of achieving my dream. From your exceptional edits to the gorgeous book cover, you have far surpassed my vision and expectations for my debut novel. From the bottom of my heart, thank you for sharing my story with the world.

To the late Jimmy Gariepy, who passed away unexpectedly before this book was published. Thank you for the endless hours chatting with me about the proper procedures in a homicide investigation. Although my computer is littered with a suspicious-looking search history (this always makes me nervous!), you saved me from delving further into the black hole, possibly raising eyebrows even further. Your stories fascinated me, and your indelible ideas generated doubt in the wrong direction, accentuating the red herrings in the story. You were a phenomenal detective and a good man, and I'm deeply saddened that you'll never have the chance to buy the copy that you so eagerly wanted.

I wouldn't be where I am today without Mary Adkins and The Book Incubator team. When I set out to find answers to my writing questions, I found your program. Call it luck, call it a coincidence, but I call it fate. You are more than a writing coach; so much more. You are an inspiration, a confidant, and a friend—a good one at that. Thank you for all your help, guidance, encouragement, suggestions, and instruction; you are the best investment I've ever made. And to my cohorts, you all helped me, too. Alongside Mary, you lifted me up, motivating me to keep going, even in the darkest times. You all inspire me.

For my beta readers, Wendy Brown, Liana Vincini, Jennifer Barchi, and Lovell Dall, thank you for taking the time to read the raw copy of my novel. Your invaluable feedback helped mold and shape it into what it is today. I heavily considered every suggestion, so thank you for your honest opinions and input.

Thank you to all the readers for keeping the art of writing alive. Without your thirst for reading, authors wouldn't have an audience—you are the reason bookstores and libraries continue to exist. We appreciate your loyalty and the love of getting lost in another world.

Finally, to my most incredible supporters, my family, and friends. Mom and Dad, you taught me to be true to myself, go after my dreams, and never let others stand in the way of making them happen. Your lessons of hard work and perseverance pay off every day. Your tenacious work ethic flows through my veins.

Matthew and Lauren, thank you for listening to me drone on and on while plotting the story, working through the details, and developing the characters. Despite your occasional eye rolls, I had to order takeout instead of cooking because I needed to "fix one more thing."

Pat, your unconditional love is the catalyst that led me here today. You didn't blink an eye when I said I wanted to become a full-time writer. Instead, you smiled and said, "Let's buy you a desk." You continued (and still do) to encourage and support me, reminding me that these things take time. Losing that bet to you was the best money I've ever lost, and it pales in comparison to the amount of my gratitude. Thank you for the endless amount of pep talks. Yes, you are pretty awesome.

ABOUT THE AUTHOR

Gayle Brown is the debut author of *A Deadly Game*. Although she started her career as an elementary school teacher, then switched gears to work in her family's business while she raised her children, she now writes full-time and is a writing mentor for The Book Incubator—a novel writing program. Gayle's passion for writing started when she could hold a crayon in her hand, using the walls as her storyboard, and it hasn't stopped. Whether partaking in creative writing classes and workshops or writing short stories and books, she has connected pen to paper or fingers to keyboard, with some of her work appearing on blogs and parenting websites. When not reading or writing, you can find her spending time with her family in Florida.

NOTE FROM GAYLE BROWN

Word-of-mouth is crucial for any author to succeed. If you enjoyed *A Deadly Game*, please leave a review online—anywhere you are able. Even if it's just a sentence or two. It would make all the difference and would be very much appreciated.

Thanks!
Gayle Brown

Printed in the USA
CPSIA information can be obtained
at www.ICGtesting.com
JSHW020920071223
53327JS00010B/49